P9-APH-142

Priv·i·lege

☺ A Novel ☹

Jason Patrick Rothery

ENFIELD
&WIZENTY

Copyright © 2019 Jason Rothery

Great Plains Publications
1173 Wolseley Avenue
Winnipeg, MB R3G 1H1
www.greatplains.mb.ca

All rights reserved. No part of this publication may be reproduced or transmitted in any form or in any means, or stored in a database and retrieval system, without the prior written permission of Great Plains Publications, or, in the case of photocopying or other reprographic copying, a license from Access Copyright (Canadian Copyright Licensing Agency), 1 Yonge Street, Suite 1900, Toronto, Ontario, Canada, M5E 1E5.

Great Plains Publications gratefully acknowledges the financial support provided for its publishing program by the Government of Canada through the Canada Book Fund; the Canada Council for the Arts; the Province of Manitoba through the Book Publishing Tax Credit and the Book Publisher Marketing Assistance Program; and the Manitoba Arts Council.

Design & Typography by Relish New Brand Experience
Printed in Canada by Friesens

Library and Archives Canada Cataloguing in Publication

Title: Privilege : a novel / Jason Patrick Rothery.
Names: Rothery, Jason Patrick, 1978- author.
Identifiers: Canadiana (print) 20190109882 | Canadiana (ebook) 20190109890 |
ISBN 9781773370224 (softcover) | ISBN 9781773370248 (Kindle) |
ISBN 9781773370231 (EPUB)
Classification: LCC PS8635.0738 P75 2019 | DDC C813/.6—dc23

ENVIRONMENTAL BENEFITS STATEMENT

Great Plains Publications saved the following resources by printing the pages of this book on chlorine free paper made with 100% post-consumer waste.

TREES	WATER	ENERGY	SOLID WASTE	GREENHOUSE GASES
9	**690**	**4**	**30**	**3,720**
FULLY GROWN	GALLONS	MILLION BTUs	POUNDS	POUNDS

Environmental impact estimates were made using the Environmental Paper Network Paper Calculator 4.0. For more information visit www.papercalculator.org.

Canadä

FSC
www.fsc.org
MIX
Paper from responsible sources
FSC® C016245

For Griffin & Suki

"But everyone's too damned sensitive these days. I see people now, kids right out of college, and they really think they should never experience an unpleasant moment. Nobody should ever say anything they don't like, or tell a joke they don't like. But the thing is, nobody can make the world be the way they want it to be all the time. Things always happen that embarrass you or piss you off. That's life. I hear women telling jokes about men every day. Offensive jokes. Dirty jokes. I don't get bent out of shape. Life is great. Who has time for this crap? Not me."

—Michael Crichton, *Disclosure*

Prologue

Doctor Barker Samuel Stone had no idea where he was.

His first thought—froth struggling to the surface of the tar—was this: *Mexico?* Had he somehow been delivered south of yet another border?

Room drenched in tacky *Mexicana,* like an exploded souvenir shop. Honey-mustard walls dripping with sombreros, decorative plates—*Whatshisname? Enraptured flautist with the hedgehog spikes? Kinkajou? No, those were the ornery bear rats from Guatemala. Uh...Kilimanjaro?*—crucifixes of varied sizes and materials: wood, punched tin, embroidered lace...

A bubble broke through, a snippet of text—*Authentic Talavera tiles...* Burst. Irretrievable.

Article? Brochure?

Gone.

Inside: Arrhythmic thumping. *Thump thump thump.*

His heart?

Large flat-screen television mounted on the wall. A man. A face. A *familiar* face: thinning patch of shorn, blond bristle; porcine eyes restless; neck crimson, overflowing his open collar like dough; porpoise-smooth skin speckled with sweat, glistening under stark white light.

The camera zoomed out to wider shot as the man pounded his mallet-sized fist on a rostrum. Behind him hung a nondescript navy blue curtain patterned with regal-looking insignia. To his left—

a woman, hands folded primly over her pleated russet skirt, mouth clamped in a grim line. Though the TV was muted, the man was clearly shouting, swinging his arms in emphatic arcs, a conductor combatting an unruly orchestra.

The camera closed in, cutting the woman out of frame, fighting to keep purchase as the man bobbed and weaved—the pin against the butterfly.

Thump thump thump. Faster. Sharper. A staccato *rat-a-tat.*

Cardiac arrest? *Am I dying?*

The soundless television loomed. An epiphany: *I'm on the floor!* Let his head loll. *Yes. Floor.* Legs outstuck, pants bunched below his knees, limp penis sticking out of the slot of his briefs like a dead tongue. Remote control in one hand, ball of toilet paper in the other.

An echo. An unknown voice. *Sounds like a party!*

Female.

On the floor, slumped back against a bed, caped by a duvet with a faux-woven Aztec pattern—girders of rust and tan and turquoise.

Party?

Returned his eyes to the television to find the man replaced by black—*No! African-American!*—faces. Night. Buildings ablaze. Everyone angry, yelling. Raised arms and pumping fists. Cut to a police cruiser engulfed in fire, objects hurtled—Bricks? Rocks?—at the flaming carapace. Plastic bags wind-whipped through the frame. Cut to a high angle, helicopter hovering over the cauldron of chaos. Spotlight tracking haphazardly scuttling figures, arms laden with spoils. Barker struggled for coherence. What was this? Protest or plunder?

Pounding more insistent now: *Thumpthumpthump! Thump-thumpthump!*

Have to get up. Hospital.

Thumpthumpthump! Thumpthumpthump!

Thumbed the remote to turn the television off, unmuted it instead, flooding the room with a concert of disorder: chanting, burning, shattering, sirens. Instinctually flung his arms in front of his face, sending the remote pinwheeling into the wall. Heard the cover spin off with a *crack*, the batteries clatter across the tiles like tossed dice.

The blare abruptly broke off, supplanted by the soothing, sing-song timbre of a male news anchor—face thick with foundation, hands firm against his desk. The speakers crackled as he spoke.

Thumpthumpthump!

Barker resolved to stand, to lift himself out of oblivion.

Sounds like a party!

Who was she? What party?

Hands on the floor. To his left, cool (*Talavera!*) tile, to his right, a patch of lumpy muck. Lifted the sodden hand, dripping yolky slime, sensed another bubble straining to the fore. Pushed it back down.

The *thumping* morphed, no longer seemed to emanate from within...

Wiped his hand on the duvet, reached up under his shirt and pressed it flat against his chest. His heartbeat, steady as a metronome.

...Stone?

His name.

Was someone saying his—?

Dr. Stone? Barker?

Propped himself on his knees, grabbed an edge and pulled. A decorative plate rose before him like the sun at dawn: The hunched deity, the flautist mid-leap, in the throes of—

Kokopelli! More text materialized in his mind. *This revered god of fertility*—

His still-slick-with-slime hand slipped. Landed hard on his coccyx, grunted with pain—first *Gah!*, then *Fuh!*—rocked side to side like an upended tortoise.

Stomach lurched. Before he could stop it, the tide crested.

Vomited onto the floor. Again. Again.

Dr. Stone?

Thump thump thump!

Dr. Stone? Barker?

Thump thump thump!

The *thump* resolved into more of a...pounding?

"Doctor Stone! Are you all right?" *Pound pound pound!*

A man's voice. Did he know him?

Pound pound pound! "Open the door, Doctor Stone!"

From the television: "Joining me now is Professor—"

Pound pound pound!

"—a Civil Rights historian who teaches law at—"

Pound pound pound!

"Professor, thank you for joining us this evening."

"Glad to be here, Chet."

Using the bed for support, Barker lifted himself to standing. A mirror on the wall, punched tin frame with scalloped edges, revealed him to himself: hair pressed into oblique peaks, eyes red and sunken, skin pallid, shirt sodden with yellow.

POUND! POUND! POUND! POUND! POUND!

Tugged up his pants and shimmied for the door. Even these mincing steps made his stomach churn. Clenched his jaw and pursed his lips. *Hold it back. Push it down, down, down, down...*

"Doctor Stone! Open the door! Doctor Stone!"

Had more or less wrested his pants up to his waist when a full foam broke through: *The Fiesta Room! The keynote! The woman at the—*

Sounds like a party!

TV: "What we're watching unfold here is the unfortunate, but in many ways inevitable outcome of years, *decades*, of institutionalized discrimination and disenfranchisement..."

Took a step back.

"...the overarching goal of which is and always has been to abridge, under one guise or another, the freedoms of a particular set of people grouped per their racial heritage..."

When had he come back to his room? What had he been doing on the floor? Who was this asshole pounding on his—?

A blunt THUD. A tremor. Force meets immovable object. The door shuddered. Barker rolled back on the balls of his feet. A second THUD, this one accompanied by splintering. The door distended; a puff of dust clouded the air like cold breath.

Barker held out his hand as if to dissuade an attacker, watched as the door caved, split down the middle in a confusion of powder and plywood shards. One half of the sundered door swung dazedly on its hinges, the other toppled at an awkward, canted angle.

TV: "Excuse me for interrupting, Professor, but it sounds like what you're saying is that these people have no choice in terms of their own actions...that these acts of civil disobedience and vandalism—"

Barker froze, one hand suspending his loose pants, the other extended in self-defence. Through the rubble of the shattered door, two men appeared. Police officers. Behind the officers, a man and a woman in identical uniforms. Paramedics? A few feet behind this second duo was a concierge holding a keycard aloft like an Olympic torch, looking crestfallen.

"In many ways they don't have a choice, so thoroughly have their freedoms—in different ways, over so long a period of time—been systematically stripped from them."

The taller policeman pushed inside. Barker watched the officer's eyes scout around the room—first to this, then to that, and back to Barker. The officer's eyes narrowed, mental gears grinding, knitting every observable element into a firm narrative sheath.

"For many of these people, far too many of these people, agency is no more than this: An illusion."

Barker had to say something; stop the officer's story from crystallizing. While in certain respects, in certain quarters, Barker was considered a genius (of sorts), this was no time for showboating. All he needed was a simple and succinct interjection, a different angle, a unique twist, a contrary but equally plausible counter-plot.

What he came up with was this: *It's not what it looks like.*

Okay. Not great. But it would have to do.

As Barker began to speak, the relay between his brain and mouth fizzled.

Instead of "It's," he said "Look."

The word hung in the air. Barker gawped, considering how best to correct his error.

The officer lunged.

CAROL: Do you know what you've *worked* for? *Power.* For
power. Do you understand? And you sit there, and you
tell me *stories.* About your *house,* about all the private
schools, and about *privilege,* and how you are entitled. To
buy, to *spend,* to *mock,* to *summon.* All your stories. All
your silly weak *guilt,* it's all about *privilege…*
—David Mamet, *Oleanna*

The Tower

Barker's iPad and dog had died on the same day, and in this moment—
fortyish minutes into the second faculty meeting of the fall semester,
with his colleague Gordon Rusk in the midst of a characteristically
epic rant—Barker wasn't sure which one he missed more.

Bored as shit, Barker's scan of the assembled told him he was
not alone. Of the dozen-odd faculty, four administrators, and one
graduate student in attendance, only the student—Molly Ellen
Clarke—and Dr. Maureen Alexi, their esteemed program director,
seemed to be paying any attention to Rusk whatsoever. Barker could
tell by Maureen's two-fisted grip on her pen, and the way she chewed
on the nub of her upper lip, that she was torn between allowing all
stakeholders their time at the podium, and keeping the proceedings
on point and schedule.

Everyone else was engrossed in a device. To Barker's right, a
fidgety colleague thumbed through a social media feed on his smartphone. Others swiped and pawed at tablets. Even Dr. Siobhan Grady,

Barker's stalwart ally in arms—*Let us ban technology from the class-room forthwith!*—was typing absently away on a laptop.

Tried to catch Shiv's eye, flash her a conspiratorial glance—*Can you believe the tear Rusk is on today?*—but she carried forth unawares.

Most would have protested, perhaps, that they were simply attending to manifold professional duties. No harm no foul. After all, these meetings were procedural busywork, a diversion from the many more pressing demands on their time and attention. The students especially—as their assignments and midterms resolved from abstraction into reality, as their panic percolated. Bodily present or not, the student corpus was always *there*, always *felt*; a moon exerting its pull on the tide.

And sure, to be fair, under desperate circumstances, Barker might avail himself of a tangential discussion or classic Rusk crusade to field an inquiry or two. No one, himself included, was perfect.

But by and large, students were an excuse. *Professional duties* a deception.

"That's not the point," Rusk responded to a comment or query Barker had missed. "These companies are trying to use common carriage as a Trojan horse. They're contending that, basically, they control the means of distribution, the *pipes*, but have nothing to do with the content flowing through them."

Barker shook his head to himself, irked that his colleagues—all of whom were waging the same impossible battle to beat back the horde of devices inundating their classrooms and lecture halls—were so indifferent to their own hypocrisy, sitting here in the selfsame thrall of the selfsame machines they bemoaned in the hands of the kids. *Who of us*, they seemed to say, *has the fortitude to ignore the siren call of possibility, of taking up throne and sceptre in our own mini media fiefdom?*

Sure, faculty meetings were dull as fuck, but that's why they got paid the big bucks, right?

"Isn't that a good thing?" asked Fidget, setting his phone face down. "I thought common carriage protected these companies from being held liable for questionable content, illegal content...?"

Nothing to be gained by calling anyone out. What was that Goethe quote? The futility of trying to change someone's *fixed inclination? You will only succeed in confirming him in his opinion...or drenching him in yours!* You could only lead by example, stand as a paragon of restraint; silently and civilly declare your allegiance to the cause of *Paying Fucking Attention to Other People While They're Talking.* Only one of the litany of social compacts and courtesies—*Holding the Door Open for the Person Behind You, Not Claiming Two Seats on the Subway*—inexorably breaking down in the mid-to-late-Anthropocene.

Don't even get me started on Texting While Walking, Barker thought, nodding in assentation with himself.

Rusk puffed his cheeks, flared his lips like the mouth of a bullhorn. "Common carriage *is* a good thing, in itself, broadly speaking. But as a regulatory mechanism, it wasn't designed or intended to deal with the degree of corporate concentration we see today. Some of the biggest *ai-ess-pees*—"

Barker mentally squinted. *Internet Service Provider.*

"—are also effectively content producers. They're the cable company and the broadcast network all rolled into one!"

Could he duck out and retrieve his phone from his office? He'd left it behind out of habit—padded his pants pockets for the umpteenth time... Yup, definitely not there—forgetting about his defunct iPad. Now his hands felt empty and restless, as baffled as a concussed bird.

Barker started to doodle instead. Struggled to render the image he'd summoned in his mind. Scratched and scribbled, shaded and smudged, erased and revised. The drawing refused to cohere, every fix compounding earlier errors. The more effort, the more distorted the features became—more melting toad than his dead dog's true face.

Rusk: "In many cases, these huge, vertically integrated companies generate the content they're distributing. I mean, look at Viacom, for example, or, or—"

Fidget eased back into his preposterously expensive ergonomic chair, shifting and sighing to signal his discomfort.

Barker tilted his pencil to fill in a shadow under a bulbous jowl. The dog had been a disaster from day one. Google suggested a digestive or irritable bowel disorder, but no amendment to the dog's diet—raw beef, organic kibble, fish oil—stymied its emissions. Both indoors and out, his dog cavalierly warped the world around him with limpid clouds of stink.

Barker had just begun to adjust to these astringent ambushes—even renewing his Costco membership to buy *Febreze* by the pallet—when the seizures started. He'd wake in the middle of the night to agonized grunts, the dog writhing around on the floor, muzzle bearded with foam, torso wrenched with bone-cracking spasms, like a senseless sequence of sign language letters.

After only a few months, the number and magnitude of "issues" left Barker reeling. Another small but significant dream crumbling no sooner than it had been fulfilled.

He'd desperately wanted a dog throughout his childhood, but was denied one by (who else?) his parents. Perpetually harried professors, they appeased their progeny's frequent (and increasingly plaintive) petitions by declaring low-maintenance animals the only possible compromise.

First fish. A small aquarium swarming with finny globs of orange and black, like leakage from a lava lamp. Barker was nonplussed, found their bugged-out eyes and emotional alterity unnerving. As if sensing his ambivalence, or in protest of their confinement—comfortable though that confinement had been made on their behalf—there was a rash of piscine suicides. He'd return from school to find yet another knotty corpse strangled in a tuft of chestnut shag. Though he cared little for the fish themselves, these recurrent brushes with the sharp cliff-edge of existence left young Barker shaken. He started avoiding the basement altogether, the stairs to which the tank—that ominous shrine to finitude—stood at the bottom of.

Soon enough his father soured on the frequent tank cleanings. *Sayonara* fishies!

Then gerbils. His mother cared for them with surprising tenderness, took Zen-like pleasure in configuring the yellow plastic tubes that protruded from the cage like ingrown plumbing; three-dimensional mazes that engendered not only latitude, but, in Barker's appraisal, the cruel fantasy of escape.

Like so many fantasies, a futile one. No matter their arrangement, the tubes always (of course) returned the gerbils to their cage, to its turd-peppered mounds of cotton and sawdust. As with the stationary wheel, a whole lot of energy expended to end up in the exact same spot. Barker detected a mounting sense of desperation in the gerbils' forays, would often observe one or the other animal in the throes of frenzied digging, trying to claw through translucent piping with tender, insufficient nails.

When the gerbils finally did escape—how this was done, and where they had gone, was never determined—his mother was forlorn for days. (Had the loss of her tube time, or the actual animals, left the deepest cut?) Barker pretended sadness, but was secretly relieved. The gerbils had rewarded his sporadic attempts at affection—cupping them in his hand while gingerly stroking their fur—by gnashing at the webbing between his thumb and forefinger.

Gun-shy, perhaps, due to these formative failures in pet-owning, it took him decades to register that, as a self-sufficient adult person, he was not only equipped, but required no one else's permission, to acquire a dog on and of his own. He struck out for the SPCA, wanting a rescue partly because purebreds were so rife with genetic defects, but mostly for the varnish of beneficence the word *rescue* accorded.

How many times had he heard *you don't pick the dog, the dog picks you?* Nope. Barker definitely picked this dog. Stooped to find, consigned to a corner, the canine embodiment of his then-current mental and emotional state: weakened and vulnerable from his crumbling marriage, harbouring early doubts about the arc of his career. This lax brown lump of inscrutable lineage—squat and stocky as a miniature ox; square-headed, stumpy-legged, with a tail as short and sharp as a quip—had clearly abandoned all hope, was perfectly content to curl up and wither on the vine.

They would rescue one another from despair.

Barker would later reflect on the conflicted look that had crossed the attendant's face when he announced his pick. Well versed, presumably, in the animal's myriad complications, who was she to stand in the way of its potential future happiness?

After purchasing the requisite accessories, Barker—pockets stuffed with biodegradable bags and bone-shaped treats that reeked of zoo enclosures—strutted off to the park like a proud parent on the first day of school. Fulfilling his fantasy in its entirety, he named the dog Atreyu, an homage to his favourite childhood book and film, the underlying rationale being that it would be frickin' high-*larious* to repeatedly yell the name aloud.

Upon arriving at the park, Atreyu, resplendent in a badass spiked collar, assumed a state of resolute inertia. Barker cajoled, lured him with treats, delivered prodding nudge-kicks to his posterior. Atreyu was as uninterested in mobility as in the brethren bounding up for their sniff, whose entreaties to scrap he outright rebuffed.

Barker put some distance between them. Enthusiastically called and clapped.

Atreyu!

Clap! Clap!

Atreyu! Here boy!

Clap! Clap! Clap!

Barker had only just caught the first of what would turn out to be many whiffs of disappointment when, momentarily distracted by the heedless owner of a shitting mutt—*You want to come back here and pick up that mess?*—he turned to find Atreyu gone. Vanished. Barker stomped through the park, his ever-more desperate cries of *Atreyu! Atreyu!* bereft of their anticipated comedic impact.

After a dozen-odd agonizing minutes, a woman appeared, cradling the stupid dog in her arms like a panting, overstuffed stomach, paws booted with muck. She'd spotted Atreyu ferreting at a rodent hole in a copse of maples—a second-hand account of energy and purpose that Barker would never personally witness—set him down, joked how those same holes drove her own dog into a similar fugue state. Overwhelmed with anger and relief, Barker was primed to deliver an appropriately jarring smack to the crown of Atreyu's dumb, boxy skull when he noticed the woman cock her head and give the air a circumspect sniff.

Grim smile. "Smells like trouble," she said.

Yes. *Trouble.*

He'd imagined an animal that would love him unconditionally, satisfy his every whim (by sensing his need/want) for affection, save him from lassitude and sadness, lick him when he was low, curl up on the couch while he played video games, or at his feet while he marked papers, fold effortlessly around the shape of his body and life, his daily routine; break up and fill out that routine, get him up off his ass, force him outside, radiate energy and animacy, pore over scents like a monk over velum, lubricate his interactions with dog-toting women. Barker endowed Trouble (née Atreyu) with all these hopes and dreams and responsibilities and more.

They never returned to that first park. It was too sprawling, too boundless, and clearly Trouble could not be trusted with too much freedom. From then on, Barker took Trouble only so far as the "park" nearest his condo complex—a fenced-in, woodchip-lined, shit-littered patch of thinning turf. (A gerbil cage for dogs!) Barker had intended it as punishment—*See what you get for running off on me?*—but Trouble evinced zero compunction. Evinced zero of anything actually, simply conceded to squander his soon-to-be abbreviated existence hunkered down on his haunches, sponging up the world's dirt and wet, secreting foul-smelling, eye-stinging, throat-throttling haze.

Needless to say, even in this inner-city dog ghetto teeming with cocksure hipsters tethered to glorified rats, Trouble was profoundly unhelpful in picking up dames.

Then seizures. These brought Trouble's signature characteristic, besides smell and stasis, into bold relief: The dog was *expensive*. Costly middle-of-the-night runs to a twenty-four-hour vet, x-rays with inconclusive results, prescriptions for pills, liquids, and tinctures with no discernible effect, that offered no alleviation.

One night the convulsions grew so severe that Barker feared Trouble might snap his own neck. The vet who typically worked the graveyard shift—a freckle-spangled ginger that looked not a day over fourteen—advised him that they were running short on options. Would Barker consider surgery? The procedure, relatively common for dogs with epilepsy, had a decent success rate, at a cost of nearly ten thousand dollars.

"What does 'decent' mean?"

"Well," the vet sighed with four a.m. fatigue, "if it *is* epilepsy..." Rubbed his eye with the heel of his hand, shrugged. "Flip a coin."

Ten grand, Barker thought, trying to appear pensive, *is a pretty hefty coin to flip.*

Technically, he *could* have shouldered the expense, but for so uncertain an outcome? Did Barker have the right to prolong this poor animal's suffering for the sake of his own selfish wants, to fill the breach opened up by a failed marriage and uncertain future?

He had half-a-mind to cart the shuddering canine back to the SPCA, preferably mid-seizure, and demand recompense. *You sold me a defective dog*, he'd tell them. *This one's on the fritz.*

Which reminded him, he needed to cancel the reservation for the kennel during the conference in November. Under Trouble's mangled portrait Barker wrote: *Cancel kennel booking.*

Underneath that added: *Write keynote.*

After the euthanization, Barker stopped by the mall and relinquished his tablet to an impassive Genius whose efforts failed to rouse the machine. He devoted the remainder of his Sunday to crafting a suitable tribute to Trouble on Facebook, one that struck the requisite balance of mourning and optimism.

Barker recounted intermittent bouts of tenderness, rare instances when Trouble consented to be held, would feint in Barker's arms, flopping his bricklike head over the crook of Barker's elbow. The way Barker phrased this affectionate quirk made it sound as if Trouble had done this all the time. A minor deception for the sake of a more moving eulogy.

Come Monday morning Barker was awash in sympathy and consolation. Family and friends and peers and colleagues and people whose names and faces he could barely place alike all rallied to his aid, bequeathing condolences and well-wishes, inquiring as to his emotional mettle, sharing pithy aphorisms, quotes, and words of wisdom. Some buoyed his spirits by recounting the loss of their own cherished companions. *It's so personal,* one wrote on his wall, *like losing a part of your self.* (Barker: *That's exactly where I'm at right now.*) Spent most of the day on the couch, nursing scotches as the compassion poured in.

The torrent tapered off mid-Tuesday. Maybe there'd been a resurgence during the faculty meeting? Patted his pockets. Right, his phone was in his office. Yes, he should definitely go and get it after all.

Shiv stared at him over the top of cartoonishly large frames, the colour and circumference of a Coke can.

Barker returned her stare: *What?*

Jutted her head.

Barker followed the gesture. Maureen was staring at him also. Had she asked him something? A prompt for Barker to do something? Say something? Interject?

Rusk's voice broke back into the forefront of Barker's awareness, "...creating and circulating content, profiting from that content, just like traditional broadcast companies—paywalls and advertising and so forth. You can't just say 'we're in charge of the pipes and whatever flows through them has nothing to do with us.' When you're granted access to public airways," Rusk repeated the words for emphasis, "*public airways*, you're subject to oversight and regulation. But more to the point..."

Rusk lost his train of thought. Maureen audibly inhaled.

"This is a distraction from the *real* crime," Rusk blurted, "that they're using this process, this opaque process, nominally for the purpose of revising common carriage regulations—and it's really troubling that the government is giving them so much leeway, basically letting them draft their own legislation—to rewrite the rules governing the neutrality of the Internet itself!"

Rusk gripped the table with both hands, as if bracing for impact. "This is the real deal here, folks! This could mean the end of the 'Net as we know it!"

The room went gauzy with silence. Fidget picked up his phone and thumbed. Barker stole a longing glance outside. Another gorgeous afternoon. Wished he were cycling. Any other Wednesday he would be cycling.

Another facial plea from Maureen. Barker was meant to manage Rusk whenever feasible, as Rusk was more liable to consent to said wrangling if it was undertaken by another man.

Barker's legs pumped restively under the table.

Something between a groan and a grunt emanated from Dr. Bertrand Shuler. With his billow of bright white hair, and the silkish scarf coiling his neck like a mane, Bert was the closest thing the program had to a grand doyen. His renown and longevity, along with his brushes with some of the greats—he'd not only worked under McLuhan, but penned the quintessential McLuhan biography, *The Message in the Medium*—granted him a nigh-legendary status.

Because he seemed to deserve it, Bert was treated with extraordinary deference. He could have retired years ago and become a professor emeritus with a tidy pension, and yet he lingered, leading the first half of the yearlong seminar for the incoming PhD cohort before jetting south for the winter. An enviable schedule, and uniquely generous of the program, but such was Bert's prestige that it was regarded as *his* generosity to *them*, and not the other way round. Even deigning to appear at these meetings—meetings at which he paid as little attention as anyone—was treated as a nigh-monarchical courtesy.

Barker liked Bert, and Bert liked Barker right back. He was a triple rarity: an iconoclast, a charming storyteller, and a lifer who'd foresworn the typically itinerant academic existence despite the fact that his clout and acclaim would have secured him work anywhere in the world.

A few days after officially joining the faculty, Bert invited Barker out for drinks. Barker couldn't help but ask—*Why'd you stay put?* "I was young, married, two kids, liked the city. Better yet, my wife liked the city. My kids…well, who gives a shit what your kids think?" Whisked his hand through the air, nearly felling his pint. "This is a big country. A long, serpentine border town. Lots of good places to be. But this," rapped his folded bifocals twice on the table, "*this* is where the action is. This city has its head up its own ass, absolutely. But not for no reason."

Barker found Bert's war stories riveting: the internecine skirmishes that had nearly toppled the department in its infancy; the subsequent purge of raucous, rebellious Marxists ("There was this unspoken agreement that, at any moment, we were prepared and more than willing to burn the fucker down"), their ranks replenished by a mosaic of "obsequious, sycophantic lickspittles" (Bert's phrasing) overly-grateful for a job in an increasingly crowded field ("Too busy ass-kissing to concern themselves with societal collapse"); the broader battles waged over political correctness in the nineties ("I wrote my thesis on McCarthy, and I'd be goddamned if I was going to sit idly by while students—*students!*—tried to resuscitate the blacklist!").

The forthrightness of his cynicism could be bracing, yes, but also refreshing. Bert made Barker feel far less crazy for harbouring his own creeping doubts. Barker's generation had been reared to believe that scoring a tenure-track gig in so intensely competitive a market was tantamount to winning the lottery; an extraordinary privilege bestowed upon a select and distinguished few. Here was a standing member of the old guard, still holding his ground against successive waves of young Turks, voicing an uncomfortable truth: It was just a job. A job with obvious benefits, sure, but a job nonetheless.

Bert leaned out of his recline, plucked his bifocals off their perch, folded them into a wand, waved the wand at Rusk. "It's unconscionable," Bert said. "We should all sign his damned letter." Bert fussed with his scarf, pruning its lint, primping it for the pride.

Barker looked to Maureen, but she was watching Bert, who resumed his former leonine repose.

Maureen's voice was calm and deliberate: "The concern, I think, is that having multiple faculty sign an open letter will make it look like the program, or the university itself, has taken a position on this legislation."

"The university *should* take a position," Rusk insisted.

Riiight, their collective silence said, *but that'll never happen.* The university had no incentive to pick a fight with the government, much less tech companies—foremost among the corporate citizens it depended on for donations. Moreover, while their feckless president inspired no shortage of antipathy, it was crucial to stay in her good graces. Putting their weight behind Rusk's cause might look like insubordination, the faculty going rogue.

Rusk knew as much, but dug his heels in anyway. Desperate not to let his sortie flag, he thrust his palms imploringly at Bert. Bert, bifocals dangling from a pinkie, interest already on the wane, tossed his hands in a *What're you gonna do?* shrug.

Molly observed straight-backed and alert. Shiv, who for no reason she or Barker could fathom had long ago earned Rusk's animus, turned to Barker and wrinkled her lower lip: *Uh oh!*

Maureen pursed her lips and flicked her eyes back to Barker. She looked tired. The last year had taken a toll, and she was obviously still feeling shaky.

Barker took a deep draught of crisp, recirculated air, felt it leech the moisture from his sinuses. "Well, the administration is going to hate this one way or another, and it does seem problematic to proceed as though we're a united front." Cleared his throat. "That said, would it be reasonable to suggest that instead of everyone signing the same letter, any given faculty member, if they so choose, is free to submit a letter independently?"

Rusk stroked the mossy stubble conquering his cheeks and wattle. "It's an option. Doesn't quite carry the same weight as all of us acting in unison, but, uh, yeah, it's an option."

Maureen took her agenda in hand. "All right, Gordon will put out a call for letters, and no one is under any obligation. You're all acting under your own initiative."

"Great," said Rusk, deflating. "Thanks for hearing me out. It's a really important issue." His tone was pleasant, but Barker knew Rusk would seethe for the rest of the day, divvying colleagues into allies and enemies, whittling down the gallery of available antagonists into the most suitable target for his contempt.

Shiv most likely.

Maureen: "Now we're going to hear from the President of the Communication Student Caucus, Molly Clarke."

Molly released the tassel of hair she'd looped round her fingers, shimmied up to the table. "Thanks Doctor Alexi." Popped open her laptop. "Hi, everyone! I'm honoured to be serving as Caucus president this year. First off, a big thanks to everyone who chimed in over the summer with keynote speaker suggestions for the student conference. We really appreciated your input. The Caucus voted on a speaker, and we're just waiting for a thumbs-up from Maureen."

Molly smiled at Barker. Barker smiled back.

Maybe not the most polished or accomplished scholar, Molly was admirably opinionated and outspoken; one of those rare students with quote-unquote "life experience." Such experience, Barker was sad to say, was an increasingly exotic quality. Most students tended not to stray too far beyond their institutional burrows, scampering from one degree to another without ever poking their heads above ground.

So why did he find Molly vaguely off-putting? That shrewd glint in her peppercorn eyes? The way she over-spiced her speech with pseudo-sanguine perk?

She'd certainly rubbed Bert the wrong way the year prior. *What's your impression of the new cohort?* Bert had pinned his bifocals in a shock of windswept white, flapped his hand dismissively. "Gender this and gender that. Aren't there any other topics on the roster these days?" Bert cinched his scarf and stuck out his tongue in mock-strangulation. "Don't mind this old goat. High time I fucked off to Albuquerque."

The culprit was obvious. Molly deftly twisted every seminar into a symposium on gender. Barker gave her a pass to the extent this was rooted in said "life experience"—laudable volunteer work with a female-owned and -operated textile co-op in Nicaragua—but found it nonetheless taxing to repeatedly replace every discussion on its respective rails.

And he hadn't quite clocked it at first, but Molly had changed over the summer. A modification not only of attitude—to wit: Her election as caucus president (last year's Molly had derided student politics as "a deplorable mirroring of entrenched patriarchal paradigms")—but of appearance. She'd arrived at the program sporting dreadlocks (one of her peers had inquired as to her position *vis-à-vis* cultural appropriation. "All culture is appropriation," had been her snappy rejoinder), and worn mainly patchwork blouses and woven shawls. Today's Molly had hacked off the dreds and replaced them with an auburn bob (not an *exact* replica of Maureen's hairstyle, but certainly in the same taxonomy); was decked out in a slick avocado suit-jacket with matching slacks and spex. The Academy was reforming her, grooming her, sanding down her coarser edges, and Molly, to Barker's dismay, was avidly embracing her own reformation.

At least it's Molly here and not Lara, he thought. *Lara would've been…tricky.*

"Conference aside," Molly continued, "the Caucus will be putting on some super fun social events. We love it when the faculty come out to these since it gives the students, especially the incoming cohorts, a chance to get to know you in a less pressure-cooker context."

We share the same campus. I'll cross paths with Lara sooner or later…

"So, please come party with us if you can!" Molly raised two sets of crossed fingers and smirked. "First up is the Halloween party. Location *tee-bee-dee.*"

Maureen: "Thanks, Molly. I—"

"One more thing—sorry for interrupting, Doctor Alexi—and to be clear, this is not directly connected to my work with the Caucus. Not yet anyway…" Closed her laptop, awaited everyone's full attention. Shiv stopped typing. Fidget looked up from his phone. Bert swivelled his chair in Molly's general direction.

"As many of you know, the provincial government recently mandated that all universities draft standalone sexual violence policies. This is a really important step, given the epidemic of sexual violence sweeping across North American campuses. I'm sad to say that our own university has a terrible track record of dealing with cases of harassment, assault, and rape."

She let the word linger. Bert caught Barker's eye, gave his bifocals a quick, tight twirl. *See? Gender!*

"The student community has asked for a meaningful role in helping to draft this new policy. This is, after all, something that impacts us directly. In collaboration with the Graduate Student Society, I spearheaded a working group to devise a set of guiding principles, and last week, we circulated a draft of these principles to staff and students for feedback. I hope all of you will take the time to look it over and share your thoughts. You can send comments to the email address included in the message."

"Molly, could you resend your draft at some point this week? Then we can all be sure we have it and know where to submit feedback."

"Sure thing, Doctor Stone. I'd be happy to."

Maureen: "This is, as Molly said, a very important issue, and a commendable initiative on the part of the students. Turning to the next—"

"One last thing—Sorry! I promise this is the last thing—it has come to our attention, the working group that is, that some university employees, including members of this faculty, signed a letter opposing some of the principles outlined in our draft."

Shiv folded her arms across her chest.

Barker leapt in. "Well, Molly, isn't that the point of...circulating your principles?"

"Of course. We're totally open to input. But this letter is...it wasn't written in the spirit of collaboration or...protecting victims. In fact, it...it kind of undermines, or goes against, the whole...the ideals we want to advance."

"Well," Maureen ventured, "as Doctor Stone suggested, I think that such a letter is part of the process, of encouraging open and transparent—"

"But that's just the thing. It *isn't* part of the process." Molly squirmed, a blush stained her cheeks.

Bertrand crouched over the table, leaning into the prospect of a second skirmish.

Molly: "I just wanted to...in the interests of open and transparent dialogue, to acknowledge that someone from our program signed a letter intended to intimidate or...or *undermine* our efforts to—"

"Okay," said Shiv, "to cut to the chase, I signed the letter. I share a concern with some of the language in the working group's draft. We initially sent a note to them in private, but they responded that they found our suggestions offensive. So, we decided that it might be prudent to air our concerns publicly. No one wants to derail or undermine the process, or intimidate—"

Molly's voice leapt an octave: "Instead of protecting the rights of victims of sexual violence, we should make sure we give *perpetrators* the benefit of the doubt?"

Shiv's face flattened, broad forehead unperturbed, eyes remote as satellites; the still, glassy surface of a deep, dark pond.

Maureen gnawed on her lip-nub.

"Victim's rights are essential," Shiv continued, "but enshrining a blanket edict that all claimants *must be believed*, full stop, has the counter-effect of infringing on the rights of the accused."

"I—" Molly started, but Shiv interrupted.

"Given the constraints of these meetings"—Fidget flipped over his phone to check the time—"I'd be more than happy to discuss our concerns with you, Molly, at a time and place of your choosing and convenience."

Beat. Molly sat back. "Thanks. I'd appreciate that." Turned to Maureen: "That's me."

Barker peeked at Shiv. She flared her eyes: *Can you believe this shit?*

"We only have a few minutes left," Maureen began.

"Thank bleeding Christ," Bert muttered.

Maureen shot him a constipated smile, "and one box left to tick, so, turning things over to Doctor Grady…"

Shiv: "Thanks Maureen, I'll be brief. I think Bert must have a flight to catch."

Bert smirked, flipped her the bird.

"I'm very pleased to announce the first scheduled speaker in our guest lecture series this year. Marjanne Abdalla is Iranian-born secularist, celebrated human rights activist, and the author of several outstanding books about—"

"Excuse me?"

Fuuuck.

"Sorry, but don't you mean *anti-Muslim* activist?"

Maureen put her head in her hands.

"Molly—" Barker began. Shiv cut him off.

"Marjanne Abdalla is a critic of *institutionalized* religion," Shiv said. "Having grown up Muslim in a Muslim-majority country, her critiques do tend to centre on aspects of that faith. I think we'd all agree that she has as much of a right to opine about oppression as we do, especially the forms of oppression she has herself experienced."

"I'm just not sure, given the number of Muslim students that attend this university, that she's the most…beneficial speaker to invite."

"Attendance isn't mandatory, and at its core the series is intended to showcase a diverse spectrum of—"

"But is she—?"

"Excuse me, Molly, I haven't finished speaking."

"I only want to ask if inviting someone so controversial—"

"If you'd let me—"

"Or, ah, *incendiary*—"

"Okay," Shiv threw up her hands, "you go first."

"—won't lead some students to think our program condones Islamophobic bigotry. Might presenting a speaker like that, with such extreme views, make some students feel unsafe?"

Bert started packing up.

"I don't get what this Abdalla woman has to do with communication," Rusk added. "Wouldn't she be more germane to religious studies? Or international relations?"

"Unfortunately, that's all the time we have for today," Maureen announced.

Shiv: "The lecture is next Wednesday, one week from today. Tell your students! Make them come! Bribe or blackmail!"

"Thanks everyone. Meeting adjourned."

As the room decamped, Maureen leaned over to Barker. "Can you come by my office when you have a minute?"

"I'm happy to talk now if you—"

"Come by my office."

"Okay."

Maureen hurried out. Barker folded his agenda, his unfinished sketch, and slid it into an inside jacket pocket.

Smiled secretly to himself as he made for the exit. *Tenure, baby! Here I come!*

At thirty-fucking-five.

Rusk was there. "What's the deal with *that?*" he asked.

Barker hesitated.

"So it's okay for *her,*" Rusk went on, "to circulate a letter about sexual assault, but I can't ask for signatories to challenge the monopolization of our communication infrastructure?"

I don't have time for this. Barker spotted Shiv in the hallway, on the other side of the glass, and manoeuvred around Rusk to bodily buffer their voices. "I think they're separate issues," Barker offered. "Shiv wasn't soliciting signatures. Someone asked to sign a letter and she signed it."

Barker suspected that Rusk suffered from an affliction common to men of a particular professional class, those that clung to the middle rungs of institutional hierarchies: A casual disdain for their female coworkers. Rusk would have vehemently denied this, of course. *Exhibit A:* His bright, successful wife, and *B:* His gifted, athletic daughter. But how else to explain his treatment of Shiv? His dismissive attitude toward Maureen? Case in point: The remedy of individual letters in lieu of faculty signatories had been proposed by Maureen to Rusk over email days earlier. Rusk had ignored her.

Wasn't there only one obvious variable?

Thought back to Bert, twirling his bifocals. *See? Gender!*

Rusk: "She signed it as a representative of the university!"

"You're free to sign that letter, or any other letter for that matter. In fact, you *have* signed those kinds of letters."

"Right, and caught no end of flak."

"Well, so did Shiv just then."

"Yeah, from a student," Rusk grumbled. "They're the only ones who give a shit about anything anymore."

Barker should have a quick parley with Rusk, warn him that his truculence was alienating him from his colleagues. Rusk would be more receptive if the caveat came from Barker. *I get that you have this chip on your shoulder, that we're these weak-kneed theorists railing against hegemony and oppression but would never get our hands dirty actually doing anything about it; that you're slogging it out in the trenches while we stay cloistered at a safe remove to quibble over communication in the abstract. But at the end of the day, we're all trying to make a difference the best way we know how.* Caution him to modify his behaviour. *So, y'know, tone it the fuck down, 'kay?*

"Listen, I've got to get to class, but why don't we grab a pint next week and unpack this a bit?"

Rusk looked visibly relieved. "Sounds good, man. Thanks for hearing me." Gave Barker's forearm a squeeze and left.

Barker darted into his office to grab his phone. Missed call from Dell. No voicemail icon. Couldn't call her back right now, would have to hustle to make it to class on time as it was.

A good sign! It was the first time Dell had contacted him since...

Rounded the corner to find Shiv and Molly still outside the conference room. Shiv spoke with the subdued deference of a customer service agent being harangued over a broken toaster, countenance devoid as the moon.

Barker tuned-in mid-sentence: "...do we right this wrong—that women have, historically speaking, been disbelieved and vilified—by swinging the pendulum all the way in the other direction?"

Quarter-turn, stared down at his phone.

"Every crime, across the board, has a small percentage of false reporting, rape included," Shiv continued. "Statistically speaking, while there are no more or less false claims of sexual assault than of any other crime—"

Molly's mouth sprang open with an audible *pop*. Shiv held up a finger.

"Which is *not* to say, of course, that the majority of claims *are* false. Far from it. The issue in terms of victim-centric approaches—this was the point of the letter—is that if we contend that victims are *always right*, that every accuser *must be believed*, their credibility unimpeachable, then in the extremely rare instance that a claim *is* false—the Duke lacrosse team, for example, or *u-vee-a*—then that false claim brings the veracity of every other claim into question. Do you see how it's a double-edged sword? Entangling the truth or falsity of one claim with the truth or falsity of every other?"

Barker turned on his heel and hastened down the hallway in the opposite direction. He'd take the long way around to the stairs.

✦ ✦ ✦

Scampered down the staircase, circumambulating Lake House's vacuous atrium. Six years ago, the program had been relocated to the university's newest building and, as so often happened in the transposition of living things with deep roots, some faculty were having difficulty adjusting to their pristine new soil.

Bert, for one, loathed Lake House's "calculated sterility," what he called "architecture by algorithm," and still, six years on, lamented the loss of his former confines. "That building had history. Character!" he'd declaimed on more than one occasion, with the full-throated indignation of the forcibly dispossessed.

Few shared Bert's nostalgia. For most, the mounting problems eclipsed any accrued sense of sentimentality. "Character, sure," Maureen told Barker. "Also black mould and asbestos. It's not like that building was condemned for no reason."

Encroaching contaminants notwithstanding, there had been rats, perennial silverfish infestations, and at least one resident raccoon that Rusk had had to fend off with a garbage pail. A vocal majority considered these altercations with assorted pests and wildlife too high a price to pay for Bertrand's esoteric appeals to "character," and—more to the point—his getting away with smoking indoors. Besides, as the program increased in cachet, and enrolment climbed, shiny new digs were all but inevitable. They needed a space reflective of their burgeoning prestige, something sleek and sophisticated, with floor-to-ceiling windows framing picturesque vistas. (Said vista, the so-called "lake," was a shallow manufactured pond lined with birch saplings.)

And that was precisely what they got: Space. Or at least the semblance thereof. Upon entry, Lake House seemed big and bright enough, its bloated atrium soaring six stories high. Upon closer scrutiny, however, this capaciousness was a mirage obscuring a net reduction in square footage, leaving faculty, staff, and students more cramped than before. True, there were several larger lecture halls, but if growth continued apace, class sizes would outstrip their capacity sooner rather than later.

Adding insult to injury, the atrium had been garnished with a *living wall.* Bert surmised that for the cost of maintaining their "gimmicky paean to eco-consciousness," the program could have hired two contract instructors year-round. The wall might have been worth the price and hassle had its plants infused Lake House with much-needed oxygen, but the processed air remained as stubbornly thin and weak as wind pumped in from a mountain peak.

As such, Lake House was more testament to the university's ample resources—*If we can blow coin on bricks and mortar of this calibre, much less a fucking living wall, need we say more about our financial virility?*—than a utilitarian milieu. Madame President loved to showcase her expensive erection by hosting all manner of events set against the backdrop of plasticine green and tuffets of tangled roots clinging tenuously to the wall above.

Towers today: distressed steel, reclaimed wood, and sexy slate in lieu of ivory.

✦ ✦ ✦

Barker steered through the quad at a canter.

With summer climes persisting into fall, all embraced the abnormal heat in shorts and tees; a splendour of race and ethnicity singing relaxed, decadent vibes: Frisbees tossed, footballs thrown, a small circle booting around a hacky-sack. Even in his hurry, Barker marvelled at the success, brought into irrefutable relief, of the multicultural ethic. *People from all walks of life, from all corners of the globe, given a common purpose, equity, and even economic footing can come together and flourish!*

Envied their chill, wished he could slow down and partake. The drumbeat of obedience instilled by their institutional educations—that ceaseless pulse of Pavlovian bells, once as central to their blinkered existences as a heartbeat—was already dissipating. Such a beautiful thing, this collective coming into awareness of their own expanding agency.

Veered inside a building, its narrow corridor clogged with students, some funnelling into a lecture hall, others slouched against brick with their phones. Raised his arms and satchel to squeeze through the scrum, through a cluster of women ensconced in black burqas, whole beings reduced to eyes consigned to slits.

Grimaced. The splendour was great, but these he detested. They screamed oppression. Tolerance had to have limits.

◆ ◆ ◆

"Afternoon, everyone!" Barker exclaimed as he entered.

Silence.

Draped his satchel over the back of a nearby chair, plugged a code into a control panel to unlock the media array—a computer, projector, and a DVD/VCR hybrid. (He'd joked to one of the kids that she should feel free to use the device if she had any DVDs she wanted to transfer to VHS. She asked him what VHS was.) The panel was finicky as shit. The pad had slipped out of synch with the circuitry underneath, and any error required re-entering the code in its entirety.

Motherfucker.

On the fourth attempt, the projectors beamed soft blue. Barker perched on the edge of a table, prompting a hurried return of phones to purses and backpacks.

As the susurrus subsided, he mentally braced himself for the three hours ahead.

"All right," he began. "Foucault."

Barker was just finding his groove when Molly arrived. She quickly and quietly—rather, a distracting pantomime of quick and quiet—slid into the nearest available seat.

"Sorry," she whispered as she opened her laptop. "I was meeting with Doctor Grady."

Less a meeting, Barker thought, *than a hostage taking.*

"So I was…right…I was saying that some of you may have noticed that—and for those of you who did your undergrad in comm, you probably noticed this a long time ago—quite a few of the thinkers we engage with are not, or would not have considered themselves, communication or media scholars. And so it is with Foucault, who was what? A historian? Please don't say that to any historians. They'd be horrified."

Silence.

"But Foucault didn't really think of himself as a historian either. He may have been doing historical analysis, but not of the sort typically associated with capital-*aitch* History. Foucault wasn't interested in a history of events, but rather a history of ideas, of *knowledge.*"

Felt their attention buckle.

"So if Foucault—as with Marx, Freud, de Certeau, to name a few—was not a media scholar, why study Foucault in a course about media?"

Silence.

Opened his thermos, took a dainty sip of still-steaming tea, surveyed their startled deer-in-headlights faces, fingers twitching autonomously over keyboards; spaced-out eyes affixed to screens, pawing at laptop track pads like rats at food dispensers. *Twitter?*

Facebook? Anything but Foucault? Others hid their hands surreptitiously under desks, eyes crotchwise.

"C'mon, Sven, we've talked about this before."

Sven pulled his phone out from under his desk, slid it into a backpack.

Barker counted. *One...two...three...four...* Trick from his TA days. Ask a question and wait and wait and wait. Let them know you're willing to wallow in awkward silence for as long as it takes.

...five...six...seven...eight...

Was irritated with Sven. *Who do you think you're fooling? What else could you possibly be doing with your hands under your desk like that?*

...nine...ten...eleven...

How fucking stupid do you think I am?

...twelve...thirteen...

You're supposed to be adults, the cream of the intellectual crop. The only way any of this works is if you come prepared with something to say; converse, discuss, debate! Don't worry about sounding stupid. We all sound stupid! It's the only escape from chrysalis, this painful metamorphosis into one who steals and synthesizes, cobbles together and generates anew; this transmutation from parrot to pirate.

"Well, Foucault kind of reminds me of Butler."

Everything reminded Molly of Butler.

Barker's mental Bert piped up: *Gender this and gender that!*

"Okay. How so?"

"Well..." she checked the ceiling, "both Butler and Foucault bring into focus the, uh, various mechanisms that exist, or that are put in place, to predetermine our actions. Like, they're both calling into question how free we really are."

"Good. But before going further, we should make a distinction between how Butler and Foucault approach this idea of social constructivism—"

"Gender performativity," Molly suggested.

Or was that a correction?

Barker knew next to nothing about Butler, except that he hated her writing, in that he could barely understand her writing. Butler epitomized academia's most egregious impulses: arrogance, myopia, intellectual elitism; ideas bent into painfully abstruse contortions; insight at its utmost remove from the practicalities and pragmatics of everyday life. To celebrate her impenetrable bafflegab was to venerate impenetrability itself; seal off the Academy from the very people—the marginalized and disenfranchised—its votaries claimed to champion.

"Yes, Butler proposes that gender is a sort of *role* we're cast in by society, by prevailing cultural attitudes; that we're coerced into playing throughout our lives."

Molly smiled.

"Foucault is not so interested in these prescribed roles or performativity *per se*, but rather how certain structures—social structures, yes, but also *literal* structures—institutional structures, architecture—impose certain behaviours, right? What's the most obvious example here?"

Sipped tea as his internal metronome ticked off the beats.

...eleven...twelve...thirteen...fourteen...

"The Panopticon?"

"Exactly." *What a slog.* "Care to elaborate?"

The kid looked unsure. "The Panopticon is, like, a kind of prison. And it's circular with, like, a pillar in the middle. And there are guards inside the pillar. And no matter where you are, because it's a circle, the guards can see you..."

Barker picked up the slack. "Good. The Panopticon was designed by a Scottish philosopher named...?"

"Bentham."

Thanks, Molly. "Right. Jeremy Bentham. And what Foucault does in *Discipline and Punish* is offer a reading of Bentham's design. How does Foucault 'read,'" pumped his fingers, "the Panopticon?"

"One of the features of the central pillar," Molly ventured, "is that the glass is, ah, opaque. So you can't see whether the guards are there or not. And Foucault says that even though you don't know whether they're there, you have to act like they are."

Replaced the plug in his thermos. "Right. Broadly speaking, Foucault's take on the Panopticon is that surveillance is something we *internalize*. In other words, if we're put in a position where we don't know whether someone is watching us, and irrespective of whether someone actually *is* watching us, we take it upon ourselves to act as though we're being watched."

"Right," Molly said. "Kind of like a performance."

✦ ✦ ✦

As the students filtered out, Barker shut down the tech, gathered his things, poured the lukewarm dregs of his tea into the trash.

Molly was waiting for him in the hallway.

"Hey, Molly. Anything I can help you with?"

"I just wanted to suggest, for next time, that there should be a trigger warning for that book."

Barker was thrown. "What book?"

She smiled. "Foucault. *Discipline and Punish*."

"A trigger warning for which part?"

"The opening section."

The opening section: Foucault's graphic descriptions of grotesque medieval punishments. Subjects tortured, executed, drawn and quartered.

Wait...

"I didn't assign the opening passages," Barker said. "Did I?"

"No. But if I have time I try to read the whole book so that I understand the assigned sections in their proper context."

"Right." Flexed his jaw. "Very industrious of you."

"Anyhow, just a suggestion. It's an amazing course, Doctor Stone. I'm really loving it a lot so far." She turned down an adjacent hallway. "See you at the Gathering on Friday!"

* * *

By the time Barker returned to Lake House, Maureen was gone. Went to his office, stuffed his satchel into his bike's lone pannier, moved behind his desk and shook the mouse. Refreshed his email: listserv alerts, student inquiries, a call for letters from Rusk, a call for feedback from Molly, a message from Hannah re: discount room rates at the Rio.

Nothing from Tatjana, his ex. Said he'd hear from her by the end of the week. *Only Wednesday.*

Clicked refresh. Still nothing.

A message caught his eye. Subject blank. Unknown name and address.

> e.robson@AlbinoRhino2017.ca

Albino Rhino sounded familiar. Couldn't put his finger on it.

Opened the message.

> Hello! I'm trying to reach Dr. Barker Stone. If this is Dr. Stone, could you give me a quick call back? Promise not to take up too much of your time!
>
> Please and thanks :)

Followed by a phone number. Signed Evan.

Dialled.

"Hello?" A man.

"Hi, I'm returning a message from...uh...Evan?"

"Evan just stepped away from his desk. Who's this?"

"Doctor Stone. Barker."

"Ah! Yes! Hello!" Burst of background clatter. "Not that one, Sadie. Hold off for...I'll be there in a second." Back to Barker: "Sorry. Bit of chaos over here."

"With whom am I speaking?"

"This is Mac. Evan just stepped away from his... Wait, I just said that."

"What's this regarding?"

"This…?"

"The email?" Beat. "Why don't I leave you my cell and Evan can call me back when he—?"

"No, it's fine. I can… Evan and I work together. We're—No, Sadie, *not* that one. Just *one second*. Literally." And back: "We work for Baz Randell. His campaign."

"The mayoral candidate?" Ah. *Albino Rhino*. Right.

"The very same."

A siren brayed in the distance. "Are you soliciting donations?"

Mac chortled. "No, no, no. Nothing like that, I… Look, this would be easier to explain in person. *Stop!* STOP! No! What is he—? *Wait!* Sorry. Like I said: Chaos."

Shiv at Barker's door. He held up a finger: *One second.*

Mac: "Any chance you could swing by our office?"

Shiv mouthed: *Luce.* Barker nodded. Thumbs up. She left.

Opened his calendar. "We could schedule something for next Monday. Maybe early afternoon?"

"It's a bit on the urgent side," Mac added.

"Right, well, tomorrow evening might be possible."

"What're you up to tonight?"

"Tonight? I'm, uh, heading to a meeting with a colleague presently."

"How late do you expect your meeting to go?"

"Eight at the earliest, maybe more like eight-thirty or nine, but I don't—"

"Perfect."

"—know where your offices are, and—"

"We're not too far from the university. We'd be happy to spring for a cab."

"I have my bike."

"Even better. Give me your number and I'll text you the map. *Put it down! Put* all *of them down!* JESUS! I will *literally* be there in, like, seconds! Okay, so we'll expect you for, say, nine-ish?"

"Sure. Give or take."

Gave Mac his number.

"Great! Thanks! Apologies for all…"

"No sweat."

"Oh, and Doctor Stone?"

"Yes?"

"If you don't mind, could you keep this on the *dee el?*"

"The what?"

"Down low. Like, for the time being, don't tell anyone about this meeting."

"Okay."

"It'll make more sense once we've spoken. See you soon!"

Click. Mac was gone.

JOHN: I believe in freedom of thought.
CAROL: Isn't that fine.

—David Mamet, *Oleanna*

The Luce

"Remind me why we come here again?"

"Because it's cheap and you can smoke on the patio."

Satisfied sigh. Shiv: "I do like smoking on the patio."

'Here' was *Lucy's*, what regulars called *The Luce*, a pub situated in an enviable juncture—equidistant from two universities and a college. Enough of a jaunt that undergrads opted for their respective campus watering holes, but close enough to not have to resort to the city's tangled transit system. Besides its academic clientele, *The Luce* cast a wide net, from white-collar banker types in glassy, hot-dick suits, to dusted construction workers in full reflective regalia. Unlike the university's narrow monochromes, *The Luce* broadcast the full spectrum of the workaday world, a babel of backgrounds and experiences—Grand Central Station with beer and poutine.

Shiv accused him of slumming among the *hoi polloi*.

"Just *hoi polloi*," he told her. "There is no 'the.'"

They claimed a table in the semi-basement, the faux-gaslights brushing the walls with undulating amber.   ·

Minimal kitsch, mainly movie posters, mainly in Italian. The largest of these—*Il buono, il brutto, il cattivo*—crowned the hearth of a gaping fireplace that evoked the British pubs, *authentic* pubs, Barker had frequented while traipsing through England and Scotland a few lifetimes ago. With its rough plaster walls, warped and perma-sticky tables, and awful service, *The Luce* lacked all the pretension secreted by your typical wine bar or gastropub. And they served proper twenty-ounce royal British pints, not those bullshit fourteen-ounce sleeves so many establishments tried passing off as pints nowadays.

Bonus: Not a single godforsaken TV to be found.

Bliss.

Shiv: "I feel like a chaperone at a high school dance."

Barker took stock. Relatively full (per usual after five), mostly students, mostly with phones in hand, faces blue ice.

Shrugged, scanned the menu.

"If we went somewhere slightly farther afield," Shiv continued, "we wouldn't have to worry so much about running into..."

"Into...?"

Leaned forward conspiratorially: "One of *them*."

"Our students?" Snorted.

"I don't want to worry about being found out in my natural habitat. I want to chillax."

"None of your students are within half a kilometre of here. It ain't no thang."

Peered over the top of her cherry-red rims. "'Ain't no thang'? Little early to be whipping out the Ebonics, don't you think?"

"Onion rings?"

"Sure. With the...?"

"Curry sauce."

"Yes! The best."

A server arrived. Semi-regulars though they were, to the best of their recollection, Barker and Shiv had never had the same server twice. "It must be an awful place to work," She'd commented once. "Hipsters don't tip. Big mistake putting *pee-bee-ar* on tap."

Here stood latest in the carousel of fresh young faces, a stunning woman of South Asian descent, sporting a sleeveless tee emblazoned

with a slain smiley face, exed-out eyes and lolling tongue—Nirvana!
No way she's old enough to know Nirvana—hem knotted into a taut bulb.

Alas, after tonight, he'd never seen her again.

"What can I get you to drink?" the server asked, teeth a start-ling white.

Barker: "Do you still have that cask ale? The *ai-pee-a?*"

"Fable?"

"That's the one."

"Great pick."

Thank you. I'm something of a connoisseur. And your name is…?

The server revolved her lighthouse beam smile to Shiv. "And for you?"

"What do you have for wine?"

Shiv knew exactly what they had for wine.

"There's a house red and a house white."

"It's a *pub*," Barker said in mock-exasperation.

"Pinot Noir?"

"Uh…" the server glanced to the side, as if in search of an unseen ally. "I'm not sure. I can check."

Barker stared at Shiv.

"Y'know what, house white will be fine. Thanks."

"Great." She snatched up their menus and turned to leave.

Barker: "Excuse me?"

Turned back.

"Could we also order some of the onion rings with the…uh…the sauce? Whatever that sauce is they come with?"

Lips polished an autumnal umber. "Sure thing." Left.

Shiv burst out laughing. "'The…uh…the *sauce*…'"

"What?"

"'Whatever that sauce is.' Yeah, what *is* the name of that sauce?"

"Your insinuation being?"

"Barker, you're allowed to say curry to a brown chick."

"That's not—"

"You think 'curry' might come across as what? Culturally insensitive?"

"The hell should I know?"

Shiv laughed harder. Nearby faces snapped up from their phones. "They invented curry, Barker!"

"Okay—"

"It's on the *menu!*" Daubed the corner of an eye. "You're precious."

"*Okay!* Yeesh. This is probably her first shift. She might not have even seen the menu yet."

"First and last if she, y'know, keeps forgetting to take food orders."

"All part of the ambience." Twirled a coaster on its axis. "And you don't have to be such a dick, by the way."

Eyebrow arched. "'Scuse me?"

"You know they don't have Pinot Noir."

"*I* do, but *she* apparently doesn't. Consider me part of their training. If they can't deal with me, then they're not cut out to work here."

The server returned, set two coasters on the table. "Oh, you've got one already," she said to Barker.

Say something clever! Face a billboard broadcasting his crush.

Set the coaster aside, put his hand on his throat.

"Fable *ai-pee-a.* House red."

Shiv shot Barker a look. "Thanks so much."

"Let me know if you need anything else." Gone.

Shiv raised her glass. "Cheers!"

"Salut!"

Clink!

"This wine comes out of a box."

"Boxed wine has come a long way."

Despite the swiftness with which they'd become friends—drinks they day they'd met, immediately following their first faculty intake session—the relationship was strictly platonic. Shiv was married. Dan was older by a decade at least; good-natured, taciturn, worked odd hours. He designed and consulted on websites for clients with enhanced security needs—government agencies and proprietary corporations, "of the *if I told you I'd have to kill you* variety," he joshed—was sometimes on call for days at a stretch. Liked to fish.

On the few occasions the three of them had spent time together, Barker got the impression that Shiv and Dan were caring and considerate partners with divergent needs and lifestyles. As such, Dan appeared pleased that his more sociable wife had a companion with whom to relieve some of the strain his sporadic schedule and solitary nature induced. Barker, for his part, appreciated Dan's cavalier attitude. Having always preferred female friends, Barker was accustomed to sporadic bouts of alpha-male teeth-baring and was plenty practised at calming the silverbacks. But Dan was evolved enough to know Barker was no usurper.

Yeah, Dan was cool.

Barker had male friends, but truth be told, he was far less comfortable in their company. Men made him feel like there was some kind of code he was meant to have internalized and finessed at some point. During his first year of grad studies, he'd cut short a blossoming friendship when the companion in question, the two of them shambling from bar to bus stop, proceeded without prompting to chronicle a slew of sexual exploits undertaken in public sites in their immediate vicinity: a blow job here, a dry hump there. It was this (albeit impressive) tally, and not the excess of beer and ill-advised Jäger shots, that Barker blamed for planting the sprig of nausea that came to full bloom during the ride home.

Women were easier, less obvious, more interesting. A preference not without its complications, but those situations worked themselves out one way or another.

"The fuck did I ever do to that guy?" Shiv said.

"He's just..." Barker wasn't sure what Rusk was.

"A misogynist prick."

"I think Gordon just likes to sulk. He's one of those guys who, no matter how much he's got, thinks everyone else has it better."

"I saw you run interference when Molly had me buttonholed in the hall."

The server appeared, face lathered in buttery light.

"Another round?"

"Up to you," Barker told Shiv. "I have a meeting to get to, but I could do one more."

"Sure, one more of the same. Thanks!"

Checked his phone. "Oh, it's early!" A text. Directions from Mac. Barker replaced the phone in his pocket.

"A meeting tonight?"

"Yeah."

"Who with?"

"I'm not supposed to say. Sorry."

"*Lah-dee-dah.*"

"Weird last minute thing...that call I was on when you came by my office. I'll tell you about it as soon as I can. Promise."

"Like I care." Checked her phone. "Then fucking Molly. I was taking it from all sides in there. Last letter I ever sign, I swear."

"It doesn't matter."

"It *does* matter. Our employer does indeed have an unblemished record of fucking up sexual violence complaints—I mean, Molly's entirely right on that count—and now it's doing this weird knee-jerk *cause-more-problems-than-it-solves* thing."

The server delivered their round. Barker watched her go. *I like Nirvana too. You think grunge will make a comeback?*

"Then the students get all up in arms because—I don't know if you've noticed this as yet—they're not exactly ones for nuance." Sipped wine. "If Molly starts to stir shit up..."

"I'm only saying don't let her get to you so much."

"I'm not letting her 'get' to me. I took on the lecture series to help Maureen. She's still not quite *back* from last year, if you know what I mean. And to kiss a bit of ass. I want a job!" She slapped the table. "A serious, all-in, tenure-" (Barker's spine tingled at the utterance of the word) "-track position. Not this sessional nonsense. Once they start to see you as contract, you're toast."

"Granted, but in terms of all of that, Molly doesn't matter."

"You're wrong, Barker. She does."

"How do you figure?"

"Are you kidding me? She makes trouble. Draws attention. Turns her warrior army against me."

"Little overdramatic." *Grunge is an underrated genre. I miss plaid shirts and wide-leg jeans. When did all the jeans get so skinny?*

"Maybe you're being a bit naïve?"

"Maybe. They do get riled up."

"I'm just saying, she decides to go after me, after Marjanne, whether it's payback for the letter thing or not, I'm not sure what I'd do."

"How so?"

"I mean I might have to cancel the lecture."

"Cancel? Because of Molly?"

"Sure, if she kicks up enough dust."

"Molly is trying to…fill a role, okay?"

"I get that. Doesn't mean she can't do some real damage."

"Let her swing her arms around a bit. She'll tire herself out."

"What do you think I've *been* doing? With Gordon? With Molly? Am I not up against the ropes while everyone throws punches? Am I not the epitome of Socratic calm and reason?" Shiv removed her Coke can glasses, her suddenly shrunken eyes sucked into the surrounding tissue. "And I like Molly. Wish we had more students like her. People with goddamned opinions." Breathed heavily on the lenses, polished them with her sleeve. "Was that your strategy with the whole unisex bathroom debacle? Lean back and take the hits?"

Plucked another coaster out from between the salt- and pepper-shakers, tore little strips off the edges.

Shiv: "Look—you're tenure track. Not to mention your stupid book."

"You love my book."

"I haven't read your book and I never will. I don't give a shit about video games."

"It's less about video games and more about how our contemporary conception of agency is being redefined through our relationship with media. But hey, *potato, potahto*."

"My point is you're golden. I'm not. Faculties used to be eighty-ish percent tenure, twentyish percent sessional, now it's the reverse. Inordinately female, next to no job security or departmental support, make less money, and teach the biggest classes with the highest-maintenance students. I'm easy pickings. One bad crop of evaluations can slay me, with ten thousand out of work *pee-aitch-dees* who'd jump my corpse in two ticks. So what incentive exactly do I have to be a hard-ass instead of handing out As and A plusses like cinnamon hearts? My number one priority is to ensure that my students *like* me. Is that some asinine, Junior High *bee-ess* or what?"

"It is. It's bullshit, it's..." The server, tending to a nearby table, leaned over to clear glasses. The back of her tee hiked up, revealing a tattoo—some twisted, thorny abstraction—on the small of her back.

"If universities would just own up to the fact that they're corporations, and that students are—as they themselves already believe—consumers, then we could all go about our business of ensuring their satisfaction without the undue burden of challenging them in any way whatsoever."

Replaced her glasses, eyes re-inflating to regular size. "Which isn't even to say that profs are immune. How many of you have gone down in sudden hails of gunfire lately? Dude fired for using anti-Semitic epithets in a course about Nazi propaganda? The one who got turfed for telling a male Muslim student that he was obligated to join a working group that might include bona fide females? Allah forbid!"

"I think he was reinstated."

"Gender pronoun guy over at, uh...?"

"He pulls in, like, fifty *kay* a month on Patreon."

Set her wine aside, pitched forward, dropped her voice. "I don't even know what I'm supposed to… Am I even allowed to say 'he' and 'she' anymore?" Drained her glass. "You heard about the Harvard lady who got taken to task for teaching rape case law because it's a potential trigger? Feminists fought for fucking *decades* to get rape included in law school curricula, and now…" Pressed her hands into her temples. "They want it taken back out! Not that learning rape case law might come in handy if you're, like, a lawyer who has to try a rape case!"

Shiv rooted around in her purse as Barker stole a sidelong glance at the server. *Couldn't help but notice your tat earlier. Yeah, I have one too. Funny story…*

"She was advised against using the word *violate* in class. As in *violate the law*."

"Why?"

"It's a trigger!"

Barker polished off his pint.

"Aha!" Shiv thrust a pack of cigarettes into the air. "Smoke?"

◆ ◆ ◆

They stood beside an ancient barbeque, smoking and nursing fresh drinks procured en route. With its potted trees, braids of ivy, scattered stone ornaments—including a birdbath that doubled as an ashtray—and off-white Christmas lights woven through a high-set trellis, the patio had a *secret garden*-ish vibe.

Barker marinated in forbidden lust. *It's impossible! Server-customer dalliances are a fantasy. They charm and seduce for the sake of their tips. Let her go, man!*

"We're talking about a woman who receives death threats on a daily basis, has been shot—not *shot at*, but *actually* shot."

Who was this?

"Last year someone tried to throw battery acid *in her face*. And that, by the bye, was in *England*. Not Iran, not Syria, not Afghanistan, but *down*-fucking-*town* London. And it's the students who need a safe space?"

Right, Marjanne Abdalla.

Contemplative drag. Barker: "What happened to them? Every year I get more and more anxiety disorders. I don't mean to belittle… Granted, there are serious afflictions we never used to acknowledge as such. But when did anxiety become a disorder? Where did all the anxiety come from?"

"Helicopter parenting? Coddling a generation of special snowflakes?"

Barker thought back on his own childhood. He'd assumed his parents were supervising him to some extent, but he'd always felt free, the world a bounty of paths, friends, bicycles, backward folds in chain-link fences…

"I can't help but think that diagnosing them…having an adult appear at your, y'know—you're eleven, twelve years old—you're having a rough time, or…you're cracked out on sugar and television and you're—"

"Video games."

"Sure. You're going through, or you're on the precipice of, puberty—not the most orderly part of anyone's life—and some adult, some person in a position of authority, pulls you aside and says: You have a capital-*dee* Disorder. For the rest of your life you will have difficulty interacting with other people. You will find social situations unbearable, will be incapable of dealing with demands and deadlines. You *internalize* that shit."

"Take these pills."

"Right!"

A bird alighted on the rim of the birdbath, sorted through the butts. Barker imagined a nest built of bent and lipstick-stained stubs.

"Also, of course, the first generation to grow up in the shadow of nine-eleven," Shiv ground out her spent smoke with a heel. "They were, what, four or five? The outset of their conscious lives, immersed in looming, all-pervasive dread."

"Two wars."

"Hurricanes."

"Mortgage crisis."

Pulled two more cigarettes out of her pack.

"I'm good."

"For later?"

The bird, butt in beak, flitted off. "Sure. Thanks." Tucked the smoke into his breast pocket. She lit up.

"Lot of anxiety-inducing shit in pretty quick succession," Shiv mused. "We don't know what it was like to grow up with all that. Probably not fun. Probably a lot of freaked-out, fucked-up parents trying to shield their brood from the worst of it.

"Generation Can't Make Eye Contact," she added.

They considered the assembled twentysomethings.

Barker's pilsner tasted skunky. *Do you know how often they clean the taps? Oh, right, you're new here. Are you a student? Where are you from, originally?* Wait, you weren't supposed to ask that. It tacitly implied they were from elsewhere, an "other." Microaggression. *Are you new to the city?* Better.

Shiv: "And what do they have to look forward to? A turbulent climate? A disintegrating European Union? Right-wing fucknuts seizing the reins of power? Explain to me how we elected the most progressive federal government in twelve years—*finally* rid of Flinty McDeadeyes—and yet somehow this city is poised to sweep a populist blowhard into power? It's not like we're, I dunno, the fifth largest economy in North America or anything. What could go wrong?"

I've only lived here a few years myself. Me? I'm a professor of communication and media. My research?

"To say nothing of the goddamned calamity unfolding down south."

I use video games as a vehicle to explore contemporary conceptions of agency.

"Barker?"

Broadly speaking, agency means our capacity to act. Bit tricky to explain. Why don't you give me your number and we could—

"Hell-oo?"

"Sorry?"

"I can't believe he's going to win. It's a travesty."

"Who?"

"Randell."

"The election's a month off. Anything could happen."

"Not looking good."

Wanted to spill. What could his campaign possibly want to talk to me about? Resisted. Keep it on the dee-el.

Instead: "Youth is wasted on the young, and democracy is wasted on the stupid."

"Don't make this about class."

"What does stupidity have to do with class?"

"Intelligence is tied to educational resources, and educational resources are still largely determined by your economic stratum."

"No economic stratum has a monopoly on stupidity. Isn't Randell the perfect case in point?"

"Last week you said he stands to win because the hicks will turn out in droves."

"I think he stands to win *in part* because the hicks will turn out in droves, but he stands to win *mostly* because of the amalgamation of the boroughs. It's demographics. Suburbanites and urbanites with totally different priorities forced to vote in the same election. Our priorities are affordable housing, bike lanes, and Pride. They want to know who's picking up the bag of leaves they left out last night. What time is it?"

Checked her phone. "Eight thirty." Flicked her spent cigarette at the birdbath. "Despite it all," she gestured at the gathered youth, "they seem pretty content, don't you think?"

"I'm going to hit the can. Meet you back at the table."

"Still," Shiv said, following him inside, "why go to a pub just to play with your phone?"

◆ ◆ ◆

Barker knew part of the answer to Shiv's question, though if he explained, she'd instantly lose interest. He recognized the signature stance assumed by some of the phone-wielding patrons, a set of idiosyncratic gestures, the way they jerked their shoulders back in unison as if dodging invisible slings. They were playing an Augmented Reality Game. Barker had yet to play the third and final entry in the *Killing Time* trilogy, but he was astonished by the craze his friend and former student Cooper Coates had whipped up.

I owe Coop a congratulatory call, he thought as he ambled up to a urinal, assumed the stance between a set of chest-high partitions. *Unisex bathrooms. An infrastructural solution to a complex sociocultural issue.* That was enough to set the whole stupid fracas in motion. *At the end of the day I'd really just prefer to go to the bathroom by myself, thanks!*

A man arrived at the adjacent urinal. He and Barker studiously avoided acknowledging each other's existence. Barker focused intensely on the ad fixed to the tile before him.

Fluflexazine. Erectile dysfunction? A satisfied woman, draped over a couch, wrapped in a white sheet, long legs tantalizingly askew, suckling a (presumably post-coital) cigarette. The slogan: "Room for seconds?"

Zipped up.

◆ ◆ ◆

Slid into the booth opposite Shiv. "I should head out."

"I just ordered another round."

"I'll settle up, and we'll, y'know, chug it."

Carried his second skunky pilsner to the bar. A specked mirror framed a choir of spirits, and a thick brass banister lined the countertop. The manager was at the other end, chatting with a pair of women.

"How's the thing with the cop? What was her name?"

"Dell." Fuck. He'd forgotten to call her back. "Could go either way. Long story."

"You fuck it up somehow?"

"Maybe. I'm not sure. I don't really want to get into it."

"'Kay."

Tried to catch the manager's eye. "I like her, though. Easy going enough for, y'know…"

"A cop?"

"We've been keeping things casual."

"How many dates?"

"Four. Five, maybe. I'm not entirely sure what counts as a date these days."

"No sex?"

Nodded. "It's not a thing, just…"

"Keeping it casual."

"Yeah."

"And no…lifestyle differences as of yet?"

"Like am I concerned about her finding out I smoke pot?"

"And whether she'll arrest you if and when she does, yes."

"We had a conversation pertaining to the use of illegal narcotics."

"She's aware that pot is being decriminalized?"

"And yet that does not seem to have softened her disposition. I believe her exact words were 'It's illegal now.'"

"Amnesty for those previously incarcerated being out of the question?"

"Yup."

"Well, good luck with that then."

"Like I said…"

"Casual."

The manager: "What can I get for you?"

"Can I settle up?" Barker handed over the bill. On the back: *Thank you!!* in a looping, free-spirited script that Barker found inordinately arousing. Then: *Anita* ☺

Signal? Invitation?

Anita. You don't look like an—

No! Microaggression!

"Two shots of tequila," said Shiv.

"No!"

"Too late. Already happening."

Dug into her purse. "Let me give you some—"

"I'll get this one. You got the last one." Rolled his fingers on the brass. "Tequila's the worst."

"Hey, wait, we never got our—" Shiv was jostled forward as a woman pushed into her from behind.

"The fuck?" exclaimed the woman, a thin blonde in a tight white halter top. Halter Top spun to confront her assailant, a black (uh, of African descent?) woman in some kind of sports jersey, hair plaited in serrated cornrows.

"The fuck is wrong with you, Melinda?" said Halter Top.

"Luwanda," said Luwanda. "You know the fuck my name is, slut."

"If this is about Travis—"

"You suck his dick?"

The crowd opened up to make space for the spar.

"None of your fucking business." Halter Top thrust a finger in Luwanda's face. Luwanda swatted it aside like a bug.

"Don't fucking touch—"

"Next time you go out shopping for some black dick, make sure that dick is still for sale, bitch."

"Then tell Travis to keep his dick off the shelf."

Several things happened in quick succession: Luwanda took Barker's pint right out of his hand, tossed its contents into Halter Top's face. The manager leaped over the bar, hooked his toe on the banister, flopped onto the floor. Luwanda swivelled at the sound of the manager's fall, accidentally smashing the now-empty pint glass against the piping. It shattered into a flurry of shards. Halter Top, wiping beer out of her eyes, heard the glass smash, saw its jagged remnants in Luwanda's hand, lunged and swatted Luwanda in the side of the head. Luwanda crumpled into a defensive crouch. Halter Top kicked at her back and torso, was grabbed by a muscular man. Arms wrapped around Halter Top's waist, Muscle Man swung her away from Luwanda, now sprawled across the floor. Suspended midair, Halter Top thrashed, sending one of her shoes soaring through the air in a parabolic arc. Barker watched the shoe twist and tumble and vanish underneath a table. Muscle Man, taken aback by the force and ferocity of Halter Top's flailing, spun her back toward Luwanda, now on her knees. Luwanda seized one of Halter Top's ankles mid-kick and yanked. Now the object of a tug-of-war, Halter Top redoubled her resistance. Luwanda lost her grip, and all three popped apart like a split atom.

Back on his feet, the manager limped over to Muscle Man and Halter Top and ushered them toward the patio. Luwanda followed. Barker blocked her path.

"Get the fuck outta my way."

"I can't do that," Barker said.

She was giddy with rage, pumping short, shallow breaths through bullish nostrils. Slivers of glass in her hair winked amber.

"I said get the fuck out my way."

Barker scanned the surrounding circle. The crowd stood mute, curious as to how these new hostilities might escalate.

He looked to Shiv for support. She watched, mouth slightly agape.

So much for backup.

Luwanda tried to deke past. Barker matched her movements in reverse. Pushed her face into his, cocked her head. He held her gaze, close enough see the engorged capillaries in her eyes.

"Listen motherfucker—"

The manager grabbed her, hauled her aside. "The police are on their way. So get the fuck out or go to jail. Your choice."

◆　◆　◆

Streetlamps hummed overhead. Light rain spotted the pavement.

"You were saying?"

Shiv finished lighting a cigarette. "What?"

"Before the... You were saying something. We never got our what?"

She smiled. "Onion rings. Curry sauce."

"Ah."

"Share a cab?"

"No, I've got my—" Was going to say *bike*, but Shiv cut him off.

"Right. Your *secret meeting*."

Donned his helmet and fastened the clip, stuffed a pant cuff into his sock.

"Don't do anything stupid," she said.

"According to you I'm too privileged to be stupid."

"You're not bad looking. Not to my taste, obviously, but insofar as the available metrics..." Caught herself slurring her words. "You're what my *baba* would have called a tall drink of water."

"What's this about?"

"We live in a world flush with hot young things who have more control over their own lives than ever before. They want to fuck and drink and do drugs. They think they're super smart and super savvy. They're coming into their *power*."

Was she telling him something?

"All I'm saying is, the atmosphere is volatile. Don't go lusting after any...y'know..."

Holy shit! Did she know about Lara?

"I'm thirty-five, I'm—"

Shiv snorted, flagged down a cab.

"You're a dying breed, Barker." Tossed her smoke as the cab

quickened to the curb, reached for the handle and stumbled. Barker moved to catch her, but she waved her hand to fend him off, braced herself.

"I'm good. I'm good." Opened the door. "Stupid-ass boxed wine."

As the cab shouldered into traffic, the window opened. Shiv stuck out her head.

"Sorry about your dog!" she yelled, the cab's red taillights the eyes of a retreating predator.

CAROL: What I "feel" is irrelevant.

—David Mamet, *Oleanna*

The Meeting

It was nearly ten when Barker reached Randell campaign headquarters. The route from Mac was more convoluted than it first appeared. Barker's GPS tried to coax him into a sketchy-looking alley that would have required hoisting his bike over a sagging chain link fence. He balked when he heard furtive rummaging from an unseen source. The subsequent detour trapped him in a whirlpool of one-ways that, even on his bike, took some effort to escape. He then managed to ride past the building twice before realizing that this indistinct two-storey strip mall, squatting on the edge of the city's industrial decay, was his intended terminus.

Called Mac. "I'm outside."

"Groovy. See the door between the dry cleaners and notary public?"

"Sure. Do you buzz me in, or—?"

"Door's open. Second floor. Come on up!"

The brief burst of rain had lathered the sewers, leaving the air ripe with funk. Seeing no rack, Barker propped his bike against a bent aluminum strut capped with a no parking sign, then pulled his satchel loose of the pannier to get at his lock. He spotted a gang—*no, gang is pejorative; a* group—of black teens in puffy jackets loitering outside a convenience store, music with an uncertain beat jerked out of tinny speakers.

On second thought, the strut looked flimsy. He'd bring his bike upstairs instead.

Wheeled it to the door, hefted it onto his shoulder. As he opened the door, the wheel caught, driving the chain ring into his abdomen. His satchel slid off his shoulder and into the crook of his arm. Tried to pull the bag back up and lost hold of his helmet. It struck the cement with a CLACK.

A teen in a bulbous roast-ham jacket split off from the pack (*Group!*), slouched over, trailing a scarf of pungent smoke, eyelids so heavy they were practically closed, said something.

Barker: "Pardon?"

"I said it look like you in a predicament." He scooped up Barker's helmet, held the door. Barker shuffled the bike and satchel as the teen placed the helmet into his open hand.

"Much obliged," Barker said.

"Have a good one, brother," he sang, loping back to his fellows.

A steep and narrow staircase. Barker twisted into his bike and sidled. Halfway up, a pedal dug into the drywall, leaving a fat grey gouge in its wake.

At the top he turned into the only available entrance. Desks, computers, phones, and placards emblazoned with *Baz Randell: Albino Rhino 2017!* commingled with more banal signage with blue backgrounds and basic yellow (Impact?) font: *Stop the All-You-Can-Spend Buffet!* Cubicle partitions were tipped against one wall like feltish dominoes.

A young woman: "Barker?"

"Yes."

"Katie." She extended her hand. Barker shook it. "Evan and Mac are waiting for you. You can leave your bike by that desk if you want. I'll be out here."

Barker followed her through the disarray, wishing he'd turned down that last beer. The surge of adrenaline from the fight at The Luce was fading, and the alcohol settled back over his mind like silt.

Worried he reeked of booze, he searched his pockets for a stick of gum or mint.

Shiv's parting comment—*Don't do anything stupid*—rankled. If she'd found out about Lara somehow, why not come right out and say so? Nothing untoward had happened. No need for code. *A consensual sexual relationship between two mature adults!* That Lara was a student, a *graduate* student, was neither here nor there. Barker had never been her professor, so there could be nothing transactional. No grades for sex. Yes, he'd been serving as Interim Program Director at the time, but there was little for Lara to leverage there.

And sure, okay, they'd kept their libidinous side venture secret, but only because they valued discretion, shared an aversion to office gossip and had no desire to become an object thereof. If there was one thing to be said about the whole inconsequential whateveritwas, one empirically indisputable fact, it was this: *They'd done absolutely nothing wrong.*

Besides, it was over. Given the brevity of the affair, it barely even ranked as a breakup. *An abrupt but amicable parting of ways.*

Shiv and Lara weren't friends. They didn't socialize. Lara had no earthly reason *to* tell Shiv.

The obvious conclusion: Shiv *didn't* know, and Barker was projecting his guilty conscience. Well, not "guilty" *per se. Regretful.* Lara had simply proven more emotionally immature than her age and intellect implied. Sure, he should have known not to get involved in the first place, but at least he'd ended it as soon as he had.

Katie brought Barker into a room at the back. Eight people encircled a long folding table strewn with coffee mugs, soiled Styrofoam, pens and markers, papers and folders.

"Ev?" she said. The room hushed. "This is Barker."

"Doctor Stone!" Evan clapped his hands and sprang to his feet. "Welcome!" To the assembled: "Let's clock out, everyone." Checked his phone. "Yikes! It's after ten. Let's sleep in a bit tomorrow, hey? Six thirty instead of six?" A communal groan. "Mac, can you stick around for a few?"

The lone lingerer, knees propped against the table, face in his phone, tossed Evan a two-fingered salute.

"Evan Robson." Took Barker's hand in both of his, gave it three firm pumps. "Thanks so much for coming."

Barker turned. "You must be Mac?"

Without looking up: "Good to meet you."

"Please, have a seat," Evan said, reclaiming his own. "Mac, maybe we want to close the door, hey?"

Mac extended a blind arm, fumbled for the edge, swung the door shut.

"Y'know what? Long day. I crave a libation. Barker?"

"Water would be great."

"No prob. Mac? I'm having a scotch."

Mac: "Groovy."

To Barker: "Sure you don't want something stronger?"

Barker set down his bag and helmet. "Uh, yeah, I'd join you for a scotch."

"Neat? Rocks?"

"Rocks if you have some."

"We probably don't, but I'll scope out the sitch. As a heads up, it isn't good scotch. We just pilfer from the interns, what they stash in their stations." Left.

Mac: "Irish whiskey most likely. Rye if we're lucky."

"Sorry I'm late," Barker told Mac. "Bit of trouble finding the building."

"Ain't no thang," Mac replied, eyes fixed on his screen. "Lots to do around here."

"You mentioned something about chaos."

Mac smirked, heaved his chest in a silent laugh. He had a bushy black beard and horn-rimmed glasses. His dark hair shone with product, raked to the side in vinyl-like grooves. The rolled-up sleeves of his maroon plaid shirt revealed spiralling tattoos. Barker spotted a chain dangling off his waist.

Evan returned, closed the door. "Irish whiskey."

"They're interns," Mac shrugged. "We don't pay them anything."

Evan grabbed three mugs, dumped their contents into a nearby trashcan. "No rocks, I'm afraid." Poured, set one mug in front of Mac, held another out for Barker.

"You may detect a subtle note of stale coffee. I assure you this is exactly what the distiller intended."

Mac chuckled. "Irish coffee!" *Heave! Heave! Heave!*

Har! Har! Har! went Evan. "Nice one!"

Evan exuded prep-school polish: loose name-brand threads, head mossed with dirty-blond Brillo pad coils so compact you could scrub pots. He looked like a character straight out of *Archie*.

Evan sat. "First off, kudos for taking the time to meet. It's late, and this isn't the easiest bunker to find."

"I was just apologizing to Mac for—"

Evan waved him off. "Not at all. We appreciate you making the trek."

Barker sipped.

"Before proceeding, we want to be clear that you need to hold this conversation in the strictest confidence." Evan slid a folder across the table.

Barker opened it, scanned the document inside.

"A non-disclosure agreement?" Beat. "You want me to sign this?"

"If you don't mind."

Barker closed the folder. "Before signing anything, I'd appreciate a bit of a briefing. Like, what's this all about?"

Mac glanced up at Evan. Evan's smile was impeccable.

"Fair." Took a swig, grimaced. "This, as you have no doubt deduced, is the scrappy shoestring operation working around the clock to elect Baz Randell as the next mayor of this fine city. I'm campaign manager and chief strategist. Mac is deputy campaign manager and director of communications."

Mac pinched an invisible brim, mimed tipping a hat.

"Is Barker okay, or do you prefer Doctor Stone?"

"Barker is fine."

"Barker, have you done any consulting work before?"

"I've...yes. For software developers and video game publishers. Once for an advertising agency. I've never consulted on a political campaign before. If...if that's what you want me to do. And if so, I'm not really sure I have anything to offer."

"Let's park that for a minute. Let me ask you this: What do you know about Baz Randell?"

There was the standard-issue playlist of scandals and offenses, the self-inflicted wounds and unforced errors that'd plagued Randell throughout his tenure as a city councillor: drunkenly castigating a couple at a baseball game; arrested for drug possession in Florida; calling another councillor a "glorified coat rack." (Like most, Barker had little idea what the insult meant, only that it was intended as one.) These and other antics inspired no end of head shaking and hand wringing. The local intelligentsia was always already aghast at Randell's undignified *beneath-the-office* breaches. Though none would have admitted as much, their disgust was at least partly rooted in Randell's bulk and shambolic dress. Balding, beefy, and looking like he'd just rolled out of bed after a bender, Baz possessed neither patience for the tedious mechanisms of governance, nor any apparent awareness of his own girth—even occasionally bodily bashing into others unawares.

What really twisted one's knickers, though, was that none of Randell's blunders ever punctured his support among the devotees. Not only was his base—the so-called *Rhino Republic*—indifferent to his mischief, but Baz's support often *increased* in its wake. The more missteps, the more fallible, the more human, the more *like them*. (This despite the fact that Randell had been born wealthy, white, and in all other respects privileged.) The boroughs ate up his *man of the people* shtick. Randell could do no wrong.

They were a city divided, and Baz was the line in the sand. You couldn't not pick a side: Boorish bully, or flamboyant folk hero?

But did Barker know anything substantive about Randell's policies? All his campaign rhetoric harped on taxes. Case in point, the slogan splattered across the signage: *Stop the All-You-Can-Spend Buffet.*

Drained his mug. "Not a lot. The controversies of course. But in terms of the campaign...? The buffet thing, I guess."

Mac screwed his face into a rictus of mock pain, mimed slitting his wrists, hissed and flicked his fingers—blood spraying from the wounds—placed an invisible gun against his temple, pulled the trigger, snapped his head back, let it hang.

"That's all Baz." To Mac: "You've got to admit, bro, it's working awesome sauce."

Mac rolled his eyes.

Evan: "We're all of us aware of the...shortcomings of Baz's style. Those of us that stuck with him have had to accept that there's not a lot we can do to change him, or his approach. And while we know it's hard for a lot of people to stomach, it's actually his...unconventional style that his supporters like the most. Baz says what he thinks. Doesn't play politics. He's unfiltered—"

"Authentic," Mac interjected.

"He truly is a *team of rivals* kind of guy."

"He doesn't come across like that at all," Barker ventured.

"We know. It's a problem."

"Look, I shouldn't have... It's not my place to Monday morning—"

"No, Barker, we want you to be candid. You're not much use to us if you aren't."

Evan topped up his own whiskey, then reached across the table and refilled Barker's mug. Mac put a hand over his. Barker looked to the ceiling. One of the halogens was flickering, emitted faint crackles and spits.

"You work for the Communication and Media department, correct?" Evan asked.

"Well, technically we're a program, but..." A thought occurred,

"Listen, I'm a theory guy. If there's a…scandal or something, if you need advice on how to manage the media, the news media, then you need someone with a background in *pee-ar*, or—"

"We don't need another *pee-ar* hack. That's what Mac's for." Mac flipped Evan the bird. Evan made a jerking off gesture.

"I could recommend some colleagues. People with expertise in damage control—"

"You're cross-appointed, correct?"

"Uh, yes." Okay, Evan had done his homework.

"In video games?"

"Yes. Sort of. There's no official video game… We're an ad hoc branch of Digital Humanities."

"You study how media control people, yes?"

There it was. Barker's entire academic career distilled into a single pithy pull-quote. *Ultimately, we may want to investigate how our media control us, and not the other way around.* A throwaway line he'd added at his publisher's behest to spice up the epilogue. Was it the best or worst fate that could befall an academic? Remembered as a rube, but at least you were remembered!

Leave them with something to chew on.

How long had it been? How long since he'd scrapped his first project mid-way through his PhD? A sprawling exploration of so-called *configuration-dominant* video game narrative: *Far more germane to* improvisational *or oral* storytelling systems. *Think, per Lord, of the "singers" of Homeric epics, drawing upon a "fund" of characters and plot points, tailored to the time and place of their telling. These epics were not, at their inception, the sort of "fixed" texts that contemporary narratology fixates on.* Couldn't contain it. Couldn't devise a workable thesis. When had he pivoted to the as-yet neglected (at least in terms of the cut he intended to make) analysis of media and agency? *Per Giddens, agency defined as* the capacity to act. *Per Ahearn, agency as* socio-culturally mediated. *Per Bandura, agency as a matter of* perception. *Per Stone, agency as* discursively constructed.

We might consider agency as the discursively constructed capacity to act.

Nine years? Ten? And already so much chewing.

See, here, this ad for the Atari 2600. The slogan: Don't watch TV tonight. *Play it! It is the media* user, *not the* machine *(i.e., the television), that the discourse implies is transformed by the console. The formerly "passive" watcher of TV elevated into an "active" player of video games. Whether the medium—the Atari itself—can be said to "truly" deliver agency is irrelevant. It is the player's perception that the console "grants" them agency, and how that perception is shaped or altered, that demands scrutiny.*

And how do we know that advertising, this culturally omnipresent discourse, has the power to shape or alter perceptions? Look at the controversy over Mass Effect 3. *The marketing promises players unparalleled influence over narrative outcomes:* "Experience...an emotional story unlike any other, where the decisions you make completely shape your experience and outcome." *Further:* "choices drive powerful outcomes...including relationships with key characters, the fate of entire civilizations, and even radically different ending scenarios." *Decisions! Choices! Ending scenarios! The game fails to fulfill these promises of* meaningful *narrative agency, and the players revolt!*

Refashions his diss into a book. *Agency in Play.* The publisher is pleased. "Catchy title." The reviews are middling. Initially, to no one's surprise, *Play* vanishes into the void, as most scholarly tomes do. Then—Glory be!—a resurrection. His book cameos on course syllabi, first in boutique grad seminars, then undergrad courses. The kids dig it. (All well and good since they are being forced to buy it.) It speaks to them. (A generation, after all, for which video games are a, if not *the,* cornerstone of social and cultural existence.) It's quote-unquote "accessible." Barker wins the strange fame accorded to otherwise obscure warrior-heroes unique to every self-contained tribe, sub-culture, and clique.

And then that fame overflows its intended brim. He goes

mainstream. Magazines. Documentaries. *Colbert*. (This latter appearance, as surreal as anything Barker has ever experienced, makes him a god among grad students.) He is exalted, but also reduced, like rich broth into saline glaze. As with the lucky ones that came before—you know, that's *Hacktivism* lady, he's *Convergence Culture* dude—Barker is pigeonholed as one of the *that* guys: The *Media Control People* guy.

The blowback begins. First polite but prodding inquiries. (*Are you sure you didn't overemphasize such and such?*) Then ever-more emboldened counterarguments. (*Did you ever consider this other thing? Have you read so-and-so?*) Followed by emphatic picking apart and full-throated critique. (*Stone utterly fails to acknowledge…!*) They pile on. Friends and peers, esteemed colleagues, fellow warrior-scholars. Had any of them read *Play* in its entirety, or just bits and pieces? The intro and conclusion? Or had they only heard the aphorism? *…may want to investigate how our media control us, and not the other way around.*

Chew, chew, chew, chew, chew, chew, chew…

Is he not aware that such a claim is not only hackneyed, but historically untenable? Theoretically unsustainable? A throwback to an arcane era of communication studies, one infatuated with propaganda and passivity, with media that *brainwash* the masses—an innately sticky notion that took extraordinary effort to dispel? Why bring *brainwashing* back up? Why lend it new credence? Why turn the conversation back seventy-odd years?

Chew, chew, chew, chew, chew, chew…

The situation is only exacerbated by the book's foremost champions: Undergrads. The kids stuff their assignments chock-a-block with exuberant but unsophisticated summaries and appraisals. They less cite Stone than hack away at *Play* like blind butchers, chopping it into slipshod chunks that must then be digested by TAs and sessionals and (occasionally) professors, who find it unappetizing gruel indeed.

Chew, chew, chew, chew, chew…

Distressed that the impressionable youth under their tutelage are rallying around Barker's vapid screed, the gatekeepers redouble their defense. The scathing analyses and glib dismissals intensify as the book's popularity soars. Bashing him becomes fashionable. *Expected.* Every Q&A at every panel at every conference is now an inquisition, whether his presentation has anything do with *Play* or not.

Chew, chew, chew, chew...

As the chorus of detractors swells, Barker performs the expected role—grins and bears it, stays gracious and self-effacing in the face of their flak. (Isn't this what it's all about? Dialogue and debate? Reflection and refinement?) Hates it. Hates back-pedalling, equivocating, conceding. To every thrust, a feeble parry: "Thank you for your question. You make an excellent point." Such is the etiquette governing scholarly knife brawls.

Chew, chew, chew...

All the while secretly thinking: *Fucking ticks. Have your fill. Feast till you bust.*

Chew, chew...

Eventually *Stone fatigue* sets in. This is an actual phrase he overhears. Instead of being attacked, he's ignored.

It is a relief.

Gulp.

At first.

Now bouts of self-pity. Was it not enough endure the PhD itself—the isolating research, simmering tensions with his supervisor, a defense nearly gone off the rails due to pushback from a renegade external? Four long years of insecurity and alienation, of whispers that his project was not only meaningless, but nonsense—that he was a fool and the enterprise proved it; awkward family gatherings (*What is it you're studying again?*), the gloss of confusion-*cum*-boredom that overtook the faces of women he tried to chat up at parties or dog parks. No matter how simplified, his pitch always got the same response: *I don't think I'm smart enough to understand all that.*

His protests—*It isn't about* intelligence, *academia just has its own vocabulary*—grew feebler. *Maybe it is about intelligence.* Maybe he was, well, *smarter* than most other people. Ultimately, Barker concludes that all the consternation and contempt has nothing to do with his book or the arguments therein—the nuance and complexity of which were wholly depleted in their distillation into a dictum—and everything to do with envy. He'd been reared in their august cradle, welcomed into their rarefied ranks (not *an academy*, but *The Academy*), only to (inadvertently) betray their trust. Did he not grasp the paradox? That so serious an undertaking required modesty? Humility?

And if he *were* to be found worthy of inclusion in the canonical, the foundational; to nudge human knowledge along an inflected course, then he'd have to do better than *media control people*. Is that what passed for groundbreaking these days? Beatification did not come at such a pittance.

I mean, nice try no cigar.

But look, Barker wasn't hard done by. To the contrary, highs and lows aside, he'd be the first to admit that his was a decadent station. Paid to study and write, offered the first professional post he'd ever applied for, taught and travelled, still cashed out not insubstantial royalties. It was just that he sometimes struggled with the fine print: Constantly taking heaps of shit from innumerable jealous asshats.

Here was Evan—politico, operative for the odious Baz Randell—posing the question Barker dreaded above all others.

"You study how media control people, is that correct?"

The tendrils of his fame-slash-infamy now reached far wider than even he himself had realized.

"Yes and no," Barker replied.

"Oh, well that clears that up," Evan joshed.

Barker let his eyes drift. They crimped at the magnesium pulses from the bulb above.

"That's a sort of bullet-point takeaway from my book, which is primarily about video game advertising."

"I'm a video game guy. Mac too."

Mac: "I'm playing a video game right now."

"I only put it forward, the question of control, as part of a larger… constellation of ideas."

"What's the constellation?"

Barker's stomach pitched. (When had he last eaten? Felt a flash of retroactive annoyance with the server for forgetting his food.) Now a fissure would open up between them, with Barker on the far side of the confusion.

"It's…difficult to explain. Academia has its own nomenclature. Language. I'm sure that politics has its own language, its own shorthand I wouldn't understand."

Evan sniggered. "That's the nicest way anyone has ever called me stupid."

"No, no, it has nothing to do with stupidity." Felt more like a lie every time he said it.

"We watched your TED talk."

"*I* watched your TED talk."

"Mac watched your TED talk and explained it to me."

"Sort of."

"So we're a little bit up to speed. I don't mean to put you on the spot. You don't have to take us all the way into the weeds, just… How would you sketch it out for your students?"

"Okay," finished his whiskey, felt the grit of a few nomadic coffee grinds rake his tongue, "first I'd ask you this: How do you know you have agency? The capacity to act? What capacities do you have? How did you get them? In ancient Greece, agency was endowed by class and social station. Philosophers and soldiers had different capacities. In the Dark Ages you have *no* agency. From the moment you're born, God has foreordained the arc of your life, and there's nothing you can do to change it. Then Marx steps into the fray. How, he asks, can a person reared in and through a set of social structures turn around and upend the very society, the very structures, that produced them? How can we revolt against a society that made us who we are?" Beat. "With me so far?"

Evan nodded. Mac, still hunched over his phone, peered in Barker's general direction.

"This all takes an interesting swerve with the advent of so-called 'interactive' media. Digital media, especially. The more widespread these devices become, the more scholars start to wonder about agency. If a medium such as *tee-vee* presumes a *passive* viewer, then digital media demand a more active form of engagement. Put simply, if 'interactive' media provide new opportunities for action, new capacities, then are they, in a sense, *giving* us agency?"

A familiar rush: A heady surge of blood accompanied by an acute emptiness, like Barker was a conduit through which greater forces flowed.

"So this, then, is the central dispute: Is agency the property of a person—like, something we intrinsically possess—or can agency be delivered by a medium?"

Evan's eyes skewed. Mac held his head at an angle.

"Does that make sense?" Barker asked.

Evan: "I think so..." Stretched the word into uncertainty: *thi-ink so.*

"Essentially, I pick up on this notion that thinking about agency as a *property*—something that can be...

"Keep going. Just coming around with a top up."

"...can be, uh, possessed or conferred—isn't all that useful. Instead, I wanted to examine how we come to form conceptions of our agential capacities, are *conditioned* to form those conceptions."

"So..." Mac's unseen lips split into a smile—wet bone in black brush. "What does this have to do with video games?"

"Video games are an especially popular form of interactive media. For lots of people, consoles were the first computer they brought into their home, and this…absorption of video games into our daily lives was attended by a glut of advertising. Basically, I wanted to examine whether all that advertising, all that discourse, over forty-odd years, could have persuaded us…or, altered our perception of, what agency is; convinced us that digital media are capable of giving us agency. That's what I meant by agency being 'discursively constructed.'

Evan poked his tongue into his cheek. "I get it."

Mac squinted.

Barker: "You know the Atari twenty-six-hundred?"

"I have one!" Mac exclaimed. "Not an original, one of the reissues."

"When the Atari launched, the slogan was, 'Don't watch tee-vee tonight. Play it!' So this ad, this discourse, says that when you plug the Atari into your television, it doesn't transform the machine, it transforms *you*. *You* morph from a passive watcher into an active player."

"Love it," Evan said.

Barker rubbed his sockets, searched for something steady to look at. Every object on the table pulsed. Twinge of nausea. Suppressed it. "This is where Foucault comes in."

"Panopticon!" Mac pumped his fist. "Wow, I never thought that shit would come in handy." Put down his phone. Barker locked onto it—its even geometry and smooth granite finish.

"Pretty standard approach to torturing undergrads," Barker conceded.

Evan: "Panopti-what?"

"The perfect prison or something, right?"

Barker set his mug aside. "You're definitely on the right track." Wrap up, go home, eat. "Foucault is interested in power. Not power in the sense of the strong controlling the weak, but power as a network; how power is subtly calibrated in relationships between people, between people and institutions.

"If advertising can change how we think about agency, then the purveyors of that discourse are effectively acting upon our agency by recalibrating or orienting our perception of it, yes?" Stomach frothy. "Ultimately, wanting us to think of media as the benefactors of…or as, like, liberatory…a natural or proper source of agency…" Acid rising at the back of his throat. "Even though, I mean, media appear to give us all these choices, they're also making a lot of choices for us; limit our control the same time they expand it." Jesus mother of fuck, that light! "Is this, then, real agency, or simply the illusion thereof?

"We must ask in whose interests…multinational corporations… to legitimate this idea…" Bile, rancid apples. "…that media are the proper source of our agency, uh, serve?" Emitted an *Mm*. "*That* is the…the…spirit in which I posed the question—and the full quote, the one that tends to get truncated into the…uh…which still doesn't quite make as much sense as it would in the context of… Doesn't matter. I really never said media *do* control us, I just wanted people to think about whether media can really be a, uh, an aquifer of…or a *source* of our agency, or if that's simply what powerful companies want us to think, or believe, our media do: Give us power, put us in control, set us free. Making us *think* that, *believe* that…that's the kind of control I'm talking about."

Evan and Mac stared, unsure, perhaps, as to whether Barker had finished.

Lifted his mug. His stomach heaved in dissent. Set it back down.

Evan nodded at the folder. "You'll want to sign that now."

◆ ◆ ◆

Leaving Randell campaign HQ, manila envelope secreted inside his satchel, Barker asked Mac how they'd found him.

"One of your students." Mac relayed the name.

Of *course* it was her. Made no sense. Made perfect sense.

Without prompting, Mac helped Barker lug his bike down the narrow stairwell. Once outside, Mac lit up a wine-tipped cigarillo.

"Any chance I could bum one of those?"

The heavy smoke made Barker's head swim. Mac scrolled through light and infinity. It was a warm night, the concrete shed shy whorls of steam.

"We're not ideologues," Mac offered without looking up. "We don't necessarily believe the same things as Baz, or condone his behaviour. *Alleged* behaviour."

"I hadn't assumed…"

"I know Evan comes across as a huckster. He *is* a huckster. But he's a good guy. He hired me. It's a good gig: High profile, good experience. But, yeah, for most of us, just a job." Grinned, eyes hidden behind plates of white. "I'm a mercenary."

A whirl of blue and red lapped at the brick. Over Mac's shoulder, Barker saw that the group from earlier had dispersed, but for one of their number spread eagle against the hood of a cruiser.

Mac clocked the scene, turned back. "Just that kind of neighbourhood."

◆ ◆ ◆

Back at his condo, Barker sloughed off his panoply. Trouble's leash and collar hung by the front door. References with no referent. Signifiers lacking a signified. Baudrillard's pooch.

Packed a bowl. Poured two fingers of scotch over three cubes.

No new responses to his tribute to Trouble. *I guess that particular high has peaked.*

Porn aggregator. Plugged *trib* into the search bar. Nothing grabbed him. Tried *teen* and *orgy*. Added *gang bang*. Too extreme, too dark and sloppy.

Closed his eyes and summoned Lara, hair tied back in an inky plume. His kitchen. Behind her. Hands searching inside her shirt, sliding up under her bra, probing the crotch of her jeans, her breathing short and shallow…

Cleared his cache. Opened iTunes. Clicked on a twenty-minute jazz piano rendition of *Paranoid Android*, lit his pipe.

Privileged.

Though…as much as he liked, often loved, his simple and stream-lined neo-bachelorhood—doing his own thing, never answering to anyone; his uncluttered condo with its unblemished upholstery and gleaming appliances; the silvery aviator-sunglasses-lens tint to his windows; keeping everything arranged in straight *just so* lines—it wasn't like he never got lonely. Bored. Hard to confess to those tilting at irrepressible mortgages, deteriorating marriages, the vicissitudes of child rearing (*The fuck do you have to complain about? I'm literally covered in shit, piss, and vomit right now*), hard to admit to these occasional ruts of sameness and repetition, his toys and trinkets emptied of allure, how tedium could overtake his life like a stain. He'd prowl, stalking inspiration, his inner monologue looping, solipsistic: *What am I doing? What is any of this* for? As insubstantial as a shadow in an eclipse, his mood an open wound—he could only sit and fester. Nothing to do. Nowhere to go. A cavity crumbling into a gaping abyss. Swallowed up in the sensation of rising altitude, teetering…

Talked himself down. *A life of extraordinary abundance! Heretofore unknown but to monarchs and gods!*

As soon as the burn hit the back of his throat, he knew the pot was a mistake. The room started to…not spin so much as skew and skip, an image broadcast over a bad antenna. Glass of water. Leaned back on the couch, eyes closed. An internal ocean of sickening lurches. Buzzing and crackling, a synesthetic translation of that stuttering halogen, fire gnawing damp wood: *Hm-BR-kk. BRR-kk-BRR-kk-mm.*

Envisioned himself as a solid and coherent thing, a barge skimming over choppy waters, contents a mess of competing pulls. The crates the vessel carried, the cords that bound them, slid and jostled and rubbed. With every shift, the lashings pulled tight, slackened, strained. Had to become the calm he coveted; the cords, their intersectional strength, the ebbs and flows of of tensity…

Beelined for the bathroom. Bent over the toilet.

Finished. Rinsed. Retrieved the manila envelope from his satchel, set its contents on his ottoman.

Evan: *You're the eighth person who now knows this material exists. Per the terms of your* en-dee-a, *if you share the contents of this envelope with anyone, if anyone so much as glances in their general direction, we will sue you until you die.*

Hadn't said much more than that. *Once you familiarize yourself with the material, call me and we'll discuss how to proceed.* If Barker was reluctant, wanted out, all well and good, no harm no foul.

But given his areas of expertise, they hoped he might have fresh insights to share.

Spread and sorted through the sheaf, but a few minutes later his focus collapsed. He didn't understand what he was looking at. Page after page of cartoon bubbles filled with juvenile banter—a graphic novel awaiting illustrations. Saucy wordplay between—best guess—Junior High school students. All *tits* this and *cum* that.

Set the papers aside. Refreshed his email.

There it was. Right at the top.

His ex-wife, Tatjana Stone (née Petrovic). A few days early, bless her.

Subject: Re: Lawyers.

Stared at it.

Closed his laptop.

Went to bed.

Interlude: The Jungle

Finishes his thesis in the dog days of summer, sets immediately to work devising a project for his PhD. Ploughs through a backlog of material he'd flagged but didn't have the time or wherewithal to grapple with during his MA: Peters, Jenkins, Anderson, Gitelman, Foucault... Prepares and submits applications. While awaiting the results, he will travel.

Inspired by friends who spent their honeymoon volunteering—rather voluntouring—at an elephant sanctuary in Thailand, he seeks out a similar opportunity in Central America. Finds a sea turtle sanctuary in southern Guatemala. He's never forgotten the documentary he saw as a child, the gauntlet of horrors the neonate reptiles must run to get from the sandy pocket of eggs to the first crust of sea foam. Contacts the sanctuary. *Sorry*, they say, *no turtles right now. But we operate another center in Péten. Wildlife refuge. They always need help.*

Books flights. Feels dizzy.

Renews his passport. Buys a sixty-gallon backpack, mosquito netting, money belt. Is vaccinated for Hepatitis A and B and typhoid, is prescribed malaria pills. Absorbs the standard warnings: *Don't drink the water or anything with ice. Don't eat anything washed in water, like salad.* Leaves his computer and phone behind (the computer might be stolen, the phone won't work anyway). Buys a decent digital camera, promising ample documentation for family and friends.

He is terrified.

Overnight layover in Houston, lands in Guatemala City, catches a connecting flight to Flores. It is dark when he arrives in the concrete bunker they call an airport. Exits into a screaming throng of gypsy cab drivers. Hears his name. A man takes his backpack, tosses it into the back of a battered black jeep. They ricochet over dirt roads. Through the window he watches the blur of an alien world.

The jeep arrives at an embankment. He and his backpack are transferred into a small skiff with an outboard motor. They skim the water in pitch black, the driver navigating with a headlamp. On shore, he is led up a sloping gravel path lined with rocks. *For snakes,* the driver says.

Hits him: *I'm in the jungle.*

A dorm. He meets the other voluntourists: a Canadian, a Frenchman, a Dane, Americans and Germans. The Dane suggests drinks. Despite the darkness and what feels like days of travel, he retrieves his own headlamp, follows the willing down the sloping path. Scythes of primordial foliage conspire above. Casting about his light reveals a glittering gemstone cosmos.

Spider eyes, the Dane tells him.

The "pub" is a shack with a driftwood porch. The owner sells them beer and snacks through her kitchen window.

Wakes in the middle of the night to an impossible cacophony. Terrific growling and huffing and screaming. Giant lizards locked in murderous combat.

I've made a terrible mistake, he thinks. *I'll book a flight back home tomorrow.*

Six a.m.—starts his stint as an itinerant zookeeper. Showers underneath an enormous spider suspended over the nozzle like a clenched fist. (Whether the fist is alive or dead is a matter of ongoing speculation). Cleans his teeth (*Don't run your brush under the water!*), and dresses. By six-thirty he's chopping fruit and veg, delivering victuals to parrots, kinkajous, spider and howler monkeys. (At some point he is told that the howlers were the contestants in the late-night lizard battle. Their bushy black beards are actually air sacks, and their pitched exhortations can be heard upwards of ten kilometres away. The sounds they make, many a proud Guatemalan will boast, were used for the T-Rex roar in *Jurassic Park*.) Cleans out a cage full of wild turkeys, heads festooned with orange globules.

He ponders the evolutionary advantage of orange globules.

In lieu of the odd jobs that typically occupy the voluntourists' afternoons, he's given a tour of the compound. The animals are all rescues, seized from poachers. Many have been abused, and arrive angry, scared, malnourished. While the centre's mandate is to gradually re-acclimate the animals to their erstwhile environs, many of the residents are too dangerous or damaged to be rehabilitated or released and will stay here until they die.

Keel-billed toucans, wood storks, white-tailed deer, opossums, wild pigs, crocodiles, musk turtles, iguanas, foxes, porcupines, and a solitary jaguar in a chain link cage. The jaguar is one that can never leave.

Work ends at three. The voluntourists change into swimsuits, amble down to a dilapidated dock, leap recklessly into the water. The French guy dons a skullcap and goggles and swims laps from dock to shore.

He's frozen in fear. Water is the enemy. *Poison.*

Or…has water been made to embody the myriad fears and dangers of visiting this unknown place? Of *foreign*-ness? *Other*-ness? Scolds himself for being so easily intimidated. Covers his mouth and plugs his nose and jumps.

This is his life for the next two weeks. From six-thirty to noon they feed the animals and wash out their shit. He develops an affinity for many inmates, the howlers especially, but loathes the parrots. They lunge and peck at his (already leaky) galoshes, kamikaze dive-bomb his head, squawk insanely, as if galled by the removal of their copious excrement. It's by far the worst shit to clean, adheres to the concrete like paint primer.

On Tuesdays and Thursdays the voluntourists are ferried across the water—shore leave to replenish supplies. The center feeds them, but the meals are bare bones (the morning coffee is called *brownwater*). Many opt to cram a small stockpile of instant coffee and boxed milk into one of the two available refrigerators. Due to unspecified past troubles, alcohol is banned. If they can make their own way back by boat taxi, however, these sojourns also present a second opportunity: To drink.

They pile into a *taberna*. Meat smokes and sizzles over a pit. They order dirt cheap beer. A drinking game is introduced. The night dissolves into frivolity and flame, scenes from a badly edited film.

In his morning stupor, he leaves a cage door ajar. A spider monkey makes a break for it. The veterinarians rally, capture and replace it. The vets are angry. *Seething.* There is much ado about the stress that such tumult causes these already anxious animals. Though everyone knows who the culprit is, no one points fingers. Later, in private, he is only mildly rebuked. He infers that the centre can't afford to alienate any Westerners willing to devote a miserly few weeks to chipping parrot shit off concrete. (The whole operation is severely underfunded—tools literally held together with tape and bailing wire, rakes and knives broken and repaired many times over.) Feels awful for causing a crisis.

That weekend he takes a shuttle to Tikal. Marvels at the scale, meditates on the ephemerality of civilization: *When it ends, the jungle will fucking erase us.* At the top of the tallest temple, he eavesdrops on conversations about *Star Wars.* This was a watchtower of the original rebel base. Stays to watch the sun set—a split yolk puddled into orange haze.

An hour after dinner, his bowels loosen. Spends most of the night on the toilet, listening through paper-thin walls to a busload of Scandinavians watch *Apocalypto.* In the morning, an older Canadian couple ascertain his state, fill him with Imodium and Gravol, force him to eat a pancake. Sweats the whole way back to Flores. Allocates every spare shred of energy to keeping his winkle clamped shut.

The refuge is not the same the second week. The Dane and the French guy, who now feel like old friends, depart. An easy-going Coloradan arrives. They reminisce about microbreweries. Several German teenagers join the crew. One of them is stunning. He cannot talk to her. (She takes a shine to the Coloradan anyway.)

Finishes his stint and ferries to Flores. At four the following morning, he is rushed into a car by a manic Guatemalan man (cocaine?), then delivered, with two other intrepid travellers (an Australian and another Dane), to a bus depot in San Benito. They board a shuttle, soar over pocked roads, bounce around like balls in a bingo cage. Three hours later, they arrive in Carmelita—shacks crowding a dirt airstrip—are served a meagre breakfast by their emaciated guide before following him into the jungle.

They walk all day. The guide describes which critters to watch out for. Recounts a story about his father—a guide before him—who absently put his hand on a tree and was bitten by a baby coral snake. With mere seconds before the venom entered his bloodstream, dad chopped off his finger with a machete.

The Dane instigates a discussion about which body parts they'd be willing to cut off of one another should the need arise.

They set up camp in a clearing, are taken to the top of a nearby temple, marvel at the endless green while guides raise cell phones in search of a signal. After spaghetti and sauce, a scorpion scuttles onto the site. Their guide admits that the venom is a fine thing to roll up with tobacco, milks a few drops out of the thrashing arachnid's tail. The guide gets his fix. The scorpion dies.

The next day they arrive at *El Mirador*, a sprawling Mayan ruin that, unlike Tikal, has yet to be pried loose from the jungle's grip. They are shown facades bearing faint scuffs of their original lustre, whispers of the resplendence that once adorned the stone.

They play basketball with a rusted hoop over tamped grass.

They eat spaghetti.

Two days later they re-emerge. Are returned to Flores. He doesn't care if he ever sees the Australian again, but has breakfast the next day with the Dane. The Dane is off to connect with a woman he met a few weeks back. There are entreaties to meet up. *Come find me in San Pedro on Lake Atitlan*, says the Dane in inflected English. Email addresses are exchanged. They hug and part ways.

Takes an overnight bus to Guatemala City, AKA *The City*, and boards a shuttle for Antigua. The vehicle skirts a diorama of disorder. Feeble early morning light paints the shambles a dismal yellow, while bandana-clad figures armed with bricks and bottles hunt. Minutes later the shuttle pierces an invisible partition. Dereliction coheres into clean, calm streets gilded with familiar Western riches: Pizza Hut, McDonald's, Starbucks.

Arrives in Antigua. Peaceful and composed. All tight, stony streets, faded colonial architecture, acrid smoke from burning garbage. Eats well, is increasingly comfortable deploying his rudimentary Spanish: *Hola! ¿Cómo estás? Estoy bien, ¿y tú? Café con leche y azúcar. Dos cervezas, por favor. ¿Cuánto es? Muchas gracias!*

Everything feels *more* here: the cities more big, the bus depots more grimy, the scenery more stunning. He is more himself, he thinks.

Joins a group hike up a volcano. Weighted with gear, the winding ash-slick incline makes for a slippery ascent. Some in his fellowship struggle. Having already done El Mirador, he feels like a badass. Freight and ash are minor nuisances. He's already survived the jungle unscathed.

Twice.

They set up camp on a plateau near the summit. A precipitous drop in temperature. Everyone layers up. They reach the summit proper in under thirty minutes. The moment they arrive, the adjacent volcano—Fuego—erupts. A tower of ash spits into the sky, followed by a concussive blast like a cannon shot.

Scream and cheer.

In the morning they practically ski down the path, kicking up more ash than the volcano could ever dream of.

Back in Antigua, he finds an Internet café. Message from the Dane: Not a win with the girl. Going to the Lake. San Pedro!

He's already booked accommodation in a different village. Going to check out another place for a few days before heading to San Pedro. Safe travels!

A shuttle to Panajachel. Finds the dock and boards a skiff. The hostel is perched on the edge of the lake, beneath Santa Cruz la Laguna up and to the north.

Five days. Waiting to check in. She is in front of him in billowing silk pants, a loose-fitting leather corset, a diaphanous turquoise scarf as thin and crinkly as tissue paper. Slung over a shoulder are two small silver canisters linked by a chain.

Glances at him over her shoulder. He smiles.

Trivia night. They end up on the same team. One of the questions is, *What causes the northern lights?* He suggests *God.* She snorts.

That night they smoke pot on the dock, tracing the top of the lake with their toes. They talk until very late.

Five days. Morning. Coffee on the patio. She joins him. He asks about her silver orbs. *Poi pots,* she tells him.

She dances with fire.

They rent kayaks. It's a blustery day, the lake choppy. They abandon the kayaks and hike to nearby Jaibalito. She is barefoot, stops to pick bits of wood and glass out of her exposed soles. He frets. She puts her hand on his shoulder and says not to worry. Well worthwhile to feel the earth underfoot.

Five days. They drink coffee, hike, smoke pot, talk and talk and talk and talk. They attend a cacao ceremony in San Marcos. A muddy concoction with a dash of chilli. The American ex-pat wears his grey, grassy hair in a ponytail, back curling into his stooped neck like a human apostrophe. Some of those present are stalwart apostles. As the conversation devolves into morbid pontificating on death and the cosmos, they make their escape.

They buy space cookies from a street vendor, scale a modest cliff, climb trees at the top, make insane cartoonish dashes for the ledge, pretend to hurtle themselves into the water below.

Five days. He can't remember ever having felt so completely comfortable with another person. They *connect.* The adventurous heart and the taciturn head. Effortless.

That night they have sex. Nice, but not necessarily good. It's been a long time, he comes almost instantly, is embarrassed by his humdrum performance. She wraps herself in his arms. They sleep. Again the next morning. No better. He's overcome with worry. Is this how she'll remember him? A fleeting disappointment? A mediocre meal at a restaurant you know you'll never return to?

Five days. They take the boat taxi to Panajachel. A desultory town, all sad greys and mottled concrete. She stops to pick pieces of glass and wire out of her soles. Keeps his fretting to himself. They buy potato chips and wine. Back at the hostel, after dinner, they hunker down in the side room with the TV, flip through the huge folder full of bootleg DVDs. She's never seen *Field of Dreams.* As they watch, their bodies embraid.

They are too tired for anything but sleep.

Breakfast together. *Five days.* Wait on the dock. She's on the boat. She does not wave. He does not wave.

Gone.

Here's the refrain: *Aren't travel relationships the best? You meet and fuck and move on.* Did that explain the comfort, the ease? When we travel, we are singularly open, unencumbered, uninhibited. We leave real life behind. Slip inside a liminal space, the closest thing to true, pure freedom—from our normal lives and selves. *That* is what you were drawn to in each other. Nothing more. Besides, it is only an elision of the real. The real will, *must,* reassert itself. *No ties! No consequences!*

But there is a consequence: He can't forget her. Can't forget her comfort. Can't forget the night she lit her pots and danced—chain invisible, the still turning point in the whirl, two red-orange galaxies fighting the pull of a black hole, or atoms sprung suddenly into fission. The more people say *Aren't travel relationships the best?*, the dumber he feels. Why is he so stupidly sentimental? Fuck-induced infatuation. A dog pledging devotion to whoever tosses out some scraps. Five days. That's all it was. Five days. A travel thing. Nothing more. Five days. He has to let it go. He lets it go.

Sends her an email:

> Just a quick note to say how amazing it was to meet you and have a great rest of your trip.
>
> I hope our paths cross again someday!

No reply. Lets it go.

Well, one more message a week later.

> Where are you?

No reply. Lets it go.

Receives offers from several PhD programs. Holds Skype meetings in Internet cafés. Speaks with fusty graduate supervisors framed by imposing bookshelves.

A glimpse of his future?

Ends his trip in Belize. Sticky hot, sun incessant, air humid and immobile with a fruity perfume smell. Every meal comes with pounds of rice and beans. A constant frothy feeling in his stomach. The beer is flavourful. There are Mennonites.

On the bus, he reads the billboards hovering over corrugated tin rooftops. *God created* MAN *and* WOMAN—*Genesis* 2:22. And: *Advertise or* DIE SLOWLY. (A billboard for billboards!) And the omnipresent pun: UN-BELIZEABLE!

Caye Caulker, all white sand and conch shells and Caribbean water. Snorkels. Swims up to manatees, among nurse sharks and manta rays, overtop a bull ray the size of a dining room carpet, through reefs teeming with coral and eels, past parades of fish of every conceivable colour.

And then back. A months-long dance of planning and packing. The last night in his apartment, almost entirely stripped of his presence—as if he were little more than a layer of surface grime—he drinks wine and looks through pictures.

There she is. Just one shot.

Stares at the photo for a long time. *Fuck it,* he thinks.

I hope it doesn't seem too strange to reach out to someone you spent five days with in the middle of Guatemala. Maybe it is strange. For this moment, I'm going to not care if it's strange or not.

Here's the deal: I've moved around a lot in my life, as a kid and as an adult, which has made me sentimental about the people I've met. You are one of the people I'm sentimental about.

There are two reasons for this.

First, though I've met many fantastic people, there are so few people in this world that we meet and truly connect with. There are times when I forget that those kinds of connections exist.

Which is to say thanks. Thank you for reminding me what that feels like. For reminding me it's possible.

Second, the people that I do seem to connect with are passionate people. People who live by and through their passions.

This is what I admired about you the most—that you were so obviously and unabashedly following your bliss.

I'm moving to the west coast to start a PhD. This is, I suppose, my own passion for the time being.

I hope that, wherever you are, and whatever you're doing, you're still living that passion.

I hope I get to meet more people like you.

Reads it once over. Irredeemably cheeseballs. Doesn't change a single word.

She writes back the next day.

Sorry for not responding to his earlier messages, was winding her way through Scandinavia. Volunteered at an orphanage in Switzerland teaching circus acts to kids.

She is—his jaw literally drops—moving to Vancouver Island. Something has happened with her mother in Serbia (no details provided), so she's going to live with her father and stepmother and two half-sisters outside Victoria.

She hates the cold, but doesn't mind rain. Has been promised mild (if damp) winters. She'll give it a year and see how it goes.

Is this, she asks, near to where you will be going to school?

✦ ✦ ✦

Once settled—he in his basement suite, she on the Island—they arrange a visit. He takes the ferry over for the weekend. They meet in Victoria, spend the evening haunting fog-shrouded streets. The next morning, they reconvene for coffee, browse used bookstores, wander into several of the city's signature *Lovely Little Parks*, take refuge from the sun under ancient trees, find a bench and talk for hours and hours. At first everything feels uncertain, tentative, as if each were a test for which the other is inadequately prepared. Then a sort of muscle memory kicks in, or a gravity reasserts itself, and they slip back into each other's orbits.

He catches the latest possible ferry back to the mainland.

A second rendezvous. This time she visits him in Vancouver. Walking. Chatting. She reaches out, winds her fingers into his. She's meant to stay with a friend of her stepmother's, but after a gut-busting dinner, returns with him to his suite. They do not have sex, but fall asleep on the futon in his living room. In the morning he makes pancakes with lemon and sugar.

A drizzly day. They transit to the endowment lands near campus, mosey over spongy moss and sucking muck, under a cathedral of trees that race the sky. Their clothes soak through. Skin clammy.

Bones cold. At home they strip and make love. Love is what it feels like. It's good. Better, for sure, than their first few fumbles. They lie there a long time, bodies clasped, as if either one let go, the other would evaporate.

Within two months she's moved in. She has few possessions of practical use—no furniture or appliances—to contribute to his already overstuffed suite, but brings four milk crates brimful with books. He never asks where they came from. (Shipped from Serbia?) As soon as they're shelved, interspersed among his burgeoning collection of academic tomes (yes, on a makeshift cinderblock bookcase—the bohemian student special!—which he suggests ironically, but she sources the materials for and assembles with gusto), it feels like her books have always been there.

The bookish gypsy, he calls her. She smiles.

In the evenings, after he's finished school stuff, they drink beer or cheap wine, smoke pot and watch movies. Their suite is in a house owned by a couple with an adopted son (El Salvador?), whose morning routine consists of stomping and thumping, amplified by their ceiling into a stampede.

One night they watch *The Princess Bride*. She has, inconceivably, never seen it before. Halfway through, she points at the ceiling and screams *Prince Thumperdink!*

At Christmas he drives her through the Rockies to meet his family. She embraces his stoic parents, says, *So wonderful to meet you! I am the bookish gypsy.*

They love her.

(*Everyone* loves her. While he puts little stock in notions of charisma or energy, she has some kind of power. *Charming* is how he most often describes her, meaning its etymological root: Someone who uses incantations or magic spells. It is this that sows the first seed of doubt. Is it *they* who are in love, or is he simply the next link in a long chain of the similarly enchanted?)

A Spartan existence. The city is rich in fresh veg and seafood.

She has an old, brittle Serbian cookbook. They endeavour to cook every dish therein.

His scholarship covers their modest expenses, but she tires of barren days while he's on campus, or at home buried in books. She goes round to the local-area arts organizations, is excited to discover a school of circus arts. They are not hiring. She shrugs off her disappointment, decides their work is unimpressive, their attitudes brusque, would not have deigned to work there if they'd begged.

She's hired as a receptionist at a travel clinic. Sits beside the doctor, Janine, as Janine doles out advice and administers vaccines. As the patients wait, with Janine out of the room, she asks them about their upcoming travels. She enjoys this immensely at first, being regaled with accounts of impending bespoke adventures: *First Columbia, Chile, maybe Bolivia... Wind our way north and do the Camino-Santiago descent... Didn't want to die never having seen the Congo, so we're going!*

After a few months the stories start to grate. *I have itchy feet*, she confesses. *Wanderlust.*

They emerge from a dark and dreary winter. The city comes alive with crocuses. Cherry blossoms fill the air like confetti. While he considers the temperature comparatively warm (he spent his teens in the prairies after all), she is finding it hard to adjust to even these moderate climes. One night, they pull her worn, anachronistic atlas off the cinderblock bookshelf, flip through its yellowed pages, marvelling at the vanished, vanquished nations.

Yugoslavia, she exclaims.

The Union of Soviet Socialist Republics, he exclaims.

Next year, he'll be done course work and starting his second comprehensive exam. He'll have a stack of books to read, but she is an experienced transporter of books. They'll abandon the basement suite and buy one-way tickets to Thailand, and from there explore Cambodia, Vietnam, Laos, Myanmar, maybe the Philippines and Malaysia. He will read. She will dance.

Finally meets her family. Her father picks them up in a tiny red car with a sewing machine engine that belches blue fumes into its slipstream. Upon their arrival, her father squeezes out of the car like a chick from an egg. A spectacled, barrel-chested Serb imposing enough to wrestle alligators. He's crushed in her father's embrace. The garrulous, gregarious Serb holds him out at arms length and says *Welcome!* The glint in his eye says *If you fuck with my daughter, I'll eat you for supper!*

Three wonderful days. The house is bordered on two sides by orchards—apple and peach trees in full splendour. Her sisters are young—four and seven. The younger one takes to him instantly. He pushes her around on a plastic truck. They play cards. He lets her win, feigns aggravation. She giggles.

Her stepmother is warm and considerate. Her father is funny, laughs uproariously at his own jokes, punctuates many of his gut-jiggling displays by slapping his daughter's boyfriend on the back.

Sincere camaraderie, or simian code?

The plan: Work all summer—he on his second comp, she at the clinic—and save as much money as possible. In September they'll store their belongings in her father's basement and head overseas. He wants to buy their plane tickets, but she wants to hold off for a seat sale. *Patience*, she tells him.

Near to the end of July, he receives a call from the Associate Dean. Due to an unspecified emergency, they need an instructor to teach a course in the fall. A relatively unheard-of privilege for a second-year PhD. Not only is the pay marginally better, but it will make a sterling addition to his cv.

When he sits her down to talk, he pretends he has not already said yes.

We could leave right after Christmas, he says.

Of course you must do it, she says.

Is she secretly disappointed? He can't tell.

A few weeks later, he realizes that it is, in fact, a full year course.

Another sit-down. Thailand is postponed until the following spring.

With only this one course to teach, he spends more time at home. Reads indefatigably. A machine. She works nine-to-five, Monday-to-Friday. Cooks dinner while he works. After: beer or cheap wine, pot and movies.

Having made every meal in her Serbian cookbook twice over, he buys her a new cookbook for her birthday. Her face sours. Their first fight. He's trying to domesticate her! She is not his *wife*, not his *servant!* He's stung, meant it as an extension of a beloved ritual. They apologize. He's been taking her for granted. She feels trapped behind her desk, inundated with fantastical stories of amazing adventures to be.

Over Christmas he concocts a secret plan. They will leave for Thailand at the end of April, as soon as his grades are submitted. He will propose at the airport. The trip will be like a pre-honeymoon.

He wants to buy their tickets. *Patience*, she tells him.

Reading break. They pop down to Seattle. Just as cold and dreary there, but a welcome change of scenery. They visit the Experience Music Project. She gushes admiration for the pioneers of hip-hop. *These are the true cultural revolutionaries*, she insists. *These artists and their music have done more for the oppressed than you academics ever will.* Outwardly he ignores the slight, but it lodges. A little shard.

Two weeks later—vomiting. Pregnant. He's overjoyed. She seems uncertain. He's terrified. *Do you want to keep it*, she asks. *Yes yes yes*, he says.

Is it safe to travel? Janine advises her to wait. In the first trimester there's a risk of miscarriage.

She thinks Janine is being over-precautious. Furthermore, Janine prescribes too many vaccinations and antibiotics, exaggerates the dangers of travel, instils fear for the sake of profit. (The first hint of a burgeoning mistrust of Western medicine, vaccinations primarily.)

He does not want to take the risk. Convinces her to wait. They can just as easily go in the fall.

Miscarries. *See,* she says, *it would not have made any difference after all.*

She becomes silent. He works at a manic pace. She stays in. He goes out. They exchange temperaments. She goes to bed early. He meets friends at pubs and drinks.

Routines fall further out of synch. He finds excuses to stay on campus, to work at nearby coffee shops. Tells her this is how it always is in the final stretch of a big project, but the truth is that her silence and solitude have thrown him. He can't concentrate at the house.

Defends his second comp. The dean offers him another course for the fall. He'd happily turn it down. They can travel while he starts preparing his dissertation proposal. She's emerging from her funk, tells him to take the course. *I would rather be gone for the winter, if it is all the same to you.*

Concludes it's all the same to him.

She books two weeks off at the end of August. After a few days with her family, they load up rented bikes with the least possible gear, and cycle from island to island. They eat sun-warmed blackberries straight off the bush (*a miraculous taste,* she says), collect clamshells and gnarled wands of wood, watch sea lions sunbathe and patrol the beaches—oilslick-lightbulb eyes surveilling these hopeless water-logged chimps. They defy campfire bans, smoke pot, cook sausages, eat chips, drink cheap wine and mead, hike and cycle and take surf-ing lessons. He's lukewarm—the board is too unsteady, his centre of gravity elusive—but she dives in with glee; just another dance already inscribed in her capacious muscle memory. They find a secluded inlet and launch into an impromptu faux-tango, scoring the sand with sinuous script. Dogs steal his sandals. They scour used bookshops from which she never emerges empty-handed. He buys gewgaws for her sisters. It is the closest they've come, he realizes, to being on a real trip together since those first five days a lifetime ago.

A tension releases. An invisible coil unwinds.

On a beach, passing a bottle of wine between them. Low clouds caress the trees, the setting sun edges the water with Matisse-like pastels. They reminisce about their now-entwined lives. Can they believe it's been two-and-a-half years since they met? Can they imagine life without one another? They smoke up, follow some locals into the cold, black ocean. When they splash, the water bristles green.

Bioluminescence, he tells her.

Magic, she tells him.

They return to their site, towel off, have sex in the tent—slowly, quietly—as a playful rain tickles the fly. After, in the pitch dark, he proposes. Just this: *Marry me*. This wasn't the plan—he had quite the preamble prepared—but it feels right. She says nothing for a long time. Asleep? He's about to ask again when she lifts her head and whispers, *Of course*. As if it were a *fait accompli*. As if he needn't have asked in the first place.

A few days into the fall semester, she abruptly quits her job. Intimates, in her roundabout way, that she was hopelessly bored. *Same people, same stories, over and over.*

He asks if something happened with Janine. *Janine is Janine.*

Burns through two jobs in as many weeks. The first, a bagel and coffee shop, she leaves after six shifts due to the ungodly early morning hours. The second, a boutique bakery and café a few doors down, she quits because of the manager's transparent efforts to screw over the (chiefly immigrant) kitchen staff. He worries this will become a pattern, that she'll hopscotch from job to job. Her third attempt, however, sticks. She takes a position as a nanny, caring for the children of a nearby couple who work from home, but whose successful web design company requires respite from parental duties. The wage is decent, and she quickly comes to love the kids. Two boys, eight and five. The exact same ages, he notes, as her half-siblings.

The course is a slog. After his introductory lecture, he's approached by three separate students. Two inform him that they have anxiety disorders, deliver letters exempting them from deadlines, permitting them to submit essays and write exams on discretely devised schedules. Internally he considers their diagnoses preposterous—Doesn't everyone get anxious over deadlines?—but is obligated to follow administrative diktat. The third is transitioning. *My preferred pronoun is* he, he says.

He's not as interested or invested in the material, the students are aloof and distant. Of his two TAs, one is fine, the other a dud. When the first assignment is handed back, there's a flurry of complaints from the dud's discussion groups. He's forced to re-grade nearly thirty papers.

She loves her job. He hates his. They're on top of one another, the suite suddenly too small, too subterranean. The days shorten. One point of concord—keeping their wedding small—unravels. They'd conceived of a free-spirited bacchanal—barefoot on the beach, fire jugglers, poi and hula-hoop dancers, a ukulele serenade as vows are exchanged on a gently bobbing pier. (They will not be one of *those* couples that waste years planning an expensive and ostentatious ceremony, but keep it simple, ensure it's uniquely *theirs*.) Her father intervenes, insists on invitations for some of her more diffuse relations, aunts and uncles and second cousins, some of whom neither she nor her father have laid eyes on in decades. Even a few her father isn't certain are still alive. Her father assures them that while most of these relatives will likely not attend, they'll be insulted if they do not receive the courtesy of an invite.

The more he watches her and her father interact, the more he understands the distance she'd formerly put between them, the dark side to her father's conviviality: Overbearance. She seems incapable of denying his manifold demands.

He, her betrothed, makes a reasonable suggestion: That she tell her father to back the fuck off. An argument. A real paint peeler. He does not propose this strategy again.

While there is never an official discussion re: Thailand, it seems obvious that, given the dilating guest list and expenses—the beach is scuttled, how can her elderly relatives traverse the sand?—the trip will be postponed. Thailand has become their vanishing point, their Zeno's paradox, the impossible to reach end of an infinite corridor.

Sex is a chore. Every effort a backslide toward their two initial lacklustre attempts. She can't climax. He goes down on her for twenty-, thirty-minute stretches. They buy toys, confess secret fantasies, quasi-jokingly ponder the logistics of threesomes. On a rare restaurant outing, she surreptitiously removes a two-six of rum from her purse, spikes their drinks under the table. Much to their server's bewilderment, they get sloshed. At home she straddles him on the couch and *fucks* him. He knows she's fucking him because she says, "I'm fucking you! I'm *fucking* you!" Can't come. Is embarrassed. They curl up and fall asleep watching *The Daily Show*.

Starts staying up after she's gone to bed to poke around less savoury corners of the Internet.

The gruelling course wraps up. He opts for a multiple-choice exam requiring not a whit of work from his TAs. (The dud *still* complains about proctoring so close to the holidays.) Her nanny family departs for a three-week jaunt through—guess where?—Thailand. She fumes. Thailand was *their* trip.

A pleasant six days in the prairies with his parents. Though their veneer of laid-back politesse never cracks, he can tell his folks are shocked by the still-ballooning roster of her extendeds, especially since they're covering the bulk of the expenses. "We'll be outnumbered," his mother comments innocuously.

With no winter course to teach, he commits to finishing his dissertation proposal. She nannies. Life regains an easy cadence. They stop having sex altogether. *A lull*, he thinks. *Couples have lulls.*

Passes his proposal defense at the end of the spring. They are married mid-summer. It is a nice ceremony, if maybe nicer for their families (well, *her* family). They exchange vows in an Orthodox Church—he's agnostic, but it's a fight he decides not to instigate—before a mass of observant Serbs and a polyp of Canadians. Reception at a local community center. Her father insists on cooking all the food, assisted by a gaggle of withered women in honest-to-goodness shawls.

Tosses the bouquet, removes her shoes, lobs them into the crowd as well.

They dance. They drink. No issues. No incidents.

Cottage on an obscure lake. Wake to the calls of loons, read magazines, pick fruit, fires in the fireplace, watch movies from the 80s and 90s drawn blindly out of an abandoned box of VHS tapes. *Sixteen Candles* and *Nightmare On Elm Street 3: Dream Warriors.* They go for aimless walks. She collects bulbous mushrooms and curious stones. He finds a walking stick as tall and bent as a wizard's staff. They borrow the neighbour's canoe. One afternoon, while washing up, two big black paws scrub the window over the sink. He scrambles for a camera. The photos are blurry, the bear a smudge. The mosquitos are prolific. A run into town to buy coils of chemical incense, and netting that they secure over the squeaky bed like a royal canopy.

Sex. Finding each other again. An expedition through familiar tundra anonymous from fresh snow.

A few weeks later they are pregnant. At once a reprieve and pivot. Sex between married couples is not only for pleasure, but *procreation*. Isn't this the point? From a strictly biologistic vantage, isn't the meaning of life to make babies, extend their braided lineages, ensure the safe passage of their genetic gospel into a turbulent and unknowable future?

Nine months. With a bit of luck, just enough time to finish his diss, or at least get through the heavy lifting.

Nine months. She embraces surrogate motherhood anew, takes the boys to parks, aquariums, science centers, and on forest hikes. She clothes and feeds and bathes them while their parents stay plugged into their respective digital looms.

Nine months. He teaches. Finds a groove.

Nine months. Routine. That's what life is, really. Everything out-side of routine is an anomaly. They are good with that.

Nine months. They enjoy each other's company. Eat good food. She has the occasional glass of wine, but no pot. He smokes only intermittently, the aftereffects proving increasingly strenuous. They have their circle of friends, supportive families on the periphery. They are comfortable.

Nine months. Baby books, advice, warnings, advice, spare strollers, second-hand clothing, toys, toys, toys. And advice.

Nine months. They kiss their underground life and floor-thumpage goodbye. The books are replaced in their crates, the cinderblock bookshelf dismantled. They move into the spacious main floor of a duplex one block off a street known as *The Drive.* The owner is a single, middle-aged woman who lives upstairs but is often out of town, knows they're pregnant, *loves babies to no end* and *sleeps like a rock.*

Nine months. Makes secret pilgrimages to antique stores, not knowing exactly what he's looking for, but finally finding it: A bookcase. Cherry-wood. Merlot sheen only slightly scuffed. Has it delivered while she's out with her kids. Her books fit perfectly. Her eyes mist when she sees it.

Nine months. Sex is sporadic but good. Brains and bodies reunited.

Eight-and-a-half months, near to the end of March, a routine appointment. The doctor cannot detect the heartbeat. Their daughter—it is a girl—has gone silent. The doctor tells them not to panic. These things happen. Come back tomorrow.

They panic. Back first thing the next day. No heartbeat.

Life breaks down. Shatters. You have seen these scenes in movies? The ones with broken mirrors? Shards litter the floor, the character stares unblinkingly at the mess, at themselves in pieces. Un-whole. Strewn across a field of missing space; overlaps and repetitions where the fragmentary reflections are doubly or triply there. This is how he will remember this time. A mangle of film spit out of a disgruntled projector. A *too-much-ness,* the world washed out in overexposed light.

They lose her.

Their girl.

A—. She names her A—.

(*They told us to name her. Why? It is an it. Incomplete.*)

That small dark room. That bilious orange light.

Her stepmother: Weeping. Hands balled.

Her father: Wailing. Literally beating his chest.

His parents: Uncertain. Austere. Uncomfortable with the operatic display of grief unfolding beside them. Wishing they'd ordered seats in a less rowdy section.

He: Blank.

What is this? All of this? This room in this hospital in this city in this country? So-called Western medicine. So-called civilization. What had it done for them? Nothing. Nurtured *complacency*. Instilled the *illusion* of safety. Their so-called privilege was a fake. A sham. They're hut-dwelling peasants at the mercy of a capricious umbilical cord.

A—. His girl. His daughter. Holds her.

Are they sure? She seems so…

(To this day he wonders: *Were they* sure? *Were they absolutely* certain?)

Leaves the small room with the orange light, enters into a changed world.

Seems the same or similar at first. At first, but only on the surface. Before he starts to notice the tweaks. Physical laws subtly recalibrated. Reality's axes off-kilter. Skewed.

At first he assumes it is *he* who has changed. That his trauma (*Is that what it was?*) has made him impervious, granted him the power of *perspective*. He's been *enlightened*, the world's inner-workings *revealed*. Sees it all so clearly. *That*—trivial and mundane! *This*—significant and profound! He has been crowned a philosopher king, singularly equipped to rule.

Yet when he expounds upon his ordeal, his hard-won serenity

and insight, the world's altered forces exert disorienting pushes and pulls. Tries to pull *toward*, they push *back*. (*Were you not reaching out?*) Proximity is pressure. New barometric imbalances rob them of the oxygen necessary to speak. Space and time thicken.

(What should they say? There's no script for this. No fund of available platitudes.)

Everything happens for a reason.

(Bullshit.)

Thanks.

(Things don't happen for a reason. We make reason out of the things that happen.)

Realizes his enlightenment has only exposed the flimsiness underneath, loose springs and cracked gears, strain and smoke. He's been reborn as an anarchist in a world of well-oiled systems, solid institutions, suits and stability.

And this: Though no one dares say it aloud, he knows what some (*all*) are thinking: *Could have been worse.*

Yes, he *has* changed, but only in this way: He's angry. Angrier than ever. Anger of a special vintage: lacking a focal point; no key culprit or scapegoat; unfocused and isomorphic and impossible to orient, channel, burn off.

Stops driving his car. To drive is to rage.

They are supernovas of sadness. All must shield themselves from the glare.

They retreat. Go mute. Dumb. Become invisible. Bend reality around themselves. Refract light. Learn not to bring it up. If it comes up—deflect. Become expert subject-changers. (*Believe in reality as you wish it to be.*)

The few times they capitulate it is a blitzkrieg. Cities reduced to rubble.

Can't keep doing this.

Rebuild, reconstruct, avert further bombardment.

Subsist and survive.

Inside: A repeat performance! The inverted temperaments return. She: Silence! He: Study! She stays in. He goes out. She reads grim-looking books about grieving and loss. They join counselling sessions with similarly stricken couples. She goes to bed, he masturbates to online porn, sleeps on the futon, says he passed out watching TV. Outside: They grow cozy in their cloak of normalcy and similitude. Business as usual. Much to his surprise, she continues to nanny. The couple are supportive, the kids affectionate. She frequently stays for dinner. (*Cool, I have more work to take care of.*) They assure her she's indispensable, part of the family.

She travels to the Island. He finds excuses to not go with.

One weekend, while she's away, and he's under the weather, he buys a stained paperback of Stephen King's *Misery* from a street vendor. Like playing an ironic joke on himself. Reads it over two days in a fluish fugue, wholly identifies with Paul Sheldon, the crippled (*Don't say crippled!*) *injured* author ensnared by his number one fan. Can't sleep, tosses and turns, wracked with febrile ideations: Marriage is hobbling by another name! They tricked one another! Now they are well and truly *trapped!*

Works works works works. While waiting for feedback on his chapters, he rewrites those same chapters, trimming the more recondite jargon into something slightly more accessible, more mainstream. Contacts publishers. Scours job postings. Applies, almost on a whim, for a tenure-track position he lacks the credentials to win, at a prestigious university out east.

Is it summer now? Fall? Turns down a course. Too close. Sees the light, completion tantalizingly within reach. Replies from university presses trickle in. Lands an interview with the prestigious university out east. She is…somewhere. Doing her thing. They're two tenants boarding together. Air traffic controllers ensuring their paths don't cross and cause a collision.

In February he flies out for his first ever job interview for any job whatsoever. Having no frame of reference, he has no clue how it goes. Flies home. A defense date is set. An offer to publish is tendered. Gets the job.

Inconceivable! she says. Rare moment of levity. High-five! He rushes out to buy pizza and cheap sparkling wine. In his brief absence, she contemplates the as-yet-non-negotiated details. Are they moving out east? Does she *want* to move out east? What are the winters like there? (*Right, the winter thing...*) Very cold. Very snowy. Dealbreaker? Could she move so far away from her family, her *families?* And wait, why hadn't they discussed any of this earlier? (His first interview ever! A *coup!*) Did she want him to turn down the position? *Could* he turn down the position? (Insanity! He'd won the lottery!) He should reject 80K *per annum*, benefits, and (potential) ironclad job security so that she can pull in eleven-fifty an hour watching other people's kids?

The sparkling wine goes unopened.

A détente. A plan. He'll take the gig. She'll stay, gradually acclimate the children to the hard fact of her impending departure in six months or so.

Signs a contract to publish his book.

Summer. They fly out east to scout for lodging. He puts down a deposit on a spacious (if overpriced) loft-style condo. Stainless steel and exposed brick. They're assured it's a safe, clean neighbourhood. Lots of Ukrainians.

They fly back. For the next month, he toggles between rewrites and packing. A quick trip out to the Island to visit her family. He's struck by how much older her half-sisters seem. The eldest charges full-bore into pubescence, worries her MySpace account like a dog with a blanket, pesters her perplexed older sister for hair care product recommendations. Her father cooks and chortles and wrangles the willing for card and board game sessions. Already feeling the tug of his impending deadline, he rejects these entreaties to chip away at his manuscript.

The night before his departure, she invites a cohort of good friends over for a barbeque. Bit of a downer. People drink too quickly and eat too much. A pall settles. They make their excuses, wish him luck, leave early. After dishes, she invites him to bed. He begs off for an hour to work on his book. By the time he wraps up, she's already asleep.

Initially, all indications are that The Plan is working. Distance makes their hearts grow fonder. Long, involved conversations over the phone, late into the night like lovelorn teens. On the eve of her first visit, over fall break, he sends off the latest rounds of revisions to his editor, sets his email to autoreply, buys a bottle of not-so-cheap wine, picks her up from the airport, cooks a decadent meal. They fuck like lovelorn teens. Takes her sightseeing: the art gallery's astonishing *Group of Seven* collection; the museum's assortment of dinosaur skeletons; the elephants at the zoo that made such an impression on him as a boy. They ascend to the top of the great tower, hold hands as they step onto the glass floor, can barely bring themselves to look at the vertiginous plunge below.

That night, after much wine, she confesses that Christmas might be too soon. Too hard on the kids. Late spring would be better. She doesn't see them as much over the summer anyway. They are less dependent on her. It'd make for a better break.

His knee-jerk reaction: This emendation is an affront to The Plan.

Talk it out. *Sure. Yeahyeah. Makes sense.*

All in all, a lovely week. A renewal. Drives her to the airport. They embrace. There are tears.

Slowly, though, the distance ossifies. Becomes a border. Not impregnable, but present. They live different lives in different spheres. Speak alien emotional tongues. She has a good or bad day with her kids, he has a bad or good day with his. They report to one another as if reading off a list. Calls grow fewer and far between. Stop checking-in every night. Go two or three days without speaking. A whole week.

Christmas in the prairies with his parents. It's fine. Strained. Friction over something trivial. Resentment lingers longer than it should. His parents act weird, give them both a wider berth. She plays *happy* for them. He resents the performance, that his folks (pretend to?) buy it. Counteracts by sulking.

His book drops. No shits are given. Two reviews—both exegetical, both middling—in Podunk academic journals. (He Googles one of the reviewers, clicks through to her Facebook, writes a scathing retort, deletes it.) Pats on the back from his new colleagues. Commended by the Program Director. She appreciates the balance of theoretical rigour and mainstream accessibility. Feels damned by faint praise, but congratulates himself on, if nothing else, an earnest first effort.

He's young. He'll bounce back. More books to come.

The calls grow tense. She admits she's made little-to-no preparations to move, has neglected even to inform her surrogate family that departure is a possibility. While they're on the topic, what has he done to spur her to make these preparations? Admits he's kind of enjoying his neo-bachelorhood. A workable model, perhaps, for their marriage? Just because almost every other couple co-habitates doesn't mean they have to.

Maybe... she says.

They agree to approach The Plan in more pragmatic terms. The Plan becomes bureaucratic, a plan for the sake of *having a plan*. A plan instead of *no* plan. Meetings and consultations, recommendations and negotiations, but no concrete steps toward implementation. Their marriage has become an institution whose only purpose is to perpetuate its own existence.

They feel less and less like a couple, and more and more like a contract.

Her next trip out east is delayed. The younger boy fell at (well, *off*) a playground and broke his wrist. The family must cancel a planned vacation to France. She feels like it's her fault, offers to bear the brunt of the boy's care while he convalesces.

It's only for a week or two, she tells him. *Maybe a month.*

Maybe… he thinks.

Decide to take a break and see how they feel. One month later, they formally separate. *Five years to the day we met,* he tells people. An exaggeration. Not entirely true. Solace in the symmetry of numbers. *Five* years. *Five* days. Surely one could read some cryptic universal decree in the tealeaves of such curious numerical coincidences? *Hm?*

She moves out of the duplex, lodges with a female friend. He calls. No one answers. Voicemail informs him that the two of them are travelling.

Guess fucking where?

Several boxes of stuff arrive. In one he finds small silver orbs linked by a long chain.

Feels wrecked, lacerated. Knows he's being irrational, hypocritical, but self-awareness does little to staunch the emotional bleeding. Scandalous threads start to weave into an epic mental tapestry ecstatic with ageless themes: *Betrayal! Duplicity! Abandonment!*

Before a sturdy fabric forms, something unexpected happens.

His publisher calls. His book is selling. Is he available to do an interview?

CAROL: I have a responsibility, I...

JOHN: ...to...?

CAROL: To? To this institution? To the *students*. To my *group*.

JOHN: ...your 'group.' ...

CAROL: Because I speak, yes, not for myself. But for the group,
for those who suffer what I suffer.

—David Mamet, *Oleanna*

The Gathering

Jet engine. *Fuuuck*. Clawed at the blinds. Person, machine strapped to their back, clearing dust and debris off the walkway criss-crossing the courtyard. Exercise in fucking futility. Following their violent displacement, the leaves and rubble—he'd seen it all before—would be raked. Dust would slather the roof in sheets for a future rain to drive back down, coating the walkway anew. This was nothing but noise for the sake of itself.

Bent the slats for a full minute, shooting savage daggers at the oblivious agitator and raging turbine.

Released the blinds, sank back into bed, pulled a pillow over his head. Too late. Hive abuzz. No one to complain to. Condo board composed of well-meaning elderlies who were all probably up by now regardless. His breeder friends would grumble that seven *was* fucking sleeping in. Could hear the chorus of clucking already: *Quintessential white person problem. Check your privilege, bro. Cushy job! Home-ownership! Independence! Up late drinking and smoking pot?*

Sorry we woke you. What's next, venting your spleen over watermelons with seeds?

Shoved the pillow aside. Neck tight, head humming with dull pain, mouth cotton-swabbed and stale (*stupid cigarettes*), brain unspooled cassette tape. Two ibuprofen with tap water, scolded his past self for inflicting unnecessary pain on present Barker.

Coffee. Couch. Tried Dell. Voicemail. Probably on duty. Apologized for not responding sooner, had the evening free if she wanted to grab dinner or drinks.

The manila envelope, contents smeared across the ottoman, baffled him. What was all this? *Rightrightright*: the email, Mac and Evan, the mysterious (but extremely volatile) package. If he divulged anything, if he even divulged that there was anything to divulge, lawyers would muster.

Recalled having tried and failed to decrypt the nonsensical but somehow nefarious cartoon bubbles. Picked up some papers, flipped, squinted at the pseudo-sexy teen-esque banter. He'd call Evan. Admit defeat. What was Barker meant to make of this shit, and what did any of it have to do with Baz Randell?

◆ ◆ ◆

Another balmy day. Geared up and cycled to campus. Arrived to find a dozen students loitering outside the lecture hall.

A brawny, sloe-eyed male with a lopsided ear that tapered into a pink taffy twist looked up from his phone and gave Barker one of those jaw-jut things. Barker jaw-jutted back. The student—*Matt? Mike?*—nodded at the closed door. "Herstory," he said, rolling his eyes.

Barker peered through the small window, inch-thick glass inlaid with wire: A woman at a lectern pointing at a projection. The card on-screen: *Herstory.*

"Kind of stupid," Matt or Mike stated flatly.

Barker set his satchel down. "What do you find stupid about it?"

"It's just, like, who are they trying to fool?"

Checked his phone. The class should be clearing out any minute.

"I'm, like, a feminist, right?" The easy way the kid said it, his rolling baritone, made the statement sound not entirely unconvincing. "I believe in equality and equal rights and all that. But..." Second sidelong glance through the window. "I guess I don't get how changing the word history into herstory does anything. Isn't history just, like, history?"

"Well, I think it's intended to make a point, yes? Your being a feminist is commendable, but supporting equality today doesn't in itself rectify the abhorrent treatment of women in the past, does it? A big part of contemporary feminism is grappling with both present-day *and* historical injustices, don't you think?"

Mattmike watched him, eyes skittish and noncommittal.

"Women didn't even have the right to vote until the early twentieth century."

"They have the right to vote now."

"Sure, but not without a lot of struggle. Granted, on its surface, maybe amending the word *history* looks superficial—academics have a penchant for these sort of silly portmanteaux and neologisms—but taken symbolically it does draw attention to, or asks us to consider, the extent to which history is itself gendered...a set of narratives told by and about men that exclude or elide the significant contributions made by women."

"Like, history is written by the victors?"

"In a manner of speaking, yes, if by 'victors' you mean white, heterosexual men of means. And, to take it farther, think about how language, the very word we use to describe the stories we tell ourselves about our past, our predecessors, still bears the obvious markings of that once-entrenched patriarchy. Could even be said to *enforce* that patriarchy."

"Huh," Mattmike said.

"I don't know what class this is," Barker said, "but I imagine that this is what the instructor wants to underscore. The word herstory is a sort of a platform to tell stories about historically important women neglected by male-centric accounts."

Mattmike nodded. "I get it."

Barker gave himself an internal pat on the back. This is what made it all worthwhile. Not only inspiring, but changing young minds. Opening their eyes to new possibilities, historical imbalances of power, unseen mechanisms of oppression. Giving them the tools to apprehend and evaluate the world, their place within it, in new and important and complex ways. Fulfilling an edict dating back to Socrates: Teaching them not *what* to think, but *how* to think.

It was an awesome, humbling responsibility.

♦ ♦ ♦

The ibuprofen had softened the throb. Barker massaged his left temple with one hand as he unlocked the media array with the other. Third and final class of the week, *Games, Geeks, and Gizmos*. "These are the themes we'll be exploring throughout the semester," he'd told the kids during his intro lecture a little under a month ago. "We'll look at games as media, as a type of structure, or what would most commonly be referred to as 'rules'—you might take a moment to contemplate the difference between *games* and *play*—as well as the material objects we use to play games, from rudimentary items such as cards and tokens and dice, to complex machines like computers and consoles. These, of course, are the *gizmos*. We'll also be looking at the people who play games, how games and gaming scaffold identity—how we understand ourselves and others. Games are not only lucrative objects *within* culture—think of all the stuff produced by major corporations: Nintendo and Electronic Arts, Sony and Microsoft—but are also a catalyst for the formation *of* culture. The power of games and gaming to bring people together into discrete communities. The geeks!" Thrust a fist into the air. "I proudly count myself among their number." They stared, looking stunned, then typed in unison, filling the room with the patter of soft rain. What kind of note-taking did Barker's declaration of solidarity inspire? *Prof = Geek. Proud!*

The projectors whirred, opened their pale blue eyes. "Today," he began, "as a means of delving into this question of community, we're going to peer into one of the darker corners of gaming culture. How many of you are familiar with GamerGate, or were before last week?" A few limp noodle arms wafted upward. "So what do we make of Golding's argument, by way of Bogost, that this controversy represents the death of a so-called 'gamer identity'?"

One...two...three...

At fifteen he threw them a bone. "We might add that this so-called 'identity' is predominantly...or, rather, let's say *presumably*, white, straight, upper-middle-class, and male." Even the keeners stayed mum. "Is this fair in and of itself? Is this category representative of gamers, both historically and today?"

A hand. Her. *Of course it was her.* "Ophelia?"

"Maybe it was true moreso in the past, but I think that more and more females today play games."

"Any guess as to percentages?"

"Like...?"

"Like, what percentage of gamers today are women?"

"Oh, um, I dunno... Maybe twenty-five percent maybe?"

"Good guess. I'd probably have guessed even lower. It's actually closer to fifty."

Tappity-tippity-tip-tap.

"Gaming has gone mainstream, yes? And that is partly due to what?" Held up his smartphone. "Because of this, right? Because this gizmo, this mini supercomputer, can be used not only to make telephone calls, send text messages, surf the web, but also, maybe especially, to play video games."

Stared.

"So say the actual number *is* closer to fifty. It sure feels like there are way more male gamers than female ones. Why?"

Mattmike raised his hand.

"Yes?" *Maybe Mitch? Or Mark?*

"We don't take them seriously."

"Okay. Can you expand on that?"

"It's like women might play games as much as men, but I think men think women aren't as serious about games. They, like, play puzzle games or fashion games. They're not playing *Call of Duty* or whatever. They're not real hard-core gamers."

"Like men?"

Mattmikemitchmark: "I guess so, yeah."

"That's totally unfair, though," Ophelia jumped in.

Barker: "How so?"

"Who says that women take games less seriously than men? That's just the, uh, that just perpetuates a stereotype about women being weak and, uh, like, frivolous or—"

"*I'm* not saying that," said Mattmikemitchmark. "I'm talking about a *perception*."

Ophelia: "A stupid perception."

Some students swivelled.

"To be fair to..." *The hell was his name?* "...your colleague here, I think he's speaking to a fairly common perception, however unfair, that women, though they comprise half of the gaming community, are somehow less serious about video games than their male counterparts. There's even a term, a *gendered* term, that encapsulates this discrepancy..."

Bueller? Bueller?

"How many of you have heard the term 'casual gamer'?"

A few heads bobbed like wave-ruffled buoys.

"This term is largely applied to women, to female gamers. Why?" Looked at Mattmikemitchmark. "What was it you said before?"

"Oh, yeah, well...*casual* makes them sound less serious." He glanced sheepishly at Ophelia. She crossed her arms. "Even though it's a totally unfair assertion."

"Right, so here we have this acutely gendered conception of gamers that parses men and women into categories of serious and non-serious respectively. If you recall that section of *Console Wars* from two weeks ago, when competition between Nintendo and SEGA intensified, both companies worked hard to cultivate this concept of the *hard-core gamer*. You see this clearly in their marketing materials at the time. This video game player is technically savvy, prefers graphically violent content. Gaming is more than a hobby, it's a lifestyle, even an addiction, one so powerful they'd rather play than eat. This *hard-core gamer* is predominantly what? Ophelia?"

"Male."

"Male. Caucasian. Privileged. Pretty striking contrast with the term 'casual,' which frames gaming as more of a lifestyle quirk, something to pass the time because, what the heck, we all happen to have a smartphone on hand. Just another accessory, right? Like a makeup case. *Casual* gamers aren't serious about games, not in the way your average *Call of Duty* aficionado is."

Moved behind the lectern, opened a window on the computer. "This is where Golding's piece and the GamerGate controversy come in. Even though the gaming community is more or less evenly split gender-wise, it's nonetheless perceived as a male domain. So what happens when women—as game designers, players, critics—start to question male-centric conceptions of games and gaming? Even—and this is the video I'm going to share with you this morning—how women are portrayed within games themselves? How many of you have seen the *Tropes vs. Women* series?"

Stared.

"All right, well, what I'm going to show you is part one of a two part series."

Started the video, sat off to the side so as not to obstruct anyone's view. Watched, impressed, as always, by the force of Sarkeesian's argument, her trenchant appraisal of the appalling violence perpetrated against female video game characters. A parade of eager whores and prostitutes weathering cavalier beatings and abuse; each glib, garish death—no, *murder*—a damning indictment of the culture's rampant misogyny. Moreover, the discursive emphasis on the impossibility of alternatives or escape; recursive cycles of violence implicitly reinforcing the idea of punishment and slaughter as somehow innate to the female experience. At once sterling scholarship and populist polemic. Also, to her credit, very hard to watch. Disturbing in the extreme.

What stung, if he was honest, was how many of these games Barker himself had played. Not only played, but cherished, considered classics—from triple-A titles like *Bioshock* and *Dishonored*, to indie darlings like the second *Killing Time*.

Rustling behind him. Barker checked over his shoulder. One of the students was packing up. She approached, knelt, said she was feeling ill and had to leave. He nodded.

Wait…is she ill-*ill, or is it the video?* Should he have more thoroughly vetted the contents? Did it merit a trigger warning? *Is she one of the anxiety disorder kids?* Cartoonish or no, much of the violence was levied from a first-person perspective. Every chainsaw grinding through flesh, every gush of blood and spatter of gore, every burst head and evisceration immediate and intimate, emphasizing the player's compliance and culpability.

Stopped the video, hit the lights. "Like I said, this is one of two parts, and I highly recommend every entry in the series. But that's enough, I think, to give you a taste of her thesis. So my question is basically—and keeping in mind what Sarkeesian says at the outset: That she is herself an avid video game fan, but reserves the right to critique that which she loves—what do you make of her argument? Agree? Disagree?"

One… Hands shot up. "Yes?"

"I disagree with what she's saying a lot," said one.

"Okay. Why's that?"

"This whole idea that men want to save or, like, rescue women," averred another, "that's a good thing. That's an idea in tons of stories."

"Fair point, and something she discusses at length in a different episode."

Another: "Video games are a business, businesses do what they need to make money. These are the kinds of games that audiences want and it's lame to criticize a business for making money."

"We're saying that any content, no matter how retrograde or reprehensible, can be excused provided it's profitable?"

Another: "It's not fair to blame all men for how some games depict women."

"Is that what she's doing?"

Another: "There are lots of games with strong female characters." The student named several. Others chimed in with their own examples.

"I don't think she's saying that every portrayal is negative. A more relevant question might be whether those examples are the exceptions or the rule?"

On and on. Initially, Barker was surprised, even impressed, by their enthusiasm. Then unease set in. Only *male* students were speaking. And, yes, there were more men in the class than women, but still, they were monopolizing the conversation, acting defensive. The girls kept quiet. Some bodily slouched behind their desks.

Barker looked at Ophelia, laptop open before her. A barrier.

Should he do something? Mollify the men without making it seem like that's what he was doing? Pose a question to one of the women directly? Would they feel singled out? Was it already too late?

"Let's leave it there for today."

◆ ◆ ◆

She was waiting for him. Always waited for him. First class—a sunny *Just wanted to introduce myself!* Both lectures thereafter.

The week prior they'd stumbled into a long (nearly thirty minutes) and involved (she divulged personal details about her family, her father) conversation. Barker dispensed platitudes about life's strange and uncertain turns (*no reason to make any concrete decisions about school, like, today, especially since it sounds like you've been through the emotional ringer*), grad school advice (*if that's something you decide you want to pursue, after you've done the travelling you talked about*), offered his services as a mentor (*happy to write letters, put you in touch with people, or if you just need someone to spit ball with…*).

That would be sooo amazing.

Round four felt less like coincidence and more like a pattern. Well, no harm in that. Student-professor infatuations were nothing new. A tired cliché. Older than Aristotle. Some kids just latched. Given the situation with her dad, she probably wanted or needed a surrogate. And besides, Barker was one of the good guys, one of the few that gave a shit. He liked the kids, most of the kids, despite their quirks and quietude. And in the end it wasn't about winning over the whole class—no point waging *that* war—but only a handful, those special three or four. They needn't necessarily be the smartest or hardest working. Curious and engaged sufficed. *You* gave a shit because *they* gave a shit.

"Hey Professor!"

"Hi Ophelia." Straw-blonde curls, ersatz stud nested in an elfish nose. (Were the kids still into facial piercings? *Sooo* nineties!) Behind thick glasses—aquamarine eyes framed by starfish lashes. (Wait, wasn't her hair straight last week? Had she been wearing glasses before?) Today it was all black attire that reminded Barker of—an antiquated reference even for him—Janet Jackson circa *Rhythm Nation*. (These Millenials. So pomo. Identity tourists trying on personalities like they were outfits, and outfits like they were personalities.) Leather vest festooned with snaps and buckles, form-fitting yoga pants, Adidas ball cap with a ponytail springing pertly out of the sizing band at the back. Per Rabin, a *manic pixie dream girl* for the scholarly geek set. "How's it going?"

"Good good good." Puffed her cheeks. "Already with the midterms, so there's *that*."

"Yeah, they creep up on you. Hard to believe we're almost half-way through the semester."

"I *know*. Crazy!"

Loved her for sparing him a teeth-grating *cray-cray*.

Barker: "So, I had an interesting night last night."

"Yeah?"

"Yeah. Mysterious email that led to a mysterious phone call followed by a meeting at the campaign headquarters of a certain mayoral candidate..."

"*Yesss!*" Pumped her fist. "They called you?"

"If by 'they' you mean Mac and Evan."

"Ha!" Another pump. "High-*larious!*"

"I have to say, I was surprised to find out they got my name from you."

"I didn't mean to...I mean, I hope it's cool I gave them your email. I didn't think that crossed a line or whatever."

"It's fine." Moved for the stairs, she followed in overextended strides. "I just meant that I didn't take you for a"—almost said *conservative*—"political person."

"Oh, I'm pretty political. I mean, you kind of have to be these days. *Omigosh*, I hope you don't think...I don't *agree* with his, like, policies and stuff. I mean, Baz is a nice guy, *waaay* nicer than you'd think, but I'm not, like, ideologically *with* him or whatever. I disagree with most of that stuff. *Derp! Then why do you work for him? Derp! Derp!*"

Barker grinned.

"I want to work in politics. It would be one potential route anyway. I thought it'd be good experience to work on a campaign, and my mom knows some people who know some people who know Ev. So *yeeaah*, that's how that happened."

"You didn't mention politics as a potential career path the last time we talked."

"*Naw*. It's my dirty little secret. Well, now it's *our* dirty little secret."

She winked.

(*Did she?*)

He held the door, she scampered through. "Ta! I've just had one too many awkward conversations about it. A lot of my, uh, peers are pretty opposed to him, and even though I tell them I'm only doing it for the experience, they think its sort of like a kind of *betrayal*, or, like, why would I devote my free time to the breakdown of democracy or whatever. Whew! *That* was an extremely rambly explanation of why I didn't bring it up. Sorry!"

They cut across the concourse.

"Sooo…?"

"So?"

"How'd it go? I mean, I don't actually know what they wanted to talk to you about. They just let it be known among the rank and file that if anyone knew anyone who worked in media, and I was all like *yeah, I think I know a guy*…"

"To be honest, I'm not entirely sure what they wanted to talk to me about either."

"Hm. *Mysterioso!*"

They arrived at the bike rack.

"If there's one thing we've all learned about Baz, it's that just when you think they've found every skeleton in his closet, you realize his closet is *waaay* bigger than you thought. He's like…I dunno… Again, I actually like him as a *person*, but… What's the term, when you can't, like, progress beyond a certain age? That sitcom?"

"Arrested development?" Freed his lock.

"Yeah." Snapped her fingers. "Like *that*. He's got *that*. Like Baz made it to Junior High and got stuck. Or decided to stay there or something. I dunno. Maybe that was a good time in his life and he never wanted to move past it. Or something."

Barker rolled up a pants cuff, donned his helmet.

"So nice out." She sounded forlorn. Shielded her eyes from the sun. "Are you going for a ride?"

"Thinking about it."

"Cool." Beat.

"Was there something you wanted to ask me?"

"No. I mean *yes*, but it's kind of stupid."

"For some reason I doubt that."

"Not *stupid*. It just doesn't have anything to do with anything."

"Now I am truly intrigued."

She smiled, kicked at something on the ground. "Do you know David Mamet?"

"Sounds familiar."

"He's a playwright."

"He wrote, ah, wasn't it *Sexual Adventures in Chicago?*"

"Close! *Perversity*." Another wink. (*Was it?*)

"I'm directing one of his plays for the Undergraduate Drama Society."

"You're directing *Sexual*, uh..."

"No, not that one. A different one. *Oleanna*."

"I don't think I know it."

"It's great. Really, really good. It's about a professor who's accused of sexual harassment by one of his students."

"Ah. Timely."

"*Super* timely. I mean, I think that that's why they picked it. *I* didn't pick it, they just asked me to direct it."

"An iron in every fire."

"What?"

"You're a third year with a full course load interning for a political campaign while directing a play on the side. How do you find the time?"

"Who has two thumbs and was a huge-ass drama geek all through high school?" Thrust her thumbs at herself. "This guy! Hard to believe, I know. But, yeah, I really like it. *Oleanna* I mean. *Such* a good play. Really topical, and timely, like you said. And super basic. Two hander, minimal set..."

"What seems to be the issue?"

"Ugh, it's *so* dumb, I'm so sorry to bother you with this, but I just really appreciate your advice. *Ya! Obvs!* So, right, so the other day I get this message signed by both student associations, the undergrad one and the grad one, expressing their *concern* over *my* choice of material. Meaning *Oleanna.* I almost write back to say it wasn't me who picked the play, but then I get worried, 'cause I don't want to get the *u-dee-ess* in trouble, or make it seem like I'm ratting them out or whatever. So I send back a message asking what their concerns are. And they write back that the play, uh, denigrates victims of sexual assault, or something like that. So I write back to say I don't think that the play is meant to denigrate anyone, more like it's about how these situations—accusations of assault or, uh, in the play it's more like harassment or whatever—can, like, spiral out of control, and how there are two sides to every story, and sometimes the person who gets accused is put in a position where everyone assumes the worst and it can get really hard to defend themselves, because there's this sort of assumption that they're guilty even though we're *supposed* to assume they're innocent. I mean, that's the whole point of a *fair trial*, right? So I sent *that* message, and worded it really nice and polite and everything, and then just, like, *this morning*, they sent me *another* message telling me that I was…hold on a sec…" Lifted her phone, thumbed the screen. "I was, quote, 'drastically misrepresenting the sadistic glee Mamet takes in demonizing women in his grossly misogynistic…' What's this word?"

"Polemic."

"Polemic." Rolled the word over her tongue, like tasting a fine wine. "Right, *polemic*, 'and any suggestion of duplicity on the part of victims of sexual assault, or questioning the validity of their claims, does an immense disservice to all victims.'" Deep breath. Exhaled. "*Whoa!*"

Fuck. He'd forgotten to check in with Maureen.

"That's a mouthful."

"True say. And then some. I was wondering, I guess, I dunno... What do you think? I mean, should I write them back again? Should I drop out of the show? I'd *hate* to do that, to not direct the play. I *like* the play, even if, I mean, I see their point. The female character, Carol, *is* kind of manipulative. But it's not like the professor, John, is totally innocent. And it's more about the position they're put in by, like, the context of the university at that time. And it's just such a topical, *timely,* uh, topic."

"What does the drama group think? Did you speak to them about it?"

"They said it's about free speech and I should ignore the student societies. Maybe they're right. Maybe it was dumb to write back in the first place. I just thought this could be part of the conversation, y'know? Doing theatre isn't *just* about putting on a play. It's about starting a, yeah, a conversation."

"There's certainly something to be said for opening up a dialogue. And for free speech, of course. It also seems that, rightly or wrongly, you've been singled out as the standard-bearer for the show. It doesn't seem fair for the drama people to hang you out to dry over the play *they* chose. They need to have your back here."

"See, I said something like that at our production meeting this morning, but they said I shouldn't have responded in the first place, and so anything I write, or the back and forth, is on me basically. They think if I stop responding the whole thing will blow over, and once the play is up no one will care anyway."

Barker untwisted the strap of his satchel, smoothed it flat across his chest.

"Well, I'm sorry you're in this position. Harassment is an important issue, obviously. Also tricky to unpack in any venue, including theatre." Straightened his helmet, fastened the clasp. "I have to admit, I'm a bit out of my element here. I don't really know anything about theatre, or that play."

"I know. I'm sorry. It's stupid. I *said* it was stupid."

"No, no." Reached out and put his hand on her arm, right under the shoulder. She didn't flinch. Drew his hand back, slid his thumbs under the strap. "Listen, why don't you give me the weekend to give the play a quick read. I'll check if the library has a copy I can—"

"Here," dropped her bag and knelt over it. The lapel of her jacket flopped to the side, revealing a black tee underneath, V-neck dovetailing at the cleft of her cleavage.

Averted his eyes.

She stood and handed him a slim, mangled codex.

"You don't need it?"

"I have another copy at home."

"Okay, great. Give me the weekend to give it a read. I'll let you know what I think and we can take it from there."

She beamed. "Thankyouthankyou*thank*you. You're probably super busy. If you only have time for a quick scan or whatever. Any advice you have I would really, really appreciate." She put her hand on his forearm. A welter of heat. Stroked his wrist with her thumb. (Maybe not. A digital twitch?)

"Happy to help."

Wrinkled her nose. "Seeya!"

"Yeah. Seeya."

Ophelia left. A moment later, Barker turned toward Lake House to track down Maureen.

♦ ♦ ♦

Barker was flying, or at least the closest approximation to flight a human being could attain. Forget the frictionless lift of an airplane. Skydiving was just gravity. *Cycling* was true independent bodily propulsion through space.

Cleared the city as rush hour hit its manic peak: sidewalks clotted, streets a crush of syrup-slow cars, drivers lurching into lanes, panicked swivels around idling cabs making ill-advised curbside pickups, indifferent to the squeals of abuse their infractions inspired.

Threaded through them all.

Shot out onto a major artery and ended up playing leapfrog with a city bus. The bus blasted by uncomfortably close, buried him in a cloud of opaline exhaust, pulled over to offload and pick up passengers. Barker passed the bus as it idled, gaining a block before its grunting bulk heaved past him once more. So it went, two intertwined trajectories, jockeying for position, the gap between them collapsing and pulling apart like an accordion.

Veered off in search of an alternate route.

Felt good to be out. Scratch that, it felt *amazing*. What a boon this late season warmth was. (*Is this what they used to call an Indian Summer? Can't use* that *term anymore.*) And no end in sight!

You had to find the sport your body was made for. Basketball was an early fit before Barker realized he was only tall *for his age*. When his peers hit puberty, his advantage evaporated. Despite decent hand-eye coordination (cultivated, he believed, through countless hours of video game play), his high waist and ambiguous centre of gravity rendered him increasingly haphazard, all flailing limbs, as flappable as an inflatable tube man at a used car lot. His first instinct was to persevere through sheer will and pluck. Bucking the counsel of family and friends, he tried out for the high school team.

He wasn't part of the first round of cuts. He *was* the first round of cuts.

Scratch basketball.

Swimming didn't stick. Water made him panicky. Jogging was a no-go. Hated how it jarred his knees, aggravating the shin splints that had plagued his aborted basketball career. Cross country skiing? Fun, but it took too long to drive out to a decent park, and you were too much at the mercy of the elements. The last time he'd made the effort, the weather had spiked from arctic to tropical, the groomed track crumbling into an impassable mush.

Of course he'd had bikes growing up, but that was simply autonomous transportation. In his mid-twenties, the Swedish girl with the long legs convinced him to invest in a real machine. He dropped a full sixth of his student line of credit on a bright red road bike with white sabre detailing. Properly calibrated to Barker's physical proportions, it felt like a prosthesis, an extension of his body. His formerly unwieldy legs became pistons, knees bulged, calves winnowed into upside-down Ts. While on principle he was opposed to the accessories that proliferated within a given sub-culture, inside of a month he'd purchased a pocketed jersey, diaper shorts, aerobars, clip-in pedals, and a compact wireless computer (elapsed time and max speed tracking, GPS, speedometer, odometer, altimeter, and calorie consumption gauge).

Still, he reserved the right to judge the poseurs, decked out in decal-clad spandex, chugging away astride bikes worth more than Barker's first car. (Shit, their *wheels* were worth more than that car.) A declaration of means, a roundabout way of buying your way into a taste preference fraternity. Got cash? Great. Done some tours? Nice. Can't summit that hill? Fuck off.

Owning the bib doesn't put you on the team.

How often was it these same clowns screaming past on a straightaway, or plummeting down a hill, whose velocity disintegrated at the scarcest hint of an incline? *Climbing is part of the deal,* Barker would think as he hammered nonchalantly past another pretender to the priesthood, maybe tossing them an encouraging nod or *Nice day today!* to complete the overall appearance of minimal effort.

While his dalliance with the Swede was as short-lived as her legs were long, cycling stuck. Became an infatuation. Was he trying to outpace the indecencies of aging—his thinning crown and budding paunch? Maybe. But so much more than that: Being the engine of his own momentum, the impossible tilt of every turn, cruising up inclines.

Crushed inclines. Barker was built to ascend.

Loved biking in the fall—the rust infusing the leaves, like blood becoming; the earth a decanter of decay suddenly unstopped, its pent-up entropy released, the air ribboned with fruity rot. Drank it in deep draughts—the fungal musk, the vaporous algae sliming the ponds—huffed life in the thick of ferment.

Cycling was also, as late, the only thing that got him out of his fucking head, subdued the ecstatic filaments of his neural network, leaving him free to exist in material space as a purely physical object hurtling through that space.

Once he'd breached the city limits, it was ninety minutes and change to his favourite bistro. The city felt all-encompassing from the inside, but from this particular patio it looked distant and shrunken, the size of a quarter between extended fingers, a squishable pimple of glass and mortar dotting the horizon.

Turned into a park. Picnicking families. Kids playing soccer. Doddering elderlies. Passed a couple pushing a stroller the width of a Roman chariot.

Taut leash. Rang his bell. *Dingding!* Dude yanked the dog aside. Barker flicked his hand in a little wave.

Flagged an errant toddler listing drunkenly toward the path. Pumped his calipers, downshifted, throttled his speed. *Dingdingding!* Parents sprang into action, snatched the kid. Little wave. Mother scowled.

It's a shared path, *bitch.*

Cyclists ahead riding two abreast. *Dingdingding! Dingdingding!* Ignorance? Inattention? "On your left!" One grudgingly squeezed in beside the other. Wave. Barker torqued the gearshift, hugged his ram-horn handlebars.

Couldn't get out of his fucking head, kept replaying snippets of his earlier meeting with Maureen.

"I don't have to tell you, Barker, that even the spectre of impropriety..."

Am I in trouble?

The low-slung sun, the smog soaking up its light tinting it an early-morning amber, pressed into his forehead like a compress.

If only I'd been prepared. If only I'd seen this coming.
Fucking Lara.

Ratted him out? Maureen was Lara's supervisor, so Lara had not-infrequent opportunities to divulge details; intimate that she and a *certain male professor* had engaged in a *certain sexual something.* If Lara *had* confided in Maureen, then the crucial question was why? To what end? What did Lara have to gain? Embarrass him? It wasn't like she could get him fired. Could she? Lara didn't come across as devious or vindictive, just immature; like so many of their students, had never not been in school. A striking intellect with no sense of the world outside the tower's well-padded walls. Veal intractably softened by the crate.

Snaked through a forest of skinny birch, through swarms of insects huddled inside thick slats of sunlight. They pelted his arms and chest like rice at a wedding.

Lara's romantic history, once he had an inkling, made him even more mindful. Not that a lack of experience was bad, but at twenty-five, she'd had all of three sexual partners, none of them especially serious. In the midst of their second fuck, on her pristine white duvet, she confessed to feel a *spiritual connection.*

Christ, he thought, *I haven't even come yet.*

(The next morning, she found a toothpick-thin shit smear on said duvet. Said nothing. As Barker would quickly learn, there was usually a lot of something in her nothing.)

But of course Lara was exactly the type to mistake infatuation for love, because this was something you could only learn through experience: fucking people, falling for them, consolidating your stuff, growing apart. That kind of shit.

Something bigger (a bee?) hit his lip like a bullet.

And if Lara *hadn't* told anyone? Who else might know? How had they found out? Why come forward now? And again, to what end?

Two consenting adults!

Careened through a set of concrete pylons marking the periphery of the park. Dropped sharply off the curb, swerved into an empty side street, stuttered over an asphalt moonscape, skidded to a stop, waited for the light to change.

From the beginning... Lake House. Maureen's door is ajar. Knocks. She ushers him in with her usual warmth. (He did her a solid last year. She feels like she owes him. She doesn't, but that's how she feels and she won't be dissuaded.)

Achievement in research evidenced primarily by published work?

Check!

Effectiveness in teaching demonstrated in lectures, seminars, and tutorials as well as in more informal teaching situations such as counselling students?

Check!

University service? Does a whole year as Interim Program Director count?

Check! Check! Check!

"Doctor Grady tells me you broke up a bar brawl last night."

Barker almost launches into the story of the catfight at The Luce, but stops cold. The details are all wrong. He can't portray the actors accurately. Halter Top would sound unhinged and hysterical, the bla...of African decent one violent, deranged, the undeniable aggressor. Their language—too crude, too vulgar, too laced with profanity. Both portraits, the altercation itself—*All over a man!*—were profoundly problematic, reductive, demeaning. It might sound like Barker was actively perpetuating retrograde gender and racial stereotypes.

"She's overstating my role. I only stepped in for a moment. Besides, I'm sure the good bits are already up on YouTube. What did you want to see me about?"

Green light. Barker took the left onto a narrow shoulder.

Maureen closed the door. "I hope I didn't lure you here under false pretences. Your tenure portfolio is still under review."

"Sure," he said, going for *chipper*. "What can I help you with?"

"I received a complaint regarding your having had an inappropriate relationship with a student."

"Which student?" Having just come from his chat with Ophelia, his knee-jerk was that someone had spotted them, maybe noticed a pattern of after-class interactions (four wasn't necessarily a *pattern*), mistaken their platonic arm-patting.

"I hope there isn't more than one." Squeezed into her seat.

"I didn't mean…" Almost protested—*There aren't* any!—but saw how awfully uncomfortable she was. A pang of guilt. Not because he'd done anything wrong, but for having inadvertently put her in this position.

"You know I like you." Looked down at her desk, rubbed at something there with her thumb. "But I'm your boss right now." Clasped her hands.

"Understood."

Left into a cul-de-sac, re-joined the path nestled between white picket fences, tore past a house that looked like a child's drawing of a house. Then a playground—multi-coloured monkey bars and a yellow slide.

"No formal complaint has been submitted, and hopefully one won't be. For the time being, this is an internal matter, and I think we'd like to keep it that way. Yes?"

Path clear, wind at his back. Clicked into his highest gear.

"Okay." Beat. "I'm not sure what to say."

"You don't have to say anything."

"Until I know what I've been accused of, I don't want to say anything that could…I don't want to incriminate myself in the event that…" *lawyers get involved.* Christ, between this and his divorce, how many lawyers was he liable to have to retain?

She sighed.

"Maureen, I don't know what you've heard, or been told, and I'm sorry that you've been put in this position, but I can say unequivocally that I haven't—"

Shook her head. "Barker—"

"No, I want you to know that—"

"Stop. Just stop for one second."

Lungs bellows, legs derricks, heart combustive, mouth a vent. Once more into the woods, layer upon layer of scrolling pole-like trunks. Light spotted the path, strobed his eyes. The lake beyond flickered salmon-pink static.

Arched his back, dropped his head, tucked into himself.

Maureen: "You know this is a...sensitive time for the university. There is a general perception, not entirely unfounded, that we have a sorry track record of botching cases of sexual assault."

"*Assault?* Is that—?"

"Let me finish."

Was the machine an extension of him, or was he an extension of the machine?

"Being sensitive to such a perception, and even moreso to public relation boondoggles, our overlings are in a bit of a tizzy. Lots of things happening at once, including the draft policy Molly mentioned in the meeting yesterday. We are meant to intensify our efforts to take these problems very seriously, or at least appear as though we're doing so." She sat back in her chair. "All to say that they are looking for a win. They might not know when and how this win will come, but do not doubt that they want to bring the hammer down on someone. Hard."

Perfect. The temperature of the air harmonized with the heat of his skin. Impossible to tell where Barker ended and the world began.

As Maureen continued his mercury started to mount. Either Lara was acting petty and vindictive and emotionally immature, or one of his colleagues was. Ratting him out. *Subterfuge.*

Conjured Lara in a post-coital tableau: naked, reclining, arm folded under her head, resting at forty-five degrees; chestnut eyes expectant, mascara smeared across her marble skin; Cleopatra bangs—less haircut than coronation—a child's scribble of inky strands. Traced the geometry of her face with his eyes: wide crown, high cheekbones, tapered jaw and speartip chin. Even her nose— what his mother would have called a *fine Roman nose*—bent at a sharp, precise angle. He found the order and exactitude of her countenance—every orthogonal and diagonal, every fractal facet—incredibly comforting.

"Pythagoras would have a field day with your face," he said. A compliment.

All her angles shifted. "What's that supposed to mean?"

A fight. She is a skilled instigator. Seize on a perceived slight or trivial infraction—or, fuck it, make one up—blow everything out of proportion. Escalate. Talk her down. Tears. Sex. Lather, rinse, repeat. *I thought you'd talk me out of it.*

A long, hard day. Stops by her apartment (as always smelling slightly antiseptic, bleach and vinegar masking something warm and waxy, like hot crayon) to drop off a treat. Surprise cupcake from the fancy cupcake shop. *So sweet! Can he stay? I thought you were busy?* She'll take a break and cook some food. *We both have to eat.* He's famished. Sits him down on her couch, puts the remote in his hand, tells him to enjoy some Netflix. Thirty minutes later, dinner is ready. She won't talk. Or only barely. Miserly, monosyllabic replies. He's thrown. Is something wrong? No. Presses. *I just don't think we're communicating.* Why? *You sat there watching tee-vee while I cooked dinner.*

See: *Put the remote in his hand*, above.

Okay, let's unpack this.

Are things moving too fast? Shouting. Tears. Sex.

How long had it taken to see that *this* was her drug—caprice, conflict, hysterics, sex—that her entire emotional spectrum—concern, offense, rage—was counterfeit. Feelings were utilitarian, useful only insofar as they could be used to manipulate and provoke, to harvest attention and sympathy for herself. She was only ever citing emotions she'd observed in others elsewhere.

Barker was erect. Maureen was no longer speaking. Crossed his leg over his knee, folded his arms over his lap.

Barker gave Maureen a broad sketch of his short-lived fling with Lara Kitts. He was Interim Program Director. Lara was acting caucus president. They met occasionally to hash out the details of the graduate student conference. Lara started attending Gatherings. (Maureen winced when he said this.) Barker gave Lara a lift home after the caucus Christmas party. (Was he in any condition to drive? Irrelevant.) Parked outside her apartment complex, in his idling car, commiserating over long-distance relationships, the out of town boyfriend she was in the process of breaking up with, Barker's own ruined marriage. A *connection*. Sex. It ended roughly three months later. Late March.

"*Ended* ended?" Maureen asked.

"Yes."

"Then, mid-April, you offered her a teaching assignment?"

Ah.

"I did, yes."

"Even though she was only going into her third year? Even though she hadn't defended her dissertation proposal yet?"

"Maureen, Lara was a superstar when she got here. You busted your ass to court her. She's been angling for a teaching assignment since day one. Besides, we all know the *a-bee-dee* thing is more of a guideline than a hard and fast rule, *and* we both know she has the chops." Pressed his momentary advantage. "Are you saying you *wouldn't* have assigned her a course if you'd been here?"

"The problem isn't the course, the problem is the perception that you, having been in charge of assignments at that time, gave her a course *because* the two of you were in a relationship."

Finally saw it clearly. A misunderstanding. If anything, the course had been an olive branch—not that Lara didn't deserve it, not that she wasn't ready—a *Hey-no-hard-feelings* type deal. There was no *trade*, no *exchange*. No untoward transactions.

(And so what if they'd fucked four more times over the summer. It wasn't an official renewal, just a flare-up snuffed out as quickly as it'd kindled.)

"Well then some wires got crossed, because we were no longer *in* a relationship when I assigned her the course. Honestly, Maureen, I thought I was being magnanimous. I was actually worried I might seem...I don't know...petty if I *didn't* offer the course. Besides, I thought she was the best candidate, and she obviously wanted to teach, so..."

Sharp decline. Felt his guts drop as the path plateaued.

"Should I be looking for a lawyer?"

Maureen's gaze drifted to the window. "I really don't think it'll come to that. And it's good to hear your side of the story. This sounds more and more like a misunderstanding, as you said. I appreciate your time, Barker." Smiled and stood. "And your candour." A fatigued parent conceding the round to an insubordinate child. *Can I go to bed and cry myself to sleep now?*

Teenagers stumbled out from behind a bush onto the path.

"Whoa! WHOA!"

Several synaptic galaxies went incandescent. Crushed his brakes, tacked hard to the right. Front wheel slammed into a splay of exposed roots. Everything went up, floated in a lurching pirouette. Gravity snatched him back. Fought to right a precarious wobble, skidded to a stop on a slick patch of grass.

Breathed.

The fuck?

Their phones. That stance. Those moves. Cooper's fucking ARG. KT3. *Remember to tell him his goddamned game almost got me killed.* Wobbled his head, gave his brakes a few useless squeezes, lifted his bike around, wheeled it over to the quartet.

"The hell, you guys?"

They guffawed.

"Hello?"

One with a cleft lip and oily sand-coloured hair oozing out from under the brim of a ball cap peeled his eyes off his screen, gave Barker a fuzzy look.

"Hey?"

"Didn't you see me coming down the path?"

Cleft Lip elbowed his closest companion—oblong head, brown hair flicked into pert quills. "You see this guy on the path?"

"Huh?"

"Look, one or all of you could have gotten killed just then. Not to mention killing *me* in the process."

Oblong Head: "Huh?"

"Technically I'm a motor vehicle, okay? Even going twenty-five or thirty kilometres an hour..." Useless. Snapped his foot into the pedal with reproachful CLACK! "You all need to pay more attention next time," he said, but they weren't even paying attention *this* time. Cleft Lip was already back at the game. Oblong Head looked from Barker to the path and back as if trying to solve a math problem.

"Like, you ever learn to look both ways before crossing the street? Same idea." Kicked off. Under his breath: "Fucking morons."

Behind him, as he rode off, one of them yelled, "Fag!"

◆ ◆ ◆

Home by sunset, faint stars dotting brackish blue, tendon in his left leg twanging like a plucked string.

Fucking morons.

Shower. Scotch. Called Dell.

Drinks. Not at The Luce, Barker had never even suggested it, like a single parent wary of introducing his kids to a new flame. What if she didn't like it? What if it didn't like her? No, too soon. He didn't even know if he and Dell were dating. Sure, they'd engaged in activities typically referred to *as* dates, but either he had way less game than he thought, or hers was a glacial pace. He'd confessed the lack of sex to Shiv, but in truth there'd been little of anything at all. Peck on the cheek at the close of their third date-type-thing, perfunctory hug at the end of the fourth. Shouldn't this be easier in your mid-thirties? Didn't adults know what they wanted and bypass the rigmarole? Wooing was for twentysomethings. Let them fuss like birds of paradise over elaborate installation art sculptures, doing desperate jives to catch the eye of a passing chick.

The thing was, he liked her. Liked spending time with her. Liked her wiry hair, cappuccino skin, acorn-brown eyes. She'd modelled a bit in her twenties, but burned out on the scene. Turned to film and TV, and after a few gigs as a stand-in for a big-deal star, fell in love with stunt work. Suffered an injury while training for a Western— thrown by a horse—that laid her up for six months. By the time she'd recuperated, had basically lost interest. Having worked security in the interim, she took the advice of a retired cop colleague, and applied to join the force. She'd put in her twenty years, retire, travel.

He liked her indifference to her archaic flip phone ("It came free with the contract"), her cursory responses, sometimes arriving several days later. The lag was worrisome at first—Were his texts not getting through? Was she ghosting him?—but now he kind of appreciated the delay, the release from obsessively awaiting a response. Occasionally he'd forget he'd even messaged her in the first place, her eventual replies a nice surprise.

Never set her phone on the table, splitting off to tend to its clingy bleats and blinking, leaving him adrift—one buoy bobbing among the multitude.

Added bonus: Dell evinced next to no interest in his work. The *kids these days* were common ground of sorts, as she also dealt with her fair share of miscreants (though chiefly of the drug- and alcohol-addled kind). But his research? Gave zero shits. Midway through sketching out the thrust of his book during their second date-type-thing, she cut him off with an "I don't get it," changed the subject, never brought it up again. And neither had he. Refreshing not to have to talk shop, sure, but for some reason he found her disinterest strangely sexy, as if some vestigial lizard-brain instinct had kicked in.

Why were the ones you had to work for always the most alluring? She was as indifferent toward his job as he was enthralled with hers. Policing was so *tangible*, so *gritty*, so *basic*. Keep the peace, catch the bad guys, put them in jail. *This* was where the rubber met the road. *Real* people. *Real* problems. *Real* world.

On their first date-type-thing (more of a casual rendezvous, a *nice to meet* you between friends of friends. *Knew her from high school. Moved back a few years ago. Think you two might hit it off*), he'd relished the tales of her training, the final gauntlet the recruits had to run.

"You mean, they actually tased you?"

"Oh, yeah. Then, very next station—pepper spray."

"And neither one of those, like, put you down for the count?"

"The point is to push through and subdue your assailant."

"Wow!"

"I'd take the Taser over pepper spray any day of the week. Felt like the skin was melting off my face."

Later: "What was the strangest moment of your training, do you think?"

"One of the first things they ask, during intake, is whether you're willing to kill someone."

"Wow! Huh. I'd have to think about that one." Flexed his jaw. "I'm not sure how I'd answer that, actually."

She shrugged. "I said yes."

Later still: "Has it changed, do you think, how you see the city?"

Puckered her mouth, in a hushed voice said, "It's awful to say, but...the Indians." His expression must have given him away. "I know, I know. It's just hard to be super sympathetic when one of them has just puked all over your pants."

That was it. *That* was real. Barker roamed spheres of grey, of gradients and granularity. In his world, binaries were objectionable, reductive—the world as either *this* or *that* way—shifting sets of standards or forces that could only said to be "true" (or "normal," or "natural") in and of their counterposition to one another.

Take Foucault's famous analysis of madness. Who, Foucault pondered, defines this "sanity" against which "madness" is measured? Revising the binary gives birth to new institutions (hospitals, asylums), forms of expertise (doctors, psychiatrists); regimes of thought and truth (what "madness" means in a particular time and place). To push back against binaries was, in a sense, to expose their contextual specificity, the actors and networks of power complicit in their initiation and proliferation.

But in Dell's world, binaries were key: cop and crook, good and bad, free and not.

The one time he'd questioned the black and whiteness of her worldview was when they'd tripped over the subject of cannabis. They were commiserating over *the kids these days*, and he was on a righteous tear re: their lack of focus and preparation. All that being said, however, he had to admit that if they weren't showing up to class stoned or drunk, then they were one step ahead of where he himself had been the first year of his own undergrad. Dell stiffened, a cold look frosted her eyes. Had he offended her? *No.* Should he not have mentioned doing (er, *having done*) drugs? *To each their own*, she offered.

Wait, weren't the feds planning to legalize weed within the year? *When or if the codification of the drug were to change, the police would adjust at that time.*

Dropped it. But who took so rigid a position on so benign a substance? So many people these days smoked up, at least semi-regularly. When the drug was legalized, should those who'd been convicted on pot offences be set free? *No.* Why not? *They'd broken the law at the time, and changing the law didn't retroactively alter that.*

What about the larger hypocrisy of drug laws? For example, the exponentially harsher sentences meted out to primarily black users of crack contra the far lighter sentences given to Caucasian users of cocaine?

And while they were on the subject, hadn't criminalizing marijuana been a *de facto* effort to keep itinerant (primarily Mexican) labourer populations in check? Punish them? Strip them of a traditional, and relatively harmless, indulgence?

And why *this* drug and not *that* drug? Why keep alcohol and tobacco legal when they killed the population of a medium-sized city every year?

And what about the drugs that weren't classified as quote-unquote "controlled substances," but were nonetheless addictive? TV? Shopping? Facebook? Fast food? Wasn't heart disease still the number one cause of death in North America?

And, and, and, and, and, and, and.

Grey zones. Gradients. Granularity.

It was against the law. Full stop. He hadn't budged the needle one iota, her opinion as incontrovertible as a feature of the landscape; a tree or canyon.

Dumbstruck. Had she always felt this way, or only since joining the force? An effect of inculcation? "I believe what I believe," she'd said. "I prefer not to talk about it."

Dropped it. *Would* drop it. But before dropping it, howsabout a final ill-advised quip, one last caustic curtain-closing *bon mot* to drive home the irrationality, the ahistorical untenability, the categorical *unfairness* of her position. "Miscegenation used to be against the law too."

Put down her tea with a *ping*. "What?"

"It used to be illegal for people of mixed race to get married."

Expressions rippled across her face like a sheet in strong wind. "I know what miscegenation means."

Inside he curdled. Couldn't believe his own stupidity. Who was he to lecture her? What did he know about the tribulations endured by a white woman in a relationship, much less having a child, with a Haitian immigrant in the nineteen seventies? What right did he have to use that—whatever pain that had caused, whatever strife Dell and her parents had suffered, none of which he had any firsthand experience with—to score a cheap rhetorical point in a spar he'd incited?

It was dumb, and stupid, and he knew it.

And maybe she noticed him know it, and maybe that explained their current date-type-thing, in one of the city's legion of gastropubs—glossy granite walls, a geometric flotilla of clamshell-white Danish lamps overhead—sharing a half-litre of Australian Shiraz and grilled calamari.

Seized the first lull. "I wanted to apologize."

Her eyebrow arched.

"For what I said the other night. The mixed-race thing. That was really, really, uh, idiotic. And thoughtless. And stupid."

One lip corner curled. "Ah. That."

"I was trying to make a point, and I did it in the dumbest possible way. I have no idea what your parents went through, or what you went through, and it was insanely patronizing to try to use your experience, and your parents' experience, to justify my position on the legality of pot."

"Been planning that speech for a while?"

Prodded a yellow rind with his fork. "Gave it a bit of thought."

"Okay," she said. "I appreciate the gesture. And you did have a point."

Beat. "I did?"

"Sure. There are lots of unfair laws, laws that have changed over time. And that's a good thing. If I'm being honest, I guess part of our training is designed to…constrict our thinking. We have to accept and uphold the laws as given. We don't have a lot of time for nuance. We're mostly concerned with not getting shot."

"Or puked on."

Covered her mouth, laughed like a flooded engine: *Hurr-hurr-hurr.* (He could get used to that laugh.) "Or puked on. And," speared a ring of squid, "it's not like I don't know I can be stubborn. That's *not* something they had to burn into me."

Sipped wine in unison.

"I was thinking too, that, uh, I haven't told you very much about myself. I...like spending time with you." Beat. "So...there was a thing, a short thing a couple years ago. Guy I met in training. I ended it quickly. I don't want to go into the details. He's not in the city anymore, but it isn't done yet either. I mean, I'm done with him, but he's not done with me. I'm dealing with it. You don't have to worry. It's being dealt with."

"Okay."

"I think that this...situation has made me less, uh, open than I normally am. I'm having what the kids these days might call *trust issues*."

"I think anyone would call it that."

"But, yeah, I like you, and I thought maybe I should go out on a limb and, I dunno, open up. Or something. Tell you a little bit more about myself, about my family."

"I'd like that," he said.

So she did. Told him about her mother's American upbringing. How her maternal grandfather, a Quaker appalled by Vietnam, spirited his family northward. Dell's mother, Judy, had been fifteen and about to start her senior year of high school. Arriving from a milquetoast, white-bred borscht belt state, she was blown away by the city's diversity. Instead of a melting pot, they found a mosaic. And the food! This was her family's first, and perhaps most significant, connection with their adopted city—its wealth of culinary riches.

Petrified to start at a new school, Judy joined the marching band. Technically this was not allowed, but Judy's mother petitioned the music director, promoted her daughter's nonexistent drumming abilities. *Why drumming?*, Judy asked. *It's the easiest instrument*, her mother responded.

Drumming wasn't easy. But with bandmates who'd been plugging away for a few years at least, it was sink or swim. After an awful first month she began to find her footing, fell in love with the preposterous costumes. Naturally shy, the whole outfit—plumed shakos, striped pants, crisp gloves, buffed shoes—not to mention the crackling purr of the suspended snare, felt liberating, made her bristle with confidence. By the end of the school year, drumming was her passion. The director suggested Judy check out a Sunday afternoon drop-in drum circle in a park near Kensington Market. Maybe she should go see what was what?

What turned out to be Parson, a Haitian émigré. By day he worked odd jobs for a rotating stable of local contractors ("Never have you seen so pristinely tiled a bathroom"), and spent nights and weekends drumming and dancing with a cohort of ex-pats from countries Judy had never heard of: Cameroon, Barbados, Côte d'Ivoire. Parson was recruiting an ensemble to perform at the city's burgeoning assortment of fairs and music festivals, to hire out for parties and corporate gigs. Judy agreed to administrate the fledgling company Parson had dubbed *Afri-Can Dance!*, while he hustled for gigs.

The gigs were surprisingly plentiful. Festival organizers were eager to showcase the city's flourishing diversity. A *right place right time* deal. Dell's parents moved into a small apartment, ran their embryonic business out of a converted closet with a desk, calendar, phone, and cranky Burroughs comptometer salvaged from an alleyway. They spent their winters rehearsing new material and the rest of the year performing it. By year three, *Afri-Can Dance!* was doing so well—even scoring occasional out-of-province gigs—that they devoted themselves to the troupe full-time. Married bought a house, drummed and danced. Then, without consulting his wife, Parson decided he was going to raise birds in their basement. Lined three walls with cages and filled them with a cacophony.

Incidentally, he did this—began installing the cages—a week after Judy found out she was pregnant. ("My therapist has some theories about that.") This was also when the abuse began. ("Judy doesn't like to talk about it, and I don't like to ask.") After they split, the company foundered. Parson tried to reverse his declining fortunes by changing the name. *Afri-Can Dance!* became *Carnival Conga Line*, but lacking his wife's administrative acumen, CCL folded a few months later. Dell had no contact with her father currently. As far as she knew, he still lived in her childhood home, with a new family, tending to his cellar-dwelling flock.

The server stopped by. Dell ordered another half-litre. In the interlude, she commented that one of the reasons she didn't like talking about her father was that she hated feeling like she was per-petuating stereotypes about violent black (her word) men beating up vulnerable white women. ("Judy's anything but vulnerable.") There are enough land mines, she stated, that come with being mixed race without reinforcing preconceptions about the inherent volatility of blackness.

She might have some theory in her after all.

More to the point, she hated when people read her decision to join the force as some sort of latent saviour syndrome, an effort to retroactively "rescue" her mother. "It was random," she told him. "It isn't my 'calling.' It's a good job with good pay and decent benefits and a pension. That's all."

Besides, she continued, growing up it was Judy she'd clashed with most; who could be cold, distant, brittle. ("She's warmed up since.") Dell had often wondered if her mother even *liked* her. By contrast, her memories of her father were mostly warm ones. "He was the caring, outgoing parent. He was the one I was close to."

"You don't think your mother's mood, her behaviour, were symp-tomatic or a side effect of the abuse?"

"I think there was a period of time when she definitely felt power-less, or at least didn't know what to do. She couldn't take out her frustrations on him, so she took them out on me instead. And look, I admire her, I'm sorry she went through all that, but we've never had the best relationship. I blamed her for the divorce. In my early life, well into my teens, my dad seemed like the way better parent."

The server sashayed past. Dell: "Can we grab the cheque?"

She pushed the plate aside—"Anyway, long-winded way of saying I didn't become a cop to save my mother"—and emptied the decanter. "It's complicated."

Before they left, she told Barker one last story. Last year she's walking down a street, wanders into a pet shop, buys a bird. A budgie. "Totally random. Totally unlike me." After a week of insane chirping and squawking, she drives it out of the city. "What did I think I was doing? Setting it free to live in the forest? Like, make friends with Bambi or something? It was a *bird* raised in a *cage*. It was going to last a day, maybe two, tops."

Pulled her jacket off the back of her chair.

"So what did you do?" he asked. "With the bird?"

"I snapped its neck."

◆ ◆ ◆

How did she end up at his condo? *Share a cab?* Sure. *Nightcap?*

How did they start making out on his couch? He with his scotch. She with more wine. Arm outstretched, his fingers skating across her exposed shoulder. Legs tucked, one of her knees touching one of his.

"You have a dog?" she asked.

What had she seen? He thought he'd stored or tossed all of Trouble's stuff. What had he missed? A rawhide stick or biscuit? An errant toy? A lingering odour he could no longer detect?

Should he tell her? Recount his recent loss? Would it be weird to fling open a compartment of his life she knew nothing about, hadn't even known was there? Would it arouse suspicion, like there were other secrets he was keeping? Or like he'd been hedging his bets somehow? Would it come across as trying to garner sympathy for himself? Would it spoil the mood?

"No," he replied.

How did they move to the bedroom? How did two people cross that boundary? A kind of cartography. A map unfolding before you. The map, like the body, is a familiar medium, but the space it shows is foreign. An intuitive roaming, trace tentative routes—from here to here to here. Why this path? The shape of the lines, their curves and turns, folds and furrows, conspire to chart your passage.

The best we can do, *all* we can do, is submit.

On his bed. On her back. Asks if she is sure.

Body tense. Resistant. Tight and out of tune. Then: A melt. Snow in sun. They soften. Press into and around. Warm wax. An imprinting.

Flow. A completed circuit.

Inside it all, for a second of a second, he sees the fallen flap of a leather jacket, a V-neck tee, the cleft of soft, white cleavage it reveals...

◆ ◆ ◆

She is buttoning her blouse.

Are you leaving?

I have an early shift.

His hand on her arm. *You should stay.*

Turns her head.

Are you sure?

Of course.

I'll be gone by the time you're awake. Smirk. *I'm guessing.*

I don't mind.

Unbuttons and sets her blouse aside. Lies supine, pulls the sheet up over her breasts, like they do on television. Modesty for the sake of the censors.

Sweet dreams, he says.

I won't make any noise, she says.

◆ ◆ ◆

And she didn't. Did he brush up against consciousness as she gathered her clothes? Did she kiss him on the cheek, the eyelid, light as a moth's wing? Did she whisper "Don't wake up"?

A dream?

Coffee. Culled junk from his inbox. The unopened message from Tatjana (Re: Lawyers) already sinking in the accumulating sediment. Clicked on an inquiry about essay instructions (subject: "ASSIGNMENT!!!??"). The student-hosted Facebook group usually devolved into just this sort of confusion: If you read between the lines in the instructions, then *such-and-such* actually meant *some-other-thing,* ergo everyone should make sure they did *X* instead of *Y.* This generation had conspiratorial minds, was always trying to crack a nonexistent code.

> Hello, thank you for your message. I can assure you that the instructions are the instructions. Please follow them as written and you'll be fine. Promise ☺

Message from Jacob, a TA. Follow-up about a family emergency. Had to leave town a few days before fall break, would miss his last two discussion groups. Molly was covering for him. Right, they'd had this conversation.

Barker: "But Molly doesn't *tee-a* for this course."

Jacob: "She *tee-aed* for you last year, didn't she? She said she'd be happy to do it. She still has her notes and knows the readings, so she said she could jump in no problem. Unless you think there's a problem. Do you?"

There was. Jacob's students would be submitting their essays in his absence, essays he was meant to mark. Could Molly collect the assignments and mail them?

> Hello Jacob, thank you for your message. I don't like the idea of mailing the assignments. If they get lost, that will be a capital-H Headache.

Maybe Barker was feeling magnanimous. Maybe that magnanimity was related to skirting the edge of disaster with Lara. (The more he ruminated, the more he saw how ruinous the Lara thing could have been, however that grit had slipped into the administrative gears...) Maybe it was the afterglow of his night with Dell, skin and sinew giddy with endorphins.

Whatever the reason, he told Jacob to have Molly collect the assignments, then give them to Barker to mark.

And please let me know if there's anything else you need.

Send!

More coffee. Couldn't think what he'd meant to do next. Mug in hand, blowing the steam into sunlit swirls, and tried to—*Right!* Baz. Leafed through the papers, the cartoon dialogue bubbles, the asinine textspeak.

- what r u eating 4 breakfast?

- cereal and sum melon.

- u like melon?

- i looooov me some melons. yumyum.

- what kindz??

- jucier tha better :)

- I happen 2 hav some melons right here 4 u ;)

- Yah! plump?

- yeah. supra juicy and plump

- Id squeeze those melons goood.

- LMAO

Retrieved his phone (smiley face from Dell), meaning to call Evan and admit that, accomplished academic though he was, Barker had no idea what he was...

The tumblers dropped. What had Ophelia said the day before?

Like Baz made it to Junior High and got stuck. Or decided to stay there or something.

He'd been reading them as saucy exchanges between teens. But what if one of those "teens" was Baz? An exchange between Baz and...a woman?

A *girl?*

The more he read and re-read, the more he knew he was right. What unchecked entitlement! What pathological impulsiveness! Baz's conviction—tried and tested over a lifetime of privilege—that he could pull off something as sleazy as sexting with a girl—an *under-age* girl?—and get away with it.

Didn't Baz have a young daughter? Could he be so utterly depraved as to carry on such correspondence, complete with winking intimations that they devise a time and place of consummation, with a woman, a *child*, possibly barely older than his own? It was not only ethically reprehensible, but catastrophically stupid. Yet if Baz had proven anything over his decade and change of public service, it was that he could set the bar as low as he pleased, and vault to ever-greater heights.

- Where would u take me?

- nice hotel baby.

- what would u do 2 me?

- all sorts of stuff. you wouldnt walk 4 weeks ;-0

- iz tht supposed 2 b my o face?

- you wud have so many ooooooooos

- mmmmm! cant wait :-0000

Baz couldn't get away with *this*, though, could he? Not if the girl was as young as she read. Surely this was beyond the pale. Surely this would end his campaign, his career. It was, if not outright pedophilia, then far too close for even his most ardent supporters to abide. Wasn't it?

Mayor! He wanted to be *mayor!*

Barker set his coffee down, leaned back, covered his face with his hands, wanted to wring every gross, greasy word out of his sullied dishrag brain.

What Ophelia had said was so wise, so observant. Baz *was* an overgrown kid. (He'd have to find a way to coax her away from the campaign, the predatory Baz, without divulging anything specific. Work-study gig?)

What could Barker possibly have to offer here? Evan *must* have misunderstood the ambit of his work, needed an expert in PR or crisis management. Granted, they were desperate for some black swan spin, but this simply wasn't Barker's bailiwick.

And if Evan *had* specifically sought him out...?

No. No way. I will not be sucked into this vortex of debauchery. Baz can burn in hell for all the fucks I give.

"Mac here."

"Hi, Mac. Barker Stone."

"Good morning to you, good sir. Patching you through to Ev. One sec."

Rustling, like Mac had the phone up against his chest, receiver rubbing against fabric, spits and hisses like wet wood kindling, then: "Hello? Barker?"

"Doctor Stone here." Brandished his honorific to remind this muck-dweller, this *consigliore*, that Barker was a professional. Sanctified. A scholar.

"Have you had a chance to look over the material?"

"I have." Let it hang.

"And?"

"Just to be clear as to what we're—"

"Let's—sorry to interrupt—let's please be, uh, circumspect, given our current mode of communication."

"Okay. To be clear, these are messages between...your candidate and...another person."

"Correct."

"And this other person is a female."

"Yes."

"And she...is her age a matter of speculation?"

"Fourteen."

Barker held the phone away from his head. Brought it back. "Well. That's..." A storm of profanity blew through his mind "... disappointing."

"Yes."

You whore yourself out to this...maybe he's not technically *a child molester, but same goddamn ballpark.*

"Now that we're on the same page," Barker strove to keep a neutral tone, "I don't have anything to offer."

"One second." More rustling. Muffled speaking. A door closed. "You aren't on speaker, but I asked Mac to give me the room. Like I said, you're in on a very small loop here, but that won't be the case for long. We were contacted by a journalist from a major metropolitan newspaper. You can probably guess which one."

The city had two dailies, the conservative *Herald* and the liberal *Tribune*. The former covered Baz like the second coming, the latter like the antichrist.

"They didn't share specifics, but made it clear they're sitting on something explosive. We think we have one week, maybe two. That's our assumed timeline. This story breaks two-to-three weeks before the election."

The election is over. *Don't you see that?*

"There are boilerplate strategies for framing this thing, but..." Beat. "Yeah, we're in the market for outside the box thinking."

"That's why you approached me? I'm outside the box?"

"I'm going to say something now and trust you won't repeat it."

"If we're not already in that deep then I'm not sure where we are right now."

Evan chuckled. Overemphatic. A forgery. "Fair. Like we said the other night, he's a good guy, really, heart in the right place. But he makes mistakes. This being the biggest by far. It's because he's a *kid*. Part of him is a big, dumb kid, and when the opportunity presents itself to act like a dumb fucking kid... Like he can't resist."

"That's a very generous appraisal."

Beat. "If we were speaking under different circumstances, I might be more severe in my wording."

The constipated codespeak was starting to grate. "To cut to the chase, what might outside the box thinking, from me, look like?"

"Say someone can't help acting like a dumb kid. Given certain conditions. Given certain *toys*."

"Toys?"

"Such as, for example, a smartphone."

Barker's eyes bugged. "You want me to say that this...that the catalyst...that this *situation*...was caused by his phone?"

"We want to know if there's an argument to be made. You are, after all, well known for having made similar assertions."

"That it's the phone's fault?"

"That media have the potential to control us. Determine our actions."

Fuck me. Fuck my book.

"As I already explained, that isn't at all what I meant."

"Due respect, it's what a lot of people *think* you meant. I'm...to be *crystal fucking clear*, I'm not excusing *anything*. But my job is to protect my candidate. The public gets to decide his fate, not me."

"I can't help you."

"Barker—"

"Doctor Stone."

Beat. "Sorry, Doctor Stone—"

"Has he done anything else? Taken this further?"

Silence. A fetid swamp of incriminating silence. "No."

"You're sure?"

"Yes."

"Because you *know*, or because that's what he told you?"

151 Jason Patrick Rothery

"Same difference."

"No, it most certainly is not."

"I respect your view, but given my position and experience, it absolutely is."

Standstill. Stalemate.

"I'm going to end this conversation now."

"Doctor Stone, please think about it."

"There isn't anything to think about. I can't help you. I *won't*. If not for the *en-dee-a* I'd be calling the police."

"Just—"

"I'm sorry, I—"

"One second, one—"

Rustling again. Barker nearly hung up, thumb suspended over the icon...

Muffled voices. Something like stomping. A tremor.

"Doctor Stone? Are you still there?" Evan's voice, far away.

Hang up! Hang up hang up hang up!

Lifted the phone to his ear. "Yes?"

"I have Baz here."

A new voice—high-pitched and pinched, almost bashful-sounding—squeaked through. "Hi, this is Baz!"

Uncanny, like being talked at through a TV. He could practically *see* Baz on the other end: tie loose, collar gaping, shirt sweat-drenched.

"Mr. Randell."

Baz sounded breathless. "I hear our boys asked you for help with our little predicament."

You mean your trying to fuck a teenager?

"They did. Asked if, ah, I could consult, I guess." His fingers tingled.

"Good of you to spare us a second thought. We appreciate it big time."

Baz didn't sound like the jackass from the texts, or like he did on television, all forced umbrage and blustery one-liners. *Time to stop the all-you-can-spend buffet, and send these councillors back to the kitchen to do their own dishes for once!* More like the ranchers neighbouring his parents' prairie homestead. Folksy. Genuine.

A put on! A performance! A charm offensive! Resist!

"Well unfortunately—"

"Sorry to cut you off. I don't want to waste any more of your time than we have already. We've got all the respect in the world for you and your work, and I'm sure you've got a lot of irons in the fire you'd like to get back to tending. *We* sure as hell do."

"Ah, yes, well—"

"If I could only confide one thing about this mess—and don't think I don't know what I've gone and gotten myself into, this is what my dearly departed mother would've called a sticky puddle of pigeon shit—it's this: I had no clue, not an inkling, not a sneaking suspicion that this woman was so young. I can almost always trust my gut—I mean, you've seen my gut, who could argue with that?—but my intuition failed me here. Big time. This whole texting thing is new to me. Didn't even *have* a cell phone until last year. If you saw the bills my colleagues rack up. *Whoo!* We're talking tens of thousands of dollars a year. For *phones!*"

Barker ground his teeth.

"Can you believe it? That's *taxpayer* money. And when each and every councillor already has a perfectly functional land line in his or her office!"

"That's…."—What? The cost of doing business? The elected representatives of the country's largest city should have cell phones, shouldn't they? Still…that was a lot of money. (Provided the figure was accurate, and not a random number Baz was pulling out of his ass.)—"…crazy."

"*That's* the word. Crazy! That's *exactly* what it is. Anyways, my nephew, he convinced me I should get one. A phone. Said it was just… what were his words? *A necessity of life in the modern age.* He's nine!" Tittered at the recollection: *Tee-hee-hee.* "I pay my own bill though. Every cent of that expense comes out of my own pocket."

"I…appreciate that."

His family's rich! He and his siblings inherited millions.

"This sort of thing, getting these messages out of the blue—I don't even know how they get my number!—it happens a lot more often than you'd think, especially for a man of my, well let's say *girth*. *Tee-hee-hee!* Ninety-nine percent of the time I don't respond. Straight-up delete them. But that other one percent, *ho boy, that's* where I get into trouble."

Barker tried to latch onto that word, that metonym—*trouble*—and everything it implied.

"I'll repeat it 'til the day I die: There's no excuse. I get stressed as much as the next guy, but I'm not a *coal miner*, if you get my drift."

"Sure," Barker said, smiling despite himself.

"I've never been good with stress. Not one bit. My dad, bless his soul, when things went south, he'd drink. I guess, growing up, I learned that booze was as good a way as any to deal. And *unlearning* that—I'm sure my dad would've done anything to save me and my siblings from that same fate, from *alcoholism*, I'm not ashamed to say what it is—unlearning that lesson is the hardest thing I've done my whole damn life. Hell, I'm *still* doing it. I slip up on occasion, just like the next guy."

Wait, what did Baz's alcoholic father have to do with texting underage girls?

As if reading Barker's mind: "I digress, *as I tend to do.*" Titter. "All I mean to say is that at certain moments—when I get stressed, or sad, or lonely—these messages from these *anonymous* women are kind of like a lifeline. A release valve. Not unlike reaching for that bottle. You tell yourself you'll only have the one, next thing you know you wake up covered in your own puke."

Barker had never fallen quite that far, but he was no stranger to a nasty hangover.

"I can't tell you how much I regret reaching out to this woman, this *girl*. And if you believe anything I'm telling you, believe this: I had *no idea* she was underage. Nada. Zero. Just kind of thought everyone texted like that, smiley faces and slang. I was flirting, sure, but that's all it was. I'd've never taken it further than that, on my father's grave."

The idiom took Barker aback. Baz's love for his father was legendary. He'd been openly crushed by the man's death. Even Baz's fiercest adversaries had attended Gregor Randell's funeral to comfort his distraught son. Baz clung to each like a drowning man moving down a row of rafts. The scenes played on the news all week, amid speculation that Baz would take a leave, or resign altogether. True to form, he showed up Monday, five minutes late, characteristically bedraggled and spoiling for combat.

Hard to believe Baz would invoke his father only to yoke him to a lie. Barker could give him that much at least.

"Here's the thing, Barker… May I call you Barker?"

"Sure."

"None of us wants you to invent an excuse out of whole cloth. I made my bed and I'm prepared to lie in it. I've already confessed to my wife, and hers is the judgment I fear the most. Her love and trust are far more important than being mayor. No contest."

Because Nialla Randell mostly stayed out of the limelight, when she *did* deign to cameo in one of Baz's pageants of contrition, it meant something. She was calm and concise, seldom spoke for more than a few minutes, ferociously defended her husband, took no questions. The press, so vociferous when it came to Baz, pretty much gave her a pass. Why interrogate her? She'd done nothing wrong. Let her walk away with whatever dignity she could retain intact.

"If I lose because of this mistake, so be it. That's on me, and I'll do what I can to make it right with the people I've hurt, all the people that put so much blood and sweat into my campaign already. If I let them down, that'll be a bitter pill indeed."

Deftly deployed every cliché, made each stale turn of phrase sound somehow fresh. *For all his hustle, the guy has a gift.*

"But I'll also have let down all the people I could've helped. All the folks buried in taxes, who don't have the transportation system they deserve. Immigrants who came here for a better life and can't access amenities you and I take for granted. Did you know there's whole districts here with no dentists? Did you even know that disparity existed?"

"I...no. I didn't."

"You need to catch a bus, transfer to a streetcar, then the subway, just to get your kids' teeth checked. That can mean a whole day worth of travel, meaning a day you can't work, a day you don't get paid. Easy to see what a burden this can be for some of our most vulnerable citizens. *Those* are the people I want to help, the people my opponents don't even pay lip service to. If I don't get the opportunity to serve because of my own stupidity—and it will be because of that and nothing else—then those are the people who will get short shrift for the next four years. At *least*."

Barker had nothing. Yes, Baz had fucked up, but who hadn't indulged in a bit of innocent flirting with an anonymous stranger or two? When things with Tat had hit their nadir, Barker had devoted many a late night to an MMORPG, messaging with members of his clan. Was there one in particular he'd become close to, had almost— as in *nearly bought a plane ticket to Atlanta*—set up a rendezvous with? Had he confessed any of this to his then-wife? At the time, he hadn't thought there was anything *to* confess. Closed his account. Deleted the game. But...was Barker really as innocent as he thought?

What was that adage about the beam in your own eye?

"That's my case as best I can make it," said Baz. "The rest is in your hands. All we'd like is for you to loan us that big brain of yours to see if there's something to be said for me being not only a gigantic jackass, but a jackass new to cell phones."

"I'll see what I can come up with," Dr. Barker Stone responded.

"Thanks, Barker. Thanks a million. I'm gonna have Ev here give you my personal number, so you can call me direct if you have any questions or concerns, or, hell, if you just want to shoot the shit. Full disclosure: I'm kind of running for mayor right now, so I might not have a ton of time to chat, but I always at least try to pick up."

"All right, that's—"

"Speaking of, Ev looks like he's about to have an aneurism over here. Probably about me burning through his data plan or something. I'll pass you back."

Barker slumped.

Evan: "Doctor Stone?"

"Yeah?" Barker heard himself sound dazed.

"You're willing to give us a hand?"

"I...yeah. I'll start thinking through... What's your...?" He needed paper, a pen. Something solid to hold in his hands. "You said your timeline is...three weeks?"

"One-to-two, best guess."

"Let's say for now that you'll keep me in the loop, and I'll start outlining a strategy. Can we connect in a few days, in person, and I'll have something to share with you then?"

"Sounds good. In the interim, I'll have Mac send over a contract. It'll be a boilerplate *el-o-a* for a consultant. We'll say it's for *pee-ar* or whatever. There's a set fee, plus expenses. Let me know if it's acceptable. If not, we can negotiate."

"I'm sure it'll be fine."

"Let me know in any case."

"Okay."

"Have a good one!"

The line went dead. Barker found a pen, but as soon as he had it in his hand, didn't know what to do with it. Stared at a blank piece of paper, confused.

His phone buzzed. A text.

- Baz!

Barker saved the number, typed Barker into the response box, tapped the paper airplane icon.

Realizing that his name and number were now stored in the same device, the same circuitry, that Baz had used to court his underage crush, Barker winced.

✦ ✦ ✦

Ride. Bite. Shower. Gathering.

It had started innocently enough. Barker was a neophyte faculty member, his book had yet to begin its surprise ascent, and his *Media and Agency* course, four students strong (initially six, but two dropped out after the first class), was scheduled as late in the week as could be—Friday afternoons, two-thirty to five-thirty. The introductory lecture was over in under an hour, and the students scuttled. The following week, after putting in a full three hours—and maybe a little lonely, what with his wife on a faraway coast—Barker wondered aloud if, in lieu of braving rush hour, they should all grab a quick drink? Unfamiliar with the on-campus pubs, and having not yet discovered The Luce, he mentioned a nearby Legion. His grandfather had been a pilot in WWII, so Barker was permitted to sign in a few guests. The beer was bad but cheap.

Anyone care to gather for a pint or two?

One of the kids seized on the word. "Let us gather!" he proclaimed with faux medieval pomp. "A great and glorious gathering shall be had by all!"

And The Gathering was born.

Had that first year of casual, semi-regular Gatherings, with that small but motley cohort, been the most fun? Had they clicked, *bonded* in that special way that nomads, in serendipitous conjunction, sometimes do?

All he knew for certain was that once his book did what his book did, both the class and The Gathering got a lot bigger.

As attendance swelled, The Gathering became more about Barker himself. The students grew less inquisitive, more ingratiating. *Needy.* (While Barker had never actually worked in the video game industry, they assumed he had connections. A residual effect of his research, perhaps, steeped as it was in industry gossip, arcana, and intel. An ostensibly *insider perspective* gleaned, in actuality, through many mind-numbing weeks burrowing through quarterly financial reports and board meeting minutes.) They knew he was busy, but could he possibly serve on their committee? (*Let's set up a meeting to discuss it further.*) Might he be available to supervise their dissertation? (*I'm somewhat tapped out at the moment, but send me a synopsis and we'll take it from there.*) Was a reference letter out of the question? (*Happy to help in whatever way possible.*) Well, what they *really* wanted was to work for a video game company. (*It's a thriving industry.*) Hey, wasn't he buddies with Cooper Coates? (*A student of mine back in the day...*) What was it like being on *Colbert*? (*Uh...fun. Weird.*)

It wasn't like he'd been angling to hold court, but he did miss his wife (even in the midst of one of their frequent impasses), and his friends out west; was grateful to feel integral to, even the reluctant leader of, a new (if ephemeral) tribe.

And hey, why not indulge—if only a little—in his newfound fame? Such fame was so fleeting, so parsimoniously doled out. What harm was there in bending a little light through his prism so that all could marvel at the splay?

At its peak of thirty, The Gathering crossed a line. He noticed a man in a cap at the bar, glowering as Barker's coterie shifted tables into new Formica continents. Later, upon exiting the bathroom, the man pinioned him in a tight crook; pushed a fat, carroty finger into Barker's sacrum.

"This isn't a public house," the man spat, breath a bouquet of oral negligence.

Barker swooned with indignation as the old man dropped his finger and tottered off. But then...the man was so old. A tree bent by centuries of wind. Stiff, shuffling gait, barely strength enough to push through the restroom door.

Should Barker follow, protest that his own grandfather was a veteran? Or was this merely a technicality two generations removed? Valour wasn't genetic. And how to excuse the horde whose entry he'd secured by leveraging his grandfather's service? This invasive species he'd let infiltrate the ecosystem, whose numbers far outstripped the natives, who had no direct affiliation with the bloodshed this edifice stood in honour of, had rearranged the furniture to suit their needs, their chief concerns being cheap beer and Barker's good graces.

Closed the proceedings down early, picked up the tab. (Incidentally, only a few dollars shy of his most recent royalty cheque. An appropriate penance, he reckoned.) After ushering out the stragglers, he found the old man, apologized for his thoughtlessness, assured him it would not happen again, offered to buy him a beer. The man put his hand on Barker's shoulder like an old friend, searched his face with cloudy eyes, and—apparently uncertain who this odd young man was, or what his offence had been—took him up on the drink. Barker almost mentioned his grandfather, but held back. It would be self-serving. Exploitative. Undignified.

He'd seen the old man during subsequent Gatherings, alone at the bar, a bony huddle enfleshed by the light of a cathode ray TV. Barker never spoke to him again, guessed the man wouldn't remember him if he did.

From that point forward, Barker capped attendance at ten.

The problem: Thirty still wanted to come. Instead of announcing Gatherings, he extended clandestine invitations, rotated the stable—these ten one time, another ten the next. But this, alas, required excess administration.

Leave it up to student initiative? Invite the first ten to ask?

Word got around that Gatherings were first come first served. The inevitable result of limiting a desirable resource: That resource gains value. Now The Gathering was elite. Exclusive. Obviously Dr. Stone was being more judicious, more selective as to whom he doled out wisdom and guidance. University itself might be an orderly reserve, but the outside world was a jungle. Survival wasn't guaranteed, so you'd better bare your teeth, unsheathe those claws, and draw some blood.

For better or worse, this was the tenor of Gatherings today: A glorified career fair with but a single booth. No shortage of sucking up, currying favour, jockeying for one of ten golden tickets. (Well, six actually. Barker reserved three for the students he supervised, and one for caucus president. This only seemed fair given how much time that person volunteered. Plus, it made Gatherings an opportunity to tackle caucus-related minutia without having to schedule a slew of separate meetings.)

Hated it. Hated feeling like he was picking favourites, leaving people out. Was tired of his oracular appointment, their hungry, reverential looks, being seen as a bridge to better, brighter futures. He sympathized. The job market sucked. You couldn't blame them for seeking leverage. But too much worship and wantonness simply killed the conversation.

Tonight though, several pitchers in (the whole consort, not Barker alone), he was having fun. Felt relaxed. The table was split between two convos. At one end, a debate roiled over a competitor from an online fighting game infamous for throwing matches to his opponents when he felt wronged by his teammates.

"If the system permits it, it isn't cheating. The rules are embedded in the code, and violating the code is not possible."

"He's a bag of dicks, granted, but he isn't cheating."

"Cheating would mean you alter the code itself somehow."

"Code can be hacked."

"That's *modding*. That's different."

Barker, Molly, and two MA students, Danica and Liv—this year's student conference co-chairs—were talking keynote speakers. Over the summer, the incoming chairs had drafted a list of candidates, the caucus had voted, and their top three picks were submitted to Maureen. At the first faculty meeting a month back, they'd discussed the students' list, and other names were offered and forwarded to the caucus for consideration. *If anything*, Barker thought, *we're doing a good job training them for a life of bureaucracy.*

It was, of course, the one name the faculty had rejected outright—a popular cultural studies prof who wrote autoethnographic accounts of *Twilight* fan cultures (Rusk: "So she, what, goes to comic book conventions dressed up as a werewolf?")—that the caucus wanted most. Broadly speaking, certain faculty (*cough*Rusk*cough*) considered her acclaim unearned, theories hackneyed, methodologies rehashed, and output unworthy of serious scrutiny. In other words: Another pretender to the pantheon. Another poseur. Another Barker.

Is that why Barker was making a point of running defense? Did he feel some sense of solidarity with this unfairly maligned woman and her research? (Well, not *unfairly per se*. Her book was fine, but he didn't disagree with certain criticisms levied against it.) Lobbied Maureen: It's the students' conference. They should invite the keynote they want most. Besides, given her recent surge in popularity, this particular professor was unlikely to be available anyway. Where's the harm? Give the kids a win, and when the prof turns them down, encourage the caucus to run with the faculty's preferred candidate.

But just as the students dug in their heels, certain faculty members (Fucking Rusk) dug in theirs, were adamantly opposed to even extending an invitation. "What that woman does is *not* scholarship," Rusk opined.

Molly seemed willing to concede the match, the co-chairs not so much. Didn't caving send a message that their conference wasn't just the department's by proxy? And if so, why should they do all the grunt work to run it?

"Doctor Stone?"

Barker was ruminating on his phone call with Baz. What if he could help Baz overcome this crisis? What if Baz was elected and, against everyone's expectations, turned out to be a good mayor? A *great* mayor? Less taxes! Better transit! Dentists for disadvantaged immigrant children! Barker would end up a key player in history. Municipal history, sure, but history nonetheless.

"Hm?"

Molly: "What do you think?"

Danica and Liv were watching him.

"Sorry, I missed that last part."

"Danica's suggesting that we submit the student pick and faculty pick to an across the board vote, and tell Doctor Alexi that the outcome is binding. That way everyone feels like they got to have their say."

"And," Danica chimed in, "it's super democratic."

Barker set his jaw. "I like that it opens up the process, and democracy is always a good angle. Two issues. The first is that students outnumber faculty, so a vote could be seen as a tactic to skew the results in your favour. Second, Maureen isn't being a control freak here. Some faculty aren't fond of this particular professor, and unfortunately universities aren't majority rule."

Danica's grin went limp.

"That blows," Liv offered.

"My suggestion is for the three of you to assemble a dossier. No need to go overboard, bullet points are fine. Take that to Doctor Alexi and make your case. Right now all you have is a name. A well-known name, sure, but one that comes with a lot of baggage. If you lay out your thinking, why this is your ideal speaker—not just that she's your favourite, but why her work is a good fit with your theme—then you've equipped Maureen to go to the holdouts and protest on your behalf."

Molly turned to Danica and Liv, arched her arrowhead eyebrows: *Well?*

"I'll give you a minute to talk amongst yourselves while I replenish the supplies." Emptied a pitcher into his glass, approached the bar, raised the empty vessel. The bartender held up a finger: *One minute.*

Barker smiled: *No problem!*

Which stool had it been? All the same. Interchangeable. Where had he been standing? Here? Last February. Lara's second Gathering. Well, the second after they'd started fucking. She'd been a regular since the fall, since beginning her stint as caucus president. Ever conscious of hosting, Barker opened conversational doors she rarely walked through. Introvert? Antisocial? Intimidated?

She loosened up once their...thing was underway.

February. At the bar with an empty pitcher. Exchanges it for a full one. Turns. Starts. She is startled he is startled.

Snuck up on me, he says.

Can we talk? she says.

She sits up on a stool. This one here? Next one over? He sits too, sets the pitcher on the bar. *What can I help you with?* Her pale skin absorbs the television's light. She looks translucent, skin fluid with colour. A chameleon.

Food.

For the conference. The caucus has to order food from the campus catering company, but it's overpriced and underwhelming. They can hire someone from the outside, but this will contravene the company's contract with the university. It can be done, but it will take some finagling.

As she speaks, she hikes up her long skirt until the hem ripples across her knees, reaches between her legs, pulls the crotch of her panties aside as casually as parting a curtain.

Flinches. Will others see?

Draws his hand down. Between. Holds it there. Not pushing. Not pulling. In tension. Extends his middle finger, skims the ridges, lets it alight on the crest, tremulous with anticipation. She folds his pinkie and ring finger into his palm. Leads him inside. Her eyelids flutter. *Food, catering, contracts.* He is still. Uncertain. What if someone sees? Slides her hand up to his wrist. Little tug. Hitch in her speech. Sharp intakes of breath. She recovers her cadence. Curls his fingers inside of her. Probes above. Slick with her wet, her warmth. Her grip tightens: *There. Yes. There...*

Contracts. Catering. Food. Worth the hassle?

Push and pull. The pulse of the tide.

Sees something over his shoulder. Rather, something already in his field of vision racks suddenly into focus. First year MA. Exchange student from...Iran? Yemen? Gay kid from a Muslim country that treats homosexuals severely. *Sam.* Not his real name. His *North American* name. To blend in. Camouflage. He can be open here, but can't disclose his orientation to anyone back home, through any available medium. Could be under surveillance. Could be flagged. If he's flagged, and tries to return, bad things could happen. Might be disappeared. Such a nice guy. So friendly and outgoing. Everyone loves Sam. Everyone's surrogate son or sibling.

Sam is looking at him. At *them.* What can he see from that angle? Nothing. Lara's back. Barker's brow over her shoulder. Nothing. Interim Program Director, student caucus President, talking catering contracts.

Barker jerks his hand away as if from a snapping maw. Lara gasps. He grabs the pitcher. *Let's rejoin our friends.* She looks suspicious.

One of these stools. *Fuck you chemistry.*

Might Sam be the secret informant? Barker looked over his shoulder. From his vantage he saw Molly, sitting more or less where Sam had been. No, Sam couldn't have seen anything incriminating. Besides, even if he had, he wasn't the type to snitch. Wasn't that exactly the kind of persecution he'd been fleeing? Intrusive and unwarranted surveillance? Punishment brought to bear on another person's private sexual conduct?

Private? You were finger-banging in a bar!

Besides, Sam was gone, graduated…

It occurred to Barker that he should invite Ophelia to the next Gathering. If she was serious about pursuing a Masters, she might enjoy a little taste of grad school life.

The bartender arrived with a fresh pitcher of bad beer. "Tab?" he asked.

"I'll get this one," Barker said.

◆ ◆ ◆

The festivities wrapped up. The bill made the rounds. Molly advised on amounts. Barker pitched in more than his share. They dispersed.

Delivered the cash to the bar, lingered behind the old man, his onetime assailant-*cum*-drinking buddy, an ill-outfitted mannequin, eyes fixed on the blinking TV.

"Did you need change?" the bartender asked.

"No. All yours."

Beat. "Don't worry. He's got people. I know it doesn't look like it, but he does."

◆ ◆ ◆

Barker wanted a cigarette. The spare from Shiv? Patted his breast pocket. Empty. Another day, another dress shirt. Maybe he could bum one out front?

Alas, no smokers. Just a bustling sidewalk, roaming traffic, air briny with hotdog stand steam, Molly at the curb.

"Molly?"

"Oh, hi. I thought you'd left already."

"Are you waiting for the bus?"

"No, my husband's coming to pick me up."

"I didn't know you were married."

"Two years almost. It's not something we tend to broadcast. We don't even wear rings." Wiggled her fingers to display the absent band.

"Sticking it to the patriarchy?"

She smiled, eyes bright cuticles. "Mostly because we're poor, and we spend our money travelling."

"He went with you to…Nicaragua, was it?"

"Yeah. Volunteering was his idea." Blushed. "He's a really great guy."

"Sounds like. Okay. Have a good night."

"Doctor Stone?"

Swivelled. "Yeah?"

Molly waited for a chattering trio to pass, crossed closer.

"I felt weird about what happened at the faculty meeting. With Doctor Grady."

"I wouldn't worry about it. She's a big girl."

Molly's mouth cinched. Should he not have said that? Did it sound patronizing? It's how Shiv herself would have phrased it. Molly knew he and Shiv were close, right? "I mean, I wouldn't worry about offending her."

"That's not what I'm worried about," she said. "I'm concerned Maureen isn't taking Doctor Grady's choice of speaker seriously enough."

So much had happened in the intervening days that for a second Barker didn't grasp what Molly was referring to.

"Marjanne Abdalla?" she continued.

"Right." *Tread carefully.* "Well, Doctor Grady is in charge of the speaker series this year, so ultimately it's her call how to proceed, who to invite."

"Even if her speaker offends people?"

Molly's tone was warm, but the words were barbed; little fish-hooks. And her stance, its solidity—the way she pressed the tips of her fingers and thumbs together in an inverted pyramid, head ever-so-slightly aslant, eyes narrowed in defiance—made Barker uneasy.

"Isn't that the point, though?"

"Isn't what the point?"

"To be curious. Inquisitive. Expose ourselves to ideas and opinions we might not agree with. That we might, in fact, vehemently *disagree* with? Even, yes, find offensive?"

"But there's a line, isn't there?"

"What line is that?"

"Hate speech, for one."

"I hardly think Abdalla's work qualifies as hate speech."

"She attacks people based on their religious beliefs. She writes articles vilifying Muslims, a religion practised by over a billion people!"

Barker caught concerned looks from a few passers-by. He took Molly's elbow, meaning to guide her toward a side street so they could continue in privacy. She matter-of-factly shook him off.

"Sorry, I..." Some of the meandering faces warped, turned hostile. Was this lady in trouble? Was Barker a threat? A pair of women hushed, slowed their gait. Barker retreated a few steps, spoke softly: "I don't know as much about Abdalla's work as Shiv...Doctor Grady... but I don't think she's anti-Muslim. She's a secularist, yes. She considers fundamentalist Islam a threat, as many people do. Criticising a religion, or tenets of a religion, is not necessarily to criticise its adherents. Besides, she was raised Muslim, so it's not like she's unfamiliar with the issues."

"Many people also think that inviting her sends a message that anti-religious and anti-faith bigotry is not only to be tolerated, but condoned."

"What would be the alternative?"

"Declaring our unqualified support for people of all races and ethnicities to practice the principles of their faith, or lack thereof, as they see fit."

"So you're cool with women being treated as second-class citizens? Stoning homosexuals to death? Female circumcision?"

Clucked her tongue and shook her head. "That isn't what we're talking about."

"No, it's what *she's* talking about."

"And what does that kind of bias lead to? Treating all Muslims like terrorists. Mosque protests. Criminalizing minarets. What's next, banning the Burqa? It's *racist*."

"Islam is a religion, not a race. And as with any religion, if its principles are interpreted or applied maliciously, that can engender a lot of prejudice and oppression. Forms of prejudice and oppression, I might add, that any progressive person would and should be appalled by. Not to mention, isn't it kind of condescending to assume that the defining characteristic of all brown people is their faith?"

"Excuse me, *brown* people?"

"People of... Look, all of this speaks to a larger point. You say there's a line, and that may be true—morally, legalistically—but every line has to be drawn. The question is: Who gets to draw that line? According to what logic? What values? This is the very reason why academia, historically speaking, has been a crucible of ideas. Competing ideas. Because more often than not, the truth is inter-subjective; lies somewhere in between. My advice—which you're perfectly within your rights to ignore, of course—would be to go hear this woman speak, hear what she has to say, and then voice your concerns to her directly. I really think you'll find that you and Miss Abdalla are relatively aligned in terms of the types of intoler-ance she's speaking out against. Plus, if you start a dialogue, we're all the richer for it, but if you prevent a dialogue, then we'll never find out what we don't—"

"Don't lecture me."

"I...wasn't. I didn't mean—"

"This isn't a free speech issue."

"But...that's exactly what it—"

"Well, if free speech means protecting speech that is hurtful, even traumatizing, if it means espousing hateful rhetoric and creating a hostile, even toxic environment, if it means that students are made to feel less safe, even *assaulted*, in a place that's supposed to be like a second home, then maybe speech shouldn't be so free."

Barker's mouth turned as if in cadaveric spasm. A hollow plas-tic owl that had lost its ability to intimidate the sparrows. Immobile, bug-eyed, impotent.

"There's my ride!" A compact car pulled up under a streetlight. A burly man with a ginger goatee leaned out of the window and saluted as Molly hopped inside the car.

"Thanks for another great Gathering!" she exclaimed.

"G'night!" Goatee called out. A second sharp salute. They peeled off.

Call Shiv tomorrow. Send up a flare.

Watch your back. Molly's not gonna let this thing drop.

JOHN: ...that's my *job*, don't you know.

CAROL: What is?

JOHN: To provoke you.

CAROL: No.

JOHN: Oh. Yes, though.

—David Mamet, *Oleanna*

The Professor & The Student

Saturday morning, Barker snuggled up on the couch with coffee and *Oleanna*, anticipating the treat of a non-academic read. The codex seemed scandalously slight, the text spare and spread out.

Searched 'Mamet' on *Wikipedia*. Chicago-born playwright and screenwriter, author of a dozen-plus works Barker had never heard of besides *Perversity* and *Glengarry Glen Ross*, which had been turned into a movie about which he remembered nothing besides something concerning a set of steak knives, and that stupid mantra a buddy of his quoted incessantly: *Always. Be. Closing.*

Dove in, was immediately thrown by the stylized language and odd punctuation, rife with ellipses and interruptions. Standard playwriting thing? *Maybe it works better on stage, with actors...*

The more he read, the more confused he became. This was...he didn't know plays from plays, but...this was bad, wasn't it? The student, Carol—ingénue seeking private counsel from her professor,

John—is struggling. Can't grasp the course content. Initially figured as obtuse—she repeatedly chastises John for his use of esoteric words when colloquial ones would suffice—her obtuseness is inconsistent; i.e., she can't define *paradigm* or *transpire* (Really? *Transpire?*), but knows what *countenance* means. Carol then abruptly morphs into a cipher for a shadowy pseudo-feminist "Group," leveraging an innocent moment of physical contact (John's hands on her shoulders) to instigate a crisis while the guileless John, generous to a fault, naively fuels his own downfall.

Finished in under an hour, sure he must have missed something, flipped back to the beginning and read it again. Recognized, of course, that Mamet was being intentionally provocative, contesting the cultural orthodoxies of his day. And while sure, orthodoxy should be challenged—how else to ensure it's integrity?—this mirthless tirade fell so profoundly short of the insightful, nuanced, reasoned counter-argument that so sensitive and complex an issue required. Rather, *Oleanna* was a rant. A supercilious bid to frame harassment as a scam perpetrated by hysterical women against hapless men. Carol is not only (by her own admission) "dumb," but easily manipulated. Her ill-defined "Group" with its sly "advisors" meant to conjure the spectre of campuses run amok with militant feminists whose driving goal, apparently, is to have books banned from the library. (*Yeesh!*) In other words: Noxious bottom-feeder fever-dream. Correction: *Male* fever-dream. *See*, Mamet howled, *it's us men who are the* true *victims!*

Barker set the screed facedown, pushed it to the opposite corner of the coffee table like a contaminant.

Thought back to his last experience with a nineties-era anti-woman tantrum, Michael Crichton's *Disclosure*. He was eleven when he saw *Jurassic Park* on his home city's last remaining single screen theatre. Spent the rest of the summer devouring Crichton's oeuvre—*Congo, The Andromeda Strain, Eaters of the Dead*—before turning to the author's latest bestseller.

Disclosure was great. They were all great. He lapped up the deft blend of genre tropes—science fiction, adventure serials—with real-world tech. Crichton's familiarity with the latest breakthroughs in science and gadgetry allowed him to do what memorable fiction did best: Make formulae feel fresh. No less true of *Disclosure*, which the postpubescent Barker found a captivating fusion of palace intrigue potboiler and promo reel for the cutting-edge media poised to kick human-computer interface into the next gear: CD-ROM drives and virtual reality!

Clock wipe. First year of his undergrad, dating an older woman (twenty-five!) with (*Gasp!*) her own apartment. Annika is what an older generation would have called, whether in benevolence or spite, a hippie. Her apartment is a new-age collage: floors a puzzle of threadbare rugs; walls dripping prayer flags and frilled oriental tapestries; air fuggy with *Nag Champa*. She wrapped herself in silk, refused to shave her legs and armpits, dropped shrooms and wandered nearby forests in the damp and mist.

He was more of a homebody than she, or discovered himself to be when granted access to an independent domain, unfettered for the first time from parental oversight. In exchange for accompanying her on her spritely forest escapades, she indulged him in his preferred pastime: Holing up with a stack of VHS tapes. At the chain store down the block, you could rent three (non-new-release) titles for five bucks. They smoked up, unfurled across her lumpy cushion mound cocooned in knitted quilts, ate stove-popped, nutritional-yeast-seasoned popcorn, and passed out before the first flick had even ended.

A blissful few months. Barker had never done drugs in high school. Pot struck him as exotic and dangerous. (*What if he got addicted? What if he ended up in rehab?*) With Nika, his stunted Epicurean side hit a belated growth spurt. She tutored him in the joys of Chilean wine, the manufacture of homemade mead, the ritualism of absinthe. (*This isn't real absinthe*, she averred. *Real absinthe has wormwood. Trippy as fuck.*)

These imbibings precipitated a period of philosophical expansion and self-discovery. For the first time, Barker neglected his studies, skipped classes, slacked off on essays and exams. His grades took a nosedive, sure, but the litany of institutionally-mandated metrics seemed suddenly arbitrary; this pointless bevy of so-called *marks* the *masses* were *brainwashed* into believing were a person's "true measure," these insipid barometers of social valuation and self-worth; the only possible passage to secure and stable futures yoked to marriages and mortgages. *Lies!* Or at least an only partial truth. Barker's eyes had been opened to older, deeper truths. Other pedagogies and yardsticks.

He was a student in the school of life, a'ight?

Summoned to the dean's office, told he was on the brink of losing his scholarship. Stopped skipping classes and resumed regular altitude. Saved drinking and drugs for weekends. Mostly.

As he and Nika excavated the video store's vast archive three flicks at a time, he came across a copy of *Disclosure*. Might make for a pleasant diversion, an erotic thriller in the *Basic Instinct* mould. (Come to think of it, Nika hadn't seen *Basic Instinct* either. Tracked it down and added it to the stack.)

Enjoyed *Disclosure* for what it was. Not as much sex as he'd hoped, and the "cutting-edge" tech, so ground-breaking in the novel, appeared hopelessly creaky on-screen. Surprisingly shoddy special effects for an A-list Hollywood hit. Reached for the remote with a shrug.

"You liked that movie?" She sounded upset.

"I've never seen the movie. I said I liked the book it was based on."

Nika launched into a scathing critique that Barker was ill-equipped to defend (or fully comprehend). He accused her of taking it too seriously, seeing what she wanted to see, reading into it in ways that were unfair and totally subjective. "It's just a movie!" he declared with finality, exasperated. "Not everything has to be about fucking feminism!"

An irreparable rift. No more shroom-infused scampering through moist dark. Goodbye incense and nutritional yeast. Back under his parents' roof. Nose back to grindstone.

A couple years later they ran into each other at a party, met the next day for coffee. She'd chopped her hair and moved provinces, was back in town to see her grandmother (stroke), and touch base with a few friends. She lived on a farm now. (Well, a *co-op*, whatever that was.) Chickens, pigs, alpacas; two cats and two dogs that slept in a furry clump in a nook under the stairs. Grew their own vegetables, made their own yogurt, dined together family style.

"Sounds like bliss," he told her. *For you*, he thought.

As their coffee wound to an organic close, she mentioned offhand the argument over *Disclosure*. For whatever reason, he hadn't given it much thought. The male friends to whom he'd pled his case assured him he was absolutely in the right. (*Dude, she always puts her own feminist shit onto everything. It's just a dumb movie!*) Said she didn't want to rehash the dispute, but did he regret breaking up over something so trivial?

The throb of a dormant wrong awoke. His first impulse was to defend the film anew, but it'd been so long since he'd seen it, and only ever that once. Offered an excuse instead, something like *Disclosure* was symptomatic of a deeper schism, and their divergent life-paths were proof-positive of that, no? She seemed placated. He changed the subject. A loose embrace, promised to stay in touch. Never saw or spoke to her again.

It rankled. They'd been having such a pleasant catch-up—fun, like when they were at their best; so much water under the bridge— and she had to go and spoil it by bringing up the fight that wrecked them. Some kind of test? Probing to see if he'd evolved, gained the enlightenment he lacked when they'd split?

Checked *Disclosure*, both book and film, out of the library.

The book was downright unreadable.

She was right! She'd been right all along!

What had once seemed so prescient, so exciting, so suave and incendiary, was revealed as a boorish shot across the bow; a juvenile, hypermasculine jeremiad on workplace sexual politics. The scales fell from Barker's eyes. Crichton was using his insipid story as a

Trojan Horse to sneak statistical distortions into the larger debate. Barker found himself freshly appalled by the book's callow stereotypes, its leering, lascivious attitude toward women. (Hadn't Nika said something about the tendency of male authors to detail and comment on the clothing and appearance of their female characters?) Crichton drew a direct line from his villain's cunning to her sexuality: Meredith Johnson is a sultry, scheming opportunist wielding her plastic-surgery-enhanced beauty to seduce and implicate her former lover and current subordinate, the diffident Tom. Name an odious, retrograde female stereotype, and Meredith personified it: prudish shrew, vexed vixen, promiscuous slut. (Crichton had the temerity to put the "slut" reference in the mouth of one of his few non-slutty female characters, as if figuring women as equal-opportunity offenders—not only as liable to harass, but just as prone to employ sexist slurs—somehow tempered the book's misogyny instead of amplifying it.)

How had Barker ever been taken in by this repugnant ploy to decouple harassment from historical asymmetries; posit it instead as beyond or outside gender; flatten gender to make the preposterous claim, buttressed by deranged stats, that women—given sufficient sway—offended as frequently as men? What made it all the worse was Crichton's self-aware cleverness. *Look at me, reversing gender to expose the universality of assault! Harassment isn't about men and women, you see, but* power.

And fucking CD-ROMS? Really?

Should he write to Nika? They'd exchanged email addresses—a minor modern miracle, something Barker never knew he'd always wanted, like the iPod a decade later—at the end of their coffee. It would be so easy to apologize, to tell her, yes, *Disclosure* was gross. Hadn't seen it then, but he did now.

Drafted a message. Deleted it and started over. His enthusiasm stalled. Would it seem self-serving? Like he was laying claim to the overdue enlightenment she'd expected of him earlier? In the moment, the *life-paths* thing had been a dodge, but it felt right in retrospect. They were different people whose lives were meant to fork. She'd derive no satisfaction from having been right all this time, from his conceding a bygone argument. That wasn't who she was.

Left the unfinished message unsent. Digital dust suspended in sleeping transistors—hieroglyphs in an earthed tomb.

Drained his mug, stared dubiously at the overturned script. What had he learned? That the nineties saw a swell of paranoid men bitching about their "victimized" brethren through popular/-ist art. Maybe, in the acrimonious context of, say, the contemporaneous Clarence Thomas confirmation hearings, the backlash made some sense. Not to excuse the works in themselves, only to appreciate the agitated cultural climate in which they'd been produced.

What should he tell Ophelia? That these artefacts were, in essence, portraits of particular times and places? Didn't the difficulty arise in attempting to square antiquated values and mores with modern moral matrices? Was that the boon of reviving such material—opening a window into a lost world to compare and contrast it with our own, appreciate the extent to which the seemingly entrenched is constantly slipping, shifting, changing?

Hi Ophelia,

Thank you for the opportunity to read *Oleanna*. What an interesting play! You certainly have your work cut out for you :)

Regarding your skirmish with the student societies, I wonder if you might try to make the case that art is not only about intent (intent being a by-product of the Romantic idealization of authorship), but that creative works often crystallize the prevailing attitudes and perspectives of their time. Like that mosquito locked in amber (if you'll forgive the *Jurassic Park* reference) with dinosaur DNA secreted inside its gut. We can appreciate the mosquito as both an artefact in itself (Look!

A little piece of history preserved!), as well as the carrier of raw data we can use to model something otherwise lost to us.

Isn't Shakespeare just such a vessel? Plays like *Taming of the Shrew* and *Merchant of Venice* were produced by an artist operating in a specific social and cultural context. Though aspects of these plays are considered offensive today, they're still performed, over and over. This is partly because Shakespeare's genius is unimpeachable, but might it also have something to do with our desire to peer into an increasingly distant and alien past?

What is to be gained? I'd propose that looking back is looking in. That exposing ourselves to the values and ideas of our predecessors helps us see how far we've come, and how far we've yet to go. (The assumption being that our works will be similarly scrutinized by future generations.)

If that doesn't fly, you could always just stick with your original argument: It's about free speech, damnit!

Hope that helps!

All the best,

Hesitated, then added:

Barker

◆ ◆ ◆

Opened his email Monday to find a message from the GSS denouncing Marjanne Abdalla's guest lecture (two days hence).

If Dr. Maureen Alexi, Program Director of the Communication and Media department, is at all familiar with the deplorable Islamophobia that is Marjanne Abdallah's stock in trade, then how did she conclude that this was an appropriate speaker to invite to a campus as diverse and tolerant as ours?

Called on the university admin to act if Maureen failed to come to her senses.

The GSS opposes ANY speaker, regardless of background, who spreads hate under the banner of "free" speech. We are dedicated to maintaining this campus as a safe, secure space wherein no student feels that their race, sexual orientation, gender identity, and even their RELIGION is ever under attack. We hereby demand that the university denounce Ms. Abdallah's hurtful vitriol, and rescind her invitation to speak.

Rode to campus. Spotted Maureen hastening down the hall. Barker popped his head out of his office, called her name. She flapped a hand in a *Not now!* gesture without breaking stride. Took the corner.

Barker tried calling Shiv in her office. No answer. Sent a text.

- So…how's your day going so far?

No response.

Shuttered his office early and went for a ride. Ordered beer and fries at the bistro, perched on a stool at the patio bannister, watched people stroll and jog and cycle by, the water a winking galaxy behind them. Once sated, he dumped his scraps on the pavement, drawing seagulls into gladiatorial confrontations complete with bumptious squawks and wing flaps, every bird willing to wreak a little havoc for the sake of some spare starch.

Later, back home, after his shower, the following email had appeared:

Dear faculty and students,

Due to a last-minute conflict, Marjanne Abdalla has cancelled her forthcoming guest lecture. Once her very crowded plate clears, we will attempt to reschedule her appearance so that she can share her remarkable mind, important insights, and courageous life with all of us in person.

Yours,

Dr. Siobhan Grady

Game, set, match: Molly Ellen Clarke.

+ + +

Tuesday evening's fusillade, subject: ART SHOULD BE ASSAULT FREE!!!!

It has come to the attention of the GSS that the Drama Department plans to produce David Mamet's profoundly sexist play *Oleanna*.

The message pondered why, in this day and age, anyone would produce a play portraying victims of harassment and assault as conniving liars, etcetera, then:

Locating Mamet's angry, anti-woman diatribe on the same continuum as Shakespeare is not only incredibly misguided, but is designed to frame opponents of victim-blaming propaganda as censorious. The student societies stand in solidarity in our belief that all art should be consensual. Sneaking misogyny, classism, and violence onto the stage under the banner of "free artistic expression" violates the contract that good art forges with an audience, and is no less than a form of assault.

A postscript (italics in original): *Sexual assault is never about free speech!!*

Light rain. A world of grey, lines and objects indistinct as half-formed thoughts.

Refreshed his email. A rush of responses. One questioned the previous message's use of the word "violates." Wasn't this word potentially triggering for survivors? Maybe a softer or less charged word could have been used in its place?

To this a rejoinder that, in the context of the message, the word "violates" was clearly being used in a non-triggering way.

Semantics still have an important role to play in this convo people!

To this, several ripostes that did not take kindly to the glib tone of the prior author's sign off. Irregardless of that author's linguistic bugbears, he/she should be more sensitive to the larger issue under discussion.

Who are you, the punctuation police?

asked another.

The earlier author responded to this latter critic that semantics and punctuation were two different things, and wondered, accordingly, how someone of such a limited intellectual capacity had secured admission into university in the first place.

This was followed by a civilized exchange.

Scrolled through a substantial sidebar re: the use of "he/she"—if the preferred pronoun had not been explicitly stated, wasn't it more respectful to use *they* or *ze?* To this: The notion of *preferred* pronouns was in itself presumptuous and offensive. Pronouns were innate, not a "preference." Then: A plea for the restoration of order and civility.

Sad to see what started as important discussion over protecting victims of sexual violence/assault devolve into stupid/meaningless dispute over spelling/punctuation.

A trenchant critique of the use of the word 'stupid':

Stupid is the historical equivalent of the "R" word. So maybe you're the stupid one for using that word?

Someone suggested ze go fuck zemself, told zem which fingers to use, and in what configuration.

The hell is a 'shocker,' Barker wondered.

Semantics author chimed in again to say, just to be clear, none of the preceding had anything to do with spelling or punctuation, though while they were on the topic, he had noted the use of the word *irregardless* in an earlier message, and *irregardless* was not a word.

And on and on and on, on, on.

Before closing his computer for the night, Barker spied a short interjection:

What does any of this have to do with sexual assault?

◆ ◆ ◆

Wednesday morning. A tangle hundreds of messages long and counting.

Delete!

Campus. Plugged a USB key into the dashboard, downloaded his slideshow.

"Morning, Doctor Stone." Jacob. His lean frame and loping gait as floppy as a filleted fish.

"Hey Jacob. How's everything with your situation?"

"Okay. I fly out later today. You're sure it's all right?"

"You've got Molly lined up to lead your discussion groups?"

"Yeah, she's doing that."

"As long as she knows to collect the assignments and deliver those to me, we're all set."

"You're sure you don't mind doing all that marking?"

"Don't worry about it."

"I feel really bad for dumping those on you."

"It's not a problem, really. Happy to do it."

"You're sure we couldn't just put them in the mail? We could express post them. I could leave money, or pay Molly back for the cost."

"I really don't want to do that. Too many complications if they get lost. This is the best solution."

Jacob slowly backed away. "Okay, if you're sure."

"I'm sure."

"I really appreciate it."

"Not a problem."

"Okay. Let me know if you change your mind."

"I will."

"Okay. Cool. Thanks again."

"You're welcome."

"Thanks."

Clasped a LAV to his lapel. Fiddled with a dial.

Tap. Tap-tap-tap. Tap-tap-tap.

At over four hundred students, *Introduction to Communication* occupied the university's single largest lecture hall. Probably could've gotten away with not using the mic, but some performative—dare he say *theatrical*—flair paid dividends in fora so roomy.

Tap-*tap*. Tap-*tap*-tap-tap. *Tap-tap-tap.*

Did anyone get it? Was anyone catching on?

Tap-*tap-tap*. *Tap-tap*-tap. *Tap.*

Chuckle from the gallery. With him or at him? *Old man tries to work tech.*

Tap. *Tap-tap-tap-tap. Tap-tap. Tap-tap-tap.*

"Can you hear me in the back?" Their chatter faded.

Tap-tap-tap. *Tap. Tap.* Tap-*tap*-tap.

In his most stentorian voice, with a tiny magician-esque flourish of his arms: "Today we're going to look at what is commonly perceived as a rupture in communication history. By *rupture* we mean a significant shift in the form or means of mass communication. As we saw in *Phaedrus*, Plato was concerned that the newfangled medium called writing would have a deleterious impact on cognition and interaction, on memory and co-present discourse. He worried that if his fellow Greeks stored their thoughts in text, they'd lose their ability to memorize and debate. How did text engender dialogue? When any society adopts a new medium, makes that medium central to their lives, it has the potential to not only change what and how we communicate, but to alter who we are as people, how society is organized, how we act and interact. Even how we *think*."

Typing filled the hall with soft static.

"As I noted a few weeks back, the idea of communication was once synonymous with *transportation*.

"Imagine, if you will, that you reside in a small, colonial outpost whose monarch lives across a vast ocean. Imagine this monarch, your liege lord, dies. How will you learn of her or his death? First, the news must be written down. Then this document, this piece of paper or parchment or papyrus or vellum, is given to a person on a horse. They ride for days and days until they reach the coast. The document is put aboard a ship. For weeks, maybe even months, that ship braves the water until, if all goes well, it reaches the mainland. Safely docked, the document is put on a train, which winds across a great, sprawling land at theretofore unknown speeds. The train arrives at a station, the document is handed over once again, maybe to another rider on a horse, until it finally arrives at your village. The document is delivered to one of the few residents privileged enough to have been trained in the magical art of *reading*. Only then and there do you learn that the monarch is dead. This chain of transportation, this months-long carriage of that material message through space and over time, was *communication*.

"Hard to believe today, isn't it? In our age of digital media, when all of us have one, more likely two or three, supercomputers on our person at any given moment. In an age where information flies from node to node at seemingly instantaneous speed. Hard to fathom how news could take weeks or months to reach you. And that's the best-case scenario, in which nothing disrupted or severed that communicative chain.

"Today we're going to look at the medium that changed all that. A technology some say made transportation irrelevant; that, according to Carey, *collapsed* space and time. This medium, perhaps the most significant one since the printing press, necessitated a new language, one allowing machines to talk to each other, to send and receive messages instantly and over immense distances.

"And remarkably, though it was in many ways the precursor to most modern-day media—telephones, televisions, even the Internet—this medium has itself almost entirely disappeared. Perished."

Tap. Tap-tap-tap.

"Anyone care to hazard a guess?"

A few hands floated meekly upward.

"Yes?"

"Telegraph?"

"Good."

Brought up his first slide:

"And what was the name of the language they spoke?"

Tap-tap-tap. Tap-tap. Tap-*tap*-tap-tap. *Tap-tap-tap.*

Someone shouted, "Morse code!"

"Good." Next slide: Code chart. "While some of you thought you were watching an old man trying to sort out how his microphone worked, I was in fact attempting to *communicate* with you, to send you a message using a language, a *code* that—like so many codes and languages before it—has been largely lost to us, like a sort of modern-day Dead Sea scroll."

A sudden burst of gentle rain.

"And what was the content of that message?"

A pregnant pause before the reveal. The whole room aching with anticipation; pin-droppingly quiet.

Tap-*tap-tap*. *Tap-tap-*tap.

"What I've been trying to tell you is this: *Essays due this week!*"

Basked in their collective groan.

✦ ✦ ✦

The wind was surly. Mottled leaves coated the asphalt in ice-slippery mulch.

Cut his ride short after nearly spilling out, locked his bike in his office. Quick shower at the athletic centre. Grabbed a tea and crossed the quad.

The preceding class had cleared and some of his students were settling in. Molly smiled, gave him a short, shy wave. Did he detect a smear of satisfaction across her face? Savouring her victory? What did any of this—embarrassing the department, calling out Maureen, fucking over Shiv—gain her? Ingratiate herself with the GSS? Position herself for a run at Society president next year?

The fuck was Molly's game?

Barker had half-a-mind to take her aside for a private *tête-à-tête*, counsel her in the perils of antagonizing one's superiors. *Maureen is an excellent resource who can open a lot of doors for you. So is Shiv, for that matter.* Had Molly ever heard of a pyrrhic victory?

A flash of recollection: Taking her arm outside the Legion, her wresting it away. (*To move us off the sidewalk! Away from prying passers-by!*)

"Good afternoon, everyone. Sven? Thanks. Today we're going to delve into a dispute that I'm sure was hammered into you throughout your undergrad—the good old determinism versus instrumentalism debate. Who can give me a quick breakdown?"

Molly didn't even raise her hand. "Determinism is basically the idea that media devices change us and change society. Like, they exert transformative effects, and thus constitute a form of control that, the more we use them, we are powerless to resist. This aligns with Kittler's anti-humanist theories of media."

Yes, Kittler's *so-called human.*

"Instrumentalism," she continued, "is the contrary position that media are simply tools, like any other technology. Because they're tools, they're basically neutral or agnostic, and can't do anything we don't want them to do."

Checked his phone. "Good. That's basically right. Turning to this week's readings, Carr brings an intriguing wrinkle to this debate."

Molly: "Neuroplasticity."

"Yes, and what—?"

"The basic premise being that our brains are plastic. Like any other muscle, they can bend and be built up in different ways. Basically, the more we use one part of our brain, the more that part develops or becomes dominant."

"Okay—"

"It's like that example he gives, the *smithy arm*. The more black-smiths used their hammer with one hand, the more the muscles in that arm built up, so they would end up with one really muscular arm and one less muscular arm. Carr argues it's the same with our brains."

"Great, thank you Molly. Very…thorough. That segues nicely into my next question. Can anyone else tell me—and Molly just gestured to this—what is the link Carr makes between tools and cognition?"

Molly opened her mouth. Barker cut her off. "Sorry to interrupt, I just want to see if anyone else has anything to offer here."

…*five…six…*

"Sven, I don't want to have to ask you again."

…*nine…ten…*

"Anyone? What does Carr say about how our brains perceive the tools we use? In terms of neuroplasticity?"

The students looked to Molly.

…*thirteen…*

Her hand—flat, a military salute—creeping into the air…

"Okay."

"Carr argues that our brains perceive tools as extensions of our body. When we're holding a hammer, our brain doesn't distinguish between body and tool. It sees the hammer as being a part of the body itself."

The class looked to Barker for confirmation.

"Yes, that's basically it."

"It's a sort of neo-McLuhanesque argument, right?"

"Sort of," Barker said.

◆ ◆ ◆

No sign of the ravishing South Asian woman from the week prior. In her place a pert young man in tight green shorts and a sleeveless tee. Shiv did her *boxed wine* bit. He ate it up, slid into the booth beside her, confessed he knew the wine selection here was shit (one reason why he was giving this place a trial run before deciding to stick around), proceeded to dish on better wine bars in the neighbourhood.

You ever been to such and such? Ramshackle on the outside, but inside they've got this Ottoman Empire vibe. Carpets and cushions. I assumed it was a shisha bar. I said to the server, Whip out the hookah! *He didn't know* what *the eff-bomb I was talking about.*

Or what about such and such? Towering candelabras drooling white wax stalactites? Divine. Totally divine. Best Argentinian vintages in the city.

Five minutes later, went on his cheerful way with their order. "I hope he sticks around," said Shiv, staring wistfully.

"I'd be surprised if he lasted the night," Barker said.

"Don't get snarky just because it's me that gets to flirt for once."

"I don't 'flirt.'"

Snort.

Smoking on the patio. The birdbath ashtray had been emptied. It felt wrong, like a break or rift of some kind; a clock forcibly reset.

A bird pecked through the soppy dregs that had survived the

bowl's evacuation; had fused to its blackened, mouldering rim. Finding nothing of use, it swooped off.

"I don't want to ask," Barker asked once his cigarette was lit, "but how are you doing with the whole Abdalla thing?"

Shiv smoked.

"We don't have to talk about it if you don't want to."

"No, it's fine." Her voice lifted into a lighter timbre. "I mean, it isn't fine. But we can talk about it." Beat. "I'm not sure there's anything *to* talk about."

"Right."

"Not that there isn't… I guess I mean I think we probably already agree on everything. Not *everything* everything. But this stuff." Deep drag. "There's a strain in moral psychology that says we're emotional beings first and rational beings second, that our first response to any situation, any new stimulus or information, any challenge or crisis, is emotional. We apply reason not to evaluate our emotional reactions, but to justify them." Peered into the distance. "Seems like in this new paradigm we don't even need to bother justifying our emotions, because emotion is the only thing that matters. The only thing that matters is how or what we feel. Not to get all whatever about it."

Shook her head. "Fuck me. That's what I think. Just…fuck me."

"Okay."

"I only wanted to ingratiate myself with Maureen. Gain a toehold in the department." Looked at Barker over her bright red rims. "I still have designs on becoming an actual professor at some point, you know."

"I know."

Pushed two rings through puckered lips, obliterated by a flustered plume. "Maureen isn't even talking to me right now. Won't return my calls or emails."

"It's only been a couple days. Let her do her thing. She doesn't blame you. I'm sure."

"I'm not." Rueful smile. "Nice of you to say, though."

They smoked.

"Kids these days."

"Kids these days."

"Think they know the fuck about everything. How's that scotch?"

"Fine."

"One more?"

"Sure."

Tossed her butt into the birdbath, where it rolled to a smouldering standstill.

◆ ◆ ◆

Ophelia was waiting for him in a diaphanous lace cardigan wrapped around a long-sleeved flesh-toned bodycon, peeled-away neck revealing bare shoulders, the straps of her neon pink bra. Her hair had regained its buoyant spring-like curls.

Hands clasped as if in prayer, mouth fixed in a pout, she approached apprehensively, bashful as an abused animal.

"Everything okay?" he asked.

"I'm so, so sorry about what happened, with the student society sending out that message."

"Oh…" Preoccupied with what, if anything, he could do to help Shiv—Intervene? Broker a peace with Maureen?—the *Oleanna* shit show had slipped his mind. "Don't worry about it."

"I was so happy to get your message. I appreciated it *sooo* much. I was at the campaign office taking care of some school stuff, and one of my friends, another intern, saw that I was super stoked, and asked what I was super stoked about, and I told her the whole story. She already knew most of what's going on, but I told her how you read the play, and the advice you gave me, which was *sooo* great, *bee tee dubs*, and she goes to hook up with her boyfriend and tells *him* the whole thing, and he's on student council, like the undergrad council, so *he* texts some of *his* peeps, and *they* text some of *their* peeps, and, yeah, that's how that happened."

Smiled. "That's…convoluted."

"I'm *so* sorry."

"It's really not a problem."

"I don't know if you saw, but after the *gee-ess-ess* sent out their message crapping all over the play, someone *beed* about them using the word *violate*, which started one of those leotarded cluster-effs like a million messages long."

"I feel bad also. I hoped there might be something useful in the message I sent."

"Oh, totally!"

"But I'm not sure there's anything you can run with now."

"Yeah. It's a really complicated situation."

She looked crestfallen. He checked his phone.

"I'm just on my way to grab a late lunch. There's a Vietnamese joint a few blocks off campus. You ever had pho?"

She brightened instantly. "I *looove* pho!"

♦ ♦ ♦

The restaurant was compact and bright, with chick-yellow walls and plastic-covered daisy-print tablecloths. The woman brought them plates of sprouts, basil, and lime wedges, filled their small cups with Jasmine and steam, left the pot.

Ophelia brought Barker up to speed on the turmoil that had rocked the Undergraduate Drama Society over the preceding days. Initially, there was consensus to not let the GSS derail their efforts. This was *art*, and you didn't cancel *art* because of a few bellicose agitators. That was *censorship*, the same kind of shit they used to pull in *Nazi Germany*. And we, the standard-bearers of *the freedom to express* will not kowtow to the unenlightened fulminations of a bunch of fucking *fascists*.

"They really agreed with me, with what you wrote. At first."

Ah. *At first.* As crude synopses of *Oleanna* slipped into various social media streams, the UDS gained a fuller awareness of the percolating outrage. Siege mentality crept in. Dissenting voices gained traction. *Listen, they submitted, we hate censorship as much as the next person, but is this play really worth the hassle?*

And maybe, they added, the other students have a point. Oleanna is pretty sexist. Or it could land that way if we don't do it properly.

All eyes were on Ophelia. What did she think? What should they do? Did she have the chops to pull the play off "properly"?

"Yikes!" Barker tugged a walnut-sized clump of noodles into his mouth.

"True say." Added some Sriracha to her broth, stirred.

"So...are they going to pull the show?" *Would it be the worst outcome?* Slurped and chewed, watched her carefully.

Her face flipped through a series of uncertain expressions. "I think they want to. It isn't a big group, and they're not the most, y'know, *confident* people in the world. I think they're kind of afraid of the councils."

"What could the councils do, though? Do they have the power to do anything?"

"I don't know. I don't think anyone knows."

Refilled her cup, then his own.

"How would you choose to proceed, if you had your druthers?"

She froze mid-mastication. "Huh?"

"Your druthers. Your *way*. What call would you make if it didn't matter one way or another?"

"Oh, I'd do the show. No question. It's about free speech!" Slammed the table, rattling the dishes. "But I don't want to eff over the *u-dee-ess*, or do the play if they don't want me to, and I don't think they want me to. They just want *me* to make the call one way or the other, which I don't want to do." Her eyes danced. "Wait...did that make any sense?"

"Not really."

Laughed. Ate soup. Sipped tea. Barker turned the problem over in his mind, from side to side to side, scoured the squares for a match.

Disclosure came to mind. What was Crichton's underlying conceit? All he'd done, really, was flip the genders. Put the woman in the power position, subordinate the man. Presto! Scathing social commentary.

Daubed the corners of his mouth with his serviette. "You know, it occurs to me, if worst comes to worst—and maybe it has—what would happen if you switched the genders?"

Lips parted. Eyes swivelled. "Wow. That's *sooo* like something my boyfriend said."

Barker pinned his smile in place. *Boyfriend?* "What was his suggestion?" Pretended to drink from his empty cup.

"He said I should make the teacher, John, a woman. That way it would be less like Carol is going after John because he's a man, and more like an issue of *power*. Like, an imbalance of power because of their, uh, positions."

"Right." *Smart boyfriend.*

"But what *you're* saying... If I make John a woman, *and* I make Carol a man, then...hold on...this is *sooo* good, *omigod*, you're a genius. Sorry, hold on." Gulped air, scolded herself: "*Finish your thoughts, Ophelia! And don't talk with your mouth full.*" As she said "full," a noodle shred flew out of her mouth and flopped onto the table. She clapped a hand over the offending orifice, squeezed her eyes shut, burst into simpering laughter.

Boyfriend, you say?

"Oh *no!* OH. MY. GOD. I can't believe that happened! I'm so embarrassed!" Cracked an eye, peered down at the noodle—curled up like a tortured comma—then up at Barker. "*Aaah!* Look over there!" Followed the thrust of her finger as she tried to bat the noodle off of the table. It stuck to the plastic, contorted into new agonies with every swat. "*Nooo!*" she wailed. Threw her serviette over it. "As I was saying..."

Of course she has a boyfriend. Look at her!

"If John was played by a woman, and Carol was—"

"We're going back to that? I'm still worried about the noodle."

She assumed the visage of stern parent, mouth folded in a fierce frown. "Stop it!"

"Where'd that noodle go, anyhow?"

Wagged a faux-menacing finger. "Stop it, I said!"

Threw his hands in the air: *I surrender!*

"If I switch the genders, then Carol, or whatever you change the name to, could be more of a commentary on... Wait! It's perfect! What were we talking about in class last week? The GamerGate deal?"

"The death of the privileged male identity?"

"YESSS! That! He's *that* guy. Straight, white, entitled dudebro, like...trying to resist his impending demise. Instead of militant feminists he falls in with, like, a men's rights group, or incels, or something like that!"

She looked at him in a way that, under different circumstances, he might have taken as affection. Laid her hand across the table, as if inviting him to take it in his.

✦ ✦ ✦

On the sidewalk outside. He'd insisted on paying. *It's the academic food chain,* he told her. *The person in the higher position has to buy food for all the lesser animals.* ("And I'm a lesser animal?" she'd asked.)

"You're my first Ophelia" he told her. So many strange names these days. Pop culture references and cities (sites of consummation, obviously). But Shakespeare? *Kind of weird to name your kid after a character that kills herself, no?*

"Neat!" she declared, as if it really did strike her as neat.

Exeunt stage left?

Put a hand in a pocket. Felt something crinkle. Teased out a poke of black plastic. Without thinking, said: "My dog died."

"Oh no!" Her face crumpled. "Your dog *died?*"

"Yeah. Two weeks ago."

Her hand on his arm. His whole body sighed.

"I'm so, *so* sorry to hear that. Are you okay?"

"Yeah. You know. Adjusting."

"That's so sad."

"I guess we've both being going through something lately."

Removed her hand, looked as if she might embrace him.

"Your boyfriend, he goes to school here?"

"He does. He's in the chemical engineering program."

"Ah. Something I know absolutely nothing about."

"Oh yeah. Me neither. I turbo-flunked out of high school chem. If they could have invented a worse grade to give me, they would have."

"Well, he must be a really great guy."

"Yeah," she beamed. "He is."

◆ ◆ ◆

Smoked a bowl, second scotch, surfed the web for porn. Scoured the aggregators, scrolled through the week's most popular vids, plugged combinations of keywords into the search bar: *young, teen, cute, shy, blonde, amateur, first time…*

Inspiration struck. Opened a separate browser, typed "Ophelia Souvene" into Google, scanned the links to her social media. *Facebook, Twitter, LinkedIn, Academia.edu.* Clicked on her *Instagram* feed.

The boyfriend. Dewy ocean-blue eyes. Flattish nose. In every shot, the same sloping, *aw shucks* smile. Pier in the summer, selfie in front of a shining lake wrapped inside an emerald mountain. Shirtless, torso toned as a plastic toy. Ophelia in aviator sunglasses, a wide-brimmed straw hat, bikini top. At an airport, excited, holding tickets to somewhere. A tropical village, corrugated tin shacks, residents resplendent in regalia straight out of National Geographic. Ophelia with older people (Parents?), younger people (Siblings? Friends?).

Ophelia alone.

On a bed, legs crossed, phone aimed at a mirror. Her reflection. The same diaphanous shawl she'd been wearing today, but only a bra underneath. The coy pose, come-hither eyes, ambiguous *Mona Lisa* smile. *Tasteful.* Patch of freckles on her chest, the curved horizons of her breasts, tastefully displayed through the lace.

A secret. A wink. An invitation.

Barker unzipped his fly.

◆ ◆ ◆

When the text arrived from Mac early Friday morning—Can u meet?—Barker's first impulse was to stave him off. Typed, Can we connect in a day or two? Erased it.

- Sure thing. Whereabouts?

Mac proposed a popular coffee shop. Round 1?

Barker arrived early, parked his bike, ordered a chai latte. The place was hopping. As he scanned for spots a two-top opened up in the back. Snagged it, tracked down a second chair, lifting it fully over his head to carry it across the room. Grabbed a copy of a weekly from a stack near the entrance. The cover promised to disclose *Baz's Biggest, Baddest, Boldest Blunders.* (*Yikes! Alliterate much?*)

Flipped to the spread, a collage of iconic shots: Baz tripping down a set of stairs at a municipal ceremony; barrelling into a fellow councillor in chambers; an obviously inebriated Baz, eyes red and swollen, surrounded by similarly wasted revellers.

Evan took the seat opposite him. "Busy!"

"This place always is."

"I'm gonna grab a coffee. You good?"

Lifted his latte. "Sorted."

"Don't need a pumpkin scone or gluten-free nut bar?"

"No thanks."

Evan plunged into the crowd. How could Barker dispose of the weekly? He hadn't brought a bag or pannier, couldn't return it to the stack without risking losing the table.

Folded it up and sat on it.

Evan returned a few minutes later. "Sorry about that. Some

jackass was ordering off of a fucking list on his phone." Scanned the room, as if for spies and eavesdroppers.

"Listen," Barker began, "I have to apologize, I should have given Mac a heads up. I don't have a complete strategy to propose at the moment. It was an unexpectedly busy week. I have been thinking through it all, and I have a few ideas we could toss around if you—"

Evan held up a hand. "Things have changed."

"How so?"

Another scan, quick and caj. "The reporter I told you about, the one we assumed had the story?"

"Okay."

"She doesn't have the story."

"Oh. That's good, then. Isn't it?"

"No. The reporter was a signal. A *flare*."

"A flare? From who?"

Leaned in close. "The parents. Probably the mother."

"The parents of the…?"

"Shyeah. The parents contacted the paper, told them they had a story, something Baz-related, crazy explosive. The reporter took the bait, called us." Evan tore open and emptied three packets of sugar into his coffee. "May I?" Barker handed over his spoon. "The mother is the ringleader. At least that's my impression."

"What do they want?"

"What does anyone want?"

"Money?"

Evan smiled at Barker's shock. "So surprised?"

"But if the reporter doesn't know what the story is—"

"Or even if there *is* one."

"—then why call you? Why ask you to comment when she doesn't know what she's asking you to comment on?"

"Fishing expedition."

Beat. "I'm not sure I understand."

Evan swept off the stray grains. "Mom opens daughter's phone. What's all this saucy talk! Who's this disgusting boy? He isn't a *boy*, mom! He's a man! What 'man'? I *hate* you, you're a bitch, etcetera." Smirk. "I have a daughter, I know whereof I speak." Sipped his mochaccino. "Kids?"

"Me?" Barker's mind was awhirl. "Uh, no."

"Don't bother. They're the worst. Except when they're not. But they mostly are. So mom gives the phone to dad. Daughter gets spanked or grounded or takes a time out or whatever. Dad's gonna call the police, but mom puts two and two together. *Wait a sec, isn't his family rich?* Light bulb pops, dollar signs dance in their eyes. Hold on though. What if we go to them directly and they screw us? We need an accomplice! The press! Lucky for us, the *Trib* is never not hot for this man's fuckups."

Barker's phone rang. Checked the screen. Dell.

"You need to take it?"

"No." Set it face down on the table.

"You can take it if you need to take it."

"It can wait."

"You can probably piece together the rest. Mom tells reporter they're sitting on a bombshell, but they'll only spill if reporter pays them *ex*. Reporter plays indignant. *The press does not pay for our scoops, madam!* But reporter goes ahead and contacts yours truly to see if she can suss out whether said scoop is a thing. If she gets the sense it is, maybe she can dig it up herself. Luckily I'm not what?"

"What?"

"Fucking retarded. So I call the reporter's bluff. She gets nothing, because if I know the scheming jackals at the *Trib*—and I know them well enough—they'll never stoop to pay cash for trash, violation of their ethics or what-the-fuck-ever. But now mom reaches out, now we know she means business. Option *bee* is crystal clear, and the choice is ours: Either this whole caravan rides quietly off into the sunset, or they can stop and set up and—*Hey hey hey!*—the circus has come to town!" Sat back.

"Is...if I'm allowed to ask...?"

Evan fanned his fingers as if holding an invisible platter: *Please, proceed.*

"Is...he going to pay? He is wealthy, isn't he? He has the money?"

"It's not that I can't tell you, it's that I don't know. But if I did know, I couldn't tell you."

"Okay."

Evan planted his forearms on the table, nodded for Barker to lean in. This close, Barker saw sleeplessness etched in red in his eyes, the down fuzzing his cheeks, lips edged with saline crust and fretted with dehydration.

"Listen," he said, "honest to Jeebus, I have no idea how this thing is likely to shake down. Out. Sorry. It *is* a shakedown. Yes, he has the money. I suspect he'd like to pay and put it behind him. The wife...different story. She's *steel*, man. Made of sterner stuff. She'd flay these people and make belts with their skin." At just above a whisper: "In some of my weaker moments, have I not wished it was *she* who was running for mayor? Alas..." Ground his sockets with the heels of his hands. "I should go. The office, uh, *get back* to it. The office." Drained his mug, stood.

"What do you want me to do?"

"Don't do anything. For the time being, this is all out of our control. Sit tight. Keep prepping your thing. We may need it. We may not. You'll get paid either way."

"Let me know if you need anything in the meantime."

"Sure," Evan said, the word blunt with fatigue. "Fucking..." Trailed off, started to leave, turned back to Barker. "Let me grab that."

"Grab what?"

"The paper you're sitting on."

Retrieved the weekly—a dampened Baz squeezed between the creases left by Barker's buttocks. Evan tucked it under his arm.

"We keep a collection," he said, and left.

✦ ✦ ✦

Cloak-and-daggering done for the day, Barker checked his phone. The missed call from Dell. No message.

Called. Answered.

"Day off?" he asked.

"Incredible outside, isn't it?"

"Just saw I missed you." Beat. "Hello?"

"I...changed my mind about asking you this in the middle of calling."

"Asking me what?"

"It's weird."

"What is?"

"My mom. It's her birthday today. Technically it was her birthday yesterday, but she's celebrating tonight. Small gathering with a few friends. And me."

"Sounds nice."

"It'll be quiet. And old people. High risk of Scrabble."

"I like Scrabble. Actually, that's not the whole truth, I'm *really good* at Scrabble."

"Uh-huh. I'll file that under *Things I Wish I Didn't Know About You*."

"How big is that file right now?"

"Thicker by the day."

"Just so as we're clear about what's happening right now, are you inviting me to your mom's birthday party?"

"It isn't a party, and I'm not inviting you. But if you found your way there, I would be there also."

"You *are* inviting me to your mom's party."

"It'll be weird," she said.

"Wouldn't miss it," he said.

CAROL: I don't know what a paradigm is.
JOHN: It's a model.
CAROL: Then why can't you use that word?
—David Mamet, *Oleanna*

The Break

Monday morning, mug in hand, Barker surveyed his courtyard, glazed with a rime of bluewhite frost. Some bleached tines stood startled as if caught unawares, trapped in place as they tried to flee, others laden with unanticipated freight. A harbinger of the coming plunge, of lustre lost, like a wet stone dried.

Sat down to plot out his keynote. Up until today, the conference seemed impossibly far away, but now—*Seriously, how has it been a month and a half already?*—felt inconceivably close. Yet even with only three weeks to go, and a forty-five minute slot to fill, it didn't strike him as pressing, *per se*.

Like every neophyte MA, Barker had taken a scattershot approach to conference attendance. *Find your conversation*, his supervisor counselled. So he did. A scholarly diaspora bound by the oscillating disputes surrounding the entanglement of agency and media.

American co-conspirator Hannah Stall studied the *Mass Effect* series, how players could carry over choices from one entry to the next. Alessandro Ostacolare, an Italian who lived and worked in Malta, was an Actor-Network theorist who studied batteries as a form of resistance. "Once you see the machine, and the thing that powers the machine, as part of the larger network of persons and objects," he extolled, "the *agencement*—this is Deleuze's term—then you can start to see the ways... How do you say? *Micro* ways? The *many small ways* they constrain action. *Resist* you. This object, the battery, is no less a dissident than one of your protestors in the public square."

"You're using the word 'resistance' as it would typically denote *human* action. But a battery has no will, no intent—"

"Ah, but has not Giddens split agency from intent?"

"Sure, but you're still using a word indicative of purposeful action to describe an object that has no purpose; is simply dead or malfunctioning. Isn't a broken battery just a broken battery?"

"Not," plucked his glasses off his beakish nose, polished the lenses with a sleeve, "if you drink enough beer."

This made Barker laugh out loud. A convivial clinking of bottles—*Cheers! Salut!*—like a breeze-jostled wind chime.

When Hannah and Alessandro declared their intention to mount a conference focused on their mutual affinity, how could Barker not jump on board?

Five years. Marriage skidding out, moving cities, about to claim his position on the tenure track (*The lottery! First ever interview!*), book selling better every month, a few campus magazine profiles under his belt. Alessandro called. "We are doing this thing for real. We want you buddy. We need you!"

Barker was enthused but elusive. *I don't know how much time I can commit, but keep me in the loop.* Ultimately, over that first year, in the cloud of confusion and drudgery—drafting syllabi and reading lists, faculty meetings and committees, the wellspring of student grievances, assorted nuisances (like his inability to work the fucking LAV)—he hadn't been able to contribute much. Consulted on the theme, helped circulate the CFP, chimed-in on abstracts. The real nitty-gritty, however, Barker played no part in.

In an extraordinary gesture, they invited him to deliver the inaugural keynote. He was legitimately touched, but, as the conference neared, was forced to pull the chute. "I'm so sorry," he confessed via conference call. "I'm fucking buried, and not in a place where I can give this the attention it deserves."

"It is not to worry." Alessandro offered, adding, "You Canadians really do apologize very much."

Barker was so busy, in fact, that though the conference was in nearby Buffalo, he couldn't make it down. Sent felicitations from afar.

"We missed you, buddy. It was good. Small, yes, but a very good start."

He'd attended every subsequent *Media, Communication, and Agency* conference in person. Watched it blossom from a few dozen presenters in its freshman year to twice that the next, and twice as many the year after that. Moved the conference from the spring to the fall to avoid the glut. Raised fees, apprehensive that this would dampen interest. Applicants were undeterred. (Did higher fees enhance their cachet? Make them seem more legit? "We *are* more legit," Alessandro averred.) Every year, a nicer hotel in which to host.

A running joke of sorts—inviting Barker to deliver the keynote, knowing he'd be too busy to accept. Having officially declined, he'd spearhead the committee to decide to whom the slot should be offered in his stead. (Two years ago he hadn't been especially busy, but given his dismal headspace, declined anyway.) Not this year. This year he was doing it. A kind of capstone. A circle completed. "So good of you to grace us with your presence, before you became too big for our britches," Alessandro kidded. "Long overdue, buddy. Long overdue."

As if in honour of his forthcoming appearance, this year's theme— *Agency in Games, Gaming, and Play*—was an obvious ode to Barker's book. (To tempt into attending, he supposed, a generation of students for whom he was now required reading.)

Loaded a new Word doc. Fiddled with the formatting. Stared at the screen.

KT2? No, that soil had been tilled too many times over, its fertility depleted.

Hadn't played KT3, didn't even have it on his phone. (Maybe Ophelia did? Maybe she could give him a quick tutorial?) Address the shifts in format? From third- to first-person to Augmented Reality? Was there a grand thematic motive at play behind these formal pivots? If so, what?

Something about the game's advertising, or lack thereof? How agency was constructed with so little attendant discourse?

Something about the series as a commentary on agency and time? The KT series as a comment on time-*ness*? (Already been done? Already been said?) Was that Cooper's intent? Did it matter?

Should drop Coop an email. Or call him. Fish for some angle or another.

Later.

As the coffeemaker gurgled, Barker refreshed his email.

Heya B,

Not sure if you got the note re: conference rates at the Rio. Me and A are staying there. Let us know your plans. Maybe we can take over a floor or something.

H

NB: If you need a second set of eyes on that brilliant keynote you're dutifully crafting, you know where to find them!

Replied:

Hannah!

Was chiselling away as your message popped up. Not sure where I'm staying yet, but that's an enticing offer. Will give it some thought and touch base.

Hope all is grand in the US of A, notwithstanding the empty inside-out bag of Cheetos you call a president.

B

ps—once I've banged this draft into respectable shape, I'll certainly pass it along for feedback. Stay tuned!

Send!
Message from Molly Ellen Clarke.

Subject: Halloween Party & Primer on Culturally Appropriate Costumes.

Delete!
Refilled his mug, retrieved the stack of essays from Jacob's groups. If he ran the marathon in two-hour sprints—fifteen minutes per essay, eight per session—he should be able to finish in under ten hours. Maybe less if he put his shoulder into it at the front end.

Rummaged through desk drawers. Found his red pen.

A conductor's baton, a tool of instruction; of imposing and maintaining order.

Okay, maestro, what have we got?

A familiar symphony of sloppy grammar, mangled broken-zipper syntax, baroque embellishments of anodyne words—*whilsts* and *amongsts*—that would have sufficed well enough in their pre-gilded states (*while, among*); abundant *thuses*, even an errant *alas*; bungled tense, like *lead* for *led*; malapropisms such as *for all intensive purposes* and *a feudal exercise*; relentless semicolons—an eleventh plague of punctuation.

That was the ground floor: Sheer stupidity. On the next stratum were calculated contraventions: padded margins, swollen spacing, added indents, engorged fonts. Hacks that, employed in concert, could inflate a two-to-three page paper into a four-to-five page one, inching it over the threshold, like cutting cocaine with baking soda.

Many a colleague brushed off the subversion. *They're just* kids, they'd chortle, *cut them some slack!* But slack was the culprit. They'd had so much slack for so long—little lifetimes of skimmed instructions and cut corners and lowered bars—that they instinctively chafed at a taut rein. *If they put as much effort into doing the work as they did into cheating, they'd pass no problem!*

They resorted to slack when work would be easier.

Then lapses in citation. Those who, out of naiveté or laziness, wouldn't pick or stick with an attribution style, culled direct quotes without identifying them as such, quotation marks neither opened nor closed; a dragnet of page numbers, calendar years, and author names imprisoned in parentheses.

Then straight-up plagiarism (or whatever for the purposes of avoiding a dragged-out administrative quagmire one termed plagiarism nowadays). Wholesale copy-and-pasting betrayed by sharp swerves into perfect prose, weird words in strange places. (Especially true of the ESL kids. While Barker reserved special sympathy for his foreign students—the so-called *Asian Quota*—whisked away to a distant land, charged thrice the tuition, and expected, with minimal English, to read the same books, write the same papers, contribute to the same discussions as the locals...) They cribbed mercilessly, trowelled it in like putty, but forgot to smooth over glaring giveaways—incongruent fonts, hyperlinks still intact.

This offended Barker on two levels. First, that they were plagiarizing. Second, that they were plagiarizing poorly.

At the apex: Work the student had purchased from elsewhere. Extremely tricky to diagnose. (Some schools paid for software that cross-referenced databases worth of such material. His, alas, did not.) One had to know the student, know their writing, to spot the discrepancies. While circumstantial confluences, an alignment of stars, did occasionally occur, it was next to impossible to prove. Might dock them points on technicalities, but otherwise...they got away with it. They won, beat the system, and there was jack shit he could do about it.

Cheating was such a fucking time-sink. A typical essay took ten to twenty minutes to mark, but once you caught a whiff of fraud—the stink of pristine grammar, or an alien, out-of-place word—it could eat up anywhere from an hour to two. He'd be compelled to comb through to suss out and match up every suspect section. With the evidence amassed, you took the student aside, informed them they'd received a zero. If it happened again, the offending assignment would be passed up to a higher power. *Out of my hands. You could receive a failing grade for this course, or be kicked out of school altogether.* The slap on the wrist usually did the trick—the recidivism rate was next to nil—but over the years, one or two repeat offenders had vanished altogether.

An affront: to his intelligence, his attention, the enterprise of higher education writ large. This wasn't fucking grade school, where affirmation was doled out like gumballs. No, he'd earned his *bona fides*, and they'd have to earn theirs also.

No shortcuts.

Seven essays in his patience began to fray. Took a break. Back to the stack. Decided it wasn't too early for wine. Second glass, his already loose grip on detachment slipping. Finished the first bottle. Opened another. The pen, a charged thing, left uncapped. The question marks he scrawled next to inscrutable sentences multiplied, mutated into misshapen fishhooks. Misused and misspelled words were buffeted by several scathing lashes. The conductor, increasingly flustered by his orchestra's mounting incompetencies—unpractised, unruly, out of tune—swung his baton ever-more wildly. *Disgraceful! An insult to the music of language, to cadence and rhythm and—*

Photogravure.

Photogravure?

Set down pen and wine. Midway through an especially confounding piece—the reality distortion field was already enfolding him: Maybe it was *he* who misunderstood English?—a spotless turn of phrase, that unfamiliar word.

The hell does photogravure *mean?*

Plugged the sentence in the search bar. First hit: *Wikipedia.*

Fuuuck.

An hour. Highlighting and cross-referencing. Two sections that weren't *Wikipedia,* but cut whole cloth from *SparkNotes.* Another two he couldn't locate, but were so immaculately composed that they must have been stolen from somewhere.

No works cited section, natch.

Forensics complete, handling the essay with the delicacy of evidence, he slid it into a manila envelope, segregated from the others.

Enough. He'd do the rest tomorrow.

At the top of his inbox: RE: Re: Lawyers. The content of the message was this:

???

Emptied the bottle. Picked up the phone.

"Zdravo?"

You can lead the Serbian to Canada...

"Howdy."

"Barker, *darling,* how are you?"

Moved to the couch with his wine. "I finally figured out what's worse than marking undergrad essays." An old joke: What could possibly be worse than marking undergrad essays?

Tatjana: "Calling your ex-wife to talk divorce lawyers?"

"Bing! Bing! Bing!"

"So," she began. Could hear her grin. "You got my email?"

◆ ◆ ◆

Lawyer stuff didn't take long. The sticking point, apparently, was alimony. Not that Barker was haggling, but that Tatjana didn't want any. "It's your money," she said. "Why should you give it to me?"

Her lawyer was insisting she petition for something, even a menial amount. "He thinks it looks best if we put everything on the table. This is what he says. Then, when your lawyer counters, we make you look cheap. This gives us, I take it, some sort of...leverage, he says, that makes him extremely excited." Ten years and nary a dent in her accent.

"I can afford it."

"I'm sure you can. That is neither here nor there."

"Then what's the problem?"

"That these are old, out of date rules. Why should the woman be beholden to the man? Why not *you* take *my* money?"

"You don't have any money."

"And that is fine for me! I'm perfectly content! But this...this *Shyster* says I must take yours. I *must*? It is...what is the word? *Patronizing.* The whole point is to unwind our lives—not completely, of course, you know we will be friends—but legally. If you are sending me cheques every month, this can never be the case."

Had half a mind, she said, to dump this lawyer and hire another.

"It's an option, I guess." Swirled his wine, watched the legs lap at the glass. "The problem, I'm wondering, is if you get a new lawyer, would we have to start the process all over again?" They'd spent so much already, could they stomach spending more? "I guess the question is, can you hold your nose and stick with this guy, or is it really bad enough that you want to find out what it looks like to switch?"

Dramatic sigh. "I am...annoyed by this. It seems like such a..."

"Scam?"

"Something like that. We cannot be trusted, as two adult people, to set the terms of our own divorce. *Must* defer to the wishes of these others whose only interest is money."

"To be fair, they're probably somewhat out of their element."

"How do you mean?"

"I'm guessing they're more used to bitterness and acrimony, to gearing up for battle. You know the expression about the hammer and the nail?"

"Yes."

"Well, yeah. You and I might be a bit of an anomaly."

"It isn't right. I pay him enough he should do what I say."

Barker laughed. "Fair."

"So," a flipped switch, from stormy to sunny, "what is happening in your life, Mr. Moneybags?"

+ + +

It had been a long time. Too long, they agreed.

"I'm not keeping you, am I?"

"No, no. There is nothing happening here but two middle-aged broads and their brood of cats."

"I'm not sure two cats counts as a brood."

"How out of touch you are! We have *three* cats. There are very cute pictures and videos on Facebook."

"I'm sure there are."

"You do not visit my page? My feed? Why not?"

"Makes me feel weird. It's what the kids call lurking."

Pshaw! "Kids know nothing. You are not really marking essays, are you?"

"I am."

"So you are drinking wine?"

"I had a glass.

"By 'glass' you mean bottle."

"Uh. Yeah. A bottle."

"And by 'a' you mean two."

"It's really messed up how well you know me."

"And all this wine has made you nostalgic."

Took him a second to take her meaning. "I just thought it'd be better to talk in person than get into a back and forth over email."

"Especially given how long it takes you to respond to email these days."

"Ouch."

"But this is better, of course. In person I can ask if you are dating."

"I'm gonna need more wine." Stuck a finger in his mouth, pulled it out. *Pop!*

"You are!"

"Maybe."

"One of your students no doubt."

Sat up. "What makes you say that?"

"Isn't that the point of being a professor? To have sex with your students?"

"First of all, gross. And second of all, the woman I'm seeing is a woman. An *adult* woman."

"You sound defensive."

"My students are *children*."

"What is the expression? 'Old enough to bleed, old enough to—?'"

"*Christ*, Tat! Who *are* you? What horrible alien planet do you come from?"

"Barker, please, I do not invent these expressions."

"Maybe that's how things are done in the old country, but on this side of the Atlantic we operate with a bit more decorum."

"Oh, yes, everyone over here is so very *enlightened*. You all treat women with so much care and respect."

"Holy shit, I miss you."

Belly laugh, so reminiscent of her father's back-slappy gut-busters.

"They are beautiful, no? Some of them, even though they are young? *Because* they are young?"

"I don't think of them that way. I'm their teacher."

"These juicy plums, dangling on the vine, ripe for the picking?"

"Do plums grow on vines?"

"It is an expression."

"Is it?"

"You have never, not once, of these hundreds of students, had a fantasy for one of them? And remember," she added, "even on the phone, I can see your face."

Speechless.

"Ah, you *sensitive* North American men get so hung up on the, ah, the proprieties... Is this a word?"

"Sure."

"You are all so worried about *when* and *whom* society says you should fuck, and not nature."

"In my profession we don't really believe in nature."

"This is insane! We are all of us biological beings, chemicals coursing through our veins. Estrogen! Testosterone! You say these things have no bearing on our actions? What, otherwise, would be their purpose? Hundreds of thousands of years, millions of species, chemicals directing and compelling our actions, making us *urge*. Urges we do not understand, but urges nonetheless. Go here. Do this. Fuck that."

"Urges."

"And then you...*academics* come along and say 'No no no, wait wait wait, all this is wrong. These things are all... What was the term?"

"Socially constructed."

"Good gravy!" Where had she picked up these idioms? Broads? Good gravy? From Barker? Television? Sundays on the futon watching *The Simpsons?* "You say, 'Forget chemicals, forget urges, forget everything that allows life on this planet to function, to thrive. We *really* figured it out: Gender is social construction. Sex is social construction. And *ta-dat-da-dat-da-da.*' And with this you get to make up all new rules. Tell me."

"Tell you what?" Set his empty glass aside.

"Tell me about these hot young creatures you lust after."

Barker recalled the fallen flap of a leather jacket.

"Fine," she said. "Don't tell me. But here is my advice: Whoever she is, fuck her!"

"Excuse me?"

"You're a man. She's a woman. You think she is a girl, but she is not. Yes, young, yes, but a woman all the same."

Beat. "As I mentioned before, I am actually seeing someone."

"Yes, this adult woman you are so excited about."

"Who says I'm not excited?"

"Your voice betrays you, Barker, always."

"I like her a lot."

"Good. That's nice."

Should he protest? Things were going really well with Dell, especially after meeting Dell's mother, Judy, last weekend at her awkward-but-not-really get-together. Finding an easy rapport, letting her win at Scrabble, her knowing and teasing him over it. *The best gift you could have given me.* How Dell had watched as Judy opened up to him, a brittle book at long last unlatched.

Too late for that. It was, in one respect, literally too late. If he signed off now, he could still smoke up and watch Netflix. But it was also *too late.* Couldn't bear to listen to Tatjana dismiss Dell. It would only diminish it, diminish this real thing with this admirable person. *All well and good,* she'd say. *But Barker, you don't speak of her, this* so-called woman, *with passion, with rapture. It would be so clear if only you could hear your own voice!*

And it was also too late. She'd pushed the seed (*Fuck her!*) inside the soil, initiated a process—sensors awakened and probing for nourishment, newborn roots finding purchase and anchoring. Had to stop it before the shoot broke ground. Freeze it in place like those frosted tines of grass.

"I love you, and everything you stand for, but I should go."

"More marking?"

"No. Yes, I mean, but tomorrow. No more tonight."

"How has this happened to you, darling?"

Never stop calling me that. "What?"

"These essays? I thought professors had minions?"

"Even minions have family emergencies now and then."

Pshaw! "Lies."

"Pardon me?"

"What is the name?"

"Jacob. Good kid. Skinny."

"He's on a beach somewhere while you are trapped at home, doing his work."

"O, ye of little faith."

"You have your computer?"

"What is this?"

"Go get it."

"Really?"

"Five bucks." Their usual wager. "Five bucks this Jacob douchebag is on a beach somewhere."

Could scarcely put into words how pleased he was with himself for teaching her *douchebag*.

"Fine, but you're wrong." Got his laptop.

"You have it?"

"Yes."

"Go to his Facebook."

"This is weird."

"Hey man," she said in an affected American accent, "you took the bet."

Shook his head to himself, opened a browser, clicked through to Jacob's Facebook page.

"Did you find him?"

Jacob. On a beach. Arm around an older man. (Father?) Surfboards upright between them. Sun. Sunglasses. Strolling bikini-clad women. An infinite ocean. Posted mere hours ago.

"How the fuck did you do that?"

"Ha! Wouldn't you like to know?"

"He's *literally* on a beach. No shirt. Surfboard. The works!"

Toppled from surprise into pique into anger. And, like the lies pocking the essays he'd spent (wasted!) his whole day marking, so too was this lie so obvious, so brazen, so *out in the open*. Like it didn't matter. Like Jacob didn't give a shit, happily broadcasting his ruse for all to see. *Fuck you professor Stone*, the photo said. *You bought that family emergency bullshit? Egg on your face.*

Felt his heartbeat race, migrate into his ears, morph into a squishy, ultrasound-like pulse. A tremor took his fingers as his body constricted.

"Five bucks!"

"Cheque's in the mail."

"You sound mad."

"It's fine. I'm pissed. It'll pass."

"Dearest Barker. You take everything so personally."

Rubbed his face and gnawed at his cheeks.

"It is as you said, they are children. They don't know any better."

"Yeah. I know."

Sigh. She knew this side of him, his combustive temper, his molassesy silences. (*Tell me!* Tell you what? *What you are thinking! If you are angry. Tell me or it will rot you from the inside out!*) But this was who he was, how he dealt. No more valiant attempts to coax him back from the precipice. No longer her responsibility, if it ever was. *Stand there and stare over the edge if you want, but do so alone.*

"I didn't mean to end like this."

"I'll sleep it off. I'll be fine in the morning."

"I know you will. It was good to speak. Please let's not wait so long next time."

"Agreed."

"And if you ever come out to the coast…"

"Yes. It would be good to see you. To meet Deanne in person."

"She would like to meet you too."

"Okay then."

"Goodnight, darling."

"Night."

Gone.

Stared at Jacob's gangly frame, his stupid smile, the lithe women, the white sand and perfect water.

Less an emergency, then, than a vacation.

Swung his hands through the air in a gestural *What the fuck?* Knocked over his wine glass. It tipped and chimed against the table's metal edge and burst into a billion shards that sneezed across the floor, twinkling like a field of sunlit snow. The base, the felled stem, made a stupefied semi-circle turn on the table.

"Fuck!" Stood the stem upright. *"Fuck!"* Swung his feet up onto the couch.

Could already feel the chips and shivers burrowing into his butter-soft soles. He'd have to cordon off the area, sweep, vacuum, mop. Get down on all fours with his headlamp, scour the slim spaces between hardwood slats.

Another hour of his life evaporated. Another entirely avoidable waste of time.

Jacob's fault.

With the larger fragments mounded next to the headless stem, Barker took his computer, and brought up a message window on Jacob's Facebook page.

◆ ◆ ◆

A shitty, listless sleep augured a shitty, listless week. Woke up feeling gummy. Dressed and went for Trouble's leash. Not on its hook. Where did he leave it?

Remembered.

Stripped and showered. Jacob's face. Jacob's women. Jacob's beautiful beach. *Thanks for all the extra work, jackass. And thanks for the broken glass, while we're at it.*

Moving as if through a minefield, he gave the floor a scrupulous wipe with a wad of damp paper towels, daubing firmly at the cracks between hardwood slats in a pressing-rolling motion. Once more for good measure. Still on hands and knees, inspected the floor in the stark morning sun, tilting his head this way and that to catch any renegade glints, any overlooked shards, any shards of shards, before the bastards stuck him.

Graded the remaining essays, stopping only for coffee and cereal, and finished midday. Stretched his arms in satisfaction. The remainder of the break opened up before him, a field of possibility to frolic through however he so pleased.

Too chilly for a ride. All good. There was so much more he could do. He need only decide what.

Bounced around his Netflix Wish List. Documentaries and foreign films he definitely intended to watch at some point, but wasn't in the mood for at the moment. Picked a new release on a whim. Lost interest twenty minutes in.

Retrieved the book he'd been reading last August, struggled to recall the thrust of the narrative, to reconnect with the sprawling cast, what had been happening to whom.

Wrote Shiv a text.

- Luce tonight?

Wait, she was out of town with Dan. Some cottage somewhere. *I'll sit on the shore and watch him fish.* Underneath the sardonic tone, he could tell she was looking forward to it.

Delete!

Email. Listserv spam. Message (via Facebook) from Jacob:

SORRY!!!!!

Delete!

Was it too chilly for a ride? Suited up. Rain.

Back to Netflix. The image blocky and sluggish.

Rebooted his router. No better.

Called his ISP. Complained bitterly about the half-hour they kept him on hold.

I work *from home. This is a* major *inconvenience.*

I'm so sorry sir. Have you tried rebooting your router?

Leafed through the Baz dossier. Couldn't concentrate.

Relitigated a fight with Lara in his head. A novelist friend, Regina, in town for a book reading. Out for dinner, then skating at a downtown rink. Feels nice to be out with another person, an unaffiliated third party, to lift, if only for a night, the veil of secrecy. Regina confesses to Lara that she was in love with Barker in high school. "I mean *obsessed*. And he had no idea!" Later—a blowout. What was *really* going on with this "good friend" of his? *I've known Regina for twenty years! If I wanted to fuck her, or she wanted to fuck me, we'd have fucking fucked already!*

Wrote Lara an email. Deleted it. Masturbated. (*Casting, audition, redhead...*)

The rain let up. Went for a walk.

Video game shop. Open-world sword and sandals RPG. Made swift tracks home. Cracked a beer while his console did downloads and updates. Couldn't decide where to go or what to do, couldn't get a handle on the combat mechanics, what weapon or spell or combination thereof was most effective against which enemy. The controller made his hands feel clumsy, at once agile and arthritic. Shut off the game, looked up tips and playthroughs on YouTube.

Poked at his paunch in the mirror. Checked his spreading bald spot. Squeezed blackheads on his nose. Found two thirds of a tube of Sour Cream & Onion Pringles on the top shelf of his pantry. Ate them all. Dreamt of the subcutaneous writhing of spindle-thin, maggot-white somethings.

The next day was worse. Prowled his condo, room to room to room. Stared out his window, at the replenished greenness of the grass. A tenant crossed the courtyard with a dog. The animal went up on its haunches. Shat. *You'd better pick that up*, he beamed at the owner. She did.

Broods. A muddle; old slights and squabbles; lingering resentments and imaginary disputes. Hasn't been this bad for a while. Maybe not since he and Tat had formally separated. (Hadn't felt like a formality, what with him owning and occupying property on the opposite side of the country, and her having shacked up with a chick.)

He is here. She is there. Distance and time—not to mention

her modish erotic orientation—have rendered their former pronoun, they, obsolete.

Makes a point to rally, to alchemize failure into creative fuel. Sources new furniture to replace the falling-apart and threadbare. Goodbye futon! (Not because it's "theirs," or because it reminds him of "the good times," but because the frame is prickly with splinters and the corners ooze sea foam stuffing.) In interpolating the new pieces he (perhaps inevitably) ends up rearranging everything else.

Buys a massive antique desk as bulky and imposing as a hull, plump and curvy with flimsy iron handles that chirp when tugged. And, as it turns out, a titch too big for his office, forcing him to suck in his gut to round the corners. Small price to pay, he reckons, to feel like the cigar-chomping tycoon at the helm of some turn of the century oil consortium.

Once the persnickety moving men have left, he hunkers down behind his colossal desk in his slick condo—truly *his* for the first time—and cranks out three articles (finishes two that were already underway, starts another from scratch) in as many weeks. Hems and haws over which journals will be the best fit, which journals *deserve* them, and submits the pieces for publication.

With the beginning of semester chaos abating, and feeling familiar with the routine, starts mapping out his next book. Expand the scope of his first effort, while contributing something new to the conversation. An edited collection of work relating to media and agency, foreground the advertising angle, look at agency as a marketing tactic, maybe the vernacular developed for, and deployed in, that marketing. More. Bigger. Approach his closest colleagues, Hannah and Alessandro, to submit chapters. Isn't Hannah researching agency as a design concern? How developers themselves conceive of, and implement, choice-making in video games? Doesn't Alessandro have a thing for MMORPGS? Maybe he could analyze how the valuation of digital objects, how buying and selling, one's real-world resources, were integral to exercising agency within the economies of self-governing gamespaces?

Economies of Agency!

Out of the blue, word from his agent that there might be interest from Colbert.

As in The Report?

Weird. And wonderful. And disorienting. And weird. Clearly it is happening. Is all coming together. As his book garners interest outside the standard circles, he's morphing into a professional oddity, one of those freaks who accidentally transcends his scholarly niche. Can he leverage this momentary fame to champion his friends and associates? Draw attention to their research? Be the rising tide that lifts all boats?

Economies of Agency, he has to admit, is a really catchy title.

Is as impressed by Colbert's mastery of his craft as he's bewildered when the interview wraps up, quick as blinking, certain he's hit peak surreal. (Colbert: "So, this book of yours, *Agency in Play,* which I haven't read, but I'm told your argument is basically that media control us." / Barker: "Not exactly—" / "Wait, isn't a book a kind of medium?" / "Uh, yes, I suppose—" / "So if a book is a medium, and media control us, then why didn't your book *make* me read it?" / "I—" / "AHA! Busted! Game, set, match!") Returns home to find the first letter afloat in a swamp of postal detritus. The second and third arrive early the following week. Not even *Revise and Resubmit.* All three articles—outright rejected.

It's the first time his work hasn't sailed through review, and these are journals he'd been published in several times over, are overseen by editors he knows, has grown chummy with. It's deflating. Humiliating. His first significant failure, the first sputter of his engine, the first loss of altitude.

Shelves the *Economies of Agency* prospectus. Buys a PS4. Winter is a blur.

Something of a relief, then, when Maureen confides that her husband has been diagnosed with cancer. Pancreatic. She's taking a leave of absence. Might Barker be interested in serving as Interim

Program Director for the year she'll be away? It will look mighty good on his CV, she adds, when tenure rolls around.

Not to mention how putting a bankable name front and centre might soothe your recruitment woes...

Of course he's in. It feels like a lifeline. A reprieve. He can kill a year desk jockeying. Perfect excuse not to worry about publishing anything for a stretch. A nice little break to reflect, relax, refresh.

And even after one semester, games and pot are losing their lustre; jarred him out of monotony only to become monotonous, as shrunken and mealy as any overplayed song. He, he realizes, is a *variety is the spice of life* kind of guy.

A brightening. A surge of optimism that, like any decent tailwind, makes him feel powerful, heroic, unstoppable.

An epiphany strikes: *I should get a dog!*

♦ ♦ ♦

Something pointy and metallic wedged in a crevice between couch cushions. Extricates it. Trouble's badass spiked collar. Barker holds it in both hands.

A tightness in his throat.

Chest caves.

Sobs.

♦ ♦ ♦

Dell's text on Thursday was a godsend. Something, anything, to release him from this rut.

Except it was strange. Her text.

- Can I come over?

Eight p.m. Not late for him, but late for her.

And she'd never just *come over*. He hadn't seen her since Judy's birthday last weekend, since she'd pulled into an alley en route to his condo to fuck in the back seat like horny teenagers.

Of course, he replied.

Gathered up his paraphernalia. Stuffed his pipe in the back of his sock drawer.

Buzzed her up. Let her in. She said nothing. Dropped her purse and jacket on the floor. Removed her shoes, her blouse. Let her skirt fall. Peeled down her pantyhose. Turned and braced herself against the wall. Lowered her head.

✦ ✦ ✦

Later, on the couch, legs interlaced like the tines of two forks.

"Something happened," she says. "At work."

"Tell me."

"We get a call. Domestic. Boyfriend assaulted his girlfriend. Threatening her with a gun. She calls nine-one-one. He takes off, takes her car. Second call. Erratic driver. Matches the description. We're close, me and my partner. We get in behind it. Car speeds up. Tries to lose us. Veers onto an exit ramp, slams into the railing. Car almost flips. Guy gets out. Pistol in his right hand. We're out. We draw, issue a challenge: *Stop. Drop your weapon.* He's rambling. High. Or drunk. Or both. He starts to run—there's nowhere to go, busy road and a big fence—ends up in a gully, realizes he's painted in..."

She trails off. He waits.

"Puts the gun to his own head. Fires."

"Holy shit."

"And he's fine. Can you believe it? At that range? *Right* against his temple? His hand was shaking so bad...the moment he pulled the trigger...the angle is off, like, just enough... He's fine. Laceration across his forehead, but otherwise..."

He reaches out. She doesn't get it at first, then gives him her hand.

"First time I've ever drawn my weapon. For real."

"Right."

"I'm not...whatever. I'm not... I feel fine. This is what I trained for."

"I know."

"But it was my first time."

"That's a lot to take in."

"It's what I trained for."

"Still."

She squeezes his hand, lets go. He wraps it around her ankle. Smiles for a second, wiggles her toes.

"What I don't get…is that impulse. Killing yourself. A year or two in prison is one thing, if it came to that. Domestic abuse? He might get off with a plea. Evading arrest? The gun? Probably jail, but not forever. Killing himself?" Shakes her head. "I don't get it."

"I think I do."

"You do?"

"I think so. He's not…in that moment he's not weighing the consequences. He doesn't see it as a choice. In that moment he just feels trapped."

"That's it?"

"I'm only speaking for myself. That feeling, being cornered, you panic."

"Not me."

"I used to get panic attacks. Not all the time, but occasionally. Something would happen, something emotional, confusing. If I was in a public space, or worse, a confined space… Your body rebels. Turns on you. Your heart beats too fast. You're out of breath. Dizzy. It's too much. Too overwhelming. You're trapped, betrayed by your own body, out of your control."

"This happened to you?"

"A few times. Maybe four or five times in my whole life."

"What did you do?"

"If I could, I ran. Bolted. Anywhere I could. But if I was somewhere I couldn't leave, couldn't run…"

"You'd put a gun to your own head?"

"I've never so much as held a gun. I don't know…I don't know what that would be like. I hope I wouldn't go that far."

"But?"

"All I'm saying is I think I understand the impulse. When you're cornered, when that reality hits, most of us, I think, will do whatever we can to get out."

Sat there, with one another, for a long time.

"I like you," he tells her.

"You make me feel less weird," she tells him.

◆ ◆ ◆

She was gone when he woke up.

Later that day, he tried the game again. Played all the way through the weekend.

◆ ◆ ◆

Monday was warm. Hot almost. Went for a ride. And another longer one on Tuesday.

◆ ◆ ◆

On Wednesday, in the theatre, Barker roused the machines.

"Professor?"

Jacob, hangdog look weirdly juxtaposed against his dark tan.

"I'm so sorry, professor."

Barker clipped the LAV to his lapel. "Don't worry about it."

"Did you get my message?"

"I didn't have time to read it."

Tactical error. Jacob launched into a detailed account. His father really was sick. ALS. Before his health worsened further, wanted to take his family on a last big trip. Had always wanted to surf in Hawaii. Bucket list. Bought tickets before consulting with Jacob, before fully appreciating Jacob's schedule and responsibilities. Once the error was identified, they tried to book new dates, but swapping the flights would have been prohibitively expensive, and the trip itself was already an indulgence.

"Next time just come to me. Tell me what's going on."

"I know. I'm sorry. It was stupid. It'll never happen again." His slender frame hung off his slumped shoulders like a sheet on a hanger.

"Seriously. It's fine."

"My parents feel horrible. They asked me to apologize on their behalf. My dad is going to call you to apologize in person. They want to take you out for dinner."

"That really isn't necessary."

"He feels awful. We all do."

"It's done. It's over. Let's leave it."

"It won't happen again. Scout's honour." Began his retreat. "If there's anything I can do to make it up to you, just let me know."

"Oh, Jacob?"

Hurried back. "Yeah? What's up?"

"Your essays." Barker handed over the stack, wrapped in a plastic grocery bag.

"Gotcha. Thanks so much. I owe you big time."

"There's one in there in a manila envelope. I'm not sure how to pronounce the name."

Jacob unsheathed the essay. "I think it's *She-Shay*, but I'm not super positive. Don't quote me on that."

"When you return it to her, let her know there's no grade and tell her to contact me to schedule a meeting."

"Sure thing professor. Not a problem. Easy peasy lemon squeezy. What's the...? Is there a problem with it? Her essay?"

"It looks like there's a bunch of stuff in there she pulled off the Internet."

"Shit. Oh no. That's too bad." Beat. "Uh... Professor?"

"Yes?"

"It's just...she's Chinese."

"Okay."

"I think, y'know, in their culture, it isn't necessarily considered..."

"What?"

"Cheating. It's how you honour your teacher, right? By copying what they say? Repeating it back. I think they think it's kind of the same thing."

"Well, in this culture it *is* cheating. So tell her to contact me, okay?"

"Yeah! Will do!"

Jacob took a seat. Barker tapped the tiny black cob: *Thump! Thump!* THUMP!

+ + +

The torrent hit an hour after class. No strangers to superlatives, these kids these days. One was *devastated* by her mark. Another, after declaring his unflagging dedication to the course, called his grade a *travesty*. Others petitioned for succour according to one or another plight: the time suck of part-time jobs necessary to supplement high tuition fees; perceived errors or vagaries in the assignment instructions; the bias or enmity of their respective TA. *If you can tell me how I'm supposed to get a good grade when my TA hates me, I'd like to hear it!*

When complaints began arriving from Jacob's group, Barker couldn't help but laugh when he realized that, though he'd assigned the offending marks himself, the students assumed the grades had come from Jacob.

No offence to Jacob (hes super-great), but hes really young and maybe doesnt know the course material super well?

To each and every one the same reply:

Thank you for your message. I'd be happy to discuss your mark in person. Please arrange to meet me during my regularly scheduled office hours, Mondays from 1pm-3pm.

If you're unable to meet during this time, please let me know and we can try to make alternate arrangements.

Sure-fire strategy of attrition. Of the forty-to-fifty appeals he'd receive, fifteen-to-twenty would set up a meeting. Of those, five-to-ten would actually show. This simple stipulation—that if they cared so deeply, felt so strongly, that they plead their case in person—culled the merely peeved from the profoundly tormented. Anyone could whip off an angry email, only a truly wronged party would face their professor head on.

The dirty secret was that for all the hair-pulling and pathos, they all wanted the same thing: A bump. An extra point. What's more, Barker was happy to give it to them. While hyperbole was simply a tactic for some, others saw a bad mark, any bad mark, as a terrific blow. Why not throw them a bone? It cost him nothing, and meant everything to them. They'd lavish him with appreciation: how grateful they were; how generous he was; what a relief it was to be heard.

The message from XiXe arrived early that evening.

I am concern something happen. Could we talk soon before Monday?

First I waste hours picking through your essay, and now I have to make extra time to meet with you?

Hi XiXe,

I have to return some books to the library tomorrow (Friday) morning. If you want to come to my office at 10am sharp, I'd be happy to meet then.

Seconds later:

Thank you!! I be there!

♦ ♦ ♦

She arrived at ten-twenty-five in a crisp white blouse and a navy blue tie done in a pristine half-Windsor. Apologized profusely, had never been on this floor before, had to procure directions as best she could.

Barker stifled his irritation, motioned for her to hand over her essay. Placed it on his desk, squared the edges, an orthogonal accusation. Searched her face for a twinge of recognition, for signs of guilt or culpability.

She stared back, hands clasped in the lap of her wool skirt: serene, curious, confused.

...sixteen...seventeen...eighteen...

"She...uh...She-Shay... Am I pronouncing that correctly?"

"Yes. *She*-Shay."

"Okay, She-Shay—"

"*She*-Shay."

"Yes. Uh. Do you know why I asked to meet with you?"

"No."

"You don't?"

The essay as innocuous as dirt over a land mine.

"There is problem with my paper?"

"That's right. Do you know what that problem is?" Better if she confessed, better than accusing her outright. She needed to bear the full weight of her trespass for the lesson, this teachable moment, to sink in.

"No."

"You don't?" Picked up a pen, put the end in his mouth.

XiXe stared. "Yes."

"Yes you do know what the problem is, or yes you don't know?"

Beat. "Sorry," she said.

Flipped to the third page of her essay, pointed to *photogravure*, lassoed in red, with his pen. "Can you tell me what this word means?"

Leaned forward. Beat. Sat back. "It is a term in photography. Images produce through negative. Put on metal plate."

"How did you come to know the meaning of that word?"

"It was from Wikipedia I use in reference."

Aha! Busted!

"Jacob say we are allow to have Wikipedia as reference."

"Yes, that is allowed. Technically. I'd appreciate more substantial sources, though. Academic sources. Does that make sense?"

"But it is allowed?"

"More to the point, She, uh, She-Shay—"

"*She*-Shay."

"She-Shay."

She smiled and nodded.

"Irregardless—sorry, *irrespective* I meant to say—irrespective of whether you use Wikipedia, you haven't cited this material properly. With no works cited section, how can readers differentiate your writing from the writing of the authors whose work you're using?"

"Is in works cited."

"You didn't include a works cited section."

Timidly reached out and turned the essay over. On the back was a works cited page. Wikipedia was there. SparkNotes too. The formatting was a jumble, but... *How did I miss that?*

"Good, that's... But this is only part of the issue. These sections..." Flipped from page to page, made sharp flicks with his pen: "Here... here...here... You haven't indicated that these are citations. All verbatim quotes."

"Yes," she said.

"Yes, what?"

"Yes. Verbatim quotes."

"You have to put them in quotation marks, okay? You have to indicate what material isn't yours. This is crucial. I mean, I'm sure Jacob has gone over this in group."

"No."

"He hasn't?"

"No."

"Jacob has never talked about essay formatting?"

"No."

"Have you attended every session?"

"Yes."

"Maybe you didn't…" *understand.* Could that be construed as culturally insensitive? A microaggression? *Don't get me wrong! It's commendable what you've done, coming to a foreign country to study difficult material in an unfamiliar tongue.*

Tilted her head.

"Look, whether Jacob…this is basic stuff. It's your responsibility to follow the instructions and format your essay accordingly. Especially the rules surrounding citations. It's not that… I'm not trying to be a dick here…"

Dammit.

XiXe: "Dick?"

Fuck! Rookie mistake. Unforced error. *Why did I use that word?*

"I, uh, know that in your culture it's considered appropriate to quote your teacher, to honour them by repeating their teaching back to them…"

She frowned as if tasting something rancid.

"But here, in this country…*culture* I mean, this, what you're doing here, comes uncomfortably close to plagiarism."

Her eyes widened; mouth sprang into a small O.

"Do you understand?"

"You say I cheat?"

"No. Not exactly. I'm saying…I want to give you the benefit of the doubt, and again, not to be a" *Don't say dick!* "jerk, I'm, ah, sympathetic to where you're coming from, as a foreign…an *e-es-el* student."

Her eyes narrowed in suspicion. She flipped the essay over, sharply this time. "I put here."

"Okay…look…" Barker drew the following:

"   " (   )

"Every citation must be formatted like this, with an open quotation mark at the beginning, a closed quotation mark at the end, and the source of the quote in these parentheses here, according to the citation method of your choosing. Okay?"

"Yes."

"Please go back through your essay and ensure that every direct quote, from Wikipedia or anywhere else, is formatted exactly like this. Okay?"

"Yes."

"Then re-submit the essay to me and I'll assign a mark."

"Yes."

"Great. Thanks for coming to see me."

Slid the essay across the desk. She took it, stood, left.

Sat and stared at the open door. Let his eyes relax, his field of vision bifurcate. Realized he'd been holding his pen so tightly he'd broken the casing. Globs of black ink had leaked onto his desk, stared up at him like spider eyes.

Spotted Maureen scamper past his door.

Called out after her. "Can I talk to you for a minute?"

Interlude: The Incident

Invites him to sit. *Do you know why I asked to see you?*

He doesn't.

Did you say something to your students about plagiarism? About how to plagiarize better?

That? He was joking! Playful bit of sarcasm.

I know that, the professor assures him, *but they don't. Maybe most of them do, but… Look, don't give them any ammunition, okay? Because when it comes right down to it, if they can use it, they will. This is all a game called* How To Get The Most Marks Possible.

As far as reprimands go, it's a gentle one. This is his second year serving as a TA for this prof. He likes the prof. Thinks the prof likes him. They have similar tastes and pop culture fixations. Rapport. He digs this aspect of grad school, the way the professors treat you more like an equal. Not quite a peer, but not like when you're an undergrad either, one of the innumerable throng. So maybe they aren't friends as such, but it feels like they could be some day.

But here, sitting across from him, hemmed in on either side by walls of books, taking in this awkward wrist-slap, the curtain is wrenched back revealing their camaraderie as a fraud. The balance of power, the *hierarchy*, reasserts itself, and he sinks through its strata. *I'm your boss. Step out of line, and you take the hit, same as anyone.*

And that he's being berated, however mildly, isn't the crux of the matter. The crux is that he's been *exposed*. That one of his students, one of those shitfuck mouth-breathers, ratted him out. Went behind his back. Reported him to his so-called superior. It's no less than insubordination. A breach. What right do they have to leap-frog the chain of command?

And for *nothing*. A dumb, offhand nothing of a joke; made to draw and harness their diffuse, flock-like attention, to instil a valuable lesson, to save them from calamity.

University is like this. Sucks the humour out of everyone. There's a new language to learn, new codes to adhere to. Humour is a volatile compound, its intentions suspect, its effects harmful.

Feels stupid and ashamed, chastened by this lapse in rectitude. Explains he made the aside in the context of a far more serious exegesis on the perils of plagiarism. He'd fielded a few cases the year before—the prof knows this, of course; had counselled him on protocol—noted the lure of the lowest-hanging fruit. *If they're going to go to the trouble of cheating, why cheat so shabbily? In the most obvious ways? Cribbing from the first few Google hits is not exactly sophisticated subversion, amirite?*

I know, says the prof. *I'm on your side.*

Of course it isn't the prof he's mad at—as much as he hates being upbraided—it's the fucking *kids*. The *betrayal*. If they had any fucking clue how much work he put into leading his groups, how much prep, how above and beyond to assign fair and accurate grades, they'd have carried him down the corridor like a championship quarterback. But they only cared about marks. They were all *what did I get out of ten on this* or *fifteen on that?* And, if any given result proved unsatisfactory: Beg, bribe, blackmail, whinge, whine, wail. *My TA said it was okay to plagiarize, provided I go deep enough into my search results! Ask anyone in the group! Those were his exact words!*

Sorry, he tells the professor, *it won't happen again.*

Don't worry about it, the prof replies. *Seriously. Don't.*

He doesn't worry about it. He leaves the office, leaves the building, cuts through campus like a scalpel. No, he doesn't worry about it. He *broods*. Gives resentment full reign to pulverize his mental topography. Concocts fantasies of revenge exacted upon each and every slacker, every turncoat, every intellectual dilettante. He'll stop responding promptly to inquiries, he'll be punitive with their grades, he'll...

That's it, really. These are his only avenues of retaliation. The pathetic extent of his control over their lives.

No wonder they treat him with derision, are openly disengaged, refuse to put away their gadgets no matter how many times, or in how many ways, or after how many threats, he implores them to do so. *I won't spend the entire semester policing you*, he warns before doing exactly that. He can't help it. It bugs him. Their phones, their computers, their stewed eyes and narcotized faces. They're here to have a discussion, not rake sand and shuffle stones around digital Zen gardens. They have to *be there with him*. *All* of them. Together.

And now one of the principal tools for the Sisyphean task of maintaining their attention—an increasingly rare resource—has been unceremoniously stripped away. If he doesn't have humour, can't make jokes, then what exactly the fuck is the alternative?

This is the moment, as he blows toward the student centre like a storm, the realization strikes: As much as he is policing them, they are policing him also.

He finds this epiphany unpleasant.

No, he doesn't worry about it. *Nonono*. He *seethes*.

So consumed is he with seething, so committed to the argument he's having with his psychic student proxies, so wholly *in the moment*, that he has no awareness of the telos of his trajectory until it's too late. A group or procession before him. Fluttering bedsheets strung between sticks. Flags? No—the fabric, whether white or cream or beige—is blank. As he penetrates the wall of bodies—a pair of women seem surprised, make a modest attempt to block his passage—he stumbles into a pageant of horror. Behind the women, or rather nested inside the *whitecreambeige* barricade, is a display. Placards emblazoned with images. Black and white scenes from the

Holocaust. One of those famous close-ups of Hitler, face screwed in a rictus of demagoguery. The emaciated matchstick bodies of concentration camp victims, cordwood dumped carelessly into pits. Other placards scream colour like a bullhorn blasts sound. Scorched oranges and retinal reds. Can't comprehend, can't coagulate the splattered mess in this blistered spectrum. His brain organizes the overload. It coheres as gore and viscera, as the *humanlizardalien* shapes of desiccated foetuses.

He feels bodily slammed into the here and now. It's *that* visceral—a punch to the solar plexus. Tiny severed limbs. Little broken bodies. Indescribably grotesque. The eviscerated wreckage interpolated with these iconic Holocaust photographs...a dialectic insinuating what? Equating these forms of violence? The genocide perpetrated against the Jews with a genocide enacted by...abortion doctors? Their clientele?

A cheerful young woman stands before him—he who penetrated the slapdash barrier, who is clearly in search of The Truth!—hands him a pamphlet. Lungs siphoned, hands sweating and shaking, tongue taffy—all it can do is stick. Breathes in little puffs. Should he thank her? He croaks, words are strips of tape he's trying to pull apart. Can't believe what he's seeing, what these people have done, what their display represents.

Who are they? Where did they come from? Who allowed them to be here? This isn't a city street corner, this is a *university*. Surely this...appalling affront to women, to the student corpus, to thinking people...surely this cannot be counted on the ledger of free speech. Surely speech requires some boundaries, some logic, some undergirding reason or rationale. This is is is *propaganda*. Violence of another kind. Not only offensive—deeply, intensely, *insanely* offensive—but a form of assault.

Drops the pamphlet and yanks the nearest placard off its easel. The cheer on the pamphleteer's face blasts away like sand. She starts to say something—*You can't do that*, maybe?—but he is beyond rules, beyond negotiation, beyond speech. Gripped in both hands, he tries to rend the placard in half, but the cardboard is laminated. Puts some muscle into it. The plastic warps and stretches until the webbing snaps.

Some of the barricade women take notice; cheer, point, shout to their friends.

Look! Look at him! Go, Random Guy, go!

The once-cheerful woman rallies assistance. A few allies flank her, move to intervene as he lunges for another placard (a crushed foetus in a steel tray of pomegranate jelly). The barricade women launch themselves into the fray. Protester on protester. Sets about sundering this second placard as the crowd around him churns.

Is oblivious to the ruckus, is in the eye of the storm, perfectly serene.

◆ ◆ ◆

Campus security steps in before anyone comes to blows, but not before a photog from the student paper snaps a few choice shots. One of the more industrious barricade women had joined him in his placard-annihilating efforts, and it's the two of them splashed across the cover of the campus weekly under the headline "DEFENDERS OF CHOICE!" Brother and sister in arms—she in a gleeful leaping-stomping fugue, he bearing a visage of perfect calm, neither looking like defenders of anything, and more like rioters in an arts and crafts class—conjoined for eternity in the delimited gaze of a camera frame.

Detained for twenty minutes. Short interview. The pudgy guard with blotchy skin takes his information and statement. He can tell the dude's heart isn't in it.

The photo causes such a stir that the editor invites him to pen a guest op-ed. He humbly accepts. By this time, several days after the incident, a sort of quasi-regret has set in. Not that he's in any way at fault. To the contrary: the placards, the whole display, were obviously intended to provoke the very reaction he'd had. (As such, his actions were not only justified, but basically preordained.) Rather, he regrets the lapse in decorum. This is not how citizens in democratic societies are meant to air grievances. Drafts his op-ed in this spirit, as atonement, olive branch, overture to common ground, to respectful discourse, not the confrontation the other side craved. A thoughtful, nuanced appeal to just, like, let everyone believe what they want to believe without dragging desiccated foetuses into the mix.

The resulting opinion piece, "Abort the Debate," is nigh-unanimously lauded upon its printing. Yes, there are a few dissenting voices, a smattering of half-hearted appeals to the high-minded virtues of free speech presumably compromised if his argument were taken to its utmost extreme; an invocation of that quote oft misattributed to Voltaire; i.e., *I defend to the death your right to say it.* There's also a letter from a representative of the anti-abortion org itself, a well-funded outfit headquartered in the U.S. whose *modus operandi*, as suspected, is to incite hysteria in bystanders and passers-by that can be leveraged for publicity and—if confrontations escalate—lawsuits. But these outliers are largely drowned out by venerations from his fellow righteously indignant, many of whom mince no words lambasting the university for having permitted the shameful display in the first place.

These admonitions reach such a fever pitch that he starts to worry about possible reprisal from the university. Or at least he starts to worry after he's approached by two student council representatives who suggest that the university might try to seek reprisal. *Technically speaking,* the older one says, ginger whorls sweeping across his jowls like a satellite view of hurricanes, *you violated a subsection of the university constitution that grants permitted groups the right to mount displays without molestation, regardless of content.* The younger one nods gravely. Wow, he thinks, that sounds pretty serious. *But don't worry, the councils have your back. In fact, we'd like to invite you to speak at our next symposium. Fifteen minutes max.*

He'd be glad to, of course. Not that he has anything to say he hasn't said already. Standing before both councils in the aptly named

Senate Room (after having spent the better part of the meeting internally scoffing at their doctrinal devotion to *Robert's Rules of Order*; at the pretentious pageantry and pseudo-parliamentary preening), his "speech"—which he's decided to deliver on the fly, to *speak from the heart* as it were—begins with an account of the events precipitating his sudden (and ill-deserved, he protests) attention, segues into an uninspired pander (à la *can't we all just get along*), and finishes with a meandering climax lacking any discernible theme or point.

He receives an enthusiastic standing ovation.

After the meeting, someone from a campus feminist caucus takes him aside to A) thank him for standing up for choice, and B) advise him that even if he'd "technically" broken the law, these so-called "laws" were devised by and for the patriarchy, and should therefore be taken with the proverbial grain of salt.

The next day he finds out that the American-based anti-abortion org has indeed filed a grievance against the university. The council reps return to inform him that said organization has a sorry track record in court, and will likely drop the suit as soon as any attendant publicity dissipates. Further, the university will probably hold a tribunal, but this is also principally for show, and has little-to-no binding legal or scholastic consequences. But not to worry either way, because they—i.e., the student councils—have his back.

He's called in for a sit-down with the Associate Dean of Arts, a genial but tired-looking man who tells him that the university isn't about to give this disgusting organization any assistance with their *nuisance suit* (his term). The police, he continues, are just as unlikely to press charges. And while he can't guarantee anything, once the ink has dried on the whole *imbroglio* (his word), he doesn't foresee the pro-life org pursuing the matter further. *If they do, we'll help you sort out lawyers and whatnot.* The university, he adds almost as an afterthought, will forego any kind of tribunal, and leave it up to the student councils to censure him as they see fit. (He had, after all, violated several statutes of their constitutions.)

Ginger Rep touches base, tells him that the Associate Dean's caveat was the subject of much mirth and mockery at the latest council meeting, specifically the university declining to "punish" him, as if it was *he*, and not *they*, who'd screwed the pooch in the first place.

This is, as they say, the long and the short of it. Threats of retaliation indeed come to naught. The councils decline to censure him. He doesn't see the Associate Dean of Arts again until convocation, and then only from afar.

An epilogue, of a sort, having to do with the woman with the pamphlet.

Though the group itself is based in the States, it worms its way into universities elsewhere through campus-based religious organizations. The materials and signage are shipped in from the U.S., but those in charge of mounting the displays are all fellow students.

The next semester, on a lark, he registers for a course in abnormal psychology. Second week, course in session, feels someone lean in behind him, right up to his ear, and in that ear whisper this: "Be honest, you just wanted to tear something down."

Ignores her. Or pretends to.

Her words haunt him. Get in his hair and on his skin, impossible to wash away.

Occasionally, while staring out over his abyss, he will wonder: How did she see through him? See his true self.

CAROL: Excuse me, but those are not accusations. They have been *proved*. They are facts.

—David Mamet, *Oleanna*

The Opening

Dell was on call over the weekend, and with more goodness forecast, Barker spontaneously decided to go camping. Engorged two panniers with gear, strapped his tent and sleeping bag to the rack on his hybrid commuter, and reserved a site in his favourite provincial park.

Set out first thing Friday morning, bike wobbly with weight. Took the train to its eastern terminus, turned onto an idyllic country lane—trees a skeletal canopy overhead, cracking the sky—and encouraged by a sputtering tailwind, began the daylong trek. Stopped for a sandwich at a small-town deli. Parked his bike against an elephantine tree trunk, wandered onto a beach nested inside a quiet alcove, devoured his lunch while watching white-knuckled waves claw at the sand.

Arrived at his site late afternoon, unloaded his gear, snapped his tent together. Doubled back to the store just outside the gates. (The sign on the door said they'd be closing for the season that coming Monday. He'd made it in the nick of time!) Picked up some marinated pork and Haloumi kebabs, a bag of hamburger buns, chips, beer, a pack of cigarettes, a bundle of wood. Grilled the kebabs over his fire, slipped chunks of meat and veg and cheese off the skewers with the buns, chewed and chomped and smacked and slurped, sucked fatty juices off of soiled, sooty fingers, lit cigarettes off the open flame, slathered his insides with lukewarm beer.

This was all it need be about, the prelapsarian ecstasies of fire, flesh, and fucking. How and when had it all gone awry? Agriculture? Cain and Abel? The figurative hunter-gatherer "slain" by the farmer? The mass production of food? With formerly diffuse clusters aggregating into ever-larger assemblages? With networks of cisterns, wells, canals—capillaries carved into reticent earth? Once sustenance was more or less assured, the nourishment and security of the tribe relatively guaranteed, that was when the real original sin occurred. Nothing to do with Eve or apples. No, the actual ejection was the advent of leisure time. Loosed from the yoke of survival—survival as a daily gauntlet, that is—humankind was left with a surplus of this brand new resource. What should we do with all this time? Let us think and ponder and deconstruct. *Philosophy!* Paint and sing and dance. *Art!* Throw and hit and kick. *Sport!*

Pleasantly benumbed by fatigue, by the metabolism of meat and beer in his bulging stomach (beer—there was one point for agriculture at least), by the surge of nicotine squeezing his arteries, entranced by the pulsating embers in his waning fire, Barker ruminated on the terrible mistake humanity had made.

This was all they needed. This was what they must return to.

Doused the cinders, conjuring a hissing phantom of thick steam. Zippered himself inside his sleeping bag, squirmed until he was comfortably wedged between rocks and roots. Darkness as inmost as marrow. Listened to rain rattle the fly like tuneless timpani, the plucking of dead strings.

Woke into an indistinguishable dark and icy cold. Rebuffed his burning bladder, fell into dreams of urination and relief.

Awoke again, pushed down the sleeping bag like a foreskin, shimmied over to and opened the flap, pissed out the side. Closed the flap, tried to crawl back into oblivion.

Did it work? Did he get there? Or did he lie in the black, the carousel of his mental zoetrope awhirl: Molly outside the Legion (*maybe speech shouldn't be so free*); Dell's silent stripping; XiXe flipping over her essay? Then: Dawn. Tent illuminated, fly jewelled with dew, nature's orchestra tuning.

Boiled water for coffee and porridge (how he loved the smell of butane in the morning), rinsed his dishes, collapsed his tent, packed up, rode home.

Over and done by six p.m. Panniers gutted, tent and gear re-stored. The whole trip had lasted thirty-six hours, but he felt like he'd been gone for a week. Praised himself for so abruptly breaking out of routine, from the city, from every device that daily monopolized his time and attention.

Thirty-six hours and he'd fully regained his chill.

Shower, pasta, wine, laptop.

All spam but for an invitation to the opening night of Ophelia's play, her reverse-gender *Oleanna*.

Hi Ophelia,

Many thanks for the invite! (How did it come so quickly? Time flies!) I'd be more than pleased

Erased "be more than pleased." Wrote:

love to attend—provided you can guarantee a consensual theatre experience ;)

Please consider this my RSVP for two tickets. See you Thursday!

Thanks again!

Barker

Refilled his wine, separate browser, Ophelia's Instagram feed...

◆ ◆ ◆

Sunday. Text from Mac.

- Can you meet tomorrow? Same place/time?

Being a weekday, the café was slightly less wall-to-wall. Evan was waiting when he arrived. Barker went to join him, but Evan stood and pointed at the counter.

"Let's get it to go," he said. "I can't stay long."

Evan's furtive eyes betrayed his exhaustion. Once outside, he lit a cigarette.

"He's gonna pay," he said.

"Yeah?"

"Yeah. What they're asking for, it's a lot, but not *a lot* a lot. Not in terms of what his family is worth." Killed the cig, lit another. "Fucking extortion," Exhaled a jet of roiling blue.

Barker: "I have worked up a bit of a...I don't know if it can be called a strategy *per se*, but a set of, uh, talking points, I guess, in your parlance."

Evan smirked, eyes aimless. "I dig the way you talk man. We all have our words, don't we?"

All of a sudden, Barker wasn't sure how he should stand. The coffee felt like an aberration in his hand. He shuffled his feet, leaned against a signpost, stood straight again, scratched and picked at the plastic lid. "It's not a, uh, complete set of... I'm still working on... I mean, it's getting there."

Flicked his butt to the ground. "We likely won't need it. Y'know— hush part of hush money. We'll pay you for the month, appreciate your discretion, *yadda-yad*." A collegial pat on the shoulder.

Evan took a swig, released a cracking belch, extended his hand. Three quick pumps. "Anyhow, good to meet you. Good luck with all your video game stuff." Strode off.

◆ ◆ ◆

Wednesday afternoon, Barker was in his office catching up on email. Shiv appeared at his door.

"Luce tonight?" he asked without looking up.

Stepped inside, closed the door behind her.

"I can't."

"What? This is a serious breach in protocol." Glanced up. She was not amused.

"Listen, I know you were trying to help, but next time please don't do that."

"Do what?"

"Go to Maureen behind my back."

Huh? "That wasn't *behind your back*. I—"

"I'm not a damsel. I can deal with my own distress. I can handle Molly Ellen Clarke myself."

"Shiv, that wasn't at all what—"

"I'm not accusing you of anything, Barker. I assume your intentions were good. But think, for a second, about how that made me look. The university is pissed as shit over this whole Abdalla...I don't know if *fiasco* is too strong a word, but in deference to my one-eighths Italian heritage, I'll use it."

"But that's why I wanted to—"

"Barker, please, just *listen*."

Threw up his hands, palms front, fingers sprung: *Go for it.*

"It would be nothing to fire me. No offense, but you don't know what it's like out there. I was on the market *five years* before landing this gig. Thankfully, Maureen has my back. So what do you think it looks like when, after she's already pledged her support, after we've already sorted out how to proceed, you hold her hostage in the hallway for an impromptu lecture—"

"*Lecture?*"

"—on how great and faultless and indispensable I am, and how it would be *such a shame* for the university to take my scalp because of a few uppity kids?"

She waited.

"Oh, am I allowed to talk now?"

"Don't get puffed up." Her face was an arctic front, but her voice quavered.

"Maybe like a concerned colleague sticking up for his friend and fellow faculty member?"

"It looks like I ran wailing to my *bee-ef-ef* to intervene on my behalf. It looks like I went to you—with your...your what? Your sway? Your clout?—and asked you to defend me. *Save* me."

His hackles rose. *I have neither time for, nor interest in, continuing this conversation,* he should announce. *Especially when my intentions, as you well know, were good.*

"Okay," he said.

She sat. "Do you get how patronizing that is?"

"Sure." Less a word than a sound effect; a soft, sucking *swoosh.* Hated how petulant he felt, for being so easily agitated, for the flush consuming his neck and cheeks, for Shiv putting him on the spot, calling him out when he'd only been trying to help.

"All right. Well... Maureen and I are on top of the situation. In fact, that's why I can't go for drinks tonight. I'm meeting with her and Molly."

"Glad to hear it."

"I'll see you tomorrow."

"For what?"

"Isn't it the play? Your student or something?"

Riiight. Dell was working.

"Unless you want to rescind that invitation in light of our conversation just now."

"No, of course not. It's fine. I'll see you tomorrow." Back to his screen.

"We can hit The Luce after?" Her tone already softening. Conciliatory.

"Sounds like a plan."

"Have a good night."

"'Night." Heard his door open and close, but did not see her go.

✦ ✦ ✦

The following night he was still riled. She'd insisted she wasn't questioning his intent, but it sure as shit felt like she was questioning his intent. He had half-a-mind to punish her by not showing up. Let her sit there in the theatre alone, confused, wondering where he was, gradually coming to grips with the gravity of her offense. As the play proceeded, she'd replay the encounter several times over—her words, her tone—and realize *she* was in the wrong. Would be sick with remorse. Could the friendship be salvaged? Would Barker forgive her? She'd call, maybe the moment the show ended, race into the lobby or whathaveyou. He'd see it was her, let the call ring through, let her stew in contrition, *twist in the wind* as it were. She'd leave some simpering, conscience-stricken voicemail. *I'm so sorry! It was a bad day! I wasn't thinking straight! I took it out on you! It'll never happen again!*

Waffled, resolute one moment—yes, ditching Shiv was the right move, the only way to drive the lesson home—and uncertain the next. Would he seem petty? Would she dismiss the ploy as acting out? Sulking? No, he should defer to his better angels, go to the show, support Ophelia. Ophelia was counting on him. He'd been a mentor of sorts throughout this process, or at least at a critical juncture. She wanted, if not needed, Barker to be there to cheer her over the finish line. (Come to think of it, he should ask Maureen if it wasn't too late to add this whole Ophelia/*Oleanna* mentorship thing to his tenure portfolio.) Tonight was about Ophelia, about Barker *and* Ophelia, and he wouldn't let Shiv spoil it for them.

Pink dress shirt and gunmetal grey slacks. Tie? Watched Netflix for four minutes. Picked a tie but couldn't get the knot right. Dug a pair of loafers out of the closet. Quick polish. Ditched the tie. Scotch. Email. Go? Stay? Which was paramount: The support and nurture of his student, or the teachable moment for his so-called friend?

At the last possible minute, he ruffled a pearl of gel through his hair, and took the elevator to the parking garage. Found his car under a skiff of dust. Fished a towel out of the back, gave the windows a cursory wipe. He'd forgotten about the crack in the windshield, a rock kicked up by a passing semi, every bump and shudder extending the spread like a firework in glacial burst.

Arrived to find the theatre foyer crammed. Spotted Shiv right away, but didn't recognize the person she was chatting with until it was too late.

Her hair was longer—an inky cascade plunging past her vulpine neck, tumbling over and beyond her sharp shoulder blades. Bangs a raised claw. Classy burgundy sweater under a dusk-blue jacket, oblong pendant (amber?) on a silver chain nested between the modest mounds of her breasts, matching earrings, sheer leggings, shellacked pumps that tapered into a javelin tip. Outfit as declarative statement. The whole ensemble screamed *Professor*.

Inevitable. We share the same campus, had to run into each other sooner or later. It's a miracle we made it this far without crossing paths. Not a miracle, of course. Coincidence. No one was avoiding anyone. They had different schedules. Came to campus on different days, at different hours. Things had ended amicably. Had she filed the complaint with Maureen? No. No point. Nothing to gain. Lots to lose. Had to be another explanation, another culprit. Envious faculty member. Didn't matter. It was over. Dealt with. Stamped and sealed. They weren't friends, but they weren't enemies either. He had nothing riding on seeing her or not seeing her. It was, per Kierkegaard, an *either/or* proposition.

Shiv noticed him before he could correct course and fold into the crowd unseen. Lara's head swivelled on its axis. Their conversation trailed off. Lara sniffed the air with her aquiline nose, as if tracking the contrail of vanished words. She looked at Shiv, then to the ground.

Were they talking about him? Something they didn't want him to hear?

"Hi there," he said.

"Hello," Shiv said.

"Hi, Lara."

"Hi," Lara said.

"How's your semester going thus far?"

"Fine. Yours?"

"Yeah. Good. Standard list of complaints *ar-e* the kids these days. I just had this one student, an undergrad..." Hit the brakes. He wasn't at liberty to divulge XiXe's plagiarism, if it *was* plagiarism and not a simple cultural misunderstanding. Or an overreaction. Bias. Would it seem like he'd singled her out? An exchange student with a tenuous grasp on the language, essay formatting, protocol? (*Nothing could be further from the truth!*) Besides, technically speaking, such matters should be kept confidential, shouldn't they? "Let's just say they keep things interesting."

Shiv and Lara exchanged a glance. It was good he'd decided to come after all. Shiv would've had Lara for company regardless, delaying her epiphany regarding, and subsequent regretting of, how profoundly she'd mistreated him. In the meantime, they could feign a friendly evening together. Not a typical outing, he supposed, for either one of them. He couldn't recall the last time he'd attended a play, and Shiv had said more or less the same upon accepting his invitation. Had Lara ever expressed any interest in the arts? Not really. Which begged the question: *The fuck was she doing here?*

"What brings you to the play tonight?"

Lara pretended to not have been paying attention to him. "What?"

So obvious. So transparent. "Why are you here?"

Her mouth slunk into a feline grin. "Ophelia invited me."

Beat. "She did?"

"She's taking my *Gender and Identity* course. I think she invited all her profs."

Lara's eyes skated around the room. *You're not a prof, you're an instructor,* Barker thought as he followed her gaze.

Lara: "She talks about you. Your course. She said you helped advise her on the play."

Both of them were looking at him. Couldn't read their expressions. His ears and neck felt seared.

"Yeah, she, uh..." Was there anyone else he could talk to? Cast out his gaze like a lure, tried to catch an errant eye. No bites. "We were talking after class one week. She's been through some..." Should he mention the thing with Ophelia's dad? Was he meant to keep that private? She'd *confided* in him. Would it be weird of him to know personal details about a jejune female undergrad? "...family stuff lately, and we got to talking about the show. She asked me for advice."

"Well," Shiv said, "it was nice of you to give it to her."

Give it to her? That was an...*odd* choice of words, wasn't it? Code? Subtext? *Insinuation.* Was it? Another trespass. Wasn't it? Dirty pool, no? He'd gone out of his way to *help* Ophelia, *counsel* her, offer an unbiased, outside perspective during a troublesome time, and this was his thanks? *Innuendo.* If it *was* innuendo, then it was insulting. He was insulted! Their reconciliation—*potential* reconciliation— even further out of reach. But this was neither the time nor place...

Did they just glance at each other again?

A ripple through the crowd. Everyone turned and shuffled in unison toward a pair of double doors, like filings to a magnet.

"See you after the show," Lara said.

To both of them, or just Shiv?

"Sure," said Shiv.

"Sure thing," said Barker.

Another not-so-secret look. Another unspoken something. This time he was certain. They *had* been talking about him. It was so so so *lame* of Shiv to do that, and all but a day after *she'd* accused *him* of going behind *her* back! Severe violation. Potentially unforgivable infraction.

He wanted to be anywhere but here, with anyone but Shiv.

They moved en masse for the entrance.

Perched on a tall stool to the side of the doors was a young woman in black pants, suspenders, and a ruffled tuxedo shirt under a silk maroon vest. As they approached, the usher—ball bearing eyes nested inside thick glasses, rust red hair scrunched up in a messy bouquet—extended her arm across the entrance. "Tickets please."

Shiv handed over a ticket. The usher tore it in half, returned the stub.

Barker: "Sorry, I didn't realize there were tickets. I *ar-es-vee-peed* to the email invite?"

"You have to go to will call, sir. If you *ar-es-vee-peed* then your name should be on the list."

"Where's that? Will call?"

Keeping one arm fixed in barricade position, she pointed to a table in a distant corner.

Furrowed his brow. "Is that really necessary?"

"I need to take your ticket, sir."

"But isn't everyone...this is opening night, right? Wasn't everyone invited?"

The usher canted her head.

"What does it matter if I have a ticket or not, if my name's on the list?"

"I don't know your name's on the list. I only said that if you *ar-es-vee-peed* then it should be."

"So I'm supposed to go to the back of the line, then, too?"

"I need to take your ticket to admit you to the theatre."

A *tsk* from behind. Turned to the cluster of stalled patrons, and in his most genial tone said, "Calm down, it's not gonna start without you." Back to the usher. "I mean, what does it matter?"

Shiv: "Go get your ticket and I'll save you a seat."

Flapped his hands—to no one in particular, to everyone around him. Stalked over to the will call table and the two girls manning it: A vaguely Latina-looking one alongside a rail-thin peroxide-blonde with a flat orange tan that could only have come from a salon. It stopped just short of her eyes, making them look highlighted.

"Stone." he said. "Barker."

The usher said nothing, tore his ticket, let him pass unimpeded. He found Shiv in the front row. "I forgot my glasses. Do you mind if we sit here? I won't be able to see fuck all further back."

"This is fine."

Slid her purse and jacket under the seat. Barker craned his neck. Recognized faces from *Games, Geeks, and Gizmos*, a boy that Barker knew but couldn't place, several fellow faculty—small mercy he wouldn't be sitting next to Fidget three rows back (Barker waved, Fidget saluted)—even some Communication and Media admin staff.

Not a massive house—maybe two hundred seats or so—but pretty much packed.

That was when Barker felt it, that special anticipatory energy that only certain crowds in special moments emanate. Such strange magic, this intercourse of play and patron. From theatre's inception in the cultural furnace of Classical Greece, the annual assembly of otherwise disparate city states; *warring* clans galvanized by old stories given new breath; weeping and wailing to quicken communal catharsis. Could Ophelia do that here, tonight? And if so, hadn't Barker made an invaluable contribution? Inspired her to envision the play anew? Yes, he was part of it, a part of this thing, this *larger* thing, larger than himself, than he and Ophelia both. The extension of an ancient ritual that, per Benjamin, because of its rarity, ephemerality, and proximity had its own singular aura.

The lights dimmed. Barker's skin prickled.

Spotlight stage right. Ophelia inside. She was born for that light. For all light. Ageless. *Glowing.*

Fuck her!

Hushed his mental Tatjana.

The audience broke into applause. For what? What had Ophelia done? Nothing. Everything. She was there. They were all here, together, with her. She beamed. A beacon. She was the light. It shone out of her, tapering to a point beyond vision above.

"Thank you!" The applause ebbed. "Thank you *sooo* much for

coming. It means so much to me and everyone involved in this production to have a such an amazing audience for our opening night of David Mamet's *Oleanna*."

Nothing. No applause for Mamet. They weren't here for him. This was her night. He was a relic of a bygone era, she was an invention, a manifestation, of the present.

"The Drama Society programmed this play to inspire dialogue about an incredibly important issue, an issue that affects every university and college campus today: Sexual violence and assault."

Yes, they concurred with rapt attention, *this is a* Very Important *issue indeed.*

"In this play, Mamet interrogates the prevailing orthodoxies of his day. He seems to frame contemporaneous harassment claims— such as those made by Anita Hill against Supreme Court nominee Clarence Thomas—as deeply suspect, even fabricated. If we take Mamet's *polemic* at face value—"

She glanced at him. Winked.

Polemic. Winked back.

"—then these claims were nothing short of a witch hunt perpetrated by women against men."

The silence transmuted, pooled into a palpable *Boo!*

"Well, we did *not* take his play at face value, we—"

A burst of applause. Ophelia paused, rode it out like a pro. "Instead, we decided to use *Oleanna* as a platform to explore new orthodoxies at play today—no pun intended."

Pretty creaky so far as puns went, but they laughed anyway.

"Today, victims of sexual violence, women and men alike, are often blamed for their assaults having occurred at all, much less having the nerve to report those assaults to the authorities. Luckily, thanks to activists and organizations across North America, victim-blaming is not only being openly acknowledged, but *challenged*."

Vigorous applause! Was it possible to give a standing ovation before a play had even started?

"Thankfully, a new sexual assault policy is about to be imple-
mented at this university, one that will see victims of sexual violence
given the benefit of the doubt without question or qualification.
We—"

Applause! A bit much already?

"Thank you. We wanted our production to be a part of this
conversation, to challenge these entrenched attitudes in the same
way that Mamet conceived his play as a challenge to the prevailing
wisdom of his day. So—"

It was not applause that interrupted Ophelia this time, but an
obnoxious synthetic tintinnabulation. A cell phone! Barker spun,
eyes scornful, and almost instantly realized the insolent phone was
his. Crouched, fished it out of his pocket. He'd turned it off! No
he'd only *thought* to turn it off right before running into Shiv and
Lara. Fuck! Held down the button. Fuck, fuck, *fuck!* As the screen
went black, he noticed the call had come from Mac.

Barker mouthed *Sorry!* Ophelia flashed him a *That's okay!* smile.

"In our production, the genders of the characters have been
reversed. The professor John is now *Joan,* and the student Carol is
now *Conrad.*"

The crowd snickered.

"By reversing the genders—"

A BUZZ trilled the space, amplified beyond credence by the
roomy stage. It was Barker again, of course. BUZZBUZZBUZZ!

He'd turned it off! BUZZBUZZBUZZ! No, only turned off the
volume. BUZZBUZZBUZZ!

Tickled the top with the tips of his fingers, skin slick with fresh
sweat. BUZZBUZZBUZZ! Couldn't get a grip. Stuck out his leg, sending Ophelia springing half-a-step back in surprise. Murmuring
behind. BUZZBUZZBUZZ! Groans. An exasperated *tsk-ah!* The
pocket released and he seized the quivering slab. BUZZBUZZBUZZ!
Missed call and text. Both from Baz.

- URGENT!!! CALL SASP!!!

Held the button. The phone piped a melancholy adieu. Back inside his pocket. Mouthed *Sorry!* again. Ophelia screwed up her face in an amicable *Weird!*

"I was going to save this for the end, but maybe this would be a good time to remind everyone to turn off your cell phone or anything else that makes noise, as this can distract the actors, and your fellow audience members, during the performance."

Guffaws. Fine. Fair. A joke at his expense. He'd brought it upon himself. He deserved that one. He was a big boy, he could take it. Twisted, gave the audience a little wave, a salute to his own stupidity. The moment he raised his hand, the laughter ceased.

Watch your step, the new silence said.

"We hope to underscore Mamet's point that harassment is, at its core, an exercise of power. However, we also want to point out that this particularly loathsome exercise of power afflicts women inordinately. This is to suggest, in a way, that an oppositional reading of Mamet's text can help surface these still pervasive imbalances, and how they continue to be calibrated and contested in our contemporary moment. The hysterical woman is transformed into the hysterical man, railing against his slipping stranglehold on privilege and prestige."

Ophelia peered into the house, to a precise point, and delivered a slight nod. Barker knew exactly who that nod was for. Lara had obviously helped Ophelia craft this speech, sticky as it was with big words, viscous with the overarching themes of Lara's course. It almost sounded as though Lara had written the speech (or parts of it) herself. Wasn't that plagiarism? Would Ophelia have been party to that? Cheated like this? He'd have to look into the matter further. If Lara was complicit, if she'd convinced an impressionable student to pass off someone else's work as—

What was so urgent? Had something happened? Had the payment gone awry? Did Baz need Barker's help after all?

URGENT! *All caps! Three exclamation marks!*

Shit was going down. The fate of the city could be hanging in the balance. It would be negligent of Barker to ignore such a plea. Technically he was still under contract. And while he hadn't agreed to be on call exactly, if there *was* a real emergency...

"The Drama Society would like to acknowledge..." Ophelia said as Barker stood and, half-ducking, beelined for the exit. Shiv shot him an incredulous look. Ophelia continued while watching Barker waddle, "...that this production is taking place on the unceded territory of the Huron-Wendat and Petun First Nations, the Seneca, and"—

Barker snorted.

It just kind of...came out of him.

Accidental bodily expulsion.

Nosefart.

Someone emitted a cartoonish GASP! as every eye in the room sought and locked on. He felt the silence calcify, the casting of a unanimous verdict.

Barker's sudden conspicuousness infused him with a surge of energy. He accelerated, and at peak velocity crashed through the double doors, sending one swinging wildly on its hinges, while the other rammed into a stationary object—a startled YELP! A wooden CLATTER!—and stopped short.

He found her smeared across the floor beside the fallen stool. Closed the doors gently behind him, mumbled an apology to the usher, now lifting herself and the stool upright, and—a little bit over-dramatically, Barker thought—rubbing the small of her back. As his phone booted, he surveyed the available exits. One set of doors led to an adjacent hallway, another outside.

"Will this lock behind me?" he asked her of the latter set.

"I don't know."

"Could you let me back in if it does?"

"Um. Yeah." *Yeah* was inflected like a question.

"I have an urgent call."

She rubbed.

✦ ✦ ✦

The door closed. Tested it. It opened. All the better not to have to rely on the usher for re-entry.

Tried Mac. Straight to voice mail. "Hey, Mac, sorry I missed your call. I'm available now. You have my number. Bye." Sent a text explaining more or less the same. Waited. The night had turned chilly. Paced, checked his phone.

- URGENT!!! CALL SASP!!!

Hit the number. Voice mail. *Hello! You've reached the personal cell phone of Baz Randell. I'm not available to take your call, but if you leave your name and number, I'll call back soon as possible! If this is about the pothole on Kipling, maintenance crews are on their way...*

Baz proceeded to share updates regarding two further potholes, as well as repairs scheduled for a finicky traffic light.

BEEEEEEP!

"Hi Baz, this is Barker. Stone. Just missed your call, saw that it was urgent so I'm trying you back. I'm here for you..." *Ugh!* "...for whatever you need. Call me back. At your convenience. All right."

Leaves frittered underfoot. Hugged himself for warmth, phone against his chest. *The ringer's off!* Restored the ringer, set the volume to max. Kicked at a piece of garbage. Checked the phone. Was the volume *maxed* maxed? It was.

"Hi Mac, Barker again. Just left a message and sent a text a minute ago. I'm only worried because I got a text from Baz, and he said it was urgent, so I wanted to try you again to see if I could get through. I have a meeting. I mean, I'm *in* a meeting, and I should duck back in. So call or text as soon as you get this. Let me know what's going on. Okay. Thanks."

His phone jingled. A text!

- How was the show?

Dell. He'd respond later.

Looked through a window into the lobby, the usher and will call girls candleflame smudges behind a curtain of condensation.

Sent Mac a second text:

- Have to duck back into this meeting. Text or call if you can.

Baz. Voice mail. Text:

- Missed your call. Here for a few minutes. Call back!

Stomped his feet. Pumped vanishing billows into the air. Checked his phone.

This is stupid. I'm missing the play.

Reached for the handle, half-expecting the door to have locked shut after all, but it yielded to his pull. Entered the lobby, still soupy with the fug of the recently sequestered. The will call girls were unfolding and arranging plastic tables into a row while the usher kneaded the seat of her stool with her buttocks, trying to recapture a lost sweet spot. Smiled at the girls as he strode through the room.

The usher lowered her arm like a boom gate.

"I'm sorry, you can't re-enter the theatre once the performance has commenced." Barker's eyes bugged as his brain buffered. She was *joking!* Broke into a dumb grin. What the kids called a *callback.* A friendly jab. Her way of saying that the ticket thing and subsequent knocking her off of her stool thing was all water under the bridge. (*And really, who sets their stool right in front of a door? We both made mistakes, amirite?*)

Barker reached for the door. The usher grasped the cuff of his shirt, whipped his arm off.

"Excuse me, *sir!*"

Wait, was she really not going to let him back inside?

"Are you really not going to let me back inside?"

"As I said, no one is allowed to enter once the performance has commenced."

"But I *just* left," he helpfully informed her.

"The performance has commenced."

"Ophelia is… I'm one of her profs, she invited me to—"

The usher composed a face that succinctly conveyed her utter lack of being at all impressed. "*Everyone* was invited. It's opening."

"She's giving a speech, right? So technically the performance hasn't—"

"Technically, once the doors are closed, the performance has—"

"I don't want to… Listen, if she's still speaking, then surely—"

The usher slumped back and to the side, cupped her ear against the gap between the double doors, as her eyes somersaulted in their sockets. She sat upright.

"She isn't speaking anymore."

"I'll be quiet, I promise. It was…I had a call. An *emergency*."

"Unfortunately, there's nothing I can do."

"I'll be *quiet!*" Dropped his voice to barely above a whisper, as if to demonstrate his mastery of, and commitment to, quietude. "I promise!" *See?*

"You may have noticed, sir, before you left the theatre, that the way the space is configured, irregardless of how quiet you may or may not—"

"Irregardless is *not* a word." Another unintentional eruption, regretfully stentorian, possibly slightly contemptuous-sounding.

The usher's eyes narrowed. "Irregardless of how quiet you may or may not be, you would have to cross the stage to return to your seat, causing a distraction to the actors and audience."

"Are you f—" *Easy.* "Are you *serious*? I *just*—"

"There are evening performances Friday and Saturday, and a Sunday matinee," she said, face glazed with triumph. "I'm sure Ophelia would be happy to rebook your ticket for another show."

Stood there, frozen, then started to nod. Maybe less nodding than bobbling, his head a planet with a wonky axis. Raised his hands in supplication. Retreated. The usher flattened her hands against her thighs, straightened her back, tracked him with unblinking eyes.

A respectful distance put between them, Barker turned and faced a wall, pretended to scrutinize a poster for *Oleanna* affixed thereupon. Should he leave? Should he wait? Text Shiv, apologize for his abrupt departure. (Now *he* was apologizing to *her?!*) An emergency, no choice but to go. Unfortunate. Unfortunate. He'd catch a later performance. And they should really hit The Luce some time to clear they air, yeah?

The will call girls had draped the tables with white linens, overtop of which they now arrayed black cloth napkins, offset like diamonds. On these were set assorted foodstuffs: bowls of chips, veggie platters, plates of desert squares. At the far end—trays of red and white wine in small plastic chalices.

Barker ambled up to the buffet, filled one hand with lemon torte and Nanaimo bars, slid the fingers of the other into a forest of plastic stems, lifting two chalices into his palm. The girls, now setting out stacks of red paper napkins, noticed.

"May I?" he asked.

They exchanged a look. "I guess it's cool," Puffy Eyes said.

Barker took a seat in one of the folding chairs lining the wall opposite the buffet. Licked his fingers, brushed crumbs off his collar.

Vaguely Latina caught Barker's eye.

"Those cups are made of corn," she said. "Totally biodegradable."

Barker raised his two goblets aloft. To biodegradability! To impermanence!

+ + +

There he sat, drinking wine, shifting and twitching as the awful aluminum chair anesthetised his extremities. Drained the first chalice, set it on the floor. Moments later, stacked the second on top of its predecessor. Took two more. The girls, off to the side and ostensibly engrossed in their phones, saw him replenish his supply, whispered something he couldn't hear and decided he didn't care about anyway.

Tried to discern the actors' muted dialogue, the audience's muffled reactions. Stacked each depleted cup—*Up! Up! Up!*—one atop the other. *Three. Four.* Fetched two more. *Five. Six.*

Hysterical screaming. Conrad (née Carole)? "LET ME GO. LET ME GO. WOULD SOMEBODY *HELP* ME? WOULD SOMEBODY HELP ME PLEASE...?"

Then: "YOU BELIEVE IN NOTHING. YOU BELIEVE IN NOTHING AT ALL!"

His tower of biodegradable corn began to tilt.

Raucous applause. Hooting. A dip, a momentary diminuendo before it redoubled—whistles and cheers—climaxed, plateaued.

The usher hopped off her dais and flung the doors apart, releasing a gust of heat and sound. Barker caught a glimpse of the actors sprinting back onto the stage, saw patrons on their feet. Their cries and clapping crescendoed once more.

The audience swarmed the lobby with excited chatter. Waving and flapping their hands, twisting and pointing punctuational fingers, emphatic pronouncements of *This! No, that! No, no—this* and *that!*

Shiv appeared.

"How was it?"

"I thought it was quite powerful, actually."

Lara surfaced in the swirl, smiled at Shiv and proceeded right past them, straight up to Ophelia. They embraced. Typical Lara hug, stiff and stingy, holding herself apart. *Like she's hugging a cactus.* Couldn't hear them, couldn't hear anything in the compressed cacophony. Watched Ophelia, watched her lips, watched her gush to Lara, *Thank you! Thank you so much!*

Sensed someone beside him, was almost surprised to see Shiv there, nearly bodily pressed against him in the crush.

"What?"

"You left, I said."

"Yeah." Beat. "There was an emergency."

"An emergency? What kind of emergency?"

"Nothing. It's… Let's not talk about it right now."

"Is everything okay? Your parents?"

Lara returned, flanked Shiv opposite Barker. They started discussing the show. Stranded, Barker pretended to listen, to be part of their conversation.

He silently surveilled the crowd. An opaque pillar in their midst. It all began to blur and amalgamate, animated limbs into floppy extensions. Anemone tentacles. The syncopated appendages of a fleshy assembly line.

I see you. I see you all.

A face. The familiar-looking kid from the theatre, sloped against a wall, jacket draped over sturdy arms.

Barker sliced through the lobby. The kid broke into a toothy grin.

"Sorry, are you one of my students?"

"Um, no. I don't think so."

"Ah, my mistake. What brought you to show?"

"My girlfriend."

"Oh, you came with your girlfriend?"

"Kind of. She's the director."

Ophelia's boyfriend. Her *Instagram* feed.

"Kodi," he said, extending his hand.

Shook it. "Good to meet you. Sorry, Ko-*bi?*"

"Ko-*di,*" Kodi corrected, sustaining the smooth slope of his genteel smile, radiating the sanguine laid-back well-groomed easy-goingness of the comfortably reared, genetically pristine, and self-assured; one of those blessed few, wind always at their backs, who sailed through life on unruffled waters, banging a bottomless reservoir of hot chicks; slipped into cushy, painless, well-paying careers, buttressed by colleagues who gladly took the heat for their fuckups (*Not the sharpest tack, but such a great guy!*); devoted every other weekend to downhill skiing or Ultimate; settled down with one of their interchangeably breathtaking conquests (after many a wild oat had been sown, after sweet, innocent Ophelia had been unceremoniously cast aside) with whom they'd kick out a small brood, the wife regaining her svelte, magazine model-esque figure nigh instantaneously; kids who'd excel at school, were taken out camping, then globetrotting—opulent beaches and remote villages in developing nations alike (*We want them to know what the world is like outside our privileged Western existences*)—and as he and the wife grew older, as age warped their bodies, would take up jogging, then cycling; would tighten, shed every excess shred, advise friends and family that it was simply a matter of finding the right balance of diet and exercise: *Balance*, they'd repeat for emphasis, *is key!*

Kodi would never not be beloved, would never experience, never know or appreciate, what lonely and lacklustre lives the rest of the rabble endured. He'd profess sympathy, sure, but secretly or subconsciously believe himself to be no different, his life and advantages not inherently distinct; think anyone could have what he had—namely *everything*—if they worked hard enough, treated others with uninvolved kindness, and always and unfailingly thought positive thoughts.

Barker hated him. "What did you think of the show?"

"It was amazeballs." Kodi looked up with crisp ocean-blue eyes. "She's a really special girl."

Keep coasting through your awesome life, Kodi. I'll stick around to clean up after your mess. "Yeah." The crowd was thinning out. "Well, nice to meet you, Ko-*di*."

Kodi shot him an affirming finger gun and tongue click.

Barker returned to the buffet, snatched the one remaining wine, plunged a bundle of baby carrots into a vat of dip. He noticed Shiv and Lara chatting with a handsome kid in a pumpkin silk shirt—face flush, black hair slicked back and sweaty. Reclaimed his former post beside Shiv, sipped wine, acted like he'd been there the whole time. Lara was inquiring as to the physical demands of the production.

Ah, so this was "Conrad."

Over Conrad's shoulder, Barker found a clear view of Ophelia. Even at this distance, a dozen-odd feet, he could tell she was absorbing all this admiration with grace and generosity. *A real team effort,* she seemed to insist. *I'm blessed to have worked with such a dedicated ensemble!*

Tethered his brainwaves to hers. *You're too good for him,* Barker beamed. *After that jerkwad dumps you, after you're free of Kodi once and for all, as your pain subsides, as your wounds knit and scars harden, come to me.*

Shiv and Conrad were gone. Only Lara remained. Staring at him. Staring at him staring at Ophelia. Pivoted her head with slow, protractor-like precision, back and forth, the hinge at the triangle's vertex: Barker to Ophelia, Ophelia to Barker.

Stomach lurched. Hands clammy. How many glasses of wine had he…? Looked to the row of folding chairs, but his tower was obscured.

"'Scuse me," he blurted. Dashed into a hallway, stomach seething, throat raw. Pushed down, willed the swell to subdue. Turned down another hallway. Another. Identical locker-lined walls, mesh-inlaid windows like portholes, spying interchangeable lecture halls, seats affixed in orchestral thrusts, vacant lecterns. Faster. Another corner. Spotted the male and female stick-figure shingles, those now-offending symbols of an antiquated binary, secured above their respective entrances.

+ + +

By the time he'd retraced his route, the door to the lobby was locked. Knocked. No answer. Found the nearest exit, walked the building's perimeter, entered through the doors he'd earlier paced outside of. (Still no response to those entreaties, by the bye. So much for URGENT!!! SASP!!!)

The tables had been stripped and overturned. Ophelia was nowhere to be seen. Shiv and Lara remained.

As Barker neared, Lara hugged Shiv.

"Ophelia left?" he asked.

Lara fixed him with a frown, curled her lacquered wax-figure fingers over his forearm. "Ophelia is somewhat upset with you at the moment. Give her some time to let the air clear."

Turned on her heel, strutted off.

Watched her go. Blood magmic, head a furnace. *Smug, cold, condescending—*

Shiv: "What is up with you?"

"What?"

"You've been acting really weird all night. For a while now, actually."

"I got a call," he said matter-of-factly.

"Not to mention snorting on your way out."

Felt depleted, punchy. "Oh, so you heard that then?" Checked once more for his tower. Tossed.

"The whole audience heard it. Because I know you, I know you're too smart to openly denigrate victims of colonial oppression. But for the rest of the people in there, it might have come across as kind of a dick move, don't you think?"

"Please."

"'Please' what?"

"That statement has fuck all to do with oppression."

"What does it have to do with then?"

"This isn't more of the same patronizing, pseudo-progressive bullshit you and I abhor? Fucking virtue-sloganeering? People of privilege proving how heroic and evolved they are, brandishing their self-proclaimed enlightenment like a badge of fucking superiority, like a fucking *tire iron*, out to bludgeon everyone else with it. If we really want to help"—(*Indigenous? Aboriginal? First Nations?*)—"victims of colonialism, we might have to do better than empty platitudes during the preamble to a play."

"It's a gesture, Barker. An *acknowledgement*. Not a solution, granted, but one way to open up a—"

"Sorry 'bout all the genocide and residential schools. Please accept this brief disclaimer *ar-e* the centuries-old pain caused by the ongoing occupation of your land."

"And what is it we're supposed to do, exactly?"

"Well, we could fucking *cede the territory*. Just off the top of my head. If we're serious. That'd be slightly more proactive than smiling and clapping and patting ourselves on the back."

"Please, wise white man, continue to enlighten me."

Beat. "Fuck you."

A bemused grin. Put her hand on the back of her neck. "How was the wine?"

"What?"

"You helped yourself to the wine?"

"That's what it's there for, isn't it?"

"You didn't *ask*."

"Who?"

"The two—*Barker!*—the women setting up the reception!"

"Of course I did!"

"No you didn't. You helped yourself and pretended to ask after the fact."

"This is ridiculous."

"Yes." Flared her eyes. "It is."

"How is it you know all this exactly?"

"We chatted with them while you were…in the toilet."

Pinched the bridge of his nose. "What am I missing here? I said 'May I?' That doesn't count as asking anymore?"

"They're *volunteers*. From her residence. An older man, a professor, comes up, takes two cups of wine, then another two, then *another* two, before the show is even over. What are they supposed to do? Physically restrain you? They're kids!"

"All they had to do was say no."

"And that would have stopped you?"

Sucked air through gritted teeth. "Yes. Of *course*."

"Then the thing with the usher—"

"She wouldn't let me back in!"

Shiv gawped. "You *left!*"

"There was an emergency!"

"Fine, but you left, and she's not allowed to let anyone in once the doors are closed. You can't at all see this from her perspective? You'd have had to walk across the stage, *through the performance*, to get back to your seat."

"I could have ducked!"

Shiv pulled the strap of her purse over her shoulder. "What were you two talking about?"

"Who two?"

"You and Lara. When I got here."

"What business is that of yours?"

"It's my business if it's *about* me, isn't it? If you're talking about me behind my back?"

"Paranoid much?"

"That conversation ended pretty quick."

"For the record, we were discussing my endless meeting with Molly and Maureen, and the quote-unquote 'solution' that has been mutually agreed upon. I haven't the faintest clue why she clammed up so fast. Besides, why would we be talking about you? I thought you two barely knew each other?"

The ground felt suddenly loose beneath Barker's feet.

Shiv took a step forward. "What is it about this girl?"

"Lara?"

"Ophelia. That's a terrible play, but she did a decent job turning it into something palatable. The gender-reversal thing was a good gimmick. So, what is it? Is she crazy smart? Is she your, what, your protégé?"

"No, she's…" *an unexceptional intellect, like most students are at this stage in their intellectual development.* "Enthusiastic."

"Ah." Shiv's face seemed to flutter. "So your interest lies in her enthusiasm?"

"I'm not in the mood."

"For what?"

"Sanctimony."

"Oh, this"—she drew a circle in the air around her face—"isn't sanctimony. This is me giving you a chance to come clean."

"About what, exactly?"

"Barker, you were practically eye-fucking her from across the room!"

"The hell does that even mean?"

Slight bow, quick shake of her head. "Nothing. Never mind." Turned and pushed through the doors. Through the condensation melting off the window, Barker saw her light a cigarette.

Followed. Cold pierced his shirt like quills. Felt his skin go scaly as a shiver seized and shook him.

"It was my idea," he said to her back.

Without turning, "What?"

"Reversing the genders."

"I know."

"You do? How?"

"Because," Shiv spun, "she thanked you for it *after you left!*" Long drag. "Congratu-fucking-lations, Barker. Who'd have ever come up with something as brilliant as reversing gender? Except, I dunno, the Greeks? Maybe Shakespeare? And not like Ophelia did any heavy lifting, hey? After all, she only *directed* the goddamn play."

Barker looked down at the faint fractals of frost forming on the grass. Looked up at the empty blackpurple sky, stars blotted out by the city's bloom.

"Can I bum one of those?"

Dropped her unfinished cigarette to the ground. "I'm out," she said, and left.

◆ ◆ ◆

Still fuming over the parking attendant charging him the full day rate (*twenty-five dollars!*), even though Barker was faculty ("Here, I

can prove it," he'd said, handing over a business card), and had a valid
parking pass which he couldn't find anywhere in his car and must
have accidentally left at home ("It's been so warm, I've been mostly
cycling to campus"), Barker tapped the gas a little too hard to pass
a meandering car hugging the centre line (yes, the speed limit along
this stretch was forty, but everyone in the vicinity knew that was a
soft ceiling), either oblivious or distracted or intentionally making
it difficult for Barker to get by. No sooner had he reclaimed his lane
than his rear-view lit up. Redblue pulsed through his cracked windshield like irradiated blood. A liquid BWOOP! Assuming he must be
in the way, he slowed down to let the cruiser pass, only to watch it
match his trajectory and decelerating speed.

Fuck. Of course. Of all the aggressive and incautious and
moronic drivers in this city, it would be Barker—who barely even
drove!—who'd be punished. All but a minute away from his building. *Fuuuck!*

Ground up against the curb, killed the engine. Dell. It would
be Dell. Knew this with absolute certainty. Would she be momentarily wracked? Could she shirk her sworn oath, placate her partner,
spare her boyfriend? (*Was* he her boyfriend?) No. The law will out.
Speeding ticket? Cupped his hand over his mouth. DUI?

Face at his window. Pressed the button. Glass squealed.

White guy.

"License and registration."

Wrested his wallet out of his pants, gave the cop his licence.
Opened the glove compartment, found the small plastic folder that
held his registration and insurance chits, and handed this over as well.

"Sir, this is a university parking lot pass."

"Seriously?"

"Registration?"

"Just a minute." Slammed the compartment shut, rooted around
in the map pocket on the side of the door, found a second folder,
checked the contents, passed it through the window.

The officer left. Returned a minute later, handed back the documentation. "Do you know how fast you were going, sir?"

"Forty?" he answered. "Maybe forty-five?"

"I clocked you at fifty-five." A statement of fact.

"I didn't realize I was going that fast. I was trying to get around a, uh... I apologize."

"Have you had anything to drink this evening?"

"I... Yes, I had a glass of wine. Earlier. With dinner."

A flashlight. On his face. In his eyes. He squinted.

"Could you step out of the vehicle, please, sir?"

A litany of potential parries streamed through Barker's mind. *Is that really necessary?* Or *Was I swerving?* Futile. A multiplicity of paths leading to same end.

Opened his door. Stepped out of his car.

"Could you join me in my vehicle, please, sir?"

Why did he phrase these commands as questions? Was it strategic? To lull Barker into complacency? Compliance? Make him think this procedural attenuation of his freedom was a choice? *Did* Barker have a choice, a secret set of rights or alternatives of which he was unaware, from which the cop was trained to lead him astray? Like, could he outright refuse? *No thanks! Think I'll be taking off now!*

Second officer in the front passenger side seat. It was Dell, of course. Had to be. This was how they ended. Barker tried to surreptitiously smell himself, skin pungent as a vineyard, every pore a geyser venting fine, fermented mist.

The officer opened the door. Barker crawled inside. On the other side of the mesh partition, the second officer—male, Asian, broad-shouldered, crammed uncomfortably into his seat—was typing. Whitey squeezed in behind the steering wheel, slid open a square slot in the partition, put his face in front of it.

"Sir," he said, "I'm going to ask you to take a breathalyser test. You have the right to refuse this test, in which case we will confiscate your car for suspicion of driving under the influence. If you take the test and fail, then we will confiscate your car, your licence will be suspended, and you will be asked to appear before a Justice of the Peace. Do you understand these options as I have presented them to you?"

"My options are that no matter what I do, you're going to take my car?"

"Do you understand these options?"

"And if I pass the test?"

"Then you're free to go."

"Then I guess I'll take the test," he said, a moment later adding, "It isn't really much of a *choice*, you know."

The officer removed a thick white straw from a cellophane wrapper, fixed it to a metallic box with a blinking green light, passed the box to Barker, straw-side first.

"Please take a deep breath then exhale through the straw until I say stop."

Barker obeyed. The straw whistled faintly as he blew.

"Stop."

Handed back the box.

Thirty seconds passed in unremarkable silence, broken only by the *clickity-clack* of the Asian officer's typing and bleats of bleary radio chatter in coded parley that Barker could only barely decipher.

Then: "Sir, the breathalyser test has returned an inconclusive result. The legal blood-alcohol limit is zero-point-five and under. It is a criminal offence to drive with a blood-alcohol level of zero-point eight and over. The test shows a result between these two levels."

A grey zone! He'd passed! On a technicality, but still!

"Due to the inconclusive test result, we are going to confiscate your car."

Wait! *What?* "Since when was there a *third* possibility!"

The officer gave Barker a business card. "Your car will be available to be reclaimed after twenty-four hours at this address."

"Hold on one second. I haven't done anything wrong. You said I didn't blow over the legal limit, and I'm not under arrest. What gives you the right to confiscate my car?"

"You didn't blow *under* the limit."

"So you, what"—*Don't get pissy!*—"all due respect, you create a…a…a legal, uh, a limbo between what's legal and illegal, and that gives you the right to seize my property? The personal property of an innocent citizen?"

The officer shot him a dispassionate *You're not so innocent, are you?* look. "You may exit the vehicle now. Do you have a way to return to your place of residence?"

◆ ◆ ◆

Condo all of four blocks away, Barker was home in under ten minutes, the card with impound lot address clenched inside a fist so tight it could crush coal.

He was so incensed that all he could think to do was go to bed. Didn't even change out of his clothes, just slid under the sheets and pulled the comforter up to his jaw, tense as an unsprung trap. Stared at the stuccoed ceiling, whole being ablaze with a single word: INJUSTICE.

When or how he fell asleep he did not know, but from that slumber was untimely ripped by an explosion of sound.

His fucking phone, on his bedside table, inches from his head, volume set to max.

Read the screen with a half-open eye. *Unknown number.*

Briefly contemplated hurling the phone against the wall.

"Hello?"

"Bark?"

"Yeah?"

"You *are* still at this number! I cannot believe these digits remain functional."

Who was this? Where was he?

"What it is, Barker Samuel Stone?"

Memory straining to clot. "Who is this?" Barker croaked, his words wind-rustled husks.

"It's Cooper, man. It's Coates!"

CAROL: Well, there are those who would say it's a form
of aggression.
JOHN: What is?
CAROL: A surprise.

—David Mamet, *Oleanna*

2 B

"Shit, man, what time is it where you are?"

"It's uh…" No clock in his bedroom. "Late. Early."

"Apologies. I'm in Australia for a thing. No clue what zone this is. It's yesterday here. Or tomorrow."

"Yeah," Barker wavered between states of consciousness.

"Listen, go back to sleep. Where are you next week?"

"Next week?"

"Yeah, like a week from now. Next Friday? *Your* Friday."

"I'm, uh…" Laptop? Calendar? "…around. I think. You mean here?"

"I'm in town for a thing. *Your* town. I'm taking you out."

"Uh—"

"To a show."

Propped himself up against the headboard. "What kind of show?"

"It's a play, but not."

"Like, theatre?"

"Kind of."

Molested a lamp. "I'm actually a bit theatred out at the moment."

"This is unlike any play you've ever seen. *Hamlet*, but not. It's late. I woke you. We'll connect later."

"No, I'm up." Found the knob. Twisted. Light.

"You predicted we'd see this phenomenon playing out in other media, your agency shit. Well, here it is, playing out! In a fucking *play!*"

"I'm stoked you're coming to town, and it'll be great to hang out and catch—"

"You're going, Bark. You're not *hearing* me. It's like they read your book, dude—I mean, they probably didn't, but it's like they did—turned it into this… It's called *two bee*—not the words, like a room number. Happens in an abandoned tannery. Everyone says it's full on sick. Not to be missed. We're going."

"I don't have a car," Barker said feebly, freshly stunned by the narrowness of his escape. If he hadn't gotten dizzy, hadn't made that mad dash for the toilet… The unravelling of his life flashed through his mind, a parallel timeline of humiliation and disgrace. Dropped his head into his free hand.

"I'm picking you up in a *limo*. Oh boy, Bark, it's gonna be a torcher! Now go back to sleep. You sound like ass."

◆ ◆ ◆

Folded a pillow over his head, tried to stifle the garish kabuki: Lara's smug frown and contrived pity, her polished claw clutching his arm (…*somewhat upset with you*…); Shiv's sanctimonious smirk and censorious *What is it about this girl?* It was a kind of reverse misogyny, wasn't it? To presume that male professors were incapable of counselling female students without unsavoury intent? (*Get your mind out of the gutter, Shiv. She's young enough to be my* daughter.) No, a man's motives were never pure, never genuine. Men could only ever be lustful, predatory; were always already worming their way into nubile pants.

Bilious orange light. His mind careened. The police officer's heavy-lidded look and unspoken accusation (…*not so innocent*…)

Pretty convenient to concoct this *third* category, neither guilty nor innocent. Now expected to squander his time—as valuable a resource as any other—tromping off to some seedy impound lot to retrieve his car, his personal property, appropriated by dint of invented legal limbos. It was a form of oppression. Not of the same scale as, say, slavery—one had to maintain perspective, after all—but certainly on the same spectrum. Mechanisms of punishment and discipline and control. A distinction of severity, not of substance.

Laptop. Navigated to the site for the play Cooper had gushed over. Mask-clad figure clutching a gleaming skull, foisting it into the foreground. Burned into skull as if with a brand—ribbon of smoke snaking up and to the side—was the title: 2B.

Glowing pull-quotes descended in a cascade of ever-larger fonts: "A triumph!"; "A dizzying evening of mystery and adventure!"; "2B has forever changed the art form of theatre!" Strings of stars sprinkled the screen like a Pollock painting.

Clicked on the *About the Show* tab.

In this innovative, installation-art adaptation of Hamlet, *the audience joins the drunken bacchanal immediately following the Prince's untimely death. Like his father before him, Hamlet's ghost stalks the court. As you roam among the revellers, you learn to influence their actions, shaping events as they unfold. Only the most intrepid patron will discover the startling secret that room 2B reveals...*

Intriguing enough. Great to see Cooper in any event. They hadn't spoken since the release of KT2. Three years ago? Not that so modest a passage of time mattered when it came to true, lasting friendship. What had Coop said after moving to San Bernadino? *You can't make old friends.*

Their lives had intersected at a serendipitous, maybe even necessary, moment: Barker hacking away at his PhD proposal, Coop a freshly minted undergrad. Born to West African immigrants, he had the build and swagger of a football star, but despite appearances, zero interest in athletics. (His high school gym teacher had pestered him into at least trying football, but after a single botched practice conceded that Cooper, lacking coordination and speed, and boasting an almost intrinsic inability to catch, was ill-suited for the game.) Fine by Coop. He had a vested interest in withholding his head from concussive encounters, as that casing housed the hard drive of a budding technophile. Computers made intuitive sense to him, so he taught himself LINUX and ASIC, spent his lunch hours designing puzzle games. Many of these preliminary efforts were so cryptic that they were far from warmly received, even, if not especially, by his teachers. Most of the so-called superiors with whom he shared his creations—typically without any introduction or instruction save for Cooper excitedly asking "Do you see?"—either encouraged or ordered him to focus his energy elsewhere. "Like memorizing shit for a meaningless test. Exactly what the Internet was about to make obsolete."

(One academic article read Killing Time's closing card—"Do you see?"—as a critique of Enlightenment rationalism, scientism, the veneration of sight over the other senses. "Killing Time," the author wrote, "asks whether you are one who sees; one, that is, who experiences and explicates the world principally through light and vision and spectra, or whether you are one of those heterodox actors capable of bracketing sight and foregrounding other sensory stimuli, thus invigorating deviant epistemological interrogations.")

Foreseeing the coming utopia of supercomputers in the pocket of every person, and the futility, as such, of "memorizing shit," Cooper persisted in his passion, utterly unconcerned as his grades cratered. "Dumpster fire," he said of his marks, "to the point where they had to haul me in to tell me that I wasn't going to graduate high school unless I pulled my shit together."

Set his "real work" aside, hit the books, and so thoroughly aced his finals that his average jumped by double digits. Good enough to graduate, but not to ensure acceptance into university.

Neither here nor there. Cooper was as keen on further intramural education as he was on football.

Computing aside, the only other lodestar that made high school sufferable was drama, which he chose a whim. Most of the other electives were full, so Cooper signed up thinking *How hard could it be?*

Drama, he soon realized, was a different beast altogether. Reflective of its status in the educational hierarchy, the class was held in the erstwhile boiler room—epileptic pipes and asbestos-collared vents. No desks—they sat on the floor. No tests—they memorized text: Shakespeare, Ibsen, George F. Walker. They wrote and performed their own scenes and scripts. Gum was forbidden, as was the word *skit*. "There is no such word," their effervescent teacher, Roman, informed them. Camaraderie was strictly enforced. "This will be a caring and supportive environment. If you aren't willing to extend your classmates the same respect that you yourself deserve, then don't let the door hit you on your way out."

In the fall and spring they mounted one acts in the school gymnasium before a heckling audience of their peers. "One of the kids complains that performing for that wall of raging asshats made him feel unsafe. Rome gives him this pointed look and says, 'If you ever feel safe on stage, you're doing it wrong.' You're doing it wrong!"

Cooper was a convert. Caught the bug. Drama tapped into the same creative vein as game design, but in a more social, collaborative milieu. "Instead of me and a computer, it was me and a bunch of geeks making stuff together." Where once he considered words no more than a neutral code, no different from the strings of symbols he plugged into C-prompt, drama transfigured language into a vessel for rhythm and intonation, secret subtext and motivation. Playscripts were a score whose purpose was *to be sung*. Memorization allowed him to add his voice to a chorus stretching back to Homer and beyond.

So profound was drama's impact that after graduation Cooper mostly set computers aside and dedicated himself to the craft. "It didn't feel like I was abandoning games *per se*. More like I'd been swept up in a complimentary iteration of the same bliss. Lots of obvious overlaps: the delimited space, the aesthetic realization of that space, the movement of the character or avatar, narrative and dialogue, adapting and improvising and adjusting on the fly, the interactive quality of performer and audience—albeit much more restrictive, at least in a traditional production."

He got headshots done, auditioned for professional companies around town, volunteered evenings with community troupes—working crew, running tech. In his spare time he started writing—shorts, then one-acts, then full-length scripts. To make ends meet, he took a box office gig at one of the city's prestige A-house shops. "Essentially a menial customer service gig." Cooper quickly realized that he'd joined the ever-replenished ranks of aspiring artists persuaded to work crazy hours for minimal pay on the promise of having their foot in the door. "Every company does it. Look around the room. Every admin hack, fund development grunt, box office jockey—like, name your pencil pusher. All young—twenty, twenty-five. Actors and directors and playwrights trying to 'make it.' The companies prey on that love. They're all so strapped for cash, the only way they can keep the engine running is by burning the keeners for cheap fuel. Forget donations and government grants, *passion* is theatre's real core resource. The managers were always pushing that line, what a privilege it was just to, like, *be* there."

Landed a plum role in a professional production. A small part he made the most of, got noticed by one of the more eminent critics. An adventurous indie company programmed one of his plays, let him direct. Noticing that most local companies had relatively shoddy websites, he supplemented his income by hiring out as a designer. This in itself was a minor windfall. After three years he was doing well enough, and living frugally enough, that he went full-time freelance. "Everything started to snowball. A legit *living the dream* period of my life. I thought I was a theatre lifer. I was sure of it."

On the recommendation of a respected director who'd cast Cooper in his first professional lead, he was invited to audition for the blustery AD of a popular national company who was recruiting (or, as Coop would later call it, *collecting*) an ensemble of emerging artists from across the country to supplement her stable of aging in-house actors. Successful applicants were whisked away to a weekend audition to demo their chops. "I knew I was in the second I walked through the door," Cooper told him. "First, only black dude there. They had a rep for paying a lot of lip service to diversity without actually being diverse. Second, I didn't give a shit. You've never seen so many desperate, obsequious motherfuckers in the same room. They wanted this thing so bad, and I was like, *I like my life, I like where I'm at, this I can take or leave.*"

Almost turned it down, but took a day and reconsidered. "Seemed foolhardy to pass up three years, maybe more, of guaranteed paycheques." He was also in a relationship, and they were talking about moving in together. "Maybe I was trying to prove that I was capable of embracing stability or financial security or whatever."

In a lot of ways, a rewarding experience. "We did all sorts of training I'd never done before. Techniques I'd never even heard of." Neutral mask. Butoh. Viewpoints. "All new to me." The ensemble was given pockets of time to collaborate. "We created this thing, this sort of rock opera based on the *House of Atreus* trilogy. It was supposed to be a nothing project, a trial run for something else, so the company didn't care, left us the fuck alone. We premiered it at some festival, and the *a-dee* didn't even come to see it. Like, by filling our allotted hour, we'd done our duty, and that was all that mattered."

But one of the company's top tier donors was there. "We're talking millions of dollars he's given them. Flips out. Buttonholes the first higher-up he can find, says something like, *This is the exactly the kind of work this company should be doing!* We were a hit, and *that* was when the *a-dee* took interest."

From there a perhaps predictable decline. "Now she's in the room all the time, picking the source material for our next project, 'curating the process.'" Cooper realized they were still being tested, their contracts effectively extensions of that preliminary weekend audition. "The people who were the least opinionated, the least willing to rock the boat, were being treated the best, getting the best parts. A year in it dawned on me—this isn't an ensemble, this is *Survivor*."

As soon as his contract elapsed, so did his relationship. "One had nothing to do with the other, but it was a blow. One-two punch." Moved out of their apartment, and—worried about exhausting his savings—put most of his belongings in storage and couch surfed. "I was lost, but more in a nomadic way. Because I was disoriented emotionally, the roving felt right."

In the basement of one of his sublets, Cooper dug a dilapidated PC out of a closet. With the owner's consent, he gutted and refurbished the machine. "Classic clunker up on cinderblocks on the front lawn scenario. By the time I was done, that motherfucker *hummed*." He started programming games again—"On a lark. Better to waste my time making games than playing them"—but felt sorely out of touch. "I'd been doing theatre so long that I realized I'd totally lost track of the other thing." The solution seemed obvious: Go back to school.

"My grades, if you recall, were crap." He applied to three schools anyway, was floored when he was accepted by all of them. "I guess I had a half-decent resume by then. Or maybe they were topping up some quota or another."

Barker's course was the first one Cooper registered for. "The material was advanced in terms of where I was coming from, but that didn't faze me too bad. I spent the first month quietly writing down every name I didn't know. Someone would say, *that sounds like an argument that Juul makes*, or *that's so Eskelinen or Bogost*. I'd smile and nod and casually scratch down *Juul, Eskelinen, Bogost…*"

Cooper and Barker hit it off. Partly, perhaps, because they were about the same age, but also because Cooper was a blast to teach: enthusiastic about the course content, prone to exuberant declamations ("I didn't know it was possible to *think* like this!"), and, once he'd found his intellectual footing, made inventive correlations between game theory and theatre. "We're talking about players and avatars, right? So is the question is, like, should we figure avatars as 'pure' extensions of players into virtual space, or do players maintain awareness that they're playing? Like, are we lending credence to Huizinga's *magic circle*, or are we dealing with, to Murray's point, degrees of immersion?

"Personally, I'd argue that the avatar is mostly about haptics. Puppetry. Learning and internalizing a set of controls; ambits within spheres of possibility, movement and manipulation. If you think about it, console controllers look a lot like the apparatus we'd use to operate a marionette, right?"

Cooper had more passion, more gusto, more insights in a minute than many of his more experienced, polished peers; was the best kind of student to teach: Excited and engaged and smart as shit.

As Cooper found his footing, Barker lost his. A dazed Barker returned from reading week besotted with a new release called *Bioshock.* "I don't say this lightly, but it's one of the most fascinating games I've ever played. Set aside environment and aesthetics—I'd be curious to know to what extent you detect theatre's influence; the *mise en scène*, the music, the use of light and shadow—and read it as meta-commentary on agency in play. So much scholarship presumes this arc bends invariably toward giving players more and more control, even enlisting them as co-authors or collaborators. Here *Bioshock* comes along and says: *Nope, games control players.* We may indulge in the *illusion* of agency, sure, but at any point the game can yank that control away. And all through the lens of Ayn Randian pseudo-objectivism. The world of Rapture conceived as a refuge or oasis for the industrialist to operate unfettered, now fallen into disrepair, crumbling in on itself, leaking, the inmates literally running the asylum. The game forces us to confront these extremes, total control versus total freedom. I've never played anything like it."

Barker had a perfectly respectable dissertation mapped out and ready to go, a bedrock two years in the laying, but the more he chewed on *Bioshock*, the more he lost his appetite for his current project.

"Run with it," Cooper implored.

"Run with what? There's too much there. I wouldn't even know where to start."

"You'll figure it out, but you don't have a choice. I've seen this before, Bark. A tractor beam. A force that rushes through you. It's called inspiration. Take the tiger by the tail! Swing that mother-fucker up around your head!"

Barker's supervisor was aghast, they nearly parted ways, but Barker persuaded him.

Cooper completed *Bioshock* within the week and was similarly smitten. "The question, ultimately, is how do we know we have agency," Cooper mused. "The game says, well, you don't. Not in this context. So why the need to make that point? Why do so many players go into certain games expecting the game to give them power and control?"

Barker had only just begun surveying the relevant canon. "It's an enormous topic, but once you get to media studies, the question seems to be, well, is agency the property of a person, or can it be facilitated or conferred by a machine, especially a quote-unquote 'interactive' one? But then Ahearn comes along and says *hold* on, agency isn't a property, it's about language and social interaction; contingent on how we talk about it in particular times and places"

"Okay," Cooper mused, "so is it a matter of tracing back or sketching out how a certain culture comes to think and talk about agency in a specific time and place?"

The dominoes fell swiftly. Advertising! How had interactive devices been promoted as benefactors of agency, and what kind of capacities did they purportedly confer? Could our conceptions of contemporary agency be said to have arisen, at least in part, from all that marketing? Might agency be not only "socioculturally mediated," but...discursively constructed?

That was good! Catchy. *The discursive construction of agency.* Surely it was already out there, already coined. There was a flourishing crop of analysis pertaining to representations of gender, race, class, childhood, etcetera, in video game ads. Someone must have done the same with agency.

Nothing. Nothing he could find, anyway. Eureka! A goldmine! Fresh, fertile, untilled soil!

What else could he do but swing that motherfucker up around his head?

Cooper, it seemed, had caught his own tiger in the process. "I'm out," he told Barker over their last official pint as student and professor. "This was good, but I'm gonna go make a game."

"Really?"

"Yeah. I've got one. Or the chassis of one." Cooper's serene demeanour took Barker aback. "It wasn't just *Bioshock,* though it was partly *Bioshock,* in that I think I thought of games too much in terms of puzzles, or algorithms. Problems and solutions. I forgot something essential."

"What?"

"Play. Not just play as in fun, but play as in invention. Creativity. I want to find a sweet spot between puzzle and play."

Finished their drinks, left the pub, shook hands. It seemed insufficient, so they hugged. "You're a good man. You opened my eyes to a lot of cool shit."

"It's been my pleasure. Honestly. Please stay in touch."

"You too. Say hey to Tats for me. She's a good woman. Don't fuck that up."

Two years went by in a blur. Then, within a month, Barker passed his dissertation defence, and Cooper released *Killing Time.*

Almost all agreed it was a minor masterwork. Even the title was kind of genius. The villain, Lilith, had been "killing time" by exploiting it as a resource. Players have to freeze time to manipulate NPCs and environmental assets, but this pulls the hero further out of synch with their world, and accelerates aging—ergo, players are gradually killed *by* time. Then, of course, the meta-commentary on games as wastes of time, as a form of killing one's own (otherwise "product-ive") time. Barker suspected the title might also be a sly *Radiohead* reference: *I'm not living / I'm just killing time.*

Footnotes, now, to KT's acclaim: Some charged Coop with rip-ping off *Braid*, another revered title in which players manipulate time to solve puzzles. When pressed, Cooper said, "Less 'ripping off,' more 'fleshing out.'" Further, KT precipitated a lawsuit filed by a company claiming to have trademark rights to *Killing Time*, a different game released in 1995, acquired when that game's developer, 3DO, went bankrupt in 2003. Tellingly, the lawsuit was filed only after Cooper's indie house was swallowed by a much bigger fish.

Not a runaway smash, but KT garnered praise to spare, was cor-oneted with the *indie darling* garland, graced many a year-end *best of* list. Once Barker had finished his own playthrough, he called Coop to congratulate him, inquired into how the game was selling. "Good enough to make a sequel," he said. "So…good enough."

KT2 was both an improvement and a departure. Maybe less so in terms of the puzzles, which were similar in base conception, and not quite as inspired in design, but the narrative came into sharper focus, Lilith is complexified—assumes the role of ally or villain depending on how the player engages with her. But its true bril-liance (or undoing, depending on who you talked to) was that KT2 "remembered" your "age" from the end of the first game, and carried it forward. Most players "aged out" before reaching the sequel's conclu-sion. Your only option—hack or workaround notwithstanding—was to go back to the beginning of the first KT and start all over again.

All things considered, another impressive product from a solo designer working out of his basement. KT2 was met with a level of anticipation usually reserved for triple-A titles released by industrial Goliaths with deep pockets. That may have been one reason why Cooper's fledgling company, Semaphore, was quickly bought out by one such Goliath. Several months later, it was announced that the series would once again switch formats, from KT2's first-person to Augmented Reality for KT3—surely an edict imposed by Cooper's new corporate masters, cashing in on a passing craze, ruining this cherished property in the process. (Barker sent Cooper a cheeky note to ask what it felt to be branded a sell-out. Cooper's response: "Feels like $$.")

✦ ✦ ✦

Not even six a.m. Checked his phone. No word from the Baz camp. Not for nothing, but all that so-called URGENCY had arguably initiated the chain of events leading up to and including the confiscation of his car. He'd be sure to express his displeasure as soon as someone bothered getting the fuck back to him. *And by the way, I'll be expensing you for the impound fee.*

Email. Typed Ophelia into the address bar.

Dear Ophelia,

Please accept my sincerest apology for what happened last night. The phone call that interrupted your striking introduction was an emergency requiring my immediate attention. I hope my actions in no way marred what was so clearly a triumphant premiere.

In any case, I really am sorry for the ruckus, and I'll definitely endeavour to catch an upcoming performance. If you're game, and at your leisure, I'd like to take you out for a congratulatory-slash-apologetic beverage. There's a great off-campus pub called Lucy's that I'd love to introduce you to if you haven't yet had the pleasure :)

And then, without giving it much (if any) thought, and for no particular reason, certainly no reason that would seem satisfactory in retrospect, despite pondering the matter obsessively over the following years, leaving him to conclude that—moreso than being tired or hung-over or otherwise not thinking straight, or any other lapse in judgement or forethought he could fathom—it simply fit that particular message in that particular moment, Barker employed a sign-off that he had never, not once, used in any correspondence whatsoever, as far as he could recall:

> With affection,
> Barker Stone

Reached out to close his laptop, belatedly noticed the single new email sitting in his inbox.

Lara.

Subject: 9.6.

Nothing more.

Nine six? The hell did *nine six* mean? Bible verse? No, Lara wasn't clever enough for code. It had to be something obvious.

Sent last night. The moment she got home? *You even bother kicking off those fuck-me pumps?* That pointed look—Barker to Ophelia, Ophelia to Barker—paddling the air with her shark fin nose. So... this was about Ophelia? Had Lara, like Shiv, contrived some lurid fantasy? These women! Their conspiratorial minds! Life as either soap opera or sex thriller. What was the punchline to that joke? *The pervert and the inkblots? You're the one drawing all the dirty pictures!*

Nine six. Nine six.

Hit *Reply.*

> No idea what the fuck you're

Full stop.

Nine six.

Plugged Molly into the search bar. A list of messages appeared. Clicked on Call for Comments: Draft Sexual Assault Policy. Opened the attached PDF. Scrolled.

9.6. Acts of Sexual Assault Enacted by Faculty or Staff Against Students

This is bad.
Read.
This is very *bad.*
Six-thirty-four a.m.
Fuck it. Called.
Voice mail. Called again.
"Hello?"
"It's Barker."
"I know. I have caller *ai-dee.*"
She sounded awake. Composed. Did he detect a twinge of pleasure in her voice? Was this the moment she'd been waiting for: the fly trips the web, the blink before the spider scampers, the more wriggling the better?
"The fuck is this?"
"You know what it is."
"When the fuck did I assault you?"
"At the Legion."
Jaw clamped, eyes squeezed, free hand a primed fist. "You're fucking nuts."
"You digitally penetrated me. Without my consent."
The Legion, the stool, hiking up her skirt, pulling the thin of her panties aside, his hand down, fingers in...
"You...you *wanted* me to! You...practically made me...It...it... it... wasn't coercion exactly, but it was pretty fucking close."
She sighed.
Fuck you! Fuck you and your fucking play-acting!
"You were drunk, Barker. Everyone could see. You went to get more beer. I came over to tell you we'd all had enough, that people were starting to leave. I sat on the stool, and you put your hand on my leg and reached under my dress. I took it, tried to push you back, but

you were…insistent. You grabbed the crotch of my underwear. I was worried someone would see, so I covered your hand with my dress. I asked you to stop, but you didn't hear or you weren't listening or you ignored me. I'd like to give you the benefit of the doubt. Either way, you were drunk. You're *always* drunk. It only lasted a minute, but it was a public place. I tried to cover for you, for us, make it look like we were discussing the conference. It was embarrassing. Sam saw. He asked me later what happened. I was upset. Crying. I didn't tell him anything, but obviously he knew something was wrong."

Hideous bullshit. Gross distortion of events. Indefensible fever-dream. Sick plea for attention. It was… It was… "That's a *lie*, Lara."

"No, it isn't. It's what happened."

"You *always* play the victim. It's your default strategy. The only way you can distract from what a shitty person you are. You stir shit up and blame everyone else for the fallout. You want to live out some… like you're the princess in some Disney movie." Then a line that he'd composed the day following their breakup, but hadn't had the opportunity to deploy: "You think you're Snow White, but you're actually the apple." Shuddered with a sense of long-overdue satisfaction.

Beat. "I sent Maureen a message."

Panic. "Don't, just…" Skin dewy. "Maureen and I are…" Marrow liquefied. "Give me…" Stomach cavernous. "Listen, give me a day to think this over." Tasted copper. "I'll go to Maureen. Or you and I can go to talk to her together. Just, please, don't contact her before I've had a chance to—"

"I already sent the message, Barker. I sent it last night."

"*Write her back.* Tell her you made a mistake. Or… or… or… tell her you want to hold off until—"

"No." Another insensate sigh. "I'm sorry this is how this happened, but I had to speak up before you did something similar to somebody else."

"I gave you a fucking course to teach!"

Gone.

Sat there, phone mashed against his cheek.

No longer a solid thing. Matter in a transmutative state. Jellified.

Bluffing. There was no message. A ploy. Fucking with him.

Lying. Maureen would see that. Maureen knew him. Knew he was incapable of...

Digitally penetrated.

Think of what you *know.* You *know* her. All those fights. The master instigator.

That thing with his high school friend. Regina.

First certainty: *Jealous.*

The remote control thing. Silent treatment over dinner. *We're not communicating.*

Second certainty: *Manipulative.*

That night. She comes to his condo. Acting coy.

What's that on her finger?

He came to me. Took the train. Brought flowers. Fell to his knees.

A ring. But more.

Evidence. Incontrovertible.

Proof of Barker's folly, his naïveté and ignorance.

Proof that he was, and would always be, a sucker.

Specifically: A pawn in her ploy to induce long-distance boyfriend to propose. Win her back by any means necessary.

Third certainty: *Junkie.*

Tears. *I'm so sorry I brought you into this.* Numb. *Why won't you say anything?* Leans in for a kiss.

Pushes her back.

Face curdles. Stung.

What did you think would happen when you came here?

Vamp pout. *I thought you'd talk me out of it.*

Don't do it! Don't marry him! I want you. I *need* you. I'll do *anything* for you!

Best. Drug. Ever.

And now this appalling, unconscionable, life-destroying lie.

Payback.

Shut his eyes and summoned: the Legion, Lara, sits up on the stool... The sequence suddenly hazy, jumbled. Hiked up her skirt. Was he sure? Or...did he put his hand there first? On top of fabric, or her bare leg? Who was pulling her underwear aside? What was the right order? Who'd been in control? Her hand—pulling or pushing?

I would never... I would *never*...

Pushing or pulling?

What had her hands been telling him?

◆ ◆ ◆

Maureen's office. It felt different. *She* felt different. Purged of residual collegiality. All protocol. All formality. Confessing his sins to an ATM.

"Thank you for coming."

"Sure."

What could one do but submit?

Questions: When had the relationship with the claimant started? Had he initiated the relationship or had she? How long had the relationship lasted? Approximately how many sexual encounters had taken place between them during that time? Was anyone but the two of them aware of the relationship while it was underway? Why had he not notified so and so of the relationship as stipulated in section something of paragraph whatever in the university's code of blah blah? On what date did the relationship end? Had there been any resumption of the relationship, or any further sexual contact of any kind, after that date? Was there an exchange of goods or professional favours during the relationship or resumption thereof? Had he had any sexual encounters with any other students aside from the student in question?

I covered for you! Your husband was sick and I fucking covered for you!

Deep breath. She removed a piece of paper from a folder.

"The claimant contends that you digitally penetrated her during an off-campus event, organized and sanctioned by you, at which several attendees, including yourself, were consuming alcohol, and at which several attendees, including yourself, became inebriated."

"Okay."

"Was this sexual act consensual?"

"Yes."

"You're aware that the claimant contends otherwise?"

"The act in question was instigated *by* the claimant. If there was a lack of consent, it was from me."

"Are you saying you were sexually assaulted by the claimant?"

"I wouldn't call it assault, exactly."

"What would you call it?"

"I have no idea. I'm only saying she didn't ask me to sign a waiver before she stuck my fingers in her twat."

Maureen closed her eyes and lifted her chin. "Between the end of the relationship, and the resumption of sexual activities—"

"*Brief* resumption."

"—did you extend an offer of employment to the claimant?"

I had your back, I was your friend, and here you are aiding and abetting the wolf!

Swallowed hard. "Yes."

Maureen put down the paper, folded her hands atop it, looked him square in the eyes.

"You're gonna want to get a lawyer."

◆ ◆ ◆

Stupor. Overexposed light. Hallway as soundless as space. Heart in his ears like the thrum of a flushed grouse. Lungs a cellophane tangle.

An investigation. Talk to a representative at Faculty Affairs immediately.

What had Maureen said…her caveat from their earlier meeting? (*A month ago? More like years…*)

Trawled his archive. Teased the words, her exact phrasing, out of its recesses like a hair out of honey. *They are looking for a win. Do not doubt that they want to bring the hammer down on someone. Hard.*

In his whole life, Barker had never before felt so much like a nail.

When had he started talking to Rusk? Pencil dot eyes sweating through his bottle-thick spex, eyebrows sprung in canopies of disbelief, railing against the latest affront. *If the telecoms think we're gonna take this lying down, they have another think coming! We'll make a spectacle of them at these hearings. Can I count on your support? Will you be there?* Barker nodded. The correct gesture. Rusk clamped a hand on Barker's shoulder. *That's what I'm talking about, buddy. Solidarity! Brothers in arms!* His eyebrows flattened, he leaned in close to Barker's face. *You feeling okay? You don't look so hot.*

Had Rusk caught a whiff of palace intrigue? Distract him! Throw him off the scent! Barker said words. Words about work, about a lack of sleep, about stuff. Rusk hoisted his mouth into an upside-down U of concern, scanned for an exit. *Get some rest there, hombre. We'll see you when we see you.*

Bert, scarf wrapped magisterially around his neck, a silkish volcano spewing billows of steam-white hair. He and the wife wanted to jet off early. Could Barker cover the last seminar class? *An early introduction, since you'll have them next semester.* Barker bobbed his head in affirmation, extolled the virtues of checking one's schedule before making firm commitments, but would happily oblige if feasible.

You've blanched, Bert told him.

Something I ate, Barker mumbled through a stupid smile.

Fluoride in the water, rotting out our stomach linings.

Ha. Ha. Ha. Ha. Ha.

Leaned in close. A baritone growl: *Not supposed to say anything, preliminary meeting of tenure committee, invite you to make an oral statement, get cracking, etcetera.*

A spot wavered in or around Barker's right eye. An elusive splotch, impossible to track. His family had a history of migraines, but he only ever got this—this aura, this shimmer, this jagged cut. Blotting out his vision in a jellyfish of bright. Not a thing in itself but an absence of things. The sheen spread and supplanted, left him blind but for edges, his world a penumbra.

Had to get out of here.

Plunged into a nearby stairwell. Climbed. Collapsed on the uppermost step. Dropped his head between his knees.

Phone ringing. Couldn't read the screen.

"Hello?"

"Doctor Stone?"

"Who's this?"

Chuckle. "Mac." Beat. "You don't have caller *ai-dee?*"

"I can't..." *see right now. Life in shambles.* "Having some trouble with my phone."

"Shitty balls. Got a minute?"

"Sure."

"Passing you over to Ev."

Rustling.

Evan: "Doctor Stone, my sincerest apologies for the confusion last night."

Last night? What was last night?

"What's that?"

The shimmer seemed to crystallize, a wafer-thin film bisecting his eyeball, threatening to shatter.

"Us trying to reach you, you trying us back. Baz decided to batten the hatches, hence the radio silence."

"Right, listen, about that—"

"I hope we didn't cause you any hassle."

"Well, actually—"

"Pretty major development on our end."

"Be that as it may—"

"They bought it."

"Who bought what?"

"The *Trib*. The story. Recall my assurance that, knowing that pit of vipers, they'd never pay cash for trash?"

"Vaguely."

"Colour me gobsmacked."

Like trying to solder together filaments of a dream.

Evan seemed to sense his confusion. "The *Trib* is paying mommy dearest for the texts. She wasn't playing us against them, she was playing both of us against both of us. We can all blow a fat kiss good-bye to the halcyon days of journalistic whatever. Now we pay off the blackmailer for the big scoop."

"They…?"

"You okay there, doc? You sound sick. Or high."

"Little bit under the weather."

"I was hoping you were gonna say 'high,' but that's just me projecting."

Ground a thumb and forefinger into his temples, rallied his focus, "I can meet any time to talk strategy. I have a three-point précis that should help explain how the use of the smartphone creates a certain set of expectations that we are…I don't know how you want to phrase this…*powerless* might be too strong a word, maybe *compelled to abide by*. Something like—"

"Doctor Stone, we don't need to meet."

"We can talk now if that's your preference. There's nothing incriminating about what I'm proposing. It's all pretty dry, uh, academic I guess. Which is a good thing. You want to skew antiseptic for it to land prop—"

"No, what I mean is—"

"Point one is *expectation of identity*. Essentially the idea that, contrary to the anonymity afforded by the Internet, when we interact with someone over a phone, we reasonably expect that person to be who they say they are, that there is this expectation engendered by the…by *telephony* to use the pompous term. That we are interacting with people and contacts with whom we are familiar, that we know in person. Thus we have a tendency to extend this same expectation to anyone with whom we interact through such a device. Ergo, when someone leads us to believe, through text messaging for example, that they are such and such a person, then there's a sort of unspoken assumption, a *compact*, essentially, that they really are who they say—"

"Barker."

"The second point—"

"Barker!"

"I'm sorry. I'm rambling. I have a dossier that I'll get to you so that you have all this in—"

"That won't be necessary. *None* of this is necessary. It's great. Sounds like great stuff, appreciate the effort, everything you put into this, but Baz wants to go a different route."

Beat. "Oh."

"He's on the *best defence is a good offence* train, and yeah, that train is currently leaving the station."

Aura subsiding. "Okay."

"We don't know when the *Trib*'ll go to print. Monday probably. So we're gonna try to get the jump over the weekend. I…listen, whatever happens, I want you to know that I really do appreciate everything you've done. Baz does too."

"And I'll be paid regardless." Meant it as a joke, but it didn't sound like one.

"It's been a month. Consider your contract finito."

Barker didn't know what to say.

Evan broke the silence. "Gotta run. Catch you on the flip side."

◆ ◆ ◆

Middle of the night, Barker was wracked with vicious abdominal cramps. The pain had a distinct score: rising constriction builds to climactic stab, decrescendo, *da capo*. Twisted into and away from the agony as his stomach clenched and convulsed, but no new contortion offered any relief.

Dragged himself onto the floor and into the bathroom. Squatted on the toilet, released his winkle. The throbbing intensified, but nothing emerged. Innards concrete. Slid to the tile, hugged porcelain, cocked his head like a rooster mid-crow.

Nothing.

Call an ambulance? Was this his appendix about to burst? Should he Google "appendix bursting"? Was he wasting time? Was he dying?

That would show them. Stumbling over my wreckage. If only they'd been there for me, supported me, proven to be true friends. They'd never forgive themselves.

I would fucking haunt them.

◆ ◆ ◆

Woke up on his living room floor half under the coffee table. As he stood—gently, stiffly—his stomach burbled as if to signal smoother waters ahead.

A sore and sullen Barker struck out to retrieve his stolen car. (Technically confiscated, but he now considered *stolen* the more apropos term.) Could have taken a taxi, but he wanted to maximize his foul mood so that by the time he arrived it would be crystal fucking clear what a profound inconvenience had been inflicted upon him. Took transit instead, arrived at the lot three transfers later. The clerk didn't once look up. Adjusted the petulance of his tone, but couldn't tell if she noticed, her downcast face sagging like soft wax. Because she never looked at him, she couldn't register his bug-eyed shock at the cost of retrieval. (ONE-HUNDRED AND FIFTY-FOUR DOLLARS!) Murmured menacing incantations as she processed his payment, but she either didn't hear or ignored him. Slipped his receipt and car key through the cut in the Plexiglas, advised, "Time to replace that windshield."

Drove over-cautiously back to his complex, sequestered his car in the underground lot. Killed the engine, slumped, air seeping out of him like a punctured tire, head on the crest of the steering wheel. His insides fluttered—an echo of last night's agony. Rocked his head side-to-side, feeling the wheel's knuckles press into his skin.

Brewed another pot of coffee. Wondered why he had. Dumped it. What day was it? Saturday? No point trying to deal with anything today. Faculty Affairs would be closed. He should take the day off. Relax, regroup, refocus. What else were weekends for, after all? The prospect of a blank slate diluted his despair. Today would be his free day, a day outside of days, a special, liminal space removed from the regular course of events, while still containing the promise of turning those events around. How? Who could say? But these types of crises had a way of resolving themselves, didn't they? What were those aphorisms, those pithy new-agey nuggets Tatjana tossed around whenever she was overwhelmed, stressed out, angry? *The universe is unfolding as it should*, she'd say. *Serenity in the eye of the storm.*

Okay universe, let's have some serenity.

Texted Dell:

- Sorry for the slow response. Long story. Drinks tonight?

Seconds later:

Extrapolated a trove of info from the deceptively simple glyph: *On shift, way down with drinks, will check in later to sort out a time/ place. I'll come over after and we'll fuck like bunnies.*

Cycled to a nearby deli (*This weather! This* glorious *weather!*). Baguette, Gouda, Havarti, Applewood smoked cheddar, peppered sausage, Niçoise olives, and a mango. Home. Arranged everything but the mango on a platter. Sliced the mango into a bowl, sprinkled it with cinnamon. Cracked a beer. Ate, drank, cranked up his console, roamed a simulacrum of an ancient forest, menaced orcs and wraiths and packs of wolves, instinctively swapped swords, nimbly melded steel and magic, stumbled over secret ruins, descended into murky, byzantine caverns. Hands and controller fused. Time slipped its ties. Drifted. Bleary eyes split the splendour into imbricated layers. Massaged the burning globes. Afterimages splashed into incandescent spots, pixely fireworks, film negative silhouettes.

Another shower to wash the hours of gaming away. Closed his eyes against the spray and steam. As he exited the bathroom, his phone rang.

"Hello," he said.

"Hello yourself," she said.

♦ ♦ ♦

She looked good. Really good. Wine helped. Ditto candlelight. But you had to admit—she was hot. *How did I do this? How did I get so lucky?*

"What?" she asked.

"Nothing," he answered. "Just wondering how a balding, thirty-something divorcé landed a fine fox such as yourself."

Looked away, at the table, tried to tamp down a smile, exhaled loudly, reached across the table with her hands. He took them. *Who me? This old thang? Fine fox, you say?* "What happened at the play?"

"Yes, the play."

"Is that the 'long story'?"

"Well…" It already felt distant. What *was* the story of the play? The most compelling through line? Which details should be included, emphasized, enchained? Which ones diminished, elided, or excised altogether? He'd find it in the moment, in the telling, as he riffed.

"So we're sitting there, Shiv and I, in the front row—she forgot her glasses—and then, the student, the one from my class who directed the play—"

"She has the…she's named after a Shakespeare character?"

"Ophelia. Kids these days and their strange names."

Dell giggled.

"She's doing her introduction, and someone's cell phone goes off. We're all turning and looking around…" Barker, already easing into the performance, pantomimed just that: Twisted around in his chair and looked around the restaurant. In the back, in the corner, suspended over the bar, was a flat screen TV. On that TV was Baz Randell, behind a pulpit, before a blue curtain.

"Oh no!" Dell propped her elbows on the table, used her fork to free a mussel from its carapace, sweating chardonnay cream sauce. "Whose phone was it?"

"It was…uh…so we're all looking, and, I mean, I've already judged this person, right, like *What kind of moron doesn't turn off their phone before going into a theatre?*"

She giggled and chewed. Barker peeked over his shoulder. Baz was doing his gesticulating thing, flapping his fleshy arms around.

"And uh… So we're looking around—"

Her mouth dropped open. "It was yours, wasn't it? Oh no!"

That would have been the first reveal. The first twist. The inciting incident. (Should he have started with the usher? Her initial barring of his passage?) Dell had undercut the beat, robbed him of this first important plot point.

"Yes." Recover. Regain his rhythm. "I was that moron."

"Who was calling? *Fuck!*" Covered her mouth with her hands— had he ever heard her swear before?—dropped them a few inches. "It wasn't my text, was it?"

"No, no…" *What is Baz saying?* "It was an actual call. Colleague from work." They'd jettisoned him, *dumped* him, wouldn't even bother hearing out his strategy, so assured were they of the superiority of their own. "I was *sure* I'd turned it off." Maybe if he squinted, could he read the crawl?

Dell tracked his gaze.

"Randell's giving a press conference?"

"Sorry, I'm… It's that thing…when there's a bright light in a dark space."

"It's really distracting, I know."

"Can I pause there for a second? I'll hit the washroom and see if they wouldn't mind turning it off. I don't see anyone watching it anyway."

"Sure."

Stood, dropped his napkin in a mound on the table. "Don't eat all the mussels while I'm gone."

"I promise nothing," she said with a playful shudder of her bare shoulders. As he moved past, leaned in and kissed her lightly on the lips.

"Mm," she mock-swooned, eyes closed, savouring.

Barker headed toward the bathrooms, checked to make sure Dell wasn't watching, then changed course and approached the bar. The volume was set at a low drone. He read the script streaming across the base of the screen. ...take on "Social Justice Warriors." "Identity Politics" a scourge on the proper functioning of...

Bartender polishing a martini glass. "You want me to turn it up?"

"Just a titch, if you don't mind."

"This guy," the bartender said, nodding up at the TV. "Hilarious!" He found the remote. The volume rose, Randell's high-pitched whinge crackling the speakers.

Baz: "...is *literally* affecting the city's business, how the city runs. Experienced personnel, career civil servants in their posts for ten, twenty years, *fired* for making off-the-cuff comments. Jokes! Not only do they lose their jobs, but we, the taxpayers, lose all that hard-won experience. These people can't be replaced at the drop of a hat.

"Here's where it starts: the *universities*. These once lofty institutions are now incubators for *identity politics*, and the *Social Justice Warriors* trying to shove their warped ideas down our throats. As far as these kids are concerned, the most pressing issues of the day are crazy Halloween costumes and bathrooms for transgenders. They've all been *brainwashed* by their *elitist professors*—"

The back of Barker's neck tingled.

"—to think that every problem, every issue, no matter how small, no matter how trivial, can be blown up"—swung his arms in a giant circle—"into a catastrophe. A catastrophe in which *they...are...the victim!*" Punctuated each word by striking the podium with his fist, meat slapped onto a butcher's block. "Who is at fault for their pain, according to these elitist professors?"

Barker had an inkling.

"You!" Thrust out a sausagey finger. A flurry of camera flashes. "Your fault. The hardworking taxpayer, trying to mind his own business. Your fault for *triggering* them, for making them feel *unsafe*, for not being sensitive to their *pain*. The *elitist professors* teach our kids to harangue us, attack us. Teach them that art, even something as fun as going to see a play, should be *consensual*."

The word hit Barker like a bullet.

"Maybe it's these professors we should investigate first, before dealing with the kids that fall under their sway."

That was it. *The Strategy.* An invitation. Want to lay siege? The universities' gates are wide open. Need a scapegoat? Go after the profs!

Maybe one prof in particular? A trail of breadcrumbs to—

Barker recoiled.

His email to Ophelia. *Consensual theatre experience.*

It was a joke! Clearly. The winky-face he'd affixed!

Was Baz trying to throw Barker under the bus? Pitching a parallel scandal to distract from his own? Drowning out noise with louder noise? Was this all a striptease with Barker as the pastie?

No no no. It doesn't make sense. Corrupt professors and sjws are old news. Besides, that was personal correspondence between Barker and his student.

A coincidence. That word. *Consensual.* Common. Barker was grasping at straws, making arbitrary connections.

"I've never been the most tech-savvy guy in the world," Baz eased into a lower gear, clasped his lapels with his meatloaf hands. "Many of you know that for a long time I didn't have a cell phone, because I didn't want the taxpayer to have to foot another bill, another trip to the *all-you-can-spend buffet.*

"I'll be the first to admit I should've been more careful. I mostly forgot I even had it, left it lying around unattended. I take full responsibility for letting it fall into the wrong hands, innocent hands, hands too young to know the proper etiquette."

A new chyron unspooled: Nephew took phone. Instigated exchange with girl own age…

Baz was throwing his own nephew under the bus!

Mopped at his brow with the sleeve of his shirt, and then, with the swiftness and dexterity of the athlete he'd once been, pivoted into full blown tirade, arms flailing, pink continents adrift across his globular neckface, exposed skin coruscating with sweat: "But for a once-respected paper—and you all know which one I'm talking about—to exploit this unfortunate incident to attack me and my family, not to mention drag *another* family, a *fourteen-year-old girl,* into the muck to further their own ideological agenda, is a thousand percent beyond the pale. The worst kind of ad hominem attack, the worst kind of trashy, tabloid journalism. And it's symptomatic of the larger disease. Make no mistake, this is where this social justice seed is planted: Going after a *kid* for making bad jokes. It's just plain *wrong.*" Baz trained his laser-beam eyes on the camera. "You want to take me on? Have at it. I'm a big boy." Mischievous smirk. "Obviously." Laughter coursed through the crowd like a current. "But," glowering, gravitas regained, "you go after my family? Shame on you. *Shame…on…you!*"

The room exploded with shouting and light as Baz bounded offstage.

The bartender guffawed. "What a character!"

Would anyone buy it? Unattended phone? Wily nephew? How could Baz stomach embarrassing his own family like that? And the bridge that Baz had tried to build—the so-called *social justice seed*—was way too rickety. Would the media care, or gladly traipse across, flee the improprieties of underage sexuality for a more familiar, less tendentious target: Elitist professors corrupting today's youth?

(*…as fun as going to see a play, should be* consensual…)

You want an enemy? *There's* your enemy. *Sic!*

✦ ✦ ✦

There you are, she says.

Tells her he has to go. Tells her he's sorry. There's an emergency.

Is everything okay? What happened?

Out of his control. He'll explain later.

Do you need a ride? Can I drive you?

Nonononono. Just as fast if he takes his bike. Faster even. Really nothing to worry about. Just a thing he forgot to take care of, and if he doesn't do it right away… Sorry. He'll make it up to her. Pinky swear.

It's okay. If you have to go then go.

He goes.

✦ ✦ ✦

Condo.

It won't stand.

Computer.

I won't let Baz, or Mac and Evan, get away with this.

Email.

NDA *or no, I'll find a way to leak it. Find a channel that can't be traced back to me.*

Ophelia in the search bar.

If that prick thinks he's going to get away with trying to fuck an underage girl he's got another—

Two addresses. Her student one. Her campaign one.

Barker scanned his sent folder. The invite to *Oleanna* had come from o.souvene@AlbinoRhino2017.ca. He'd simply hit reply.

We just pilfer from the interns, what they stash in their stations.
Evan and Mac had access to their email the same as their whiskey.

I'd love to attend—provided you can ensure a consensual
theatre experience ;)

The winky-face! Right there! Plain as day!
Seriously! They were threatening to toss *that* to the press? Cut
the emoticon, distort the intent? Brandish Barker as proof of professorial malfeasance? The inculcation of starry-eyed students into his
ideological cabal, bending young minds to insidious ends? *Boring!*
No way that worked! No way that distracted from the real story, not
once Barker laid out his own breadcrumbs, a trail leading to a lecherous old man lusting after an impressionable young...
With affection.
"Consensual" wasn't a threat. "Consensual" was a *flare.*
Wait...
We have your emails.
Not the same thing!
Your casual invite out for drinks...
(*Fuck her!*)
We know what you're up to, what we'll make it *look like* you're
up to.
Not the same fucking thing—
And now you know we know.
—in any way, shape, or form!
Regardless, you still want to throw the first stone?

◆ ◆ ◆

Ophelia was absent from class for the first time. Barker waited in the
hallway after anyway, in case she popped by. He could apologize in
person, ask how the other showings had gone. (*So sorry I didn't get to
see it. Next time for sure.*) Also, just out of curiosity, did she happen to
know whether, as an intern, Mac and Evan had access to her email?

◆ ◆ ◆

Molly approached as he was packing up.

"Hi professor. We missed you at the Halloween party last Friday!"

"Sorry, my Indian Chieftain headdress didn't make it back from the cleaners."

Beat. "Do you have a minute?"

"I'm late for a thing."

"No problem. I'll be quick. Do you remember when I covered for Jacob? I took over his discussion groups the week before fall break?"

Tried to slide his laptop into his satchel. It came up against some unknown blockage. "Yes."

"One of his students, I believe it's pronounced *She*-Shay," she said with the same halting inflection as XiXe herself, "she came to see me the other day. She was really worried I thought she'd plagiarized her paper."

"Uh-huh." Pried a stack of files apart, jammed the laptop between them.

"I think she thought I'd marked her essay, since I was the one she handed it in to."

"Can we cut to the chase here?" Snatched his fleece off a chair.

"Well, she said that you said that in her culture plagiarism is considered okay?"

"Nope," he said, shoving his arms through his sleeves.

"I told her I didn't think you were the type of person to cast aspersions on a whole other culture like that, but she still seemed pretty upset."

"It's a misunderstanding. You may have noticed her English isn't so hot."

Molly winced. "I, uh, told her to talk to Maureen if she had any further concerns."

Draped his satchel over his shoulder, untwisted the strap, grabbed his helmet. "Great." Zipped up. "Anything else?"

"Also, well, she, ah… Did you happen to say something to her about your penis?"

Barker turned and dove into the hall, into the shoal of students, and swam.

✦ ✦ ✦

True to his word, Cooper picked him up in a limo. Bright pink.

"Doctor Stone!" Wrapped him in a hearty hug. "So good to see you! How goes the battle?"

"Not gonna lie," Barker said, ducking into the spacious ride, "bit of a rough go lately." Dell sprang to mind. Kept springing to mind. He hadn't responded to her calls and texts (The last one: Did I do something?), didn't know what to write, how to explain. The longer he left it, the more insoluble it felt. Should he tell her everything: the fling with Lara, the gig with Baz, the blowout with Shiv, the pending investigation?

No. Impossible. She'd see him for...

She'd see him as someone else.

Patience. A remedy will present itself.

The universe is unfolding... Serenity in the eye...

"Shit, brother, that changes as of this moment." Cooper revealed a bottle of Johnnie Walker Blue, unwound the foil, poured. "For the record, this is not my favourite scotch. You can get better shit for less, *ai-em-aitch-oh*. I bought it because it's fucking expensive, and I'm fucking *rich*."

Couldn't help but laugh. "So this is your life now? Pink limousines and overpriced scotch?"

"You jest, but it kind of is. Caviar and Cubans. That," indicated a bottle chilling in a tub of ice, "is *actual* champagne. Like, from *Champagne*."

"You know I was already impressed with your life, right?"

"I'm not doing this to impress you. Well, maybe a bit to impress you. No, I'm doing this because I can. This is what happens when a bunch of corporate fuckbags unload a dump-truck full of cash on your front lawn." Lifted a tumbler of unstable amber. "Rocks?"

"Please."

"Heathen." Scooped a handful of ice out of the bucket, plopped it into Barker's glass. "Salut!"

"Cheers!"

Clink!

"What time does the show start?"

"Ten. And that is but one of several activities I have planned for us this evening."

Twenty minutes later, the limo pulled up in front of a nondescript door flanked by large panes of frosted glass. It looked like an out of business antique shop. "Best Turkish bath the city has to offer. Quiet. Low key."

"And here I forgot my trunks."

Cooper drained his tumbler, put his face inches from Barker's, bugged out his eyes. "Where we're going, we don't *need* trunks." Rapped a knuckle on the partition. It descended with a groan. "My man Carlos. Hour, give or take."

"Text me when you're ready."

"*Gracias, mi amigo.*"

"*De nada.*"

"All right Doctor Stone. *Vámonos!*"

+ + +

As derelict as the building appeared from the outside, the interior was divine. A narrow hallway fluted into a lush courtyard, walls and archways masoned in brandy-coloured brick, primordial potted palms and sharp splays of ferns like crashing green waves. Sunlight streamed in from an unseen source, a skylight set so high it was obscured by its own yield. In the centre was a shallow pond cobbled out of pastel-coloured pebbles, plump fish broke the surface like orange and black tubers. In the centre stood a roughhewn statue of a falcon mid-flight.

Barker took a draught of cool, slightly spiced air. "This place is ridiculous."

"I think that's the idea." They were greeted by a woman with sleepy eyes, a tranquil smile, and creamy date-brown skin. "Good have you with us, sir," she said to Cooper. "Your room is ready."

They were led into a warm, closet-sized space with jade tile walls and squat wooden benches. At the end of each bench was a short stack of towels. The door closed and Cooper began to strip. Barker faced the wall, removed his clothes, groped for a towel behind him.

The tiny room shook with Cooper's trademark thunderclap cackles.

"What?"

"Never have I seen a man work so hard to not see another man's dick."

Barker turned as Cooper cinched a towel around his waist. "You one of those dudes won't piss in a urinal unless there's a partition? Sneaks off into the stall instead?"

"I just don't want to embarrass anyone. Not with the heat I pack."

"I seen the heat you white boys carry. Don't keep me up at night."

✦ ✦ ✦

Steam so dense he tried to part it as he entered, heat polished his lungs—the brief smoke-like burn melted into minty cool. Barker sat on a slat fastened to the wall while Cooper picked through vials arranged on a recessed shelf, like tinctures in a medieval pharmacy. "Mind if we go a little eucalyptus in here?"

"Be my guest."

They sat in steam. Men in the heat of their cave.

"You feel your pores, man?"

"What should I be feeling in my pores, exactly?"

"You feel them opening up, dontcha? Blossoming like a flower in springtime?"

"Uh...can't say that I do."

Beat. "Yeah, you feel it. 'Course you do."

Steam flexed and swirled. Cooper stood, motioned for Barker to follow. Two buckets had appeared in the jade closet. Cooper found a hose, turned a spigot. When the buckets were half full, Cooper set the hose aside, gave Barker a broad, toothy smile. "You ready for this?"

"Ready for what?"

"Hunker down."

"What?"

"On your haunches. *Down* boy! *Sit!*"

Barker obeyed. Cooper overturned a bucket.

"GAH!" A plunge into a mountain stream. Electroshock. A brief but blissful obliteration.

"You feel those pores blossoming now, hey?"

Barker shook off his dousing like a wet dog.

"Now you do me!"

◆　◆　◆

Repeated the cycle twice over, dressed, strode through the courtyard with brio. Brothers born anew from the womb of the cave, forged in nakedness, steam, and sweat. They were the falcon—unshackled and ready to soar.

"What next?" Barker asked, beaming.

◆　◆　◆

The *maître d'* led them wordlessly to their table, pre-set with artisanal earthenware as lustrously varnished as lips. An epic mural wrought in black and white and crimson arced like a comet overhead.

"This one of those places so fancy they don't have menus?" Barker asked.

"They do, but where we're going—"

"We don't *need* menus?"

"Finally picking up what I'm laying down! We're going *omakase* style. All pre-arranged."

Barker shrugged. "Your tab, man."

Surveyed the room. Cubicled in Japanese screens—pearl seams burrowed inside black lacquered frames, rice paper depicting cherry blossom trees mid-bluster—dined a mosaic of wealth and age and race resplendent in costumes of prosperity very much cut from the same cloth. Against all that finely tuned shadow, the bar was contrastively bright—an oasis of bleached-bone marble drenched in white from a row of low-hanging pendant lights. (Sitting there, ostensibly angling for "aloof," Barker thought he recognized a female actor from one of the teen movies—something about cheerleading or breakdancing— Lara had once made him watch.) The open kitchen was a whirl of cooks and skinny knives and sudden spitting upsurges of flame.

"The guy, head chef here, trained under this dude in Japan who runs this hole in the wall in a tunnel. Master *itamae* so famous they made a documentary about him. Dude's so anal it takes four years to learn how to make rice."

The server arrived with a tall flask of *sake*. Poured and left.

"Guy a few tables to my right," Cooper tilted his head. "White geeze, curly hair?"

Barker stole a glance. "Yeah?"

"Big money donor to that theatre company I worked for back when. Bank money. *Millions*, man. This room," twirled his finger in the air, "collectively worth maybe the *gee-dee-pee* of the country my parents emigrated from."

Food arrived: *Sashimi* that melted like butter; summer-hot *wasabi*; *dashimaki tamagoyaki* the consistency of custard, a taste so elusive he couldn't tell if it was sweet or savoury.

"That's real wasabi, by the bye. The imitation garbage you've been eating all your life is horseradish with green food colouring."

The server replenished their *sake* as another round began: salt-briny *uni* served in its own halved shell; pinkish *otoro* filigreed with stark white stripes, a flattened candy cane as oilfatty as *foie gras*; small raw fillets that Cooper couldn't identify, but instructed Barker to sear over a head-sized chunk of Himalayan salt the shade of diluted blood.

"I was hoping to score you some *fugu*, but technically it's illegal here. There are only, like, a hundred or something chefs in the world licensed to prepare it."

"You've had some?"

"Bigwigs from Japan flew in to ink the contract. Show of solidarity or honour or whathaveyou. We have this signing ceremony at my offices in San Bern, then they helicopter me and my board and *cee-eff-o* to this sushi place in *el-a*. Makes this joint look like a roadside diner." Clacked his chopsticks. "They put this slimy little slab in front of me, and all the Japanese execs are grinning like…like toddlers with a secret. Just chewing and grinning, so I chew and grin back. As I'm chewing, my mouth starts to go numb. Hits me: Fuck, this is fucking *blowfish*. Took every ounce of restraint not to spit it out, not to mention keep fucking grinning. Choked it back, lived to tell the tale."

Barker pushed away from the table, let his head hang.

"Pretty decent, hey?"

Brought himself upright. "It's edible."

◆ ◆ ◆

Carlos pulled up the moment they exited. Ensconced in the limo, Cooper sabered the champagne, cheered as foam overflowed their flutes.

Removed a small plastic packet from a pocket, tapped a hillock of white into the purlicue between his thumb and forefinger, held it out.

Barker considered the mound.

"Ketamine."

"Never done it."

"Then you, my friend, are in for a special treat."

Barker plugged one nostril, snorted the bump, then did two more interspersed with Cooper's as Coop recounted a recent trip to do *ayahuasca* in Peru: "Hour three, I'm shitting and puking in buckets. Hour four, I've reconciled my entire childhood!"

They pulled up outside the theatre.

Except it wasn't a theatre. It was an alley.

"What is this?"

"This is the play."

Barker had expected a glittering marquee, the riot of lights festooning the city's razzle-dazzle theatre strip. Instead, they emerged onto an empty side street. A sputtering street-lamp dolloped sugary pink into hovering ribbons of haze. The buildings above looked abandoned and empty, looming towers of dead, oil-blue panes.

"You sure this is the right place?"

Cooper grabbed Barker by the elbow, dragged him into darkness. Barker felt simultaneously stretched and compressed, like his legs had gone stringy while his helium balloon head floated mere inches above the concrete. He concentrated on walking, on manoeuvring his limbs in the requisite ambulatory motions.

As his vision adjusted, people, a whole long line of them, coagulated out of the black, cleaved to one side of the alley, rubbing their hands and scuffing their feet against the chill.

"What is this?" Barker asked again.

Cooper clasped Barker's shoulders, brought their foreheads together. "Remember what I said about your book?"

"Not really," he said, staring into Cooper's massive milk-moon eyes.

"It's just like you wrote. Expressions of agency across the media landscape. This play *is* your book, man!"

"That's...uh...wild."

Cooper took Barker's hand, skipped him down the alley. "Wild doesn't even come close!"

◆ ◆ ◆

Shadow-strewn foyer reminiscent of a séance parlour. Cooper relayed their names to a veiled woman. She crossed them off her list, checked their coats, mimed holding out an open palm. They held out their palms. Into their palms she placed a die, mimed rolling the die. They rolled. She held out her hand, palm down. They mimicked her. She wrote the numbers their dice had shown—Barker's four, Cooper's six—on the backs of their hands, then indicated a pair of black curtains: *Please continue on your journey...*

On the other side they were met by figures in flowing dark robes who took their hands and checked their numbers. As Cooper was escorted off in a different direction, he said, "It's a play, Barker. So *play*."

Barker was brought before another robed figure, face shrouded by a low-hanging hood. The figure grasped and lifted Barker's wrists. A curtain fell as his arms were released, slid through sleeves, head through a throat, into a hood that hands around him straightened. Through this strangled aperture, he saw the figure mere inches from his face, all but chin and lips concealed. "Remember," the figure said in a monkish whisper, "they think their destiny is in their own hands." Barker was swivelled sharply to the right, saw silhouettes in a mulberry gloam. "Show them they are wrong."

Barker's hand was placed on a shoulder as he felt a hand alight on his own. That hand gave his shoulder an antsy squeeze, as if to confirm its substantiality.

The slapdash procession moved, buckled as its members adjusted their footing and pace, smoothed as they synchronized and proceeded through twilight purple. Voices filtered in. Formless sounds resolved into seething whispers, confused murmurs, glottal ejections. No sooner had he recognized the utterances as a stew of text—O, *what a rogue and peasant slave am I... Our last king, whose image even but now appeared to us... This was sometime a paradox, but now the time gives it proof... Offense's gilded hand may shove by justice... O, from this time forth, my thoughts be bloody or be they nothing worth...*—than the polyphony devolved, grew antic and erratic, words twisted into quivering laughter, laughter into cackles, cackling into shrieks. The hand on his shoulder clenched, fingers digging into his flesh. Barker realized he was doing the same, eased his grip.

Suddenly his hand was wrenched off the shoulder in front, as was the hand clamped onto his. Hands pressed into his sides and back, prompting him to stop. Stumbled, caught, righted. Breath at his ear. A soft, "Stay."

Stayed.

Silence. Darkness. Stillness. Then:

The ballroom exploded into light like a flashbulb burst. Candles set in serpentine rows of sconces ignited. Chandeliers dripping glittering red jewels flared. Thousands of incandescent bulbs whirred like incensed wasps. He winced. A banquet! Walls giddy with plaster *fleurs-de-lis* refracting a gauche gold glow across long wooden tables laden with minarets of exotic fruit; muscular ice sculptures; a colossal roast pig, apple clenched in its singed maw. Robed figures in and among statues—no: *actors, characters*—hoisting goblets and chalices, toasts in stasis. Woman bent over the banquet table, man grabbing her dress, faces locked in orgiastic glee.

They'd woken into a suspended second: Drunken feast becomes bacchanal. The costumes were a filth-patinaed gallimaufry: Elizabethan *sacques* like muddied, overturned tulips; shredded flappers shedding their beads; satin *Juliettes* sprouting mangy plumage; soiled togas; ruptured flak jackets; *Cornuti* helmets with cracked and broken horns.

A bombastic voice: "And let me speak to th'yet unknowing world how these things came about. So shall you hear of carnal, bloody, and unnatural acts, of accidental judgments, casual slaughters, of deaths put on by cunning and forced cause, and in this upshot, purposes mistook fall'n on th'inventors' heads. *All this can I truly deliver!*"

Music. A jaunty, off-kilter quartet bestirred, lurched into a sloppy *ballata*. Hooded heads turned. Four phrases in, the hall erupted into a boisterous scrum. Some danced, some ran, some chased, some stumbled and swayed; muttered and cursed and screamed and belched. The now animate man ground his pelvis into the perpendicular woman. She groaned in debauched bliss.

It was the robed patrons who were now fixed points in the festive carousing. Barker felt confused and sclerotic. Should he stay still?

Move? There was so much to look at, so much happening. Edged closer to the banquet table as several robes cloistered around the grinding couple. The man was grunting, the woman squealed, rapt with porcine ecstasy, bodice squeaking with the strain. The roast pig watched with leering sockets. Barker noticed that the mounded fruit was rotting, saw faces in the ice melting in agony. Fruit tumbled to the floor as the couple climaxed.

Some of the robes were roaming now, picking up and inspecting objects, testing their proximity to the performers who, no matter how close the patrons got, did not acknowledge their presence.

One other figure threaded through the ballroom unmolested: round, pale face; crown aslant; peach doublet splotched with blood. He seemed dazed and disoriented, reached out to nearby revellers, appeared crestfallen when they didn't "see" him. Barker followed "Hamlet" as he floated, dotting the floor with a trail of red footprints, desperate to catch the attention of his former courtiers, each of whom slipped out of reach the moment before his fingers made contact.

Surrounded and utterly alone.

Then "Hamlet" saw him. Saw Barker. *Touched* him. Put his hand on Barker's chest, over his heart. The Prince seemed stunned, overcome with relief. "Eyes without feeling, feeling without sight…"

Barker was speechless. "Hamlet's" face shrivelled. Dropped his hand. Drifted.

Characters streamed in and out of the hall, followed by robes in fluid sparrow-like flocks. Barker joined the concourse, trailed a woman in a spattered emerald green Victorian gown—hem torn and dangling, betraying ripped fishnets—as she staggered through a set of doors into a short hallway. He heard ferocious wind as the woman flung herself from side to side, into walls depicting pitched woodlands, a passenger trapped in a tempest-tossed ship. (Could he almost feel it? *Feel* the space tilt and sway?) She plummeted through white saloon-style doors. Barker scrambled in behind her as the hinges chirped.

The room was round, its cylindrical wall a luscious plum. Dead centre and set slightly askew were two top-lit cradles with a man wedged between them, naked but for a cloth diaper leaking brown sludge. Wilted with exhaustion, he kept a dutiful hand on each cradle, rocking them slowly, dolorously; a Sisyphean nanny with two boulders to tend. Infantile wails ricocheted. Several robes encircled the cradles. Barker approached and peered inside. In one, a massive twitching tongue. In the other, a still-pumping heart, blood gurgling out of its broken aorta.

Room to room to room to room, not always knowing what any one element had to do with *Hamlet*, but delighting in every detail; how striking and distinct each environment was; the proliferate objects—brittle letters, smudged pipettes, archaic surgical tools— he could pick up and play with.

One door Barker opened on a lark, sure it was a supply closet, only to reveal a votive candle cosmos and sunken floor brimful with water. The light bouncing off the pool's surface buttered the walls with undulating absinthe green. Below—a sunken mannequin in a shredded cream white wedding dress, tatters wafting like tentacles, a sodden Marilyn Monroe wig with suspended curls, painted eyes pleading, wide with distress, arms outstretched, forever yearning for the saviour that would never come.

Ophelia. Drowned.

Another and another and another. Two men in muddy jerkins and flared jodhpurs seated across from one another at a three-legged *Belle Époque*, encased in an enormous glass jar the shape of a vacuum tube. Between them floated a coin in perpetual flip.

Barker noticed figures sequestered in corners, silent sentinels leaning out of the light and action. At first he mistook them for resting patrons, seekers of momentary respite, but then noticed their masquerade masks tapered into feline tips. A robe sidled up to him (Cooper? Right height and build, but…Barker wasn't sure), and in a deep (Cooper-esque) voice said, "Don't worry about them. They're only here to make sure you don't go out of bounds. Anything else is fair game."

Bounds? Barker thought. *I have yet to encounter* bounds.

Across the room, a robe took hold of an actor's wrist, led him to a second actor who was priming wicks in a vat of liquid wax. The robe placed the former's hand on the latter's cheek. The latter set her cores aside, embraced the man whose hand had graced her. Barker looked closer. Wound round the performers' wrists were thin ropes or ribbons with raised ends. As he continued to rove, he realized that many of the performers had these wrist-ribbons, that the savvier robes were using them to direct the actors into new actions and interactions. Not all of these attempts were successful. Some suggestions were resisted, or otherwise declined. The actor's hand would hover, then slowly sink, and they would soundlessly return to whatever they'd been doing prior thereto.

Scaled a spiral staircase, found himself tromping through sand punctuated by curved bones. A man in a British bush jacket and pith helmet sat on a stool, receiver at his ear, tapping furiously on a black-encrusted Wheatstone. As Barker hesitated, the soldier leapt up from his station, took Barker by the arm, brought him to the table. The soldier reclaimed his stool as the machine chattered, spat out a strip speckled with nonsense words and symbols. Tore it off, balled and tossed it. Listened intensely to the receiver. Tapped. Another strip unspooled. Gave it to Barker.

Stones make ripples. Then Stones sink.

Snatched it back, lit a match, message engulfed in a blistering flash.

Barker retraced his path in search of the staircase, but it wasn't there, or he'd gotten turned around. Dashed down a hallway, swung left, pushed through a cloister and into sumptuous violet light. A forest of robes lined the periphery, in their clearing a brawny robe—Cooper! Had to be!—with ribbons in each hand. Under him were two women, shirtless, sprawled languidly across a burgundy velvet *chaise lounge*. "Cooper" puppeteered them like living marionettes, made them feed each other grapes. Brought one woman's hand to a bowl the size of a birdbath, let it linger until she plucked a grape from the ample bunch. Drew the hand to the other woman's mouth where the fruit was deposited into longing ice-blue lips. She clenched the orb between her teeth, crushed it with a spurt, juice dribbling down her bare chest.

"Cooper" noticed Barker behind him, moved aside, offered a ribbon. Barker took it, gave the ribbon slack. The hand descended, grazed the other woman's arm. She gasped. More slack. The hand slid down, across her oiled abdomen. Sharp intake of breath. The hand trickled onto her thigh. A gasp again. Led the ribbon gently to the side, guiding the hand under her dress. The gasp melted into a moan. A little tug, the taut link lifting silk. Fingers slithered underneath, sank inside. She writhed. Leaned up and over her conquest, as if to drive the ecstasy deeper down. "Cooper" dragged his ribbon, its hand, up onto the woman's own breast, letting her thumb knead her nut-hard nipple, then moved it across to the other's breast. As it latched, her back sprang into an arch. Both women moaning, panting with pleasure, thrusting, grinding, folding into and around…

Barker was drawn in, as if the ribbon's polarities had reversed, as if control now coursed the opposite way, as if they were sucking him into their syrup of limbs and flesh.

What could one do but submit?

Arms on him—grabbing, yanking. Robes staring mutely as his feet left the floor. Lifted, carried—away, away—across the room, through doors, down hallways and stairs. A sickening backward somersault through time. Further. Further. The entire enchantment in time-lapse reverse. Tossed into the shadow-strewn foyer. Collar clutched in a hand, a vice. Stripped of his robe. Tree-trunk forearm pinning him against a wall. He and his coat ejected into the dark, deserted alley.

The fuck? Had he crossed a line? And if so, what line? No rules had been relayed, no instructions given. How was he supposed to know what was and wasn't allowed?

Left the alley in a stupor. Carlos and the limo were nowhere to be seen. Should he try to call Coop? Padded his pockets, remembered he hadn't brought his phone, per Cooper's instructions.

Coat hanging off his arms, Barker walked. Followed the mumbles of traffic, ambled toward brighter, better-lit streets. The sidewalks started to fill out. Familiar landmarks came into focus. The sports stadium's magnesium glow pushing back black sky. Subway station up ahead. He was more central than he'd surmised. Decided to walk to the next stop. It was warm out now. A nice night. He didn't want to go home yet. Not yet.

Turned a corner to find himself thirty feet from an approaching comet—rotund core trailing a retinue of hammered hangers-on.

The core came into focus: Baz Randell. Plastered as shit.

Barker tried to get out of the way, tried to dodge the celestial object as it barrelled, flattened himself against the nearest available wall. But Baz—eyes at half-mast and misty with drink, collar gaping, shirt drenched; coterie cheering and whooping, snapping selfies and shooting videos with their phones—engulfed Barker in a sweaty, sloppy embrace.

"This guy," Baz bellowed, "I don't know who this guy is, but I fucking *love* this guy!"

The crowd roared their approval.

And as suddenly as he'd been rushed and enfolded, Barker was released.

The comet departed along its preordained path.

Nothing to do but rest in its wake and watch it go.

JOHN: They're going to discharge me.

CAROL: As full well they should. You don't understand?
You're angry? What has *led* you to this place? Not
your sex. Not your race. Not your class. YOUR OWN
ACTIONS.

—David Mamet, *Oleanna*

The Keynote

Why did I book this flight?

Smeared across three seats and wedged under two armrests in
the boarding lounge of an airport in…St. Paul? Second of two lay-
overs. A three-hour flight diced up and spread out over seven.

Why this flight? Extra time to polish his keynote in the *very
unlikely* event that it wasn't finished by the time he embarked. Now,
swollen with fatigue, every time he opened his laptop, or perused his
notes, his eyes swam and his resolve went limp as a shoelace.

But when he tried to give in to the undertow, his mind thrashed—
Maureen's ambush, Baz's tirade, Dell sitting, waiting (*Did I do
something?*), the women with the grapes—and sleep skittered off
like a startled lizard.

- Bark! Whered u go?!?

- Sorry. Got dizzy. Went to get some fresh air. Couldn't get
back in.

- U ok??

- All good. Took a taxi home.

- So good 2 see you brotha!

- Thanks for a great night. The play was fantastic. What I saw of it

- Fuckin rights! GOAT! Until anon, my friend. Much love C

Should he confide in Dell, tell her about Baz, about the dossier, put himself in legal jeopardy, risk his career (*what's left of it to risk*), jail even? *That's how much I trust you*, he could say. *How much I care. I'll put everything on the line to tell you the truth.* The whole stupid string of circumstances culminating on the TV behind him. *You see how messed up that was, right? Why I reacted the way I did? Why I fled?*

Even if that helped clear the air, what next? She was police, held a clear and unswerving sense of right and wrong, was innately a seeker of justice, had a mandate *for* justice seeking. If he told her the truth about those texts—the nephew a dodge, blackmailing Barker by mischaracterizing his (*entirely innocent!*) exchange with Ophelia—what would Dell do?

Worse yet, if Baz won, then technically he'd be her boss. What kind of position was that to put her in?

Couldn't think. Couldn't sleep.

Couldn't tell her. Couldn't explain otherwise.

And it increasingly looked as though Baz would win. Nephew or no, elitist professors and SJWs notwithstanding, the *Trib* stuck with the story as printed: Baz Randell had sent sexualized texts to an underage girl, was planning a rendezvous with said girl for the purposes of consummation.

The *Herald*, however, blasted the *Trib* for casting outlandish aspersions on the already unfairly maligned Baz. All part and parcel of a broader crusade, an axe they couldn't help but grind. Suggested, contrary to the freedoms and protections the *Herald* itself enjoyed, that such spurious allegations might merit legal proceedings in the form of, say, a lawsuit for slandering this complicated, yes, but otherwise *decent, hardworking* man, *dedicated civil servant, devoted husband* and *father of two*. And *golly gee Wilikers*, didn't it make so much more sense that the nephew—the little scamp!—had laid his sticky mitts on Baz's phone (a phone we all know Baz didn't want in the first place), had taken his opportunities when and where they came, and indulged in a bit of playful flirting with a girl a few years his senior? One need only read the messages—clearly composed by a couple of kids splashing around in puddles of incipient sexuality. Irrespective of which side or section of the ideological spectrum one fell, weren't all of us *appalled* at how low this once esteemed outlet had sunk? A formerly celebrated bastion *paying cash for trash?* Falling afoul of every sacrosanct tenet of *ethical, objective* journalism? Did the hypocritical guttersnipes at the *Trib* have no shame?

The public was split. Those who already saw Baz as a gross, boorish, opportunistic gasbag, an entitled *born-on-third-but-thinks-he-hit-a-triple* type, found the allegations more than credulous, and accordingly gave the *Trib* a pass for its purported lapse. *They put their money where their mouth was* became a common exonerative refrain. (Midweek, ostensibly in response to the *Herald's* relentless critiques, the *Trib* published a hand-wringy sidebar to plead their case: The story was not only in the public interest, but was of urgent concern given the proximity of the election; ponying up was the only available short-term means of securing the necessary evidence.) No one in the anti-Baz camp was surprised by the scandal, just saddened. Simply further evidence (as if further evidence were required) that Baz lacked the integrity and moral compass to manage a Circle K, much less helm the country's cultural epicentre and economic engine. (And *O! The irony!* of Mr. Randell, so quick to lambast anyone who dared drag his family through his muck, making a shield and spectacle of his very own kin!) If this didn't disqualify him, nothing would. And what a miserable comment on how wholly off the rails municipal governance had gone! That Baz remained a choice at all said everything that needed saying about the sorry state of the city, its leadership, and the unbridgeable chasm cleaving the electorate.

Baz loyalists, on the other hand, swiftly dismissed the so-called "scandal" as the latest in a chain of conspiracies contrived by a consortium of deranged leftists. Here was their preferred organ, the *liberal media*, doing what the *liberal media* did best: Smearing a decent, hardworking man trying to do right by his decent, hardworking constituents; claiming the moral high ground while simultaneously slipping its ethical fetters. And in service of whose interests? Blatantly fucking obvious: The elites! The sneering old money aristocracy and smug bourgeoisie and freeloading artists whose opulent lifestyles and *hoity-toity* soirées required unrestricted access to the public teat! Every stuck-up member of every snooty club that excluded the very proles who made their privilege possible. Those who loved Baz already loved him all the more for standing strong in the face of this latest cannonade. Baz was no mere mortal, but a modern-day messiah, of which this latest persecutory act was only further proof (as if any further proof were required).

As the week progressed, focus shifted from the substance of the scandal—At what time of day had the texts been sent? Could Baz and/or the pings of his phone be traced to particular locations at those times? Did those times and locations align with the home- and school-bound life of a grade-school boy, or the schedule and whereabouts of a certain councillor-*cum*-candidate?—to the chasm itself. What did any given person *believe* to be the truth, and why? "The key question," one talking head surmised, "is not whether Randell sexted with this girl…I don't think we'll ever have the proof we need to make that call one way or another"—*As if,* Barker wanted to scream, *it isn't your job to pursue that proof!*—"but how a democracy can continue to function when the public is presented with two or more separate and opposing, but in and of themselves *credible*, sets of facts?"

Because their competitor had promised not to disclose the identity of the girl (legally fraught territory), or her parents (as this would *de facto* identify the girl), the *Herald*—demonstrating no such restraint—went out in search of said parents, speculated on their political leanings (read: ulterior motives), and whether it was possible they were colluding with Baz's opponents. Following an anonymous tip, the *Herald* published a grainy long shot of a sunglassed woman striding through a supermarket parking lot under the headline: IS THIS THE MOTHER? Two days later it turned out it was in fact *not*. Despite a hasty retraction, the falsely identified woman, after weeks of online harassment, would sue the *Herald* for slander. Coincidentally, she would file suit the day after the girl's actual parents outed themselves (and by virtue their daughter) as the featured guests on a special two-hour episode of *The View*.

The maelstrom had already piqued the fancy of American late-night comics, who revelled in throwing some good-natured shade northward. Though merely a municipal election, *The Daily Show* declared the entire country an *Icicle Republic*—"We're pretty sure that's the only kind of fruit that grows up there"—while another host quipped that the scandal gave whole new meaning to the term *beaver trap*. A panel show guest asked of her coterie, "Are we really buying this? The whole *my nephew did it* excuse?" Another panellist: "You're ten, you live in an igloo. What are your options? Hockey or sexting? I'd take sexting any day of the week."

Gracing every screen: The same close-cropped pic of Baz's goofy, raw steak face garnished with a shock of corn silk spikes. *See*, the photo declared, *those Canuckleheads are as hopelessly clown shoes as anyone!*

There was so much to pick apart and pillory, so captivated was the public's attention, so enraptured was the media with its own reflection, that no one seemed especially interested in flushing any *elitist professors* out of the brush. The media would get back to stoking outrage over identity politics in due time, but for now why bother with a busker when the circus was in full swing?

Barker had started to wonder whether the whole *elitist profes-sors* thing was simply sabre rattling. Not a signal intended to spook him, but a dog whistle to rally Baz's base. Or maybe a faltered mis-sile from a larger fusillade, launched only to fall harmlessly into the ocean. As Evan had indicated, maybe the campaign had simply pan-icked, thrown everything at the wall to see what stuck.

If, on the other hand, it *was* a flare, then...it worked.

Twisted onto his other side, armrests slicing into his chest and thighs. Why had he booked this flight?

Because it was the cheapest one. Because it was the best deal.

A moment, a glorious moment of melting into mucoid black...

...a voice beckoned. The tendrils broke, released him. He surfaced.

The intercom. An announcement. His flight was boarding.

Pried himself loose. Sat spread-legged kneading his face.

Couldn't sleep. Couldn't think. Couldn't write.

His keynote, his forty-five minute vacuum in space.

How long was this last leg? An hour?

They're counting on me. My friends are counting on me.

Retrieved his carry-on from under a seat, waited for the voice to call his zone.

◆　◆　◆

Why did I take public transit?

The route had looked straightforward enough when marking it out online. Exit at the far end of the airport, catch the bus, eleven stops, disembark, head left, ten-odd minute walk to the hotel. He'd printed off the Google map, highlighted his terminus, and now vigi-lantly watched the digital display as the bus lurched fitfully forward.

Two stops. Three.

After the airport came kitsch and decay. Sultry neon fronts for liquor stores and pizza shacks, asphalt pocked and crumbly as sandstone, incongruous curbs glancing off one another like crooked black teeth.

Four stops. Five.

Having heard nothing further from Maureen—and starting to resent her for her silence, for stranding him in uncertainty—Barker continued to teach. (Ophelia returned after her uncharacteristic absence, but did not wait for him in the hallway after.) He'd spoken with a spritely-sounding woman at Faculty Affairs who confirmed that yes, they'd been notified of the investigation, told Barker not to worry, to hold tight, assured him that they—probably she herself— would be in touch in the next few days. *So sorry you're going through this,* she added in a (mawkish?) tone. *We hate to see any of our members unfairly preyed upon.*

Six stops. Seven.

Even the listservs had gone strangely quiet. Barker half-suspected he'd been lanced, his name stricken from the roster, the larger project of his banishment, his culling from the herd, already underway.

Eight stops. Nine.

The exception to his barren inbox was an invitation to attend an open forum entitled "Othering, Secularism, and Freedom of Speech," with Molly Ellen Clarke presiding, and Shiv listed as a "guest presenter." (Presumably the quote-unquote "solution" she'd mentioned at *Oleanna.*) Skimmed it:

> ...recent events that led to the cancellation of...harvest open, honest, and supportive dialogue surrounding neo-colonial preconceptions...activated audience format in which attendees are invited to comment on the proceedings in real time...

An alarm sounded in the back of his brain. He should contact Shiv, make sure she knew what she was getting herself into, what "comment on the proceedings in real time" meant. But they still weren't speaking, the catalyst of their current impasse being a similarly guileless offer of support. No, she'd made herself very clear: Shiv would fight her own battles, and Barker should back the fuck off.

Ten.

The bus pulled into a roundabout and idled. The digital display read LAST STOP. Confused, Barker fought the undertow of exiting passengers to reach the driver, who confirmed that yeah, they'd passed his stop a while back. Get off here and wait for the number such and such, then ask that driver to let him off at so and so, though if he watched for it, he'd definitely see the sign for his hotel. Hard to miss.

Why had he taken public transit? It was his first time in Vegas. The city had never held any especial appeal. He hated gambling, harboured little interest in overripe singers, circus acts he could see in his home country, or magicians. (Though he was considering splurging on a ticket to see the Rio's resident duo, Penn & Teller, more meta-magicians than magicians proper.) Weren't walking and public transit the best ways to get the lay of the land, revealing hidden sights and secret side streets one might not otherwise chance upon?

Wrested his carry-on off the rack and disembarked. The sky was a purple-grey smudge. A delirious wind snapped dust and debris through the air, flustered palm fronds like ripped flags. Barker huddled against a concrete wall, his only companion a young man in a hooded sweatshirt and enormous jeans that parachuted to the ground like elephant legs. The man paced while embroiled—as his half of the phone conversation implied—in a distressing interpersonal drama. He was sweet on some young lady, but said lady had engaged in sexual relations with another man, the very man, apparently, with whom he spoke presently.

"Nigger, wait. Wait, that *ain't* what this is."

Barker shrank from the word as if from a threatened slap.

"Nigger, *please*, she for *sharing*. She for *sharing*. But not in my house, nigger. That's *my* house!"

Ah, the crux! It was not the betrayal itself, but rather the location in which the indiscretion had transpired that had sparked the man's ire.

As the half-conversation continued, Barker melted into the nearest available shadow and listened as the man uttered *that word* with abandon, as its frivolous invocation oozed centuries of ugliness. Leavened through repetition, the word started to sound sublime, almost like spoken-word poetry. Barker nearly laughed at the thought, but strangled the emission in his throat, lest he draw any unwanted attention.

Why public transit? Because a cab would have charged him thirty bucks for the same trip he could take for two. To say nothing of encountering a few of Vegas' native sons in the process.

It was ethnography. He was an ethnographer. Of what, exactly, he did not yet know.

◆ ◆ ◆

Why did I book this room?

Drenched in gaudy *Mexicana*, like an exploded souvenir shop. Honey-mustard walls dripping with sombreros and decorative plates depicting that enraptured flautist with the hedgehog spikes— *Kokopelli* the brochure informed him, *god of fertility!*—under an army of crucifixes.

Why this room? Because it was part of the package. With the flight, a pittance per night. Because by the time he'd gotten his shit together, the conference rates at the Rio had elapsed.

Unpacked. Took the elevator downstairs. Bought a donut and a Big Mac and—ducking inside a liquor kiosk as the clerk lowered its gate—three 24oz bottles of Corona, two Heinekens, and a two-six of spiced rum.

Back upstairs he checked his phone. Nothing more from Dell, her Did I do something? already sunken out of sight.

Put his phone on silent, piled a mound of faux chinchilla fur pillows, stretched his legs over lines of rust and tan and turquoise criss-crossing his duvet. Before tucking in, powered on the flat-screen television mounted on the wall, sifted through the available channels, located a cable news outlet, and watched Baz Randell win the election in a landslide.

+ + +

Slept in fits and starts (by that point better than nothing), awoke surly and sore, stomach leaden from travel and junk food.

Showered and shaved. Hit the McDonald's for coffee and Egg McMuffins (his gut burbled in protest, but he overruled it, citing a distinct lack of options, and the 2-for-1 coupon he'd found on the counter next to his door), struck out for the conference.

These streets were not made for walking. A ways north of the Strip proper, he kept having to cross from sidewalk to sidewalk to skirt the rampant construction. Passed one half-finished edifice—gleaming bronze and sinister tint, sprigs of rebar shooting out of pilings like broken veins—that filled him with a special dread. An altar to a dark, destructive god; to ego, malice, ignorance.

Shuddered. Forged ahead.

The Strip was amok with lunatic facades and lurid doppelgängers of other, better times and places—the Eiffel Tower! Caesar's Palace!— each cartoonish tinker-toy imitation bringing into brash relief how *not* those things they were.

Strewn throughout the gloss and glitter were the desperate and disabled—shucking-and-jiving, murdering instruments, working sodden puppets. A running disclaimer that America, for all its rapturous overtures to freedom, was one of the least free countries on earth, especially if you had the misfortune of being born, or otherwise ending up, poor.

Escaped Caesar's by exiting into a maintenance bay. Slipped through a loose fence, found a sidewalk that steered him under a freeway. As he emerged from out the underpass, the Rio rose on the other side of an ocean-sized parking lot.

Wound through a smoky maze of slot machines before emerging into a concourse and spotting the registration desk. The first set of panels was already underway, and the hallway empty save for a few stragglers crouched over laptops, and someone affixing signs—"This Washroom is Now UNISEX for Your Comfort"—over every pair of pictographs. Found an impeccably polished samovar, helped himself to coffee. Relayed his name to the woman at the desk. Received a lanyard and program. "If you move to the next table," the woman informed him, "you can select your preferred pronoun badge."

The table was laden with sheets of oval stickers:

He/Him/His
She/Her/Hers
They/Them/Theirs

and a blank write-in sticker. Behind him he heard the woman say to her colleague, "I don't know why they say preferred. Isn't your pronoun just your pronoun?" Barker peeled off one of each of the stickers, stuck them to the back of his program.

The first tier of panels wrapped up. Jabbering blocs of the studious and scholarly, in suits and skirts and skinny jeans, filled the hall, promiscuous light sparked off lanyards, smartphones, and spectacles. Heard someone call his name, turned to see Hannah split off from a coterie. He closed the gap. They embraced.

"If it isn't homecoming king of nerd prom!"

As soon as the exchange of pleasantries was underway, Alessandro appeared. They shook hands and patted each other's shoulders. "I am so happy to see you," he declaimed. "It is only too bad you couldn't join us last night for the kick-off. Much wine was drank, and we were given tickets to see the performance of magic!"

Barker glanced at Hannah, her cinnamon-brown curls newly streaked with grey. "Penn and Teller," she confirmed with a grimace, brandishing that adorable gap between her two front teeth. "I'm sorry, I know you wanted to see them. The hotel gave us comps at the last minute. All you need to do, apparently, is throw them an ungodly amount of money and they'll spring for a few tickets to the house act."

"No worries," Barker said, swallowing his disappointment. "How were they?"

"Magnificent! True performers. Expert command of the audience. Masters of their craft."

"Alessandro, you're supposed to play it down a little."

"Ah," he exclaimed, cluing in. To Barker: "An awful waste of time. The best I can say is the ticket was free."

Barker's eyes pricked with tears.

"They perform most nights," Alessandro continued, "so if your desire is to see shitty magic shows, then you should have ample opportunity to do so."

"Okay," Hannah giggled, "that's laying it on a little thick."

"Besides, *they* are not the feature attraction of this hotel." Alessandro waved his hands at Barker, like a game show host revealing the grand prize. "*You* are!"

◆ ◆ ◆

Their triumvirate, origin and organizers, loitered in the hallway drinking coffee and catching up. When the second set of panels let out, they joined a pilgrimage en route to the food court. Alessandro rejected Barker's suggestion of the all-you-can-eat buffet. "This is better," he asserted. "They have very good...what is the name of that Vietnamese soup?"

After lunch, Hannah scampered off to tackle admin work, so Barker joined Alessandro for a workshop titled *Agentic Media in Marginalized Communities*, which guest-featured two tanned, thirty-something Coloradans who'd just returned from a trip installing solar panels in remote El Salvadorian villages. They wore bushy beards and ragged tees and seemed to feel as conspicuously underdressed as they were. The blond one with buggy eyes explained that they'd flown direct to Vegas, hadn't done a proper load of laundry in over a month, and apologized for any strange stains or smells they'd inadvertently smuggled into the room. The audience snickered. One woman even clapped. The Coloradans exchanged a look: *Where the fuck are we right now?*

After thanking them for their presentation, an androgynous

prof in an eggplant blazer, ears riddled with cuffs and plugs, asked the brown-haired one with the bald spot and frayed dreds in what ways he considered the installation of the panels—a medium that "read" one form of energy (i.e., sunlight), and translated it into another (i.e., electricity), albeit not without a significant degree of *biopower* (i.e., the men themselves)—to constitute a conferral of agency (i.e., enabling previously unknown capacities to act)? Dreds nodded and looked down at his shoes. "I guess that, uh, these people didn't have electricity. So...any capacity that requires electricity, I guess." The prof thanked him profusely for his insight, for everything he and his partner had done in service of disadvantaged peoples in developing countries. This incited an extended discussion concerning whether the words *disadvantaged* and/or *developing* were condescending and/or derogatory. "Against what metric do we gauge what does or doesn't constitute an 'advantage,'" someone asked, "and how does that exhume our neo-colonial biases?" As the assembled filed out of the stuffy room, Barker saw someone approach Buggy Eyes to ask if there weren't ableist attitudes afflicting their cause. "Are we to assume that only people such as yourselves, who have the capacity *to* install solar panels, can or should be enlisted to do so in...uh...such communities in such parts of the world?"

After chatting with a beanpole sporting a trim beard and fat onyx frames—"I take pictures of people taking pictures. It's a sort of ethnography of ethnography, or a documentation of documentation. I like to turn the gaze upon the gazer"—Barker begged off to find a quiet spot to "touch up" his keynote, assuring Alessandro that he'd meet him and Hannah for a quick dinner beforehand.

After a half-hour of aimless wandering, Barker spotted a craft brewery in a strip mall. Disrupted a game of beer pong as he entered. Took a stool. A lanky Asian woman with a British accent slid behind the bar, plied him with samples, indexed flavour profiles. *You might detect orange or grapefruit... Dark chocolate finish with a hint of cardamom...*

He ordered the one with the highest alcohol content.

She asked him where he was from. He told her he wasn't sure. Born in one city, spent most of his childhood in another, then flung across the country just in time to be mauled by puberty. Spent a year living abroad. Traipsed out the Coast for his PhD. Returned to the city of his birth for work, expecting to feel a long lost sense of connection. Hadn't. So…he couldn't really say he was *from* a particular place. Further, this question…he'd never been able to answer it properly, despite it being an inevitable staple of small talk. The asking made him anxious. Not because there was no answer, but because it was complicated, and complexity was not what the asker expected.

There was a lot to be said for these sorts of expectations—things you're supposed to say, to do, to be, and how fucking weird it felt not to be or do or say those things. One became an outlier not only by deviating from norms, but because norms deviated from them; denied the ease of stable ground, left stranded as continents of thought and truth regrouped.

This was maybe the foremost misunderstanding about control: That control isn't always or mostly a matter of force, but estrangement. Making the other alien so that they will crave familiarity. Control is a poison we swallow to metastasize semblance. Only by belonging— so we think—can we hold back the creeping edge where annihilation lives, muzzle the fear of how flimsy it all is: Our shared ellipsis; this mad dream that the jungle will somehow relent, will refuse to swallow us all.

The question *Where are you from?* being one tiny example. *We are all* from *somewhere, so you must be* from *somewhere too.* See? Be one of the multitude who *are from*, and as such are authorized to inquire unto others' *fromness.*

Told her about this book he'd read once, a book so good he had to stop reading it. Bad things were about to happen to one of the main characters—you saw it coming, his inevitable disgrace—and Barker couldn't bear to continue. Told her about this one part that described people with peripatetic existences, how they were defined less by *place*, and more by *events*; how hard that had hit him. Like the author had revealed a hidden truth, as internal to him as breath. He'd been mounded puzzle pieces, and here was the picture on the box! What a delightfully existential sensation that was. *I too am concocted, a set of (selectively edited) stories ("…shading into one another…")* I *tell myself about myself!* But dangerously open to interpretation. His deepest, darkest fear, in fact, was losing the thread of his own narrative, having his story hijacked, being left illegible.

Maybe, he offered, instead of asking *Where are you from?*, people should ask What *are you from?* What events made you who you are? What stories do you tell to make yourself make sense, to both yourself and others?

Actually, he didn't say any of that. When the lanky Asian woman with the British accent asked him where he was from, he said, "Canada."

She said, "Cool."

He wondered if the pun was intended.

She went back to beer pong.

Inspiration struck. Barker reached over the bar, stole a napkin off a stack and a Sharpie from its pint glass quiver, and drew.

◆ ◆ ◆

Met Alessandro and Hannah at a Mexican restaurant. They ordered sugary drinks that looked like giant Cretaceous-era plants in bloom. Hannah excused herself to go to the bathroom.

"How was your flight?" Alessandro asked.

Thinking of the man at the bus terminal, Barker smiled to himself. "Good."

"This is a distinctly *American* beverage," Alessandro said. "Not only the preposterous size, but the tiny umbrella that adorns it. Invented in the States, you know? Not the umbrella itself, of course, which dates back to ancient China, maybe Egypt, but this tiny umbrella, this unnecessary…what would you say? Garnish? Crafted by a bartender in Hawaii, or so the legend goes."

Hannah returned, sat, sucked neon orange off of her toothpick shaft. "So," she said to Barker, "what's with putting a fatuous, inebriated tyrant in charge of your city?"

◆ ◆ ◆

People filtered into the lecture hall as a technician in a black tee and saggy jeans gave Barker the rundown.

"This is the volume control panel for the LAV, these digital sliders here. Are you using a LAV?"

With its raked seating, the auditorium appeared more intimate and compact than its capacity suggested. "No," Barker said.

"Oh." Saggy Jeans took a moment, his lingering hand stroking the panel as it shut down. Used his fingers as a spindle to coil the mic cable. "Do you have your *u-ess-bee?* I can load up your Power Point."

"I don't have a Power Point."

"Prezi?"

"Nope."

Scrunched his eyes. Scratched his belly. "Were you running anything through the projectors at all, because we should probably get those humming?"

"I'm not projecting anything."

Puffed his cheeks, released the pent up air in a gust. "All right. I'm 'a go crush a butt, then I'll be sitting in that corner doing literally nothing. Send up a flare if you need me for anything."

Barker took a seat in the front row, his back to the bleachers as they filled out. Minutes later Hannah claimed the lectern. The crowd hushed.

"Good evening everyone. Thank you so much for joining us here, at the fabulous Rio All Suite Hotel and Casino for the sixth annual Media, Communication, and Agency Conference."

Applause.

"Many of you have travelled from near and far to join us tonight. First off, I'd like to thank the hotel staff for their help and assistance. It's been a blessing to host our conference at such a supportive venue.

"As you've all no doubt inferred, the theme of this year's conference—Agency in Games, Gaming, and Play—was inspired by the acclaimed book penned by our keynote speaker, Doctor Barker Stone. Barker's key claim is that our contemporary conception of agency is a chiefly discursive phenomenon; discourse such as the advertising that attended the advent and ascendance of video games.

"*Agency in Play* is as inspired as it is contentious, and has incited acclaim and debate in equal measure. As a sidebar, if you buy Barker a beer, I'm sure he'd be happy to explain how he was in no way suggesting that media control people."

She flashed him a nervous smile, a wink between friends.

Smiled back.

"Barker's monograph sent the conversation surrounding media and agency spiralling in new, fascinating, and generative directions, and has had an indelible impact on how agency is analyzed and interrogated in our field. And as if that weren't impressive enough, Barker was integral to the founding of this conference, and has been a principal organizer throughout its short but hectic history.

"Please join me in extending a very warm, and very *overdue*, welcome to Doctor Barker Stone."

Hannah ceded the platform, joined in the applause. Barker stood, turned—a respectable three-quarters full—and clamped onto the lectern's sides.

"Hi. This is my first ever time in Vegas, and I think the nicest thing I can say is that it has wholly confirmed everything I anticipated hating about it."

Couple chuckles.

"All standard thank yous apply: conference organizers, hotel staff, all of you for being here."

Patted the breast of his suit jacket.

"I originally planned to talk about the latest *Killing Time*, which has proven something of a craze among today's youth. But I haven't gotten around to playing it yet. In fact, my only exposure to the game thus far was an engrossed teenager stumbling onto the bike path in front of me, nearly killing both of us in the process. True story."

Silence.

"I wanted to say..."

This is all a sham. I'm a sham.

Cocked his head.

Admit it. Strike a match and bolt.

Looked up at the lights.

Burn the motherfucker down.

"...what a privilege it is to be here tonight."

Confronted his tribe.

"I hear that word a lot these days. Maybe it's always been there, always been so often uttered, but my ears are only now newly attuned to it. Like when you buy a car, and suddenly see that car on the road everywhere. Was it always so ubiquitous, or does it only seem so now because I am myself inside of it?

"A word, category, construct. An inflection point. The axis around which everything purportedly wrong with our world now turns.

"What privilege brought me here—to this conference, this lectern, this position of prestige? I had the privilege of being born white, straight, and male in a time and place that puts a premium on those things. Their value may be depreciating, but they are still worth an inordinate amount by any measure. I was raised by smart, successful parents who were ready and willing to have me, loved and supported me, read to me from a very young age, put me in music lessons and sports, had high expectations of my intellect and diligence, trusted me with considerable latitude. It took me a long time to recognize how special that is. Most should be so lucky.

"I had the privilege of growing up in a stable home in a safe neighbourhood in a peaceful country with universal health care, regulated banks, gun control, and affordable post-secondary education.

"I have the privilege of a nice condo, a slick bicycle, a passport and the resources to travel. I am privileged to stand on sidewalks, sit in coffee shops, and exercise my right to vote unmolested.

"These are but a tiny handful, I'm certain, of the innumerable other blessings and buffs that I inherited or claimed, or were bequeathed or have otherwise accrued to me, through little to no effort of my own."

The audience appeared to dim.

"My privilege is real. I don't dispute it. I like that we're having this conversation. It has not been pleasant, but it is overdue. I appreciate having been brought into a fuller awareness of my privilege, how I've been shaped by it, profited from it. We should acknowledge, and unpack, and analyze, and—yes—*check* our privilege. Particularly those of us who have so much."

Ran his hands along the lectern's sides.

"I like it, but I also resent it."

The height of the thing, its shape and surface, felt right, stable, soothing.

"I resent it because of everything I stand to lose. I'll cop to that. No one wants to relinquish the upper hand, even as the consequence of a necessary course correction; the balancing of historically skewed scales.

"I resent being assigned to a category I don't identify with, with people I don't like. Lumped in with history's assholes, the entitled descendants of ethnic puritans, conquistadors and colonialists taking our languid break along a bloody trail who, when asked to account for the carnage in our wake, say we weren't there, and can't see that far back, and besides, never took a scalp ourselves.

"In this sense, privilege is like putting an innocent person in a cage with criminals, and stating the crime must be equally shared.

"I resent that privilege is posited as the prism through which all light bends. I resent the assumption that I can be fully known—background and beliefs, the content of my character—by virtue of one simple, stupid label. I resent being made an exemplar of, or ambassador for, an artificial cohort.

"And I resent that so much of my privilege is outside my control. I didn't *choose* it, didn't *ask* for it. I have, further, experienced the very antithesis of it, where I was utterly deserted by it.

"Why should I be judged or shamed or penalized for things I can't control?

"To which those who have always lacked privilege might respond: *Yeah, welcome to the club!*" ·

Heady rush of blood. *So good.*

"Privilege is an old formula reframed: Who has power, and who doesn't? Who is the puppet, and who pulls the strings? To paraphrase the best video game of all time: Who chooses, and who obeys?

"Yes—if there are those who have privilege, then there must be those who lack it. As with any binary, the halves are mutually constitutive. To define sameness is to define difference. To declare who is privileged is to declare who is not.

"So who decides? Who decides what counts? Who assumes or is given the right to curate this category, to determine the relevant criteria—sex, skin, class, caste, height, health, age, anatomy—and how many points each is worth, how they stratify?

"There are obvious temptations, obvious *perks*, to this endeavour; to parcelling humanity into privileged and oppressed. You certify your own virtue and enlightenment, for one. Indeed, in terms of social and cultural capital, calling out others for their purported privilege has never been more lucrative. Better yet, you claim the right to act upon others: to chastise, discredit, chasten, dissuade, censor, stifle and silence and suppress.

"Categorization, simply put, is a form of control. As such, assigning privilege constitutes an extraordinary exercise of power.

"Is it worth noting that iterations of this project—of persecuting privilege—have been mounted many times; have led to massacres and purges and re-education camps; to killing everyone with eyeglasses? No matter the point at which any given crusade flew off the rails, however noble its incitements and underpinnings, each began as a rebalancing of the scales, as taking power away from the privileged—however 'privilege' was defined in that place and time—and dealing it back out among the non.

"This is a distinction of severity, not of substance.

"All of us—this modest gathering of the intellectual elite, our little clique, sequestered inside this expensive hotel, in an oasis of American excess—all of us arrived here, in one way or another, by dint of privilege. We who refashioned academia into activism, who celebrate diversity of every stripe except opinion and perspective, who have done so much to make privilege a *thing*—clarion call and cudgel—are indisputably some of privilege's primary beneficiaries.

"Our foremost privilege, I think, is the time to talk about privilege at all. I have visited places where people have no such luxury, whose daily lives are governed by far more basic concerns: water, food, safety, electricity. Not to say that privilege has no bearing, only that they'd be hard-pressed to find the time or wherewithal to talk about it. They might consider such a discussion irrelevant anyway.

"Or maybe not irrelevant so much as obvious.

"To which end, when it comes to determining privilege, I propose that the only meaningful metric is this: If you have time to talk about privilege, you're privileged.

"There, that should solve everything. You're welcome.

"So, yes, my privilege is real—if for no other reason than I'm talking about it right now—but I must insist that I am more. So are we all. Sums of elaborate and mutative equations, of compatible and countervailing variables—luck, chance, talent, skill, effort, experience—that propel us along our respective paths.

"And agency, of course. The choices we make. Our capacity to act. Our actions and their outcomes, intentional or otherwise."

A realization, as fleeting as a reflection in a pane of passing glass, tipped over the receding edge of conscious thought as Barker's busy mind, his inside self, finally blinked out.

This is what I was born to do.

As Barker continued ("...use this venue to defend my book, as that would only ensure our communal boredom..."), a not unfamiliar feeling took hold ("...became a locus of such intense debate..."), stiff fingers waking dormant notes ("...sprang from analysis of how conceptions of agency were..."), rising altitude, ("...raised more or less the same concern..."), hollowness—as if he were a conduit through which greater forces flowed.

"Are we in control, or being controlled?

"What I was *not* saying was that Facebook and smartphones brainwash people. They do, but that's not what I was saying.

"Rather, I wanted to understand how, in a world organized around the production of media, run mostly *with* media—media manufactured by opaque technocratic regimes, governed by oblique license agreements, inscribed with invisible algorithms and surveillance mechanisms; media we lack the tools to open, are sometimes legally prohibited *from* opening, and, either way, wouldn't have the first fucking clue what to do with if we *could* open them—how these media came to be perceived as a wellspring of human agency. I wanted to understand this gradual act of persuasion, how a new story was proposed and spread and came to seem, came to *feel*, natural and immutable.

"Once we accept and internalize such a story—one that leaves out, of course, the coincident constraints imposed upon us, all the vanished capacities, all the choices, big and small, media now make on our behalf—we are blinded to, and forget about, the motives and machinations that brought it into being.

"That's all I really meant by *the discursive construction of agency*. What stories do we tell each other, or are we told, about what agency is? Where agency comes from?

"For as long as we've had language, language has held immense power. Words are mystical, magical. They conjure, charm, invoke, incant. At the core of Christian theology is *the word. The word was with God and was truly God.* God is a self-proclaimed discursive construct that doubles down on the supremacy of words by banning competing media. No graven images! No sculptures or woodcarvings! Only words.

"I daresay no one in this room would contest that discourse can inflect, alter, enforce, even constitute reality. We need only consider the discursive transubstantiation of gender to see this phenomenon in action. *Sex*—our anatomical attributes—is delineated from *gender*— the cluster of social and cultural attitudes coagulating as *femaleness* and *maleness. Binary* was swapped out for *spectrum. Gender identity* was added to the mix: Your subjective appraisal, or an innate mental construct, distinct from sociocultural performance or physiological sex. We concocted categories reflective of gender's newfound fluidity, and pronouns and prefixes endorsing those categories. Accordingly, there are some who now contend that biological sex is a chimera. That it's culture and discourse all the way down.

"This denial of anatomy and biochemistry is, of course, insane, but in fact very few of these maneuvers were grounded in reputable science or research. As such, the discursive reconstruction of gender surfaces an important hazard where our discursive confections are concerned: That while we certainly find truth through fiction, we also tend to mistake fiction for truth.

"In a weird way, this propensity is baked in. For a long time fiction was all we had. For lack of material documentation, of pens and papyrus, myth served as our collective memory. Stories stored and transmitted information over time; were an archive of, and vessel for, truth. Truth and fiction operated in tandem; were and are entangled. Even today, our lives are governed by fictions like 'money' and 'country' and 'university.' Our poor, beleaguered brains ceaselessly sift through and sort an overabundance of input into tidy, intelligible plot points.

"Stories such as 'identity' allow the self to congeal. Stories such as 'God' or 'America' allow the group to galvanize. Stories such as 'privilege' give shape and content to nature's indifference."

His mental Molly piped up, *Don't lecture me!*

Smirked.

"Okay, I realize I'm skating around on treacherously thin ontological ice—all this arrogant blather about truth and fiction. Why further blur already fatally disfigured lines? Why endorse the instability of 'truth' itself?

"But aren't we all, as evangelists of postmodernism, at least partly at fault for this state of affairs? All reality is a construct! All truth is subjective! We're all shifting intersections in larger networks of power! Life is a zero sum outrage arms race, disparate clans locked in conspiracies to rule; culture and identity battlefields on which contests for domination between privileged and oppressed play out, with words and language, categories and constructs, our most effective and destructive artillery!

"In such a sphere, manipulating and controlling discourse, in whatever capacity, is a seductive and profound exercise of power.

"How is such power deployed? Well, you can change, revise, or invent language. Or you can restrict who is and isn't allowed to speak. Or—my personal favourite—you can police what people are and aren't allowed to say.

"A crucial front in this campaign is the purging of our communicative ecologies of offense. Offense is a nifty shortcut to the moral high ground, is impossible to deny or refute. Like privilege, offense is a trump card that automatically wins any disagreement or dispute.

"Offense is often now construed as tantamount to any other form of physical assault, as having the same effect as a real life lash. Making offence synonymous with violence, conflating harsh words and bodily trauma, fetishizes discourse as all-powerful, as constitutive of reality. Plus, just this sort of concept creep justifies pushing back against, and punishing, the oppressors in kind.

"The ultimate victory is not having to police speech at all. Per a certain someone's reading of a certain perfect prison, the most efficient exercise of power is to have a population internalize the mechanisms of it's own surveillance; to empower us, in other words, to police ourselves.

"That's why I resent privilege most of all. Because it is so often deployed as a dumb, blunt instrument to enforce self-surveillance.

"This is precisely why privilege, in fact, offends me.

"But I would argue that my being offended is good. Useful. In the same way the integrity of the immune system depends on exposure to pathogens, so too do our emotional and cognitive mettles depend on exposure to situations, experiences, challenges, problems, people, ideas, and opinions we don't like. Exposure to harmful things is advantageous. Essential, even.

"Offense reminds us where our lines are drawn, tests the integrity of the trip-wires set around our most firmly held beliefs; reminds us how and why we drew them that way, and what they were put in place to protect. Offense illuminates how words and language change and adapt, how norms and values are forever in a state of flux. Offense is a signpost that says we were once *there*, and now we are *here*. To try to rid the world of offense is not only futile and misguided, but dangerous.

"As such, anyone arrayed against exposure, who inhibits or curtails discourse, who claims the moral or legal authority to police quote-unquote 'bad' discourse—which, to be blunt, is simply speech they don't like—who evaluates discourse not on the basis of merit and validity, but ideological purity; who equates offense with assault and dissent with hate, are equivalent to the anti-vaccination movement.

"They are intellectual anti-vaxxers."

Barker reached inside his pocket...

"Like a denuded virus, the university is designed to fortify our intellectual immune system in much the same way that vaccines fortify our physical one."

...and held up his napkin for all to see.

"This is why, to return the university to its original mission, we must immediately—"

Hannah stood and ducked out the nearest exit.

Barker watched her go, and as she departed, his gaze intercepted the napkin in his hand. Except it was not a napkin, but his half-finished portrait of Trouble. The doodle's distorted visage and drooping graphite eyes ogled him from the back of his folded-up faculty meeting agenda.

"Uh…"

Dropped the agenda on the lectern, plunged his hand back inside his pocket. Dug around. Retrieved the napkin, limp with moisture, its image surrendered to illegibility.

Beat. "I…"

Inside: Nothing.

Beat. Then: …*five…six…seven…eight…*

Waved it, a flimsy white flag.

…*thirteen…fourteen…fifteen…*

Set it down, smoothed it out.

…*eighteen…nineteen…*

Alessandro, clenched in a sort of full-body fist—legs braided, arms strapped across his chest like a straight-jacket—kind of jolted out of position and began to clap. The audience followed suit, set aside their phones to free up their hands, slightly lowered their laptop screens to make their applause visible.

Whatever reaction he'd hoped for—stony silence, pumping fists, exercised academics exploding in raucous debate, spilling out into the blustery night, overtaking the Strip, three margaritas deep, horns locked in ferocious *tête-à-têtes*—they weren't having it.

Shyeah. You fumbled the ball in the end zone, jackass!

The muted applause tapered off. Some took this as their opportunity to depart.

Hannah re-entered and joined Barker at his side. "We have lots of time left for questions," she announced to those that remained.

Propped his elbows on the lectern.

"Yes," she called out, "in the back?"

A young man in a brown blazer perched on the edge of his seat. "Hi, yes, my name is Josh Parks, I'm a doctoral candidate at *u-cee* Santa Cruz. I wanted to thank you, first off, for a really, uh, interesting lecture."

Interesting. Ugh.

"Thanks."

"I was wondering...I guess I feel a sense of solidarity with some of the points you raised. I think we're all pretty concerned about how offense plays out in terms of trigger warnings and bias reports and deplatforming and all, and what this means for the future of the university. Especially those of us who, ah, are soon to be out on the job market, and want to strike a responsible balance between job security and catering to, I guess, or accommodating, maybe, the needs or sensitivities of our students."

"Okay," Barker said.

"But how do we, I guess, avoid the perception that this is just a generational thing? Like, how is it really any different than one generation, I guess, railing against the things the next generation grows up with? How would you respond to someone who asks, like, aren't you just another grumpy old man shaking his fist at the kids and their awful rock'n'roll?"

And so it began. *Thank you for your... Was wondering if... Touch on your point regarding... Considered the possibility that...*

Some confessed concerns regarding how the university ignored, even encouraged, student self-indulgence; shared their own stories of being called in by deans or department heads or ad hoc administrative committees to be wrist-slapped or interrogated for the use of such-and-such a word, or cautioned against teaching such-and-such a section, or including such-and-such a reading in their syllabus.

A woman in a turtleneck emblazoned with a seahorse: "I like the vaccination comparison. This idea of exposure is something I hear my *cee-bee-tee* colleagues bandying about quite a bit. I worry, though, that *intellectual anti-vaxxer* is precisely the kind of loaded, derogatory slur we should avoid."

A young woman with a pale blue mohican recounted finding herself on the receiving end of a bias report for criticizing a student's use of the word *hence.* "I thought it was sloppy writing. At some point they learn to clutter up their essays with all these fancy-sounding words when a simple word, even *no* word, would work just as good." The report chastened her for the tacit implication that the student wasn't sufficiently intellectually equipped to employ such specialized vocabulary. "She made it out like I was calling her stupid, when I was only trying to give her pointers on style."

"Thanks for sharing that," Barker said.

As the Q&A wore on, Barker's responses grew terse, his monotone sullen. ("I didn't claim to be an expert on that issue." "It wasn't my intent to incite an ontological feedback loop.") Hannah nudged him with her elbow as if to say, *Perk up, champ!*

Hated himself for the magnitude of his failure. It was the worst of all possible outcomes: Neither outrage nor acclaim, but a shrug. He'd had all the pieces, but hadn't properly fit them together. Should have prepared. For lack of preparation, he'd succeeded only in confirming what his detractors had always said, what he himself had always feared: He was a clown, a poseur, an imposter.

Hannah finally put the proceedings out of their misery. "Please join me in thanking Doctor Stone for such a provocative talk, and thank you all for your comments and questions. What a lively and insightful conversation!"

Applause. *Yay us!*

As people packed up and filed out, Alessandro bounded up to Barker, grasped and shook his hand. "Cool speech, buddy. Maybe a little wandering around, but lots of neat stuff in there. You should keep working on that!"

Wan smile. Solemn nod. Craved a curtained room and a soft bed.

"And now for the best part," said Alessandro, spiralling his finger up through the air. "Drinks!"

Those that noticed Barker enter the hotel lounge greeted him with smiles and handshakes, pelted him with *Great speech!*-es and *Really enjoyed that!*-s. In counterfeit deference to his stature, perhaps, a space cleared at the bar as he and Hannah and Alessandro approached. Alessandro tried to flag down a bartender as Hannah tugged at Barker's shoulder, cupped a hand to his ear.

"I'm so sorry I ducked out," she shouted. "Catering emergency. One of our payments didn't go through. Had to deal with it right away if we wanted coffee tomorrow. Nightmare!"

"No sweat," he shouted back.

They ordered beers and stayed there, up against the bar, yelling at each other over the din. Could barely hear them, barely hear himself. Tried to read their lips, nodded in mock understanding, let his eyes and attention float out across the revelry.

An expectant look snapped him back. "Sorry!" he yelled. "What was that?"

Hannah said her goodnights. She was presenting first thing in the morning, wanted to give her piece another once-over before bed. She kissed them both on the cheek, melted into the thinning crowd.

Alessandro leaned in close. "She is cute, yes?"

"Hannah?" Things between them had always been platonic. *Siblingesque.* "Sure. Of course."

Closer still. "We are dating."

"Who? You and Hannah?"

"Yes."

"For how long?"

"From the last conference."

"Why didn't you say anything?"

"Well…you know. Things can be complicated. We are living long-distance. I am still in Malta, and she is, well, *not*. There is also the issue of the conference, which we would not want to jeopardize if things went sour."

"That's wonderful! I'm so happy for you both."

"This is kind of you to say. I'm happy you approve."

"Of course I approve. You're two of my favourite people."

Alessandro hugged him. "I could cry to hear you say that. I won't, but I could."

"Let me buy you a drink!"

"Yes, I will!"

Alessandro made quick work of the pint. "I must go to see if she is really working, or if she may be waiting for me to deliver a good night kiss." Winked.

"Go forth, my friend, and prosper!"

Alessandro's eyes twinkled behind his square specs. He clapped Barker on the shoulder. "See you tomorrow, buddy!"

Barker ordered another beer. They were such good people, deserving of one another, and yet their being together, having found one another, ruffled the surface of a hidden well. His mental Tatjana scolded him to *Bless that which you covet!* Another insipid aphorism. What was it with the Serbs, always trying to put a good spin on bad omens?

He was happy for them. Wanted to be happy for them. *Would* be happy for them. Later. For now he needed to wallow. Keynote, marriage, career—*Failures!* He'd never find that person that understood him, truly *got* him, accepted him warts and all. Destined, it was clear, for a life of loneliness, of skipping across an archipelago of barren flings. So strange, in retrospect, how certain he'd been about Tatjana, like the universe's prodigious tumblers had aligned, like a great cosmic lock had been sprung.

Was she the one? His one shot? Had he had it and blown it? How many of those did anyone get, should anyone expect, in the span of one lifetime?

On the other hand, at least he knew it was possible—that feeling, that connection—because he'd experienced it, felt it firsthand. Others weren't so lucky.

Or…was it worse? To know it was possible, taste it and never get it back?

So many marriages, like his, that'd flamed out. Friends stuck in sexless, loveless couplings; who seemed incapable, despite their better judgement, of fleeing emotionally, even physically abusive partners; who for lack of resolve or resources (*Our lives are too financially entangled! It'd be too big a blow for the kids!*), wouldn't or couldn't just get the fuck out. Wasn't he lucky, on that count, that his divorce had been so painless? That they were still on such good terms?

Dell was a lost cause. (Had she ever really been a candidate? No. They were too different, their views and realities too contrastive.) And Lara…what the fuck had he been thinking? What a fucking idiot to fall prey to the trap of the tight young twentysomething. To lose his head to goddamned chemistry. He should have known better. *Had* to know better. Would right here and now resolve to learn this lesson, solder it into his brain and being: *Fine young women are way more trouble than they're worth.*

A fine young woman sidled up beside him. "Hi."

"Hello," Barker said.

"I wanted to say how much I enjoyed your keynote. It was a lot different from what I was expecting. In a good way."

"Much appreciated."

"Bit on the broad side, but I'm down with that." Beat. "This is totally none of my business, but were you…okay afterward?"

"What do you mean?"

"During the *cue-and-a* it kind of looked like you were upset or something."

"Just tired. Long few weeks. Long flight that got in late."

"Uh-huh," she said.

"To be honest—"

"Best thing to be."

"—I was maybe a bit disappointed."

"Why's that?"

"I was hoping for…I don't know. More of a reaction. Or something." Beat. "Obviously it was, well, something of a work in progress."

"Sure."

"I don't know. I guess I wanted to push some buttons. Spark something. I've been in the game a few years now, and these things—panel presentations, keynotes—are always so...reserved."

"You wanted to pull a Brecht?"

"Sorry?"

"German theatre dude. Early twentieth century. All about exposing artifice, pulling back the curtain, showing the Great and Powerful Oz for a fraud. Larger question being: Is it any different in real life? Proles in the balcony, bougies in the orchestra. Bougies would clap nicely at the end. Proles would be screaming and ready to riot."

"Hm. Yeah."

Took her in: crisp cerulean eyes, high, angular cheekbones, perfectly straight bleach-white teeth, hair in a pixie cut—sprouts of black root. "That sounds about right. Love it. Hate it. Have a *reaction*. That's all."

She leaned against the bar. Her elbow grazed his arm. She left it there, fabric lightly touching his, a whisper of friction every time they adjusted.

"I'm not sure we're the revolutionary type." Looked him in the eyes. "Do you think we're all, like, these reluctant do-gooders ready to change the world as soon as someone delivers the big, rousing speech that rallies us to our cause?"

Smirked. "What do you think? Are we?"

Tilted her head, arched an eyebrow, set her lips in a contemplative pout. "I think we're nice people who like the idea of making a difference, but we're too shy or scared or nerdy to get our hands dirty. And fuck, who can blame us? It's a good life—tenure, sabbaticals, bursaries, pensions—or at least that's what I keep hearing."

"True say."

Squealed. "*True say?* Where'd you pick up that stale old slang? *Ay caramba!*"

"My students assured me that shit was cutting-edge."

"Holy hell, did they take you for a chump."

"I paid good money for *true say*."

"Can you get it back?"

He laughed. She held out her hand. "I'm Bailey."

"If I was an asshole I'd say *like the liqueur?*"

"Good thing you're not an asshole."

"Barker."

"I know. A pleasure."

Beat.

"Can I buy you a drink?"

♦ ♦ ♦

Told him about her dissertation. Her defence was scheduled two weeks from Monday. Was she stressed? "Naw. I know that shit inside and out. Bring it the fuck on." She'd scaled back on conferences to focus on revisions and polish. "I wouldn't miss this, though. I've been attending since the third one, I think. Felt like I finally found my people. My conversation."

She'd read Barker's book. "I knew I wanted to do a games diss, but that was it. Maybe I was a bit chickenshit, too. Like games didn't count as 'serious' scholarship." Reading *Play*, she saw the light. "It was such a cool combination of history and content analysis. You made game studies seem, well, legit." Like Barker before her, she dropped the project she'd been picking away at and whipped up a new one from scratch. "You might be sick of hearing this, but you really were an inspiration."

"Not sick of it yet."

"Don't worry. I'm not some weirdo, stalkerish fangirl."

What was the new project? "It's based on *Bioshock Infinite*, how the game literally puts the player on rails. Which is in itself an interesting counterpoint to, or I would say tacit rebuttal of, this glut of exploratory, open world titles. I couch the analysis in a historical survey of the expression *on the rails*, of what I call *on-railness*, both in games and preceding games...trace it back to the development of the railway, this mode of transportation that was meant to tie together, and in that sense liberate, an enormous geographical expanse, while using essentially slave labour to construct it." *Freedom,* she mused, *always seems to come at its own expense.* "This idea of *railness* now implies an abridgement of player freedom, a lack of ambit or latitude. But then there's this great juxtaposition with, on the other, the idea of going *off* the rails, which is to sort of succumb to chaos, a *lack* of control."

"I have rum," Barker said. "In my room."

Gulped her scotch. "I'll get mixers."

✦ ✦ ✦

Took a cab to his hotel—"The *Fiesta* room?" Sly grin. "Sounds like a party!"—carried an armload of Cokes upstairs.

"Yeezus," she said. "Looks like a *tienda* exploded in here."

Gave her two plastic cups to unwrap while he jogged down the hallway for ice. Returned to find her twisting the cap off an orange vial.

"Adderall." She clocked his confusion. "I used to take it for *a-dee-aitch-dee*, but now I use it to study. Cheaper than coffee. At least the kind of coffee I like."

Ice, Coke, stirred in the rum with his finger. She crushed three pills, first with the cap, then by turning the vial on its side and steam-rolling the chalky crumbs. "You have your key card handy?" Cut the powder into four lines, bent over one, snorted it.

Barker hesitated.

"First time?"

✦ ✦ ✦

Halfway through the two-six, on the bed, talking about Baz. She was from Chicago by way of small-town Oregon, but the whole country, maybe even the whole Western world, was galvanized by the election. "You guys are so fucked," she chortled. "That guy's a grade-A train-wreck."

"To play devil's advocate, though, it's not like he's not a known entity."

"That's a problem, though, isn't it? All his shit was out in the open, and you elected him anyway."

"Not to say he doesn't have baggage, but he's been on council for years. His constituents adore him. He's got to have some idea what he's doing, doesn't he?"

"Or people are fucking morons."

"Sure. Or people are fucking morons."

◆ ◆ ◆

Straddling. Grinding into his bulge. Pulling his shirt. Tugging buttons. One pops. Slides her hand inside the slit. Rakes nails across his chest. Gasps. Thrusts his groin against her. Bites her neck.

She moans. "Purr."

Her hand on his belt.

Room jittery.

"Wait…hold on a…"

World falling away in snow-like flakes.

Pants wrested down to his knees.

"One second—"

"Relax. It's all good." Hand running up his leg, cupping the welt of his exposed briefs.

Pressing. Grabbing.

Kissing him. Kissing her.

At his ear. "I'm putting you in my mouth now."

And she does. And he is.

Room a blur of unstable geometrics.

Tongue tip tracing the ridge of his—

"*Fuuu…*"

Fingers. Wetness.

O… O… O…
Lifting her.
"Oh, *daddy*…"
Eyes open.
"Don't stop."
Daddy?
"How…old are you?"
Stroking. "Old enough." Sliding…
"Wait—"
"It's an expression."
Scrambles back against the headboard.
"No. Stop. Seriously."
Up and off. Shimmies to the cusp.
"It's your first time. Chill. Take a breath."
"Too…"
Too young. Too student. Too professor. Too…
Heart racing. *Trilling.*
"…fucked up."
"We're *adults*."
Can she read his mind?
"I can't…can't do this right now."
"Okay," she says.
"You should go," he says. "I'm sorry, I…"
Rolls her eyes.
Closes his. Wills the spin to cease, the room to still.
"I like you," he offers to the abyss. "Could we…?"
Opens. She's gone.
Washroom?
Walk-hops. Bathroom empty. *Did I pass out?*
Vial on a side table. Forgotten? Left behind?
Relief. Skin prickles.
I did the right thing. The imbalance of…
I'm a shepherd. Shepherds don't fuck sheep.

Congratulates himself on his chivalry.

Rum and remote and a handful of toilet paper. Puts a pillow on the floor against the bed. Gives his pants to gravity like a layer of shed skin. Flips through channels. Finds the pay-per porn. (*Nine dollars!*) Titles meaningless, interchangeable. Stops on one at random. Accepts the charges. Swigs rum. Watches flesh smash flesh. Swigs. Pantomimes of pleasure, vigour, climax. Swigs. Tries to coax his penis back to standing.

The taste of the rum on his tongue turns syrup sweet. A chemical sludge: medicine, perfume, a melted bag of candy.

A tremor ripples through his innards, a gust blows through the black, as the tendrils overtake him.

✦ ✦ ✦

After the cops broke down his door, after the ambulance and paramedics, after Dell appeared at the hospital, he pieced it all together.

The university had put out a press release that was, for whatever reason, picked up by the national media: Famed professor Barker Stone had been suspended (with pay) pending an investigation into allegations of sexual misconduct. Further, this was all the university was prepared to divulge for the moment, so reporters needn't bother pressing for further details. (Barker had received several messages on the matter, but had shut off his phone prior to the workshop with the Coloradans and forgotten to turn it back on.) When no one could reach him on his cell, clouds of concern began to gather. Various faculty approached Shiv. Shiv said that Barker had been acting weird lately, added that he'd been dating a police officer ("Delilah, maybe?"), so maybe someone should check in with her.

Dell was located, asked to comment on Barker's mental and emotional state as of the last week. *Well he ran out on me at a restaurant.* Why? *No idea. We haven't spoken since.* Did you try to contact him? *Yes. Several times.* He didn't respond? *No.*

Had Barker ever expressed suicidal ideations; i.e., a desire or

willingness to harm himself, to take his own life? She said *No*, then
Wait, then recounted their conversation the evening she'd watched
a man put a gun to his own head and fire. *He said something like that
he "got" it.* Got what? *The impulse to…I don't remember exactly…do
whatever it took to get out of a situation like that.* Like what? *Like, when
you're cornered.* Ashen faces and stricken glances. Was Barker capable
of hurting himself? Her first instinct was to say *No*, but…

I'm not sure, she said instead.

By this time (two a.m. EST) other parties were trying to find
Barker at the Rio. Conference organizers notified police that he'd
last been seen in the lounge. The bartender recalled serving him, but
wasn't sure when he'd left or if he'd left alone. *Bit busy here Saturdays*,
the bartender told them, *especially with a conference.*

The Rio professed to have no room booked under the name
Barker or Samuel. There was a Stone, but the first name was Carole.
A series of increasingly frantic calls were made to ascertain where
Barker was lodging.

Once this was determined, the concierge was implored to try
Barker in his room. Said concierge called several times to no avail,
but informed the police there'd been a PPV charge to the room a
little over an hour ago, so that was a good sign! Could the hotel
send someone up? Someone was sent up. Knocked. No answer. The
LVMPD dispatched an ambulance. The paramedics acquired the room
number while the concierge tried to run off a new key. (The machine
had been acting finicky all night, was still refusing to cooperate, they
were in the process of swapping it out for a new one.) The paramedics
arrived at Barker's door. Knocked. No response. The police pounded.
No response. The bulkier of the two officers kicked in the door a
moment before the concierge reached them—*Alack! But a moment
too late!*—with a newly minted key card.

Here's what the police and paramedics saw: A nearly depleted
two-six of rum, cans and empty bottles of beer, a vial of prescription
medication, a visibly discombobulated and incoherent Barker, pants
around his ankles, genitals exposed.

Here's what they smelled: Vomit.

All indications pointed to OD, the officer later wrote in his report. Barker was hauled into the ambulance. After a perfunctory physical exam—*patient's pupils dilated; trouble vocalizing; vomit soaking shirt and pants*—the paramedics administered gastric lavage. A tube was inserted into his oesophagus, and a saline solution pumped through it. They reached the hospital as Barker began to expurgate the contents of his stomach.

Notified that Barker had been found, had apparently attempted to take his own life, Dell requested two days emergency leave, packed an overnight bag, took a taxi to the airport, boarded the next available flight to Vegas.

After regaining consciousness and expelling the last of the rancid sludge, it befell Barker to explain to an officer—who kept flashing Dell incredulous *Can you believe this shit?* looks—that he knew nothing of his suspension, or a press release related thereto, or the already roiling debate concerning his purported sexual improprieties. He'd simply met a girl in a bar and taken her back to his room. Feeling queasy, he'd brought a premature end to the encounter, then taken it upon himself to fulfill his lingering arousal. (*Unsuccessfully*, he saw the officer note with a douchy grin.)

What did Dell make of this? Barker could barely bring himself to look at her. The few times he did, dared glance in her general direction, he found her staring into space. She betrayed nothing, a sphinx, her face porcelain that the details of his disgrace could not chip.

I'm just another perp to her now, he realized. *Another sad sack they pulled off the street covered in his own puke.*

Released an hour later. Leaving the hospital, there was the matter of the bill. Did he have insurance? Yes, he was covered by his union. The computer doesn't recognize the number. Did you want to call your provider? *Oh, I was just, as of yesterday, suspended. With pay,* he added, since that struck him, in the moment, as a pretty important distinction. Ah. Did you want to discuss payment options? She inflected it like a question, even though it wasn't one.

Returned to the hotel to retrieve his things. Found and turned on his phone, sent Hannah a text to let her know he wouldn't be making it down to the Rio today, was dealing with an unexpected emergency.

How about that? An actual *emergency!*

Arrived at the airport a few hours shy of the return flight he'd originally booked. Dell bought a ticket for the same flight. The agent asked if she and Barker wanted to sit together. Dell said either way worked. As they crawled through security, Barker offered to reimburse her for the cost of her flights. Dell said he didn't have to do that, but she'd accept if he insisted.

As the plane taxied, Barker reeled from the cost of the ambulance and brief hospital stay. He'd call his union first thing Monday. Surely, if he'd been suspended *with pay*, then there was no reason to cut off his insurance. Even if that was how it worked, surely he'd be covered at least through the end of the weekend. Surely there'd been a mistake. Surely.

At about the midway point in their flight, he noticed Dell flipping through the in-flight magazine, asked what she was reading about.

"Belize," she said.

"It's nice," he told her. "Chill."

◆ ◆ ◆

She hailed a cab at the airport, gave the driver Barker's address, left him to pay when they arrived.

Inside his apartment, she uncorked a bottle of wine, poured herself a glass, sat on the sofa seat opposite the couch, and waited.

He didn't know how to start. As soon as he'd started, couldn't stop.

First Lara, her accusation. Best guess: Lara was acting out of jealousy because she suspected Barker of pursuing another woman, another student. The undergrad he'd mentioned, the director of the play. And yes, Barker harboured a kind of...*affection* for said student. Nothing he intended to act upon, of course, but...it was there.

Then consulting on Randell's campaign, the NDA that legally barred him from telling Dell what he was about to tell her, *viz* the folder full of text messages between Baz and an underage girl. (This was the only point at which Dell spoke: "Oh, God."). How Barker had been tasked with exonerating Baz by proposing that his smartphone had been controlling him somehow.

Then, that night at the gastropub, catching a glimpse of Baz's press conference, realizing his emails had been going to Ophelia's campaign account, the campaign's implicit threat to leak one or some of those messages to throw the press off the scent of the sexting scandal.

For some reason, though it wasn't germane to anything—maybe he was simply on a confessorial roll—he told her about Cooper, the ketamine, 2B, the grapes, his wrenching ouster, Baz and his posse.

Everything that had gone down in Vegas she already knew.

She sat for a while, head bowed, holding her empty glass as if in supplication. Eventually said, "Let's go to bed."

She did not undress, but lay supine on her back, crossed her arms over her chest, and fell asleep.

In the morning, when he woke, she was already gone.

◆ ◆ ◆

On Monday, with Maureen's blessing, Barker stopped by his office to collect some things. As he filled his box—more to feel like there were things he needed than actually needing any of those things—Bertrand slinked up to his door.

"Barker," he said with trademark huskiness, "I wanted to tell you how sorry I am for your troubles."

Ran his finger along spines of books like a stick along a fence. "Thanks, Bert. Kind of you to say."

Bert glanced in both directions down the apparently empty hallway, then tilted his white and windswept mountain peak into Barker's soon to be ex-office.

"Not for nothing," Bert said, "but back in the day, fucking your students was kind of the point."

✦ ✦ ✦

Lake House was uncharacteristically quiet. All the better to make his escape unnoticed. *Goodbye capacious atrium! Goodbye high-maintenance living wall!* Descended a staircase and caught sight of Shiv though the porthole of a closed door.

Peered inside. Shiv stood at a lectern, Molly sat a few feet to her side, watching her phone with a wisp of satisfaction. Barker couldn't hear what Shiv was saying, but projected onto a large screen behind her was a confluence of social media streams. The collocated feeds were in full flow, columns in perpetual renewal, a vertical garden of comments blossoming into one another, floating their predecessors up and into oblivion.

- How entitled do u have to be to think u speak on be half of all Muslims?

- Exactly what happens when privilege gets a podium.

- Word to anyone being traumatized right now; You Are Not ALONE.

- Shes my instructor and she sucks this bad in class to!!

- What a disgrace. #hatespeech #endislamophobia

- Juice another spoiled member of the cis-gender sisterhood.

- This bee-yotch needs to get fired pronto, yo.

- (*Just) [[Autocorredt FAIL!]]

Shiv either couldn't see, or was ignoring, the inverse cascade, and soldiered on, face as impenetrable as a fortress.

Barker turned and continued his descent.

✦ ✦ ✦

Cycling! November and he was cycling! Decent October weather was rare, cycling in November was downright unicorn.

The initially all-consuming misery of being investigated for quote-unquote "sexual misconduct" had quickly ebbed into an undercurrent. More itch than pain. The wheels of justice turned slowly, alas. It would be weeks, even months, before verdicts were handed down. External lawyers had been retained to review the evidence, conduct interviews, and submit a (non-binding) report with recommendations for disciplinary action (if any). Nothing to do but wait for these impartial third parties to do their thing.

Yes, the wheels of justice turned slowly, but the wheels of his bicycle spun swiftly, at such speeds that their gathering gyroscopy defied gravity itself! An intricate interplay of physics that carried him through every curve and corner, angles that would have toppled any stationary entity.

What was gravity to him while engaged in the human equivalent of flight?

Barker could already see the silver lining. His most recent conversation with the woman at Faculty Affairs was encouraging indeed. Lara's complaint, she informed him, was classic *he-said-she-said*. No evidence that the incident at the Legion was assault. Lara's only corroborating witness ("How did this supposed 'assault' occur in a public setting, at an establishment full of people, with only *one* purported witness?"), the MA student Sam, was nowhere to be found. As far as anyone knew, shortly after convocation he'd boarded a flight to Yemen and hadn't been heard from since. Moreover, Sam hadn't seen anything firsthand, had only encountered Lara after the fact. Either way, the real pickle was the ostensibly *tit-for-tat* tender of an instructor position. ("Or, rather, *tat* for *tit*," she quipped.) The resumption of relations after said offer was accepted tainted Barker's assertion that no favours, sexual or otherwise, had been on tap. (Though it certainly put the lie to Lara's narrative, didn't it? If she truly considered the incident assault, then why continue the affair later on?) Could Barker produce proof—something in writing, an email perhaps—that the affair had irrefutably ended, and that the offer really was, as he asserted, an olive branch? *Yes, he said, I think so.* Surely he and Lara had exchanged a conciliatory message or two. He hadn't been able to find one yet, but there must be something in his archive somewhere.

Investigation aside, he felt showered with good luck. With Baz's first week in office offering no shortage of tumult, no one in the media had bothered to take the *consensual theatre* bait—if it *was* bait—or had otherwise made any connection between Barker and the campaign. The flare—if it *was* a flare—had served its purpose. Burned out. No reason for Evan to "expose" him for anything, much less on the basis of blasé innuendo; matters of interpretation.

(Not that the press hadn't devoted significant energy to picking through Barker's life and past for threads of disrepute. Here was XiXe on the news, alleging in nigh-incomprehensible English that Barker had asked her to meet him in his office, accused her of plagiarism—when her works cited page was *right there*, she displayed it prominently for the camera—and then made an offhand and unprompted comment about his penis. There was a newspaper article quoting an anonymous student—Jacob, no doubt—accusing Barker of posting thinly veiled threats on their Facebook wall. Everywhere, scurrilous gossip re: Barker's incessant self-aggrandizement—bragging about his "famous" book, his TED talk, *Colbert*, etcetera—his condescending attitude, his not-so-secret Islamo- and transphobia, and, somehow most insidious of all, his self-ascribed gatekeeper status, situating himself as a portal to lucrative employ in the video game industry (provided one was willing to bend the motherfucking knee), amply evinced by his exclusionary invite-only soirées. Not for nothing, but it was at just such a "Gathering" that the very as-yet-unknown-but-*definitely*-sexually-unseemly misdeed that had set the wheels of his now-unfolding disgrace in motion had taken place.)

Best of all, the university was roundly condemned for the vagaries of its initial release; had furiously back-pedalled, quickly disseminated a second statement stipulating that the first one was a rough draft, had been mistakenly sent out, pleaded with everyone—press and public alike—to just, y'know, *fuggedaboudit!* Good luck unringing *that* bell. If the university's palpable embarrassment wasn't reward enough, Barker's new lawyer considered this second "self-incriminating" statement fine evidence indeed that his employer had, in fact, defamed him.

Excellent grounds, in other words, for a lawsuit.

If the cards cut his way, his lawyer opined, he might even be reinstated with tenure. The university would look terribly petty putting him through this ordeal only to deny him his formerly impending promotion. (Not that he'd be sticking around too long, not after this particular institution had shown its true stripes.)

In the meantime: Weeks, more likely months, *with pay.* For all *intensive purposes* (*Ha!*), Barker had landed an early sabbatical. Unplanned, sure, but he could still be spontaneous. His second book, his sophomore effort, was long overdue. Enough scratching his balls in the bullpen. Time to get back on the field and pitch! And here he had a perfectly feasible project ready to go! With a bit of tinkering, his *Economies of Agency* proposal would be in fine form to submit. He could coordinate with Hannah and Alessandro, draw up a list of potential contributing authors to approach before, if necessary, casting a wider net. If all proceeded smoothly, he might be able to get the book to press within a year. Two tops. He'd write one or two chapters himself, of course; make a point to sit down at long last with KT3. Surely there was a chapter's worth of analysis there. KT3's ever-expanding in-game microtransaction marketplace—"Buy Yourself Some Time"—had been generating a lot of buzz (read: controversy). And what with his direct line to Coop, he could gild his piece with an insider perspective on the game's design and development straight from the mouth its celebrated creator.

Speaking of Hannah and Alessandro (*So happy to hear about your budding romance!*), both insisted his keynote had gone over much better than he thought, assured him they'd received, quote, "a lot of positive feedback."

(*If there's anything we can do to help in terms of your current predicament, please let us know!*)

Even his impasse with Dell, who Barker had basically written off—who, more to the point, had every right to write *him* off—was showing signs of thaw. After going incommunicado for a few days, he'd texted her to say how much he appreciated her giving him the opportunity to come clean, that he totally understood if she never wanted to speak to him again, but if she was at all open to continuing the conversation, he'd really like to do that. (Plus if she sent him the cost of her flights, he'd cut her a cheque ASAP.)

This morning: A reply! In sum: She'd been giving his situation a lot of thought, and, yes, might be open to "continuing the conversation," but needed more time. She'd contact him when she was ready. In the meantime, her flights had cost—

Holy shit they were pricey! Flying last minute was the worst. They gouged you the worst. Only people in desperate circumstances booked flights at the last minute, and the airlines knew that and took advantage. *Fuck me!*

But hey, at least his medical coverage had kicked back in. And—bonus!—his inaccessible insurance was a clerical error. Just one of those crazy coincidences. Of course they would cover his costs incurred down south. Wasn't it appalling what they charged for health care in the States? Sure, our system isn't perfect—waiting lists and whatnot—but at least no one up here goes bankrupt. Shameful that an industrialized nation, in this day and age, didn't prioritize the welfare of its citizens over corporate greed. Profiteering off the backs of the ill and unlucky, *de facto* penalizing them for having the gall to get sick, was a moral abomination plain and fucking simple.

An early sabbatical. A reprieve. A chance to rest, regroup, refocus.

Cut back on the booze and pot, junk his few remaining cigarettes, pack up the console. A chance to change.

Better yet: A chance to *choose* to change.

Life was just…strange, wasn't it? As bad as things seemed one day was as good as they seemed the next. Peaks and valleys. You just had to stay positive, keep your chin up and a *Yes!* in your heart, and never let the bastards get you—

Cycling at full musth, Barker didn't register the quartet crossing the path ahead. The closest one—the kid was just *there*—looked up from his phone and leaped. Alerted by the flail of arms, Barker swerved, choked his brakes hard. Rubbery screech like a needle scratch, back wheel levitating, bike and body bound in a lurching pirouette, succumbing to gravity's quick. Landed hard on his left, helmet slapping the concrete with a nerve-racking CRACK. Skidded a few feet before grinding to a lumpy halt.

Was he hurt? Under his bike. What was broken? A crowd congealed. "Could somebody…*fuck!*" Skin shorn off his knee and thigh, a field of subcutaneous pink, pebbles of blood like poppy buds. "Could somebody get my bike off me please?" Of the eight or nine onlookers, none moved.

Fresh pain shot up his hip as Barker twisted onto his back, used his knee to prop up his bike—rear rim banana-bent. Kicked it off. Peeled away his shorts to reveal a second sinister patch of abraded red.

"Are you okay?" someone asked.

"No," he said. "I'm fucking *not*."

Spotted the kids with the phones, the one from the path. "The *hell* were you doing?"

Dumb question. Redundant. No need to ask, and apparently no need to answer. "You were on your phones, right? Playing that fucking *game*, right?"

Stood, favouring his left leg. It felt grated, but not, miraculously, broken. The crowd had swelled to over a dozen. "I don't suppose anyone called an ambulance?"

No response. Nary a nod or shake of a head.

"That," indicated his distorted bicycle, "is a motor vehicle, right? It's classified the same as a *car*. When you wander blindly onto a path without paying any fucking—"

Was that guy filming him? "What are you doing?" One of the fuckwits, one of the original four, phone in the air, its back to Barker, bulbous fish eye level with Barker's face. "Excuse me? Guy with the haircut? Hello? Are you *filming* me?"

Lunged for the phone, misjudged the distance, handful of empty air, shifted his weight onto his damaged leg, yowled, hobbled in a circle while the pain abated. "Put that away, please. I haven't given you permission to—"

More passers-by drawn to the brouhaha, compelled to film it.

Barker spun from lens to lens. "I haven't given anyone permission to photograph me or...or...or reproduce my... If any of you post an image or video I'll sue you for—" Swiped at another phone, hooked his finger into its gel case. The amateur videographer retreated and Barker's finger snapped free.

"The fuck is wrong with you? How is this your first reaction to... to seeing someone... I mean, look at my fucking knee!"

How many now? Fifteen? Twenty? In place of faces—backs of phones. A carousel of unblinking irises.

Something inside him slipped, like a chain off its ring. "Put your phones away! Put your *phones* away! PUT YOUR FUCKING PHONES AWAY!"

The kid—the one who'd initiated the accident, who, like the rest of his posse, said nothing, did nothing, phone aloft like the others— no longer looked human. Not to Barker.

None of them did.

Not people, no.

Extensions.

Meaty prostheses.

Fucking *tripods*.

The word burbled up through the tar. A word he had never, not once, to the best of his recollection, uttered aloud. It wasn't, he would later protest, as if he *chose* the word, *chose* to speak it. (Though in darker moments to come, he would concede to himself that, given the circumstances, it was as apt a word as any other.)

And not for nothing, but the last time he had heard that word, it had been used *against* him. He'd been the "victim," for lack of a better term.

Such things were not, not always, fully under our control. Are we not more like conduits through which words, which language pass? And as with so many words, was this one not in a state of transmutation; a perpetual shedding and renewal of semantic skins? The sand never stopped shifting, obscuring old meanings while uncovering new ones. The word itself, the letters that comprised it, didn't *mean* anything in themselves; were mere carapaces, containers, signifiers standing for a roving stable of signified, like soldiers in salute, or like currency—a coin, a token whose value is always already in flux, relative, contextual. Barker had no more invented the word, assigned its content or symbolic alloy, than he'd spurred its metamorphosis. And as neither the first nor the last to deploy it, what could he be accused of, really, but being one in a chain of conduits? Of vessels? One node along the relay, a passer of the torch, an indistinct link in a glorious continuum, the endless topsy-turvy tumble of human communication.

"You'd better put that fucking phone away or I will shove it down your throat you fucking

Epilogue

► ►| 0:13 / 1:12

F&GG0T-screaming cyclist losing his SH*T

616,273 views

Hairy Coo
► Subscribe   3.2K

👍 3,902   👎 563   ➡ Share   ≣ Save

Dude skids out on his bike, starts screaming at everyone and tries to take their phones!

COMMENTS: 3,286

Ranchero Mike
totes apoplectic at 1:27. Something flighs out of his nose!
High-larioos!

Lee McCarthy
first there was the mona lisa. then there was that freeze frame.

Shakespepper
Isn't this that same dude that got fired for raping those chix?

buttbuttbutt
think u mean 4 raping chex

Captain Nuts
box of Chex? like the cereal??

BFSkinflint
Cereal rapist

Shakespepper
OOOO! SNAAAAAAAP!!!!!!!

Martinez222
Don't think he was actually fired, but he was definitely suspended.
He's suing the university or something.

MrHankey
you can sue people for being a raging lunatic asshole?!?!

Bat Eyes 4 Real
I dunno, if you got me in an accident, then didnt' do anything
except film me as I bled, Id prolly call you a fat too. (Isnt that the
reason anyone sues anyone?)

MrHankey
WHO CHOO CALLING FAT, WILLIS???

Bat Eyes 4 Real
**F@g. derpderp

Chaila
Just fighting for hiss rights not to bled to death on the sidewalk

SimonSez
Ya he's like a modern day MLK basically

duncan simard
PUT YOUR PHONES AWAAAAAAAAAAY AY AY AY ay ay ay ay eeee

wilsonleg
Nice reverb, yo!

the russian bot
I have a f@g!—MLK

duncan simard
That one day we will not be judged by the color of our skin, but by the contents of our anus!

xxyxxyxy
gross

Mel Abelle
You ARE a fag [[JJK!]]

Jarjarbee
Hes obvs using 'fag' in the olde englishe meaning of a bundle of sticks for burning.

Ed K.
Bundle of dicks.

saltriver
trundle of wicks

Greg Prescott
Grundle of Micks

wayslickz
What's a "grundle" mean?

MattnTrey
F*g is what your supposed to yell at bikers who make noise while your drinking on a patio. Have we learned nothing from South Park?!?!?!?

Cynthia Lehane
I took class from this guy. He was always hitting on my friend. Taking her out for food and sending her emails and stuff. Hot tho, in an old guy kind of way.

Bat Eyes 4 Real
U bone?

Supes Clicksalot
Also had him as a prof. This vid is waay more trick than anything he did in class. Pretty good class tho. I liked the telegraph unit, and time and space biased media. A Canadian invention!

Ty_Boo
Canadians didn't *invent* time/space-biased media, that's a *theory* of Harold Innis, who was a canadian scholar. are you sure you're getting you're money's worth at university?

Shakespepper
STFU nerd. NNNNNNEEEEEEEERRRRRRDDDDDDDUH!!!!!!
11!!!!1!!!!!!

calvin scott
I have a hairy innis.

Eloise Souvene
Anyone know his name, pls?

SHOW MORE

Works Cited

Privilege reflects a range of contemporary thinking on various subjects, to which end, I often cite real-world authors, artists, intellectuals, and academics—though not, for obvious reasons, in formal scholarly fashion.

Similarly, the text and characters often espouse or invoke ideas and insights gleaned from, or inspired by, these same (or similar) influences, but without explicit accreditation. Here I'll acknowledge sources and material not otherwise identified in the text itself.

All errors, misinterpretations, and oversights are my own.

THE TOWER

Rusk's "diatribe" is loosely based on the commendable work of Dr. Dwayne Winseck.

Shiv's argument to Molly regarding sexual assault (p. 32–33) was informed by the work of Jeannie Suk Gersen, in particular her article "Shutting Down Conversations About Rape at Harvard Law," published in the *New Yorker* on December 11th, 2015.

THE LUCE

Lamenting the sorry state of sessionals (p. 50), Shiv cites statistics from Caroline Fredrickson's *Atlantic* article, "There Is No Excuse for How Universities Treat Adjuncts," from September 15th, 2015.

On p. 51, Shiv again references Gersen. Gersen details being taken to task for using the word "violate" while teaching a class about rape case law in her *New Yorker* article "The Trouble With Teaching Rape Law" (December 15th, 2014).

THE MEETING

The onomatopoeia for Mac and Evan's laughter (p. 65), as with Dell's later on, is a nod to *Bonfire of the Vanities*, by Tom Wolfe (1987).

Barker's rundown of the history of agency (p. 73–74) is partly indebted to Martin Hewson's article "Agency," from the *Encyclopedia of Case Study Research* (2009).

THE GATHERING

The idea of university training students for a life of bureaucracy (p. 160) was inspired by a chapter by Dr. Ira Wagman titled "Bureaucratic Celebrity," from *Celebrity Cultures in Canada* (2016), by Katja Lee and Lorraine York (editors).

The notion of humans being emotional beings first, as noted by Shiv on p. 187, is a key theme of *The Righteous Mind: Why Good People are Divided by Politics and Religion*, by Jonathan Haidt (2012).

THE BREAK

Alessandro's analysis of batteries as a form of resistance (p. 200–201) was inspired by the work of Dr. John Shiga, principally his article "Translations: Artifacts from an Actor-Network Perspective," published in *Artifact* (April 21st, 2006).

THE OPENING

The "tire iron" reference, and "virtue-sloganeering" (p. 262) are both nods to Laura Kipnis' harrowing and essential *Unwanted Advances: Sexual Paranoia Comes to Campus* (2017).

2B

For the theatre-savvy, 2B will be instantly recognizable as a variation on Punchdrunk's magisterial *Sleep No More*, which premiered in NYC's "McKittrick Hotel" in 2011. *Sleep*, a sort-of adaptation of *Macbeth* filtered through a film noir prism, is the recipient of much-deserved fanfare, and continues to inspire artists operating in various media, such as Erin Morgenstern's luscious novel, *The Night Circus* (2011).

"Vamp pout" (p. 286) is one of two nods to China Miéville's *The City and the City* (2009). At the time I started writing *Privilege*, I had just finished work on a theatrical adaptation of *City*, and the book was still very much rattling around my brain.

THE KEYNOTE

The book that Barker reflects on in the microbrewery (p. 330–331) is *The Way the Crow Flies* (2004), by Ann-Marie MacDonald.

Barker's keynote draws on various indispensible sources, including Walter J. Ong's *Orality and Literacy* (1982), *The Truth About Stories* (2003) by Thomas King, *The Triumph of Narrative* (1999) by Robert Fulford, and *Sapiens* (2014) by Yuval Noah Harari.

The notion of offence as an unbeatable trump card (p. 340) comes from an article by Greg Lukianoff and Jonathan Haidt titled "How Trigger Warnings are Hurting Mental Health" (the *Atlantic*, September 2015). In Kipnis' phrasing, "feelings can't be argued."

"Guy with the haircut?" (p. 364) is the second nod to *The City and the City*.

Acknowledgments

My immense gratitude to Gregg Shilliday for taking a chance on this freshman effort, and to Catharina de Bakker, Stephanie Berrington, Mel Marginet, Sam K. MacKinnon, and everyone at Enfield & Wizenty and Great Plains who helped make *Privilege* possible. They have been wonderful to correspond with, and supportive in the extreme. I am incredibly lucky to have landed at their shop.

Lee Kvern was a tenacious editor. Whatever you don't like about this book, Lee probably tried to talk me out of, and whatever you do like, she probably encouraged me to keep.

A small circle of friends and family graciously read and offered feedback at several ungainly stages in *Privilege's* growth: Toby Malone, Erin Oke, Michael Rothery, Leslie Tutty, Clayton McKee, and Brad Fox.

Brad merits further props for all his digital heavy lifting, including the front-matter graphic, cover design concepts and consultation, and involved assistance with website development. If the Internet was moving, Brad would be that selfless buddy with the truck. He's a great cousin-in-law-in-law, and an even better zombre.

Dr. Malone not only read several drafts, but also assisted with the development of Barker's keynote, while still finding time to give me heaps of shit about Shakespearean punctuation.

Clayton McKee shared insight into the world of fine dining, sushi style. He's as awesome a friend as he is a gourmand.

Many thanks to Jacob Tyerman for consulting on the protocols and procedures of police work.

Further to Dr. Dwayne Winseck, scholarly props to Dr. Michael Dorland and Dr. Ira Wagman.

Without my parents' generous support, none of this would have been possible.

Speaking of support, I'm indebted to various hammocks throughout Belize and Guatemala that made writing the first draft of this book so damn comfortable.